Praise for *Something's Alive on the Titanic:*

LIFE SIGNS . . . AT TWO MILES DEEP . . .

There *was* a man standing in the center of the room—only a silhouette at first, but becoming more distinct as Gillespie's eyes adjusted to what his helmet light was illuminating.

A man, very definitely. Wearing the bridge coat of the Royal Merchant Marine. A black officer's cap, with the White Star insignia. Under the peaked cap was a face—square-jawed, stern, very British.

Now it was Gillespie who gasped.

On the right temple was a tiny black hole, jagged around the edges as if a bullet had penetrated there.

Into the oceanographer's numbed mind came the realization that he was looking at William Murdoch, *Titanic*'s first officer.

Murdoch, who had been in charge of the bridge at 11:40 P.M., April 14, 1912.

Murdoch, who had given the fateful command—"Hard astarboard"—the command that turned the ship into the hidden ice spur that ripped out her guts in thirty seconds.

Murdoch, who, according to several eyewitnesses, had shot himself in the temple just before the giant liner sank.

The figure was shaking its head. . . .

SOMETHING'S ALIVE ON THE TITANIC

ROBERT SERLING

ST. MARTIN'S PAPERBACKS

This novel is a work of fiction. All of the events, characters, names, and places depicted in this novel are entirely fictitious or are used fictitiously. No representation that any statement made in this novel is true or that any incident depicted in this novel actually occurred is intended or should be inferred by the reader.

SOMETHING'S ALIVE ON THE *TITANIC*

Copyright © 1990 by Robert Serling.

Cover illustration by Neal McPheeters.

Library of Congress Catalog Card Number: 90-37467

ISBN: 0-312-92999-4

Printed in the United States of America

St. Martin's Press hardcover edition/December 1990
St. Martin's Paperbacks edition/September 1993

10 9 8 7 6 5 4 3 2 1

I have never had the privilege of meeting
this man of great integrity and sensitivity,
but, nevertheless, this book is dedicated to:

Dr. Robert D. Ballard,
discoverer of the *Titanic*

"*In future, when I think of the* Titanic, *I will see her bow sitting on the bottom, dignified despite the decay and, finally, at rest.*"

—Dr. Robert D. Ballard

"*Do I believe in ghosts? No, but I'm afraid of them.*"

—Marquise du Deffand

Introduction

Her life was tragically brief; her death, immortal.

On April 14, 1912, the Royal Mail Steamer R.M.S. *Titanic*, on the fourth night of her maiden voyage from Southampton, England, to New York, struck an iceberg and sank two and a half hours later.

She carried 1,320 passengers and 908 crew members. When she went down, her sixteen lifeboats left 826 passengers and 697 crew members behind to die.

Not for nearly eight decades were human eyes to look upon the remains of what was once the world's biggest, most palatial ocean liner—at the time "the largest moving object ever created by man," her builders proudly proclaimed. In the 1980s, three separate expeditions finally located the *Titanic*, and much of the mystery and conjecture still surrounding her final moments of agony were at last explained.

Possibly.

For this is a story of what might have happened.

Prologue

William Gillespie, director of the Woods Hole Oceanographic Institution, had a personality that meshed with both his august title and his reputation as a scientist—dispassionate and totally unflappable.

Except that on this cold, blustery morning in February 1995, the mood of Dr. William George Gillespie (B.S, M.A., Ph.D.) did not fit that description. He was more than visibly upset; he was shaken, to the point where his hands trembled as he read, for the third time, the letter he had plucked from the mail his secretary had deposited on his desk less than an hour earlier.

Gillespie had been sifting through the pile, trying to decide what looked important or interesting enough to open first, when he spotted "Office of Naval Research" in the upper-left corner of one envelope. This he had torn open with the alacrity of a five-year-old attacking Christmas wrapping, but his initial reaction was dismay at the unwanted contents. A second reading had given Gillespie the urge to throw the lengthy letter against the wall, as if someone had just handed him a rattle-snake.

The letter itself was not a surprise—he had been waiting for it a long time—but what it disclosed was not what he had hoped. No, Gillespie thought glumly, Rear Admiral Roger Cornell, known throughout the United States Navy as "Jolly Roger," was not the type to bake bad news with evasive sugar coating. Cornell said what he meant and meant what he said, a trait the scientist had always admired for the more than two decades of their friendship. Gillespie suddenly wished he hadn't started the whole mess.

Should I tell Bob Ballard about this? was the next thing that sprang into his mind. No, he decided quickly. The last sentence in Cornell's letter—"I urge you to see me in Washington at your earliest convenience to discuss this matter"—dictated caution, not to mention discretion. Dr. Robert Ballard, the discoverer and first explorer of the *Titanic*'s wreck, didn't have to know until Gillespie himself was ready to tell him.

He punched a button on his intercom.

"Yes, Dr. Gillespie?"

"Mary, call Delta and get me on the first available flight to Washington tomorrow morning. And then call Admiral Cornell."

Having crossed this Rubicon, he felt a little better. Until he made the mistake of rereading the letter once more.

Dear Bill:

We have completed our investigation of the rumors you heard regarding the Titanic, *and I'm afraid there is no easy way to cushion the shock of its results. So here's the bad news.*

I regret to inform you that Ballard's 1985 French–American expedition was not the first to discover the wreck of the Titanic. *Nor was Ballard's 1986 expedition the first to explore the ship in detail.*

Before I explain those two statements, let me assure you that the investigation was conducted by top Naval Intelligence agents and that their findings have unlocked a strange story that, as of now, has no ending. It began, rather innocently, in April 1975 (the exact date has never been determined), when an Englishman named Derek Montague paid a casual visit to Southampton Maritime Museum in England. Montague happened to be a member of that fiercely dedicated breed of Titanic *buffs. His visit was a favor to an author friend who had asked him to do some research for a book the latter was planning to write on the famous liner.*

Specifically, the author had asked Montague to examine any available papers relating to the ship's cargo. He had told Montague: "See if you can find any evidence that she was carrying valuable stuff that might appear in the cargo manifest as something else."

But Derek Montague was more than just a Titanic *buff. He also was a former expert in the Government Code and Cipher School—GC&CS, the cover name for Britain's chief cryptoanalytical organization during World War II. Except for our own navy eggheads who cracked the Japanese navy's code before Midway, there was no finer group of code breakers in the world, and Montague, though young, was one of their very best.*

So it was Montague who set in motion the chain of events that constitute this incredible tale. . . .

SOMETHING'S ALIVE ON THE TITANIC

Part One

1975

1

Like so many Englishmen, Derek Montague was a great respecter of history and tradition. In fact, he mentally capitalized both words and considered History and Tradition practically synonymous, semantic blood brothers, as it were.

Which was why he didn't resent the chore Peter Groton had asked him to perform. Groton was one of those journalists who regarded their newspaper careers as staging areas for literary invasions—in other words, Peter wanted to write a book. He also believed fervently in a philosophy expounded by a certain contingent of the Fourth Estate: Sensationalism sells better than dull facts, so don't let them get in the way of your story.

"There's nothing really new about the *Titanic*," a publisher had told Groton. "We'd be interested only if you could uncover some unknown information. . . or perhaps develop a provocative theory on why she sank."

"It hit an iceberg," Groton had protested. "What the hell theory could I develop . . . that the iceberg hit the ship?"

"You don't have to prove a new theory, Mr. Groton. Just offer it in a logical, persuasive manner that sounds scientifically plausible. Or, even better, gear your research toward a mystery angle, such as the possibility that if anyone could get to the wreck, they might find a fortune in valuable jewels. There have been such rumors, y'know. That what was lost in the *Titanic* may have been worth more than the ship herself."

That had prompted Peter Groton, who enjoyed seeing his own byline but hated the ditch-digging aspects of research, to ask a favor of his old Oxford schoolmate. He knew that Montague, a widower and retired, had plenty of time on his hands.

"I'm sure that with your background, you might unearth something I'd never recognize as significant," Groton had enthused. "Come on, Derek, remember the fuss made about the supposed contraband cargo on the *Lusitania*?"

"Peter, that was in wartime. The *Titanic* went down in 1912. There probably isn't anything more startling in that cargo manifest than a crate of cheap wine disguised with fancy French labels. Besides, I can't do it right now. I'm off tomorrow for a week's holiday."

But Groton had pressed and pleaded. "I'll wait 'til you return. And I desperately need something I can turn into an intriguing mystery. Maybe the ship was carrying illegal dynamite that went off via spontaneous combustion." His eyes lit up with inspiration. "Or the dynamite could have ignited with the iceberg impact and *that*'s what really sank the—"

Montague had interrupted wearily: "All right, Peter, I'll do your bloody research for you. But don't expect miracles. I'll phone when I get back."

He hadn't bothered telling Groton that he welcomed the chance to visit the Southampton Maritime Museum again. Its official name was Wool House, for it had been built in the fourteenth century as a warehouse to hold freshly sheared wool before it was shipped elsewhere. Montague loved the old building with its Spanish chestnut roof and huge, sturdy interior beams. Now, as he sat in the section devoted to *Titanic* lore, he could glance up at those beams and just barely see the carved names of French prisoners of war, most of them sailors captured in eighteenth-century sea battles. Wool House had been used as a temporary prison then, a proud time when Britain's fleets dominated the world's oceans. Montague, whose boyhood, adolescent, and adult hero was Admiral Nelson, never could look at those conquered names without mental images of swift, slashing frigates and stately three-deckers firing massive broadsides.

"Britannia rules the waves," he hummed to himself, and then smiled at this musical manifestation of his incurable interest in naval tradition. Actually, the *Titanic* was a part of that tradition, as far as Montague was concerned—a magnificent example of British engineering genius applied to civilian ship design and construction, just as that same genius had produced the world's first dreadnought.

Never mind that the liner's design was seriously flawed in several respects. She was not as sturdy as the older Cunard twins, *Mauretania* and *Lusitania*. For that matter, she was even structurally inferior to a passenger ship built in 1858: naval architect Isambard Brunel's *Great Eastern*, which really was virtually unsinkable. *The Great Eastern*, a clumsy monstrosity only one hundred feet shorter than the *Titanic*, had a double hull compared to the latter's single-layer one. Brunel's creation also had longitudinal as well as transverse bulkheads, providing a honeycomb structure of enormous strength. Her transverse bulkheads reached thirty feet above the waterline; the *Titanic*'s only ten feet. The *Great Eastern* had once struck a hidden shoal, tearing a gash in her outer hull eighty-three feet long and nine feet deep, yet she reached New York under her own power. Taking her lesser length into consideration, the damage was as extensive as that suffered by the *Titanic*.

Titanic lovers like Montague never dwelled on the ship's technical inadequacies, however. Human errors, overconfidence, foolhardy assumptions and plain carelessness had doomed her—mistakes by men who knew the supposed "unsinkable" label was pure hyperbole. Only sixteen lifeboats and four collapsibles for more than two thousand passengers and crew, no binoculars for the lookouts, indifference to a plethora of ice warnings, excessive speed into a known berg area—these were human flaws, not ship flaws.

In fact, there were some experts who defended the vessel's construction. Yes, the bulkheads were too low, but those same fifteen bulkheads, dividing the hull into sixteen watertight compartments, had kept a mortally wounded ship afloat for nearly three hours and allowed the *Titanic* to maintain an almost even keel until the very end, thus making it easier to launch the lifeboats. Her owners were the ones who decided only sixteen lifeboats were needed on a liner designed to carry as many as sixty-four, and had even ruled against using thirty-two. Sixteen seemed adequate for a ship that couldn't sink.

Yet the mistakes and jaunty arrogance of that Edwardian era were part of the *Titanic* mystique, all woven into the fascinating mosaic that formed the *Titanic* legend, a legend born with her very death throes. Almost from the moment she sank, there had been talk of locating the wreck and recovering the fortune in diamonds and other gems that reportedly went down with the ship. In the same year of the disaster, several wealthy American families, including the Guggenheims, Astors, and Wideners, had asked the prestigious salvage firm of Merritt and Chapman to find and raise the *Titanic*—a project that quickly died when the company informed the backers that in 1912, no search-and-salvage equipment was remotely capable of accomplishing this feat.

Montague himself was totally scornful of the treasures reputed to be aboard the ship. The cargo manifest had been widely published and contained no hint of anything other than the prosaic commercial goods normally shipped on liners. The most valuable known item was a jeweled copy of the *Rubáiyát*, which had been sold at a London auction for less than five hundred pounds shortly before the ship sailed. Insurance claims had been filed for various pieces of personal jewelry, but not in astronomical amounts.

So, he asked himself, what was he doing in the museum? Groton and his damned book! Whatever Montague came up with, even some mildly suspicious (and probably easily explainable) entry, he knew Peter would ride it to the heights of wild speculation, unsubstantiated surmises, and highly dubious conclusions. He liked Groton as a person, but as a journalist Peter had the morals of a Soho whore. Yet Montague had made a promise and anyway, he had never really examined the *Titanic*'s cargo list in detail. It might prove interesting, if unproductive from Groton's point of view.

He stood up and stretched before laboriously squeezing his six-foot-five frame into the small chair allotted to a museum library study desk. Montague's height was not especially commanding, for he was built along the lines of a pipe cleaner. His face was so broad, however, it was almost intimidating, as if the imposing head had been grafted on to the tall, thin body. A shock of thick shaggy gray hair added to the cranial dimensions and his stern features gave him a look of perpetual arrogance.

He was not an arrogant man, however. He had a quick, easy smile and the dry wit of someone who did not take himself very seriously. "Curious chap" was the label most casual acquaintances pinned on Derek Montague, unwittingly applying the right adjective but with the wrong meaning. Montague was a man of insatiable curiosity, especially when it came to anything concerning the *Titanic*. So it was with a sense of anticipation that he bent over a photostatic reproduction of the cargo manifest. The original had gone down with the ship, but, as was the custom, a copy had been sent to the port of destination on another vessel—which happened to have been the famed Cunard liner *Mauretania*.

The manifest was lengthy. There were hundreds upon hundreds of individual crates, cases, boxes, and bags listed, sent by over one hundred different shippers. Consummate professional that he was, Montague would examine every name and every item. He did not really know for what he was searching. If he found anything, it probably would be from sheer instinct, born of innate suspicion. He began reading, his eyes roving each listing like a radar beam probing for a telltale blip.

Wakem & McLaughlin	1 case wine
Thorer & Praetorius	1 bale skins
Carter, W. E.	1 case auto

He stopped, smiling to himself. Carter, W. E. had struck a chord of recognition. That would be William E. Carter, Philadelphia mainliner and a first-class passenger who was one of the fortunate survivors, along with his wife and two children. Montague had once seen the White Star Line's official passenger list; it had read:

Mr. William E. Carter
Mrs. William E. Carter and Maid

Miss Lucile Carter
Master William T. Carter and Manservant

Life among the wealthy of that era, Montague mused. A ten-year-old boy with his personal valet. One of the *Titanic*'s countless legends was that younger Carter got into the last lifeboat only because John Jacob Astor, amid protests from other male passengers, had placed a woman's hat on the child's head, saying, "Now you're a girl and you can go."

Neither the Carter maid nor manservant had survived, suffering the same fate as the expensive French Renault automobile Carter was taking back to the United States—a twenty-five-horsepower job, said to be one of the fastest passenger cars in the world. Montague found himself wondering what the Renault looked like now after sixty-three years of immersion under 12,500 feet of saltwater.

Fuch & Lang Mfg Co.	4 cases printer's blankets
Maltus & Ware	8 cases orchids
Spencerian Pen Co.	4 cases pens
NY Motion Picture Co.	1 case films

He couldn't help scanning the manifest for an item he *knew* couldn't be listed.

British Museum	1 mummy case

That's how it would have appeared, except for the fact that no such artifact was ever shipped on the *Titanic*. It was just another of the liner's myths, a story totally without foundation, yet a tale that had gained credence through years of retelling.

Montague knew its background well. It had originated with an actual event the second evening of the ship's maiden voyage. At one of the first-class dining saloon tables, a prominent English journalist named William T. Stead was entertaining his dinner companions with a wild yarn about an Egyptian mummy that brought a curse upon anyone who owned it—mysterious illnesses, violence, and, eventually, death. Stead, one of the most respected writers of his time, was en route to America to address a peace conference at the personal invitation of President William Howard Taft, but he also was a devout believer in spiritualism and the occult; a skilled raconteur, he had his listeners actually believing the story.

In truth, Stead himself had planted the seeds of later embellishment. There was no such mummy; what he was referring to was an empty mummy's case owned by the British Museum—a coffin whose intricately carved cover included a face with tormented, terror-filled eyes. Stead had transferred this unhappy countenance to that of a non-existent mummy, a story that would have been forgotten if it was not for the fact that one of his dinner companions survived the sinking and related it to a New York *World* reporter.

Montague smiled to himself as he remembered how the "mummy's curse" also had survived—exaggerated and distorted with every fresh telling until it became part of the *Titanic* legend. Montague knew the ultimate version was a horror story: There supposedly was a mummy case aboard the ship, the property of a wealthy American collector who had purchased it from the British Museum and was taking it to New York. When the liner sank, the American bribed a cargo handler to put the case in a lifeboat and then bribed someone on the rescue ship *Carpathia* to take it aboard.

The case, so this account continued, stayed in the American's private collection for two years—a period marked by a series of unexplainable tragedies afflicting his family. He decided to send the artifact back to England and shipped it on the *Empress of Ireland*, a liner that on May 29, 1914, collided with another ship in the St. Lawrence River and sank with a loss of more than a thousand lives—presumably, along with the mummy case and its curse.

Marvelous yarn, Montague mused, but absolute fiction. The mummy case in question never had left England and was still in the British Museum; he had seen it himself. Yet the instigator of that wonderfully phony story had always intrigued Derek Montague. He wondered why William Stead, a true follower of mysticism, hadn't been one of those people who had dire premonitions about the *Titanic*'s voyage.

There were plenty of these: a woman passenger who tried to change her booking at the last minute because she had an uneasy feeling something was going to happen to the ship but was talked out of it by a scoffing White Star agent, the wives of several crew members who expressed similar fears to their husbands. One of them was the manager of the *Titanic*'s à la carte restaurant, Luigi Gatti; his wife had asked him not to go because she had a strange forboding. Gatti was a survivor, and to his dying day never forgot his wife's warning.

Of course, every major disaster brought premonition claimants out of the woodwork in droves. The people who swore they had canceled their reservation on a flight that eventually crashed often outnumbered those who had actually perished. Still, Montague knew many of the premonition incidents involving the *Titanic* had been verified, and that, too, was part of the ship's power to intrigue, tantalize, and utterly grip the imagination. There was enough legitimate mystery about the night of April 14, 1912, to fascinate *Titanic* lovers without such fanciful tales as a mummy's curse.

One such was the coal fire that had broken out in number ten bunker on the starboard side of boiler room six. It had started in Belfast and was still burning when the ship reached Southampton to pick up the first load of passengers and the rest of the crew. Captain Smith knew about the fire but was assured by his chief engineer and Harland & Wolff inspectors that the blaze did not put the liner at any risk. It could be extinguished fully when additional stokers boarded at Southampton, and there was no sign that it had affected the bunker bulkhead.

Smith thought so little of the incident, he made no mention of any fire in his log, and neither did the Board of Trade inspector whose final report cleared the *Titanic* as seaworthy and ready to sail. Presumably, the problem was fixed either at Southampton, when the other stokers came aboard, or at Cherbourg, where the ship picked up the remaining passengers. Putting the fire out, if it was still burning, would have been a simple task; all they had to do was remove the coal from the affected bunker and/or keep hosing it down, as they had started to do before the liner left Belfast.

Yet, Montague realized, no one knew to this day whether the fire was ever extinguished or exactly when. There were those who speculated that an unchecked bunker fire might have weakened the bulkhead and thus played a role in the sinking, the theory being that a heat-weakened bulkhead could have triggered the progressive collapse of other bulkheads under the pressure of tons of incoming water. Montague himself thought this was rubbish; the ship's surviving officers never mentioned the fire as being a continuing or even a minor problem, certainly no factor in the ship's fate. It was not even brought up in either the American or British investigations into the tragedy. Anyway, the *Titanic* sank because the bulkheads weren't tall enough, not because one of them might have been weakened.

There also had been speculation that the bunker fire would have been capable of producing deadly coal fumes, highly combustible if exposed to an ignition source like a spark—say from a spark caused by collision-damaged metal rubbing against metal. Montague discounted this theory, too; a massive explosion occurring at the moment of impact certainly would not have gone unnoticed. On the contrary, survivors testified as to the apparent gentleness of the impact.

He had read somewhere that a surviving crew member claimed there actually had been a devastating coal-dust explosion—either from a spark or the result of spontaneous combustion—that blew out one side of the ship. White Star officers who lived through the sinking, according to this wild account, invented the story of the *Titanic* hitting an iceberg to cover up their own negligence in allowing the bunker fire to rage unchecked.

Montague considered this yarn patently false; there was far too much evidence and testimony that the liner had, indeed, hit an iceberg. Any alleged cover-up would have had to involve hundreds of surviving passengers, as well as the supposedly culpable officers. There couldn't have been nearly eight hundred conspirators trying to whitewash J. Bruce Ismay's company. Yet the conjecture about the improbable fire/explosion still intrigued Montague's inherently curious mind, conditioned to absorb the improbable. He didn't believe the story, but he wondered about another possibility.

Suppose an explosion had occurred at precisely the moment the *Titanic* collided with the berg's hidden spur? Quite a coincidence, but there still were those diehards who refused to believe a ship of that size and strength could have been mortally wounded by a relatively small sliver of ice. Was it a combination of collision and explosion damage that had doomed the liner? Montague didn't really believe this, either. That collision had been the classic example of the irresistible force meeting the immovable object—46,000 tons of metal racing at more than twenty knots smashing into a frozen meat cleaver. It was the irresistible force that had lost the battle.

If only it were possible to find the damned ship, he thought. Such a discovery might solve so many riddles of the *Titanic* tragedy, answer so many questions. He had always fantasized about being on an expedition that located the liner—a foolish fantasy, he realized, because what would a retired cryptoanalyst be doing on such an expedition? Someday, somehow, however, oceanographers like his closest friend, Trevor Van Buren, might make fantasy a reality and separate all the fiction from fact.

Fiction always mixed with fact on the subject of the *Titanic*, and he found the latter just as interesting as the unfounded rumors that spawned fiction. There were plenty of facts to excite the imagination without interjecting phony "what ifs" into the story. There were many little-known facts, such as the ship's fourth stack being a dummy, strictly window dressing, because passengers of that era equated speed and power with the number of funnels a liner carried. The *Titanic* would have been just as fast with its three legitimate working funnels, or even two, but White Star wouldn't have been caught dead admitting it. Ironically, the line emphasized comfort, not speed. Contrary to accusations made after the tragedy, the *Titanic* was not trying for a speed record on her maiden voyage.

The company loved to spew out numbers, anyway—to impress the public with the new ship's size. It was proudly emphasized that she was longer than the then-highest skyscraper in the world—New York's Woolworth Building. Advance publicity included photographs of the Woolworth Building with the *Titanic* superimposed alongside, standing on one end so that the bow loomed over the top of the skyscraper. The publicized statistics prior to the maiden voyage stressed not only the luxury of this floating city but what was involved in her provisioning. The two thousand passengers would be enjoying forty-three tons of meat and fish, not to mention two thousand quarts of ice cream, fifteen hundred bottles of champagne, and three thousand cigars. The second-class dinner menu—*second class*, Montague remembered—offered a choice of four entrées (haddock, curried chicken, spring lamb, and roast turkey). The first-class buffet-luncheon cuisine would have made the chef at Claridge's envious; there were thirteen meat, fish, and fowl selections on the Irish linen-covered serving table, plus salad staples and eight kinds of cheese.

They ate well on the *Titanic*, Montague thought enviously, but deservedly so. Most of the wealth aboard was concentrated among several American millionaires who had paid up to two thousand dollars for first-class passage—the equivalent of well over ninety thousand by 1975 standards. Just thinking about their culinary luxuries made Montague's stomach churn with hunger, but he willed himself to continue with his task.

Some of the items amused him, for they bore no apparent relationship to the listed company. For example, there was the National City Bank of New York and its 11 bales rubber—what the bloody hell was a bank going to do with eleven bales of rubber? Or American Motor Co. listed for 1 package candles. Montague also deduced, rather wryly, that the *Titanic*'s cargo hold contained enough alcoholic beverages to keep half the city of New York drunk for a week. He counted 719 cases of wine, liquor, brandy, cognac, and champagne, plus three barrels of wine—not to mention four cases of opium, with the shipper unlisted.

On he read.

| Tiffany & Co. | 1 case china, 4 cases silver goods |
| Altman, B. & Co. | 1 case cottons |

Sovereign Metals, Ltd.	34 cases nails, screws and bolts
Lazard Fréres	25 cases sardines
First National Bank of Chicago	300 cases shelled walnuts
Brown Bros & Co.	75 cases dragon's blood

Montague chuckled. Sardines for Lazard Fréres, a prestigious investment firm? And a Chicago bank with what must be a year's supply of shelled walnuts! He wondered momentarily what the devil constituted seventy-five cases of *dragon's blood*, until he remembered that the term applied to a number of resinous red substances obtained from various tropical plants and trees; they were used for coloring varnishes and also in photoengraving. He had just started to read the next manifest item—318 bags of potatoes shipped by J. P. Sauers & Co.—when something clicked in his mind:

Sovereign Metals, Ltd., 34 cases nails, screws and bolts.

There was something tantalizingly familiar about the firm's name, also something deucedly familiar about the cargo it was shipping. Somewhere, sometime, he had seen both before, and not under favorable circumstances. It was like trying to recall a vague picture or face from the past—frustrating because he was so close to recognition.

Then he remembered.

"Well I'll be damned!" he blurted, more loudly than he intended. Two other museum visitors gave him disapproving stares, but Montague didn't even notice. He marched into the office of the museum curator, a friendly butterball of a man he had come to know well from his frequent visits.

"Josh, I've been looking at the *Titanic's* cargo manifest. Would you happen to have any copies of the waybill numbers from the shipments, or know where I might obtain them?"

The curator seemed mildly offended that Montague would suggest looking elsewhere. "Derek, we have everything pertaining to that ship right here in this museum, including those waybill numbers, I'm surprised you even asked. Let's see . . . well, I'd better help you find them myself. I think I know where they have been filed. . . ."

In less than five minutes, he handed Montague a thick, rather dusty folder that obviously hadn't been opened since its original deposit in an out-of-the-way filing cabinet. It took Montague a good two hours before he found the Sovereign Metals waybill for thirty-four cases of nails, screws and bolts. The first thing that struck his eye was the listed weight: 9,850 pounds. Not only was the poundage unusually high for assorted nails and so forth but Montague also noticed that in sifting through the other waybills he discovered that weights were not listed—only on the Sovereign shipment. The addressee at the port of destination was a J. Smyth, and Montague's eyes narrowed.

Then he noticed something else, significant to the practiced eyes of a former professional code breaker. He compared other waybill numbers with Sovereign's and found that the latter was the only one with ten digits instead of the usual four or at the most five. He copied down the numbers in a small pocket notebook he always carried with him and put the folder back in its cabinet.

He poked his head into the curator's tiny office just before leaving. "Many thanks, Josh. I put the file back."

"Find what you were looking for?"

Montague smiled enigmatically. "Perhaps. I'd be more certain if I knew *what* I was looking for."

He waved good-bye, the curator staring after him. "I wonder what the hell he meant by that?" he asked himself aloud.

When Montague returned to his small London flat, a one-bedroom affair whose principal features were an ancient piano and a huge well-stocked bookcase, he placed a call to Peter Groton.

"Peter, Derek here. Sorry, but I drew a complete blank. There was nothing in the cargo listings. Absolutely nothing."

Groton chirped, "That's perfectly all right, Derek. I've changed my mind about doing a book on the *Titanic*. While you were away, I decided there's been too much written already and nobody really cares anymore. Actually, Derek, I'm going after a far more interesting subject." He paused dramatically. "Get this . . . who was Jack the Ripper?"

Inconsiderate whelp of a journalist, Montague thought, but he didn't voice this opinion because he was relieved to have Groton off his back. He even felt grateful, inasmuch as Peter had unwittingly steered him to a doorway that might hide a fascinating mystery.

"A topic of eternal interest," he agreed. "I wish you luck with the project."

"I've got a retired Scotland Yard sergeant who's going to help me with the research," Groton confided. "Anyway, thanks for your trouble."

"Anytime," Montague said cheerfully, and hung up. He felt a twinge of guilt at the deception, but rationalization was easy. Groton would have embellished the slightest hint of what Montague suspected into a grievous mutation of the truth. He still wasn't sure exactly what he had found. His suspicions had been stirred by the double recognition of the name Sovereign Metals and the use of the words *nails, screws and bolts*. He had never actually seen them in a manifest before, but he remembered being warned once by a GC&CS superior to look out for them in any documents pertaining to wartime shipping. "The blokes have been using other covers," his superior had said, "but they started using this one back in 1912 and continued to use it during the Great War, when they actually caught us napping. In 1917, they managed to get gold out of here into Germany, a welcome bit of aid for the Jerries, who must have paid Sovereign dearly."

"Whose gold?" Montague had asked.

"You may find this hard to believe, but Sovereign seems to be a worldwide network of professional thieves, and very well organized. They deal with stolen jewels, bonds, securities, money—anything of value, which they always convert into bullion and contraband to willing buyers. I couldn't begin to tell you how many revolutions have been financed by these shipments, including enemies of the Crown. The bastards have used at least twenty names over the years, including Sovereign."

Montague went to a rear closet and from the top shelf removed a stack of thin bound volumes he hadn't examined for years. They were obsolete codebooks, so dusty now that he had to use a damp rag on them first. He resisted the temptation to browse, like a man rereading old love letters, for codes had always fascinated him in the same way murder mysteries intrigued the analytical mind.

The codebook at the very top provided the greatest temptation of all, an especially intriguing one based on chess terms. He remembered it being used by French partisans until the Germans cracked it. A bloody disaster, he recalled ruefully— nine partisans were executed before anyone realized the broken chess code was an invitation to Nazi firing squads.

That was the attraction of these books. He knew that almost every code would bring back memories, some glorious and others painful, these combinations of numbers and letters and words and phrases that eventually might have sent one convoy to Russia unscathed and another into ambush.

He sighed with nostalgia, sifted through the pile, and came up with several volumes titled *Nonmilitary*, which he took back to his living room. He perused their contents for more than two hours before he found what he was looking for. He had come upon one code that had a distinctly recognizable pattern—hieroglyphics to the untrained eye, but a lingual map to his. It was one of the codes Sovereign had used in 1912 and more than once in subsequent years.

Montague opened his notebook to the page on which he had copied the ten-digit waybill and studied the numbers once more: one of the simplest codes he had ever tackled and a very old one—vintage early 1900s, he knew. Underneath the ten numbers, he wrote ten letters, then went to work on the words *nails, screws and bolts*. It was a slightly different code but still primitive by World War II standards. He quickly translated them, leaned back, and whistled.

Under the ten numbers, he had written the words *via Titanic*.

Under *nails, screws and bolts*, he had written 34 *crates bullion. Cargo hold 3*.

He was excited and not a little self-satisfied. Only someone with a memory like Derek Montague's would have attached any suspicion to the name Sovereign Metals, Ltd. That J. Smyth had rung a bell, too; it was a frequent pseudonym

Sovereign used for its addressees—another thing he had been told to watch for.

He also was puzzled, however. The first two words of the manifest code—*via Titanic*—seemed superfluous, mere excess verbiage and totally illogical to Montague's very logical mind. Whoever J. Smyth was, Sovereign must have informed him in advance that a gold shipment was en route aboard the *Titanic*—probably by a cable message using the same code, he reasoned. So why repeat the vessel of shipment in the coded manifest: Was *via Titanic* another code in itself?

The solution came to him even as he pondered whether to try another decipher for those two words. It was common practice then for shipping companies to send copies of cargo manifests to other ships that might arrive before or after the vessel carrying the cargo—a precautionary measure in case the latter failed to reach its destination. He knew that a copy of *Titanic*'s manifest had, indeed, been sent to New York on another liner—no less than the *Mauretania*, at the time the fastest passenger ship on the North Atlantic. If the *Mauretania* had reached New York before the *Titanic*'s scheduled arrival, the waybill code made sense. It informed the recipients how the bullion was being shipped, without resorting to a cable that could have been intercepted by the government.

Now, Montague thought excitedly, all he had to do was find out when the *Mauretania* had docked in New York, before or after the *Titanic* sailed. . . .

The next day found him in the historical records room of the Cunard Line, examining the *Mauretania* file. The search was simple, relatively quick, and definitely rewarding. Every trip that *Mauretania* had made, from her maiden voyage in 1907 to her withdrawal from service one month short of twenty-seven years later, was recorded—including her departure for New York on April 4, 1912, six days before the *Titanic* sailed.

Derek Montague returned triumphantly to his flat an hour later and made two phone calls. Neither number he dialed was the one listed for Groton, Peter.

2

Montague watched Trevor Van Buren pour himself a fourth snifter of brandy and smiled wryly.

In all the years he had known England's most famous oceanographer, only once had he ever seen him take more than one drink during a twenty-four hour period. That happened to have been the day Van Buren received a final divorce decree ending his loveless and childless marriage to Hester Van Buren, an angular, foul-tempered shrew with the sexual appetite of a mink and a commitment to marital fidelity that could charitably be described as sporadic.

On that happy occasion, Van Buren had celebrated by consuming *two* portions of Bristol Cream sherry, the second one dissolving his carefully protected inhibitions sufficiently for him to proclaim, "Derek, my friend, I must confess I'm delighted to be rid of that bed-cruising bitch!"

The third man in the room also grinned as Van Buren returned to his armchair carrying the refilled snifter. John Hawke knew both his companions from close World War II contacts—Montague because of his code work and Van Buren because the latter had been a civilian adviser to the Royal Navy's submarine service, which happened to have been John Hawke's wartime branch of duty. Hawke, in fact, had helped develop the four-man midget submarines that in 1943 had slipped submerged into a Norwegian fjord and dropped delayed-action Amatex explosives under the hull of the German battleship *Tirpitz*. The blasts, which wrecked all three of the giant warship's engines and damaged not only the hull but her rudders and steering gear, put the *Tirpitz* out of action for four months.

Hawke not only had played a major role in the design of the midgets but had gone along on the daring raid in which six of the sixteen crew members involved died. Hawke himself was wounded.

John Reginald Hawke was a tough, irreverent maverick with a touch of working-class accent, even though he was Cambridge-educated. From his English father, a career naval officer, he had inherited a wiry, tireless physique and a love of the sea; from his Australian mother, the uninhibited friendliness of the typical Aussie, occasionally hardened into a directness that could infuriate his superiors. Of medium height and one year shy of turning sixty, he was not an imposing man except for his eyes. Deep-set, they had a chameleon-like quality, capable of changing shade with his mood—a pleasant sky blue normally but turning into the ice-coated paleness of topaz when he was angry or under tension.

Those eyes conveyed mostly a curious expression now, as Hawke studied his two companions. He was looking particularly at Trevor Van Buren, whose reaction to Montague's revelation had been so ambivalent that it produced obvious nervousness, as if the oceanographer was both excited and worried. The three men were in Van Buren's study, the most comfortable room in the small house that stood on the outskirts of Broadway, a small village in the heart of the Cotswolds.

Hawke was not the sort of man to understand why anyone who had spent his life studying the secrets, treasures, and mysteries of the earth's oceans would prefer to live in an inland town. It had taken Montague two hours to get there from London by train, and Hawke had spent even longer driving his ancient Jaguar from the seacoast city of Weymouth, where he had retired, still a bachelor, after twenty-two years in the Royal Navy. Broadway was a lovely little place, actually far nicer than Weymouth as a quiet residence, but it was too far from Hawke's beloved sea. One couldn't watch an Atlantic sunset or smell the faintly pungent salt air or walk along the shore at night, listening to the waves sigh as they rolled in. Hawke respected the sea without fearing its capacity for treachery, danger, and, too often, death. He considered Van Buren to be one of those scientists whose only real love was acquisition of knowledge, an emotionless gathering of facts that didn't warrant dilution by sentiment.

Yet Van Buren's response to Montague's cryptic telephone call—"I've stumbled on something fantastic about the *Titanic* and we must discuss it together"—had been identical to Hawke's: eager curiosity. It was Van Buren who had insisted on their meeting at his home. "A better setting for something which sounds monumental," he had explained rather ponderously.

However, now Van Buren was frowning, for Hawke had just uttered precisely what the oceanographer expected him to say after Montague's announcement: "We've got to go after the gold, of course."

"A very expensive proposition," Montague pointed out. "And even if we could organize an expedition, we might have the devil's own time finding that ship."

Van Buren's frown was interrupted only long enough for him to take a sip of brandy. "It seems to me that even if she's found, a far more difficult problem is getting down to her. For God's sake, John, the North Atlantic at the spot where she sank is more than twelve thousand feet deep. You talk so glibly about *having* to go after the gold, assuming it's there—no offense, Derek," the last prompted by Montague's slight smile—"but that code of yours is pretty skimpy evidence."

"If it was the only bit of evidence, I would be inclined to share your doubts," Montague said. "But I have been doing considerable research in the past fortnight or so. I learned, for example, that Scotland Yard was informed at the time that a huge contraband bullion shipment would be made to finance a revolution in a certain South American country. That country happened to be Paraguay. The revolt, if successful, would have been followed in turn by a war between that nation and Bolivia. Only a shipment the size of the one I believe was on the *Titanic* could have accomplished such an effort, because the rebels required a prodigious amount of arms—both for the revolt and their subsequent aggression.

"The Yard's interest was piqued originally by a number of extremely clever bullion thefts that had been occurring sporadically in several European countries during the latter half of 1911. In January of 1912, it actually began inspecting the cargoes of virtually every ship departing England, which was Sovereign's known chief base of operations. Nothing was ever found, and the Yard finally concluded it was chasing after false information—logical inasmuch as there was no sign of any revolution."

"Which proves absolutely nothing," Van Buren declared.

"On the contrary, if you will let me finish. The Yard's investigation and searches ended in March of 1912. But this was precisely when the cover name of Sovereign was first used, and the thieves began utilizing a new and at the time unknown code for its illegal shipments. It continued to use both the name and this code for several years—the same code I broke, mind you, and the code that was in effect at the time the *Titanic* sailed. This is not speculation, gentlemen, but fact."

"Then I shall play devil's advocate," Hawke said. "Why didn't anyone familiar with Sovereign's methods of operation connect the failure of the revolution to take place with the *Titanic's* sinking?"

"Why should they? Remember, the existence of the new code went unsuspected until after World War One. Sovereign before 1912 was not even known by that name. As a matter of fact, I have been aware for some time that Sovereign actually smuggled gold into Germany in 1917, and Scotland Yard seems to have assumed this must have been the same bullion reported stolen in the series of 1911 thefts."

"Perhaps it was," Van Buren said dubiously.

"Then explain to me, if you will, the fake Sovereign cargo manifest listing for the *Titanic*. Obviously, Sovereign waited for the Yard to be lulled into believing the gold was never sent. Nor did the Yard ever suspect that the gold might not be shipped directly to South America but to an interim destination for transshipment. Naturally, the loss of the bullion was never reported, it was illegal to begin with. Would you chaps listen to one more piece of convincing evidence?"

They nodded in unison. Montague smiled, very sure of

himself now. "I have spent years studying every aspect of that disaster, including its aftermath, and I recently ascertained a most interesting fact. After the sinking, a certain pseudonymous individual made discreet inquiries of several British salvage firms as to the possibility of exploring or even raising the liner. I have a copy of the letter he sent to each company. He was discouraged, of course—no such salvage technology existed at the time. That same individual was later identified as Richard Dunbar, a Welshman who was one of the principal brains behind Sovereign and may have been the ring's original organizer. In 1938, Dunbar went to prison, where he died four months later, taking the *Titanic*'s secret with him . . . until I stumbled upon that manifest item. The Sovereign gang dissolved shortly after World War Two, the major leaders either imprisoned or dead. Most of them, by the way, were British subjects, with a sprinkling of French, Belgian, and Spanish cohorts. There was one German involved in the hierarchy. None ever talked, apparently believing in the logical supposition that the gold was lost forever."

Montague leaned back in his chair. "After all I have told you, I cannot believe either of you can still dismiss all this as coincidence or conjecture."

"It is all the evidence I need," Hawke said, with a side glance in the oceanographer's direction.

Van Buren sighed. "Look, you two, stop daydreaming about gold and be practical. Water pressure increases by forty-four-point-four pounds per square inch for every additional one hundred feet of depth. The pressure where the *Titanic* lies has been estimated to be at least six thousand pounds per square inch. Let me ask you something, John. What was the maximum depth achieved by your submarines during the war?"

"About six hundred feet for our subs," Hawke replied. "But an American boat survived a depth-charge attack at seven hundred feet."

Van Buren snorted derisively. "Seven hundred feet, you say? Something of a miracle in itself, and you want to go more than eleven thousand feet deeper! Come on, John, it would be the equivalent of an elephant flattening a tin with its foot."

"Not necessarily," Hawke said quietly. "Remember the

midget subs we used to cripple the *Tirpitz*? For the past eighteen months, I've been working with the same group that built those subs—as a consultant on the design and development of a new deep-sea-exploration submersible—two of them, in fact. A two-man craft and a smaller, more simplified version that carries only one."

"How deep is deep?" Van Buren asked.

Hawke's smile was that of a politician whose opponent has led with his chin by asking the wrong question.

"We sent a radio-controlled sub down to fourteen thousand feet and kept her there for two hours. When we brought her up, I assure you she didn't look stepped on. There wasn't a leak to be found, much less any hull deformation."

Montague whistled. "Fourteen thousand feet! That's two thousand deeper than the *Titanic*."

"Very impressive," Van Buren conceded. "But all you proved was the structural integrity of the hull. What about your human environmental factors? Your life-support capabilities?"

Hawke's voice dropped an octave to add dramatic effect. "Eighteen days ago, we put a chimp in the smaller of our two subs, sent her down by remote control to the same depth—fourteen thousand—and brought it up alive and well two hours later. A postdive medical examination showed it could have stayed down even longer with no ill effects. And if you need further evidence that we have ourselves a first-class deep-sea-exploration vehicle, said evidence is sitting in this room."

"You dove it yourself?" Montague blurted.

"That I did, two days after the chimp experiment. As you can see, I'm in fine shape. A hell of a lot better shape than I was after diving under that bloody Hun battleship, I might add." He looked at Van Buren with a mischievous grin. "Sorry, Trevor, but I believe I've answered your chief objection. Unless you have a few others, which wouldn't surprise me in the least."

Van Buren's return smile was one of partial surrender. "Not objections, John. Questions."

"Such as?"

"Let us assume the *Titanic* can be found . . . a dubious premise in itself, because the accuracy of her last reported position has always been a matter of controversy. It would be like looking for the proverbial needle in a haystack. But I'll concede it's a possibility, albeit a dim one. So now we're over the wreck site, presumably with a salvage vessel that has hauled your submarines to the scene. I shudder to contemplate the cost of mounting an expedition just to find the *Titanic*, let alone recover any supposed gold. Although I must say, Derek, you have provided us with some impressive evidence."

Hawke added quickly, "That bit about the Dunbar chap from Sovereign seeking information on salvage possibilities is what convinces me it's worth the candle."

"All well and good," Van Buren said, "but you still haven't told us how you propose to pay for this. I can't imagine anyone foolish enough to back you merely on the promise that *if* you recover the bullion, they'll recoup."

Montague nodded gravely. "I only wish we could find someone to finance an expedition just to find the *Titanic*, let alone recover that bullion. I agree with you, Trevor; the cost would be staggering. We'd require far more than Hawke's splendid little craft for a successful venture. I judge we'd need at least a half-million pounds of financial backing, and that may be an understatement. Considering the economic condition of this country at present, we'd probably have difficulty raising a half-million shillings, even from private capital."

Hawke said quickly, "But also consider the stakes. What's the current price of gold on the London Exchange, Derek?"

"I looked it up the same day I deciphered the Sovereign code. It's bringing around fifty pounds per ounce. And I've already done the necessary arithmetic. Nearly five tons of bullion would be worth about eight million pounds which, by the way, may be a considerable understatement."

"Why?" Van Buren asked.

"Because it is not ordinary bullion. It is gold from the *Titanic*. Each and every bar would be a collector's dream, probably worth almost double the market value. Did I say eight million pounds? Make that sixteen million."

"Sixteen million pounds," Hawke repeated. "Thirty-two million or so in American dollars."

Montague inspected him curiously. "Do you have a point in translating pounds into dollars?"

Hawke chuckled. "Must there be a point?"

"With you, yes. For a man who's half-Australian, you do possess an unusual amount of ulterior or even devious motives. When you mention American dollars, I suspect you have something in mind."

Hawke said, "Not something . . . someone. What the devil do show-business people call financial backers? There's a word for it—"

"Angel," Van Buren supplied.

Hawke nodded. "I think I may have our angel. An American, I hasten to add. A very, very rich American. He came to mind the instant Derek dropped his little bullion bomb. Ever hear of Martin Lefferts?"

Van Buren shook his head, but Montague's bushy eyebrows lifted in surprised recognition. "Eccentric Yank millionaire, isn't he?"

"Billionaire," Hawke corrected. "And just crazy and wealthy enough to underwrite this treasure hunt."

Van Buren still looked puzzled. "I don't get it, John. He might be rich as Croesus, but what makes you think he'd be willing to spend a small fortune backing this . . . this wild-goose chase?"

"Because he's already spent a very large fortune backing similar wild-goose chases. I know the man, Trevor. Worked for him once, as a matter of fact. On one of those chases."

Montague exclaimed, "Now I remember . . . five years ago! In Scotland. You were trying to find the Loch Ness monster."

"Precisely. Unfortunately, we didn't find Nessie. But we had one hell of a lot of fun looking. That's how Martin Lefferts likes to spend his money, trying to prove the reality of myths and legends. I'd be a rich man if I had what it cost him to wander around Tibet for three months looking for the Abominable Snowman. He once financed an expedition into the heart of Africa on the strength of an ancient tribal legend that a species of dinosaur big enough to kill a hippo still existed in the area."

"The man's absolutely daft!" Montague laughed. "Live dinosaurs in the twentieth century; this Lefferts chases rainbows!"

"Not daft. Consumed by curiosity." This came from Van

Buren, and both Hawke and Montague stared at the oceanographer.

Van Buren chuckled. "Don't look so startled. I rather envy anyone who can afford to turn scientific curiosity into an expensive hobby. I'm well acquainted with that African dinosaur legend. Fascinating, actually. The story's been floating around since the late eighteen hundreds: two tribes living on opposite sides of Lake Bangweulu, never coming into contact with one another, yet telling identical tales of a beast that killed animals as large as hippos. They had a name for it: *mokéle-mbêmbe*. Not only did their descriptions of the monster tally but the descriptions themselves were that of a horned dinosaur closely resembling the prehistoric triceratops. One expedition—not the Lefferts fellow, John—anyway, this one expedition never saw the creature but obtained some of its purported droppings. They were analyzed in a laboratory and found to contain the remains of sizable fish and lizards. The droppings were extremely large, of a size associated with those of a rhino or elephant—except that neither of those herbivorous animals eat fish or lizards."

"Strange stuff for an oceanographer to get interested in." Montague smiled.

"Not so strange. Mind you, I don't quite believe it all, but there is compelling evidence that prehistoric creatures still exist in the oceans' depths."

Hawke nodded. "The Loch Ness monster is supposed to be some kind of plesiosaur that survived millions of years after its supposed extinction."

"Now that's a cockamamy fable if ever I heard one." Montague chortled.

Van Buren said soberly, "No, it's not as cockamamy as you think. Not too many years ago, a Japanese fishing vessel hauled up the carcass of a huge creature, obviously reptilian. The remains began to rot and they had to throw the carcass back into the sea. But they took photographs of it. When the pictures were developed, they showed a beast remarkably similar to the Mesozoic plesiosaur. And the Mesozoic Period, incidentally, dates back one hundred and fifty million years. As recently as the nineteen fifties, a species of fish supposedly extinct for at least fifty million years was caught alive in the Atlantic. An amazing discovery, believe me. Makes one wonder whether those old sea-serpent tales might not be more fact than fiction."

His companions exchanged glances. This was an unexpected side of Trevor Van Buren, an almost stuffy, precise little man who tried to compensate for his lack of height and flabby body with a huge, bristling mustache that would have looked more at home on the face of a Royal Grenadiers drill sergeant.

However, now they found Van Buren's interest and even belief in the bizarre as incongruous as that walrus mustache. The oceanographer apparently wasn't conscious of their stares, and he continued in his soft, almost hypnotic voice, as if he was talking to himself.

". . . you know, finding and exploring the *Titanic* would be an incredible achievement in itself. But there could be even greater scientific rewards. Who knows what kinds of creatures inhabit those depths? It would be an absolutely fantastic opportunity to study—"

Hawke brought him back with a blunt question. "Trevor, can we take it that you're with us on this project? We're going to need top oceanographers, and you're the best there is, absolutely perfect for this endeavor. Only an oceanographer, with knowledge of currents and tides and oceanographic topography could help us locate that wreck. Plus the fact that you have done a considerable amount of exploratory diving work."

Van Buren hesitated, his racing thoughts jolted like a car that has hit an unexpected pothole. "There is one thing. I am not particularly enamored with the idea of turning this into a looting expedition. That tragic ship is the graveyard of almost fifteen hundred souls, and it would be a terrible thing to desecrate a graveyard. The *Titanic* should be explored, not plundered." He turned to Montague, an imploring note in his voice. "Isn't that how you see it, Derek?"

Montague hated to answer the question honestly, suddenly realizing he already had settled in his own mind the ethical conflict that breaking the code had unleashed. He was more than just a *Titanic* buff, an expert on *Titanic* lore. He felt a reverence for the ship that went far deeper than the usual trivia of facts, figures, statistics, and nautical controversy. He had a respect based on the way she so starkly symbolized the faults and virtues of her era, simply because the *Titanic* herself was the tragic product of those faults and virtues.

What he hadn't grasped until now was that while Van Buren shared those feelings, he did so in a significantly different way. Montague's respect was historical; Trevor's was emotional, almost religious. The oceanographer had raised the moral issue that inevitably brought him into conflict with John Hawke, who by sheer force of personality, Montague conceded, already had assumed leadership without asking for it.

It was to be expected. Hawke was a natural leader, an adventurer and military man to whom sentimentality had always been a contemptible flaw because it got in the way of what he perceived as higher priorities, a man who willingly wore blinders to navigate that narrow path labeled MISSION. To Hawke, Montague realized, the *Titanic* was another *Tirpitz*; to Van Buren, she was a shrine. Montague found himself cast in the unwelcome role of philosophical mediator.

My God, he thought, what an unlikely trio. Up to now, their diversity of backgrounds and views had made for stimulating friendships. They were always arguing over one thing or another, whether it was politics, books, films, social issues, or rugby results. This time, it was more basic and intensely personal than an abstract difference of opinion, and a pinpoint of guilt pricked Montague's conscience. In the excitement of his discovery, he had discounted any possible moral dilemma.

"Well, Derek?" Van Buren said.

Montague said, not without sympathy, "You have to be practical, Trevor. This would be an enormously expensive proposition, requiring financial support from private capital . . . someone like this Lefferts. He's going to expect a reasonable return on his investment, and I can't say that I'd blame him. Only the government would finance a purely scientific venture, and I, for one, would not relish asking Parliament or even Buckingham Palace for the funding. Look, my friend, it should be entirely possible to recover that gold without disturbing the ship. Am I not correct, John?"

Hawke had the grace and also the honesty to look a little embarrassed. "Theoretically possible," he said gently. "Provided she's not smashed up too badly, of course. If we can work our way into the interior and get into that number three cargo hold without having to clear away a mass of wreckage, we shouldn't be disturbing the *Titanic* to an excessive degree."

Van Buren bristled. "Your use of the word *excessive* sounds very much like an admission that you can't possibly get at the gold without tearing the ship apart."

"It might come to that," Hawke admitted.

The soft voice was edged with emotion. "Might? I'd say you know damned well you'll have to destroy her!"

"Not unless we have to," Hawke retorted. "But I'd be a liar if I made you a flat promise not to disturb a rivet."

"Then how do you propose to enter her?"

"Naturally, I haven't had time to work out details. Derek just sprang this on us. But I have a tentative plan. We have both those exploratory subs operationally ready. The smaller, one-man boat has a very narrow beam. I figure there must have been some structural damage when the *Titanic* took that dive, enough to create some gaps in her hull. We'd use the large sub to explore her externally first, see if there are any areas for entry, maybe take some pictures for scientific purposes"—that last was directed at Van Buren and was accompanied by one of Hawke's ingratiating grins—"and the one-man sub would be used to enter the cargo hold. Both boats, by the way, are equipped with remote-controlled robot arms or pincers . . . for lifting the bullion crates. They're also handy for clearing away small pieces of debris. And the subs have powerful floodlights for illumination."

"There were thirty-four of those crates," Montague reminded. "It'll take forever to raise each one to the surface."

"Assuming there is anything left of them," Van Buren noted dourly. "I doubt whether wood could have lasted very long."

Montague said quickly, "Sovereign, according to the brief research I was able to accomplish before we met, always shipped bullion in metal containers."

"Well rusted, I fancy," Van Buren said almost triumphantly, as if the possibility had clinched his side of the argument.

Hawke tossed him the kind of patient look a teacher would use on a backward pupil. "To answer Derek's question first,

the smaller sub's primary job would be to get the gold out of
the cargo hold. The outfit that built the boats also has designed
and constructed a large steel platform that can be lowered to
the ocean floor via four steel cables attached to each end. In
this case, we'd need four reels of cable, each twelve thousand,
five hundred feet long. The smaller boat goes after the crates,
one at a time, and transfers them to the platform. When the
platform's full, it's raised to the surface and cargo winches will
haul everything aboard."

It was Montague who asked the key question, beating Van
Buren to the punch. "John, your recovery plans are predicated
on any sub, however small, being able to probe the *Titanic's*
interior. We all must face the likelihood of this being an impossibility. The wreckage debris might very well prove impassable.
Frankly, I share Trevor's concern that we'll have to destroy the
ship to get at the gold. And I'd hate to see that happen."

"Thank you, Derek," Van Buren murmured.

John Hawke rose from his chair and began pacing in front
of his two friends. It was, they knew, a sign that he was on the
verge of open anger; the pacing seemed to keep his temper
under control, like a man calming down by counting to ten.
They let him pace with the fluid strides of a caged tiger, until
he finally stopped and faced them. His eyes, Montague noticed, were a chilling blue.

"I think I've had enough of this sentimental tommyrot,"
Hawke said in a tone of deadly calm. "What in the bloody hell
is so special about the *Titanic*, anyway? She's just forty-six
thousand tons of metal. A legitimate salvage operation with a
very large pot of gold waiting for anyone with the guts to go
after it. I'll tell you what she isn't; she's no sacred shrine to the
incompetent bastards who sailed her or the rich blighters who
went down with her!"

Van Buren muttered, "It still would be akin to grave robbing."

"I don't give a damn what you call it," Hawke snapped. "I
told you if there's anyway to get inside her without mucking
up the place, we'll do it."

"And if you can't?" Van Buren asked softly.

"Then we'll attach explosives to the hull adjacent to that

cargo hold and blow a fucking hole in the side. And take that horrified expression off your face, Trevor. You're an oceanographer, for Christ's sake! This is a chance to explore and photograph the most famous ship in seafaring history. Or, and you said it yourself, to discover new kinds of marine life no man has ever seen before, or even knew existed. You're so concerned about that pile of junk at the bottom of the North Atlantic, you're forgetting this would be a scientific expedition, too. And for all we know, we might not even have to go into the ship. If she broke apart going down, that bullion could be scattered all over the ocean floor."

Montague breathed slowly. "God forbid. It's going to be difficult enough to find the ship itself without having to go groping over miles of ocean bottom for thirty-four crates."

Hawke smiled laconically. "That might be easier than trying to get inside the *Titanic*. But whether we're inside or outside the ship, no dive will be allowed to exceed five hours, and even that's cutting a bit close."

"Five hours?" Montague asked. "Why is that?"

"Dive duration is limited to the endurance of the storage batteries that power everything on those subs, from propulsion to the life-support system. The batteries have to be recharged after every six hours of use. When I say five hours, I'm allotting an hour and a half for descent, two hours maximum on the bottom, and another hour and a half for ascent."

"Still a considerable risk," Van Buren mused, "although I must say I'm intrigued by the project in general." He smiled shyly at Hawke. "You're a most persuasive fellow, John."

Montague was frowning, and Hawke said, "*Your* enthusiasm seems to have waned, old boy. If something's bothering you, let's have it."

"I was just wondering where I might fit in . . . with the actual expedition, I mean."

Hawke laughed. "You must be joking. Your knowledge of the *Titanic* is priceless, and I intend to have you participate in the fullest measure. Why, you must know every rivet in that ship, the full details of her interior, including the cargo areas, the possible structural damage we may encounter . . . good

Lord, Derek, I wouldn't dream of going without you. As a matter of fact, I insist on your making at least one dive with me. When we explore her, I need to know exactly what I'm looking at, and you would make an excellent tour guide."

The frown had left his friend's face, replaced by a look of doubt.

Hawke saw it. "You still seem bothered by something."

Montague said slowly, "As you know, I'm a devout *Titanic* buff. Have been ever since I can remember. Even as a lad, I haunted libraries trying to read every story ever written on that tragic maiden voyage. John, you're offering me a chance to actually see her as she is today, yet I have misgivings."

"About the gold?"

"Good heavens, no. The prospect of becoming wealthy intrigues me almost as much as the glory of finding the *Titanic* herself." He hesitated. "I'm simply wondering if I'll have the courage to make such a dive. You're both experienced . . . you were in submarines, and Trevor's done deep-sea exploration. But I haven't gone much deeper than the water in a bathing tub; I don't even fancy *swimming* underwater. The very thought of descending two and a half miles in a little eggshell of a craft absolutely petrifies me."

Hawke said sympathetically, "Perfectly natural, Derek. Let me assure you, however, you won't be going down in any eggshell. My subs are enormously strong. Look, safety itself is merely the art of reducing risk to the least possible chance of occurrence. Let me give you an example that may allay your fears. Suppose we're exploring the *Titanic* and we encounter some difficulty with our life-support system. Well, we've"— he gave a modest little laugh— "actually, I did most of the work, but anyway, we've developed an emergency ascent system on both submarines. Their motors are equipped with auxiliary superchargers capable of cutting ascent time to less than thirty minutes. A most welcome safeguard, I assure you."

Van Buren asked, "Why not use these superchargers on descent, as well? You'd have more time to spend on the bottom."

"Too much drain on the batteries," Hawke explained. "As

I said, they're reserved for a real emergency. I'd much prefer a slower descent and less time at the wreck, and have the wherewithal to get us back in a jiffy if need be."

"One more point," Van Buren said. "This gold you say is in a cargo hold, I shan't be surprised if the British government laid claim to its share if you recovered such a hoard. After all, the *Titanic* was a British ship. And for that matter, the White Star Line subsequently was merged into Cunard, so Cunard itself might argue for its own share."

"A point well taken, but already anticipated," Montague said. "I consulted with a barrister chap I know, an expert on maritime law." He took a sheet of paper from an inside coat pocket. "I didn't mention the *Titanic*, of course; I merely questioned him on what property rights would be involved in, say, the discovery of a freighter carrying valuable cargo that sank in international waters. He quoted me something he called the 'law of finds.' Let me read you what it says:

" 'The law of finds is operative in admiralty as an adjunct to the law of salvage, with the same jurisdictional basis. The assumption of the law of finds is that title to the property has been lost; this normally requires strong proof, such as the owner's express declaration abandoning title. The primary concern of the law of finds is title to the property. The finder can acquire title against all the world (except an owner who shows nonabandonment) by demonstrating the intent to acquire the property and possession, or a high degree of control.' "

Montague returned the paper to his pocket and regarded his companions triumphantly. "Does that resolve your doubts?"

Van Buren shook his head. "No, it does not. The language of barristers is the most convoluted and tortured known to civilized man. Would you mind translating what you just read?"

"Gladly. The *Titanic* sank in international waters, about three or four hundred miles southeast of Newfoundland. There was no effort made to salvage the ship, either by White Star or anyone else. In other words, she was abandoned by her owners, giving anyone who finds her the right of salvage. The law of finds would grant Sovereign Metals a claim to the gold, but

Sovereign no longer exists. It too, in effect, abandoned the wreck. So under both the law of salvage and the law of finds, to the victor belongs the spoils, if I may put it that way."

"Any more questions?" Hawke asked.

"None for now," Van Buren said.

"Derek, are you with us?"

Montague merely nodded. He felt oddly drained without being really tired, a vague uneasiness that somehow had washed away the excitement of his discovery and the unbridled enthusiasm and confidence of John Hawke. He found himself wishing that his wife, Beth, were still alive. Beth, that slim, lovely patrician lady to whom he could always confide his misgivings, his frustrations, his dreams. Beth, whose cool, unruffled judgment was the perfect antidote to his occasional impulsiveness. Beth, a woman of great inner strength and beauty—marvelous attributes for a mate, but pitifully inadequate defenses against the cancer that had taken her.

He was not quite sure why misgivings were coming over him now. The sixth sense of a cryptoanalyst told him something was wrong, but he could not define it. He knew he had set events with unknown consequences in motion, like dislodging a small rock that could turn into an avalanche. Was it potential danger that bothered him? No, he decided, personal fear could not be the reason for his qualms, because his eagerness to see the *Titanic* was uppermost. . . .

Van Buren's voice shattered Montague's self-introspection. "Well, what's next on the agenda?"

"I'm going back to Weymouth and call Lefferts," Hawke announced. "If he'll see me, I'll dash over to New York, and put the plan to him." His eyes, back to a softer, darker blue, almost danced. "I dare say that in a few months from now, our only concern will be how to spend our ill-gotten gains."

"Terrible choice of words," Van Buren murmured, but with no apparent rancor. "Derek, I guess you can sit back and relax for awhile."

Hawke said quickly, "Nobody relaxes. Trevor, we'll need oceanographic research on the area where she sank—currents, bottom topography, sound propagation curves. I'd like Derek to get us diagrams, cutaways, blueprints, deck plans, and whatever else is available on the *Titanic*'s interior, including the exact location of cargo hold three. Is that possible?"

Montague sighed unhappily. "We won't have the actual blueprints, I'm afraid. The originals were destroyed in World War II during a German air raid on Belfast. A direct bomb hit on the Harland & Wolff shipyard. Great historical loss; they were printed in black ink on linen, and no copies were made. Pity."

Hawke said worriedly, "Then what the devil can we work with? We can't go blundering about that wreck with no idea where to look for specific cargo holds."

"Oh, there were numerous schematic drawings made of the ship's interior, most of them published in *Shipbuilder*. These are readily available. They're not as detailed as the blueprints used in the *Titanic*'s construction, but for our purposes, they'll do nicely."

"Thank God." Hawke sighed. "For a moment, I thought we were in real trouble. So let's get cracking."

On mutual impulse, they all shook hands. It was a perfectly natural gesture that pleased Montague. The earlier angry exchange between his two friends had bothered him, but there was no sign of further animosity. Van Buren even smiled when Hawke, with his usual irreverence, said jokingly, "Now don't worry about your precious forty-six-thousand-ton tombstone, Trevor, we'll keep grave desecration to the absolute minimum."

"Actually, a bit over forty-six thousand," Montague corrected. "She displaced several hundred tons more than her twin sister, the *Olympic*."

Hawke laughed. "Ever the stickler for accuracy, aren't you, old boy?"

"There's been enough rubbish written about the *Titanic* without you, of all people, getting her tonnage wrong," Montague said, so seriously that Hawke laughed again. "It's no laughing matter, John. Not until the *Queen Mary* did we British build a larger ship. As a matter of fact, Germany launched the *Imperator*, which displaced over fifty-two thousand tons. . . ."

The lively discussion that followed, on subsequent liners that dwarfed the White Star giant, put Montague in a better mood. His knowledge of ocean liner history was encyclopedic; he was surprised and delighted to learn that neither Hawke nor even Van Buren realized Harland & Wolff had built a third sister ship, *Britannic*, torpedoed and sunk during World War I. "She was supposed to have been named *Gigantic*," he lectured, "but after the *Titanic* disaster, White Star deduced, quite properly, that any name connoting great size didn't exactly inspire public confidence. . . ."

But later, as Hawke drove him to Moreton-in-Marsh—the nearest train station to Broadway—Montague's gloom returned. It was as shapeless as ectoplasm, shimmering in his mind without ever assuming a distinct form. He finally admitted to himself what might be wrong. . . .

He had shoved that tiny rock down the side of a boulder-strewn mountain.

3

"I think I've got the kind of ship you'd need," Martin Lefferts said. "And I've got to admit this Montague seems to have latched on to something. But everything hinges on whether he actually broke a code—and that code could turn out to be complete bullshit."

Hawke laughed. "You do have a way of getting to the point. I assure you, however, that Montague's deciphering of that code is not bullshit, as you put it. As I have explained, there is too much corroborating evidence to support it."

"Could have been some kind of hoax," Lefferts suggested.

"There was no earthly reason for a hoax. Come now, Martin, you don't even believe that yourself."

He enjoyed sparring with the American billionaire. He knew him well enough to gauge whether he was interested in something. Lefferts's reaction to a proposal could be measured by the amount of profanity he directed toward it—polite, courteous inquiries were a sure sign that the supplicant didn't stand a chance. Lefferts hadn't grabbed the hook yet, but he definitely was circling the bait.

The two men eyed each other shrewdly. They were alone in Lefferts's plush office on the twenty-eighth floor of a Third Avenue skyscraper, and Hawke, a man of simple wants and modest income, envied the rich environment without resenting it. The huge room, done in muted pastels, was luxurious yet not ostentatious. Lefferts, Hawke knew, had designed the decor himself.

The incongruities of Lefferts's personality fascinated Hawke.

He had the vocabulary of a dockworker, yet Hawke had seldom heard him swear in front of women. He boasted of never having gone beyond high school, but he could discuss literature with the erudition of a college professor. He was openly ruthless in business dealings, in direct contrast to the way he treated his employees. It was said that the only cause for dismissal from a Martin Lefferts company was dishonesty, because everyone he hired was competent to begin with. The majority of his enterprises weren't unionized; he treated people too well, with dignity and compassion, demanding in return only that they work hard, and he was rewarded by what he prized most in life: their loyalty.

Lefferts was in his middle sixties and looked ten years younger. Not quite a six-footer, he had Hawke's wiry build with the slight suggestion of a paunch, kept well hidden by the double-breasted suits he wore. Hawke had never seen him in any color except brown. His sartorial tastes were definitely influenced by intense if questionable beliefs. "Fat cats and politicians wear blue suits," he explained to Hawke. "Brown's more democratic."

The suits were always neatly pressed, but Hawke had the idea they had come off the peg. For a man who could purchase a $125,000 Rolls-Royce as effortlessly as someone buying a pack of cigarettes, Lefferts had surprisingly plebian tastes. The first time they had met in New York to discuss the Loch Ness venture, Lefferts had suggested breaking for lunch. Hawke's palate was tingling; he anticipated gourmet dining at a place like the Four Seasons. They wound up at a nearby McDonald's, with Lefferts extolling the culinary virtues of the Big Mac and "the best damned French fries in the world."

During one of Lefferts's visits to England, Hawke had wangled both of them hard-to-get invitations to a Royal Geographic Society dinner. Lefferts looked dubious.

"Is this shindig formal?"

"Why, yes. Black tie, white tie optional."

"I won't go."

"You won't go? Look, we'll rent you a dinner jacket and—"

"You can buy me a tux if you want, but that won't change my mind."

"What do you have against formal wear?"

Lefferts flushed, then snarled, "I look like a goddamned penguin."

They didn't go to the Royal Geographic Society dinner, but Lefferts later learned from a mutual friend that Hawke had already paid for the expensive tickets and wasn't able to get a refund. After Lefferts departed England, a messenger delivered a package to Hawke's flat. Hawke opened it and found a matched set of seven Dunhill pipes, exquisitely grained, with this note.

John,
The food would have been lousy, anyway. Sorry.
                                                            Martin

Hawke was smoking one of those pipes right now, the fragrant smoke competing unsuccessfully with the heavier aroma of Lefferts's dirigible-sized cigar. They were staring at one another through the pungent clouds.

Lefferts said, almost casually, "This Montague guy, how good was he at his job? Breaking codes, I mean."

"He's an excellent piano player."

"Come again?"

"I was answering your question rather obliquely, but seriously. A great many men in that line of work happen to be excellent musicians. There seems to be a connection between deciphering ability and the structure of musical compositions."

"You pulling my leg?"

"No, I'm not. Your own navy had a cryptoanalytical unit based at Pearl Harbor, the one that broke the Japanese navy's code and led to the victory at Midway. The unit consisted largely of band musicians from the battleship *California*, one of the ships sunk in the Pearl Harbor attack. They were recruited into deciphering duty because of their musical skills."

"Well, I'll be damned!" Lefferts marveled. "I never knew that."

"That's the trouble with you Americans," Hawke scolded mildly. "You have an abysmally inadequate knowledge of your own history. Now Montague's piano playing may not have a damned thing to do with his cracking codes, but that's beside the point. Derek did more than break a code. His extensive research on Sovereign provides ample evidence that these thieves were involved for years in contraband gold shipments, and he hasn't the slightest doubt that one of those shipments—possibly the biggest Sovereign ever attempted—was on the *Titanic*. I know it's risky and I know it'll take a small fortune to mount an expedition, but believe me, Martin, the payoff will be worth it."

"You're damned right it'll be an expensive operation," Lefferts mused. "I'd say at least a million bucks . . . maybe more if we have to buy those subs of yours."

"The company will lease us both submarines. Seven thousand a day. Incidentally, they don't know finding the *Titanic* is our mission. I gave them some rot about diving for a seventeenth-century British warship sunk in the West Indies."

"Seven thousand pounds?"

"Seven thousand in your dollars. And Lloyds wants sixty-five thousand for hull insurance. I've already checked with them."

Lefferts snuffed out his cigar and wheeled his chair around so he was facing the big picture window that overlooked Manhattan. For a long minute he seemed to be staring into space, then wheeled back toward Hawke.

"John, I won't say I'm not tempted, but level with me. Give me the odds on both counts: finding the ship and recovering the gold. And no phony optimism."

Hawke didn't hesitate; he had anticipated the question, because Martin Lefferts always played the odds. "Finding the wreck . . . I'd say one chance out of three. Nobody's been able to locate it so far, but no one has tried as hard as we're going to, and if anyone can pinpoint where she lies, it's Trevor Van Buren. He knows ocean currents and tides like you know the way to your bathroom. Remember, we have to find her within two weeks after we commence the search. If we don't, we'll have to wait another year."

"Why two weeks?"

"It's already late April. We won't be able to get everything organized and under way until early July. Weatherwise, that's the best time of the year for the North Atlantic. Assuming we find the *Titanic* within a two-week period, we'll need another two weeks for salvage operations. Those three-to-one odds apply to establishing the wreck site no later than mid-July. If we have to stay around into August, we've got troubles; the weather's too unpredictable."

Lefferts inspected him curiously. "You're giving me the impression you're going to be the boss of this little excursion. Am I correct?"

The question startled the Englishman to the point of hesitating before he answered. It was a logical question that reminded Hawke he had automatically assumed a command role the minute Montague had revealed the gold's existence, even taken it for granted, with absolutely no discussion as far as Derek and Trevor Buren were concerned. They had accepted his leadership as if it was preordained. Hawke did that to people who were at least his peers or even his superiors. It had been that way at Cambridge and almost from the start of his Royal Navy career: John Hawke simply exuded a "follow me" air that was as much a part of him as the clothes he wore. When he was a relatively lowly lieutenant, a fellow officer of the same rank but senior to him—whom he had upbraided for some minor transgression—blurted, "The trouble with you Leftenant is that you wear that uniform like it belonged to a ruddy admiral!"

His instinctive compulsion to take command of virtually any situation had won him respect but also a few enemies in the RN hierarchy. If he hadn't been such a maverick, he probably could have retired as a rear admiral. In fact, he had never made captain, even though he had commanded two submarines while holding a lieutenant commander's rank. He regretted losing the higher pension, but he didn't regret for one moment the reason why. His philosophy was simple: "You gave me a job to do and if you don't like the way I'm doing it, kindly get the hell out of my way."

But now he was facing a powerful American with the same kind of dominating personality, the identical urge to take control. This was as good a time as any to establish the chain of command.

"Only one man can be in charge, Martin. I know submarines, I know deep-sea operations, and above all else, I know that you can't run anything this complicated and risky by committee. If you can't accept that, we might as well end this conversation right now."

Lefferts chuckled. "John, if there's one thing in this world I respect, it's a son of a bitch who's as hard-nosed as I am. I sure as hell don't run my own shop democratically. As they say, a camel is a horse engineered by a committee."

"The world's finest definition," Hawke agreed. "But mind you, Martin, there may be times when you and probably many others will challenge my authority and question my decisions. I'll welcome discussion, but the final say is mine. Understood?"

Lefferts nodded and lit another cigar. "Okay, the odds on getting the gold out?"

"At least fifty-fifty, maybe better. Personally, I'm not too hopeful about gouging our way into the interior. It's almost certain the debris we'd find would frustrate that. We'll use the smaller sub to explore any accessible areas, of course, but I rather expect we'll have to go in by blasting an entry path through the hull, a hole big enough to accommodate the one-man sub."

"This Van Buren, you told me he's not too happy about messing with the ship. Any chance of using divers?"

"Not at that depth. But I'll tell you what we will need . . . a demolitions expert."

Lefferts chuckled. "Thought you were pretty savvy on explosives yourself. You blew up that Nazi battleship, didn't you?"

Hawke smiled a little grimly. "That didn't qualify me as an expert. All we had to do was plant the Amatex under the hull and get the hell out of the way. The placement wasn't that scientific, rather haphazard, in fact. Not so with the *Titanic*. We'd have to figure out what dimensions of the entry hole would be adequate for the sub's admission. Damage to the inner section of the hull must be kept to the absolute minimum, or we'll have a debris problem. The equivalent of surgical skill will be required, using a scalpel instead of an ax. It calls for someone who really knows precise demolition techniques."

Lefferts slammed his fist on the desk. "Craig Caitin!"

Hawke observed dryly, "From the note of enthusiasm you attach to his name, I take it Mr. Caitin knows demolition."

"Hell, I'll bet he was weaned on dynamite. Got his start blowing up old buildings right here in New York. Lives over in Queens. Ended up specializing in underwater stuff, salvage and offshore oil work. I used him a few years back when I went after a Spanish galleon in the Caribbean, one that sank in 1687. She went down with a reported fortune in gold coins and jewels."

"I gather he's a good diver, then."

"The best. Ornery son of a bitch, but he's an artist with explosives."

Hawke kept his face straight. He asked innocently, "How much do you think he'd charge us for the *Titanic* job?"

"Charge *us?* You're a slick bastard. I'm the one you're asking to throw at least a million bucks down a twelve-thousand-foot hole. I'd have to be crazy to get suckered into this deal."

"Right," the Britisher agreed. "Martin, you *are* crazy. Loch Ness monster, Abominable Snowmen, live dinosaurs . . . you're a bloody pushover. That galleon you found, was there really a treasure in the captain's cabin?"

"Naw," Lefferts admitted with a sigh. "Just a few gold coins and a bunch of pots and pans. Which is probably what we'd find on the *Titanic*."

Hawke uncoiled from his chair and leaned across the billionaire's desk, their faces only inches apart. "This time, you're wrong. This time, you're going to hit the jackpot. This time, your dreams will become reality. This time you won't be fucking crazy, because this time you won't fail. I tell you there *is* gold on that ship. Almost ten thousand pounds of solid bullion. And there's a bonus, an extra dividend, if you will. We'll not only be making a fortune but we'll be making history—as the men who found the *Titanic*!"

Lefferts exhaled with a half sigh that acknowledged, even admired, Hawke's intensity. "You son of a bitch. You think you've got me hooked, and you're right."

The Englishman smiled in return. "You're an easy mark, my friend. I merely appealed to man's greatest weaknesses:

greed and ego, both qualities that you fortunately possess in sufficient quantity to be the right man to back us."

Lefferts looked a little disappointed. "Hell, John, I don't think I'm abnormally greedy or egotistical. I'm just adventuresome. I like challenge. I like achievement. I like doing things that other people just dream about doing. If I succeed, fine, give me the rewards and acclaim that go with success. But if I fail, nobody hears me whine or complain. I've got a pretty wife and a ten-year-old son who think I'm nuts, but I don't give a damn. Life's not worth living without *some* risk."

"An admirable philosophy," Hawke conceded, "and I was mostly joshing about greed and ego. So down to real business, Martin. I'd like to meet Caitin."

"It can be arranged. Word of warning, he's abrasive. Real hard-nosed type, the kind of guy who was born two hundred years late. He should have been a pirate. Makes me sound like a choirboy, and he could drink a Marine regiment under the table. Maybe you two will hit it off."

Craig Caitin joined them for lunch the next day at O'Hennessy's Irish Pub, owned by a good friend of Lefferts named Isadore Stein who hired nothing but Irish bartenders and kept discreetly in the background. Its ersatz Irish decor notwithstanding, the restaurant was an appropriate setting for Hawke's introduction to Caitin.

The explosives specialist was built like an inverted pyramid, a huge, bull-shouldered man with flaming red hair and an unkempt red beard to match. He said nothing until Hawke finished briefing him on the projected mission, during which time he consumed five shots of straight bourbon. Then he bellowed, "I don't particularly like you limey creeps, so if you're gonna run this show, count me out."

Lefferts gulped. Hawke merely smiled affably and took a sip of his scotch and water. Somehow it reminded Lefferts of a destroyer taking on fuel.

"I don't particularly like British creeps, either, Mr. Caitin," Hawke said in a tone coated with steel slivers. "Nor, for that matter, do I like American creeps. Quite frankly, I do not give one bloody damn what you think of me, because I am going to run this show with you or without you. And right now, I rather think it'll be without you."

Caitin stared at him, then turned to Lefferts. "This limey creep, I like."

Hawke chuckled. "Probably because I'm half-Australian."

"That explains it," Caitin said. "Mind if I have another drink?"

"Be my guest," Lefferts said, and in the next breath, Caitin and Hawke were discussing demolition problems as if they had known each other for years.

". . . this Amatex stuff you said you used on the *Tirpitz*," Caitin was saying, "won't work on the *Titanic*. Too powerful."

Hawke nodded. "I agree. Also Amatex-shaped charges are an implosive, directing a destructive force inward. What we're looking for is something that would blow a section of the hull so it falls outward. The less damage we create inside the ship, the easier it'll be to reach the cargo holds. How about dynamite, small charges strategically placed?"

Caitin stroked his beard thoughtfully, and while he pondered that suggestion, Hawke found himself studying the strong contours of the man's face. Caitin's granite features, Hawke decided, would not look out of place as the fifth head on the American monument at Mt. Rushmore. His eyes also impressed the Britisher; after all those drinks, they were still clear, a dark brown and curiously gentle. A good man to have around in a pinch, Hawke decided.

Caitin finally said, "I wouldn't trust dynamite at that depth. It's too tricky, and we'd be attaching it with those robot arms you mentioned. You can't get diddlysquat worth of precision using remote control. When it comes to dynamite, I'd rather work with my hands." He held up those hands, the size of ham hocks and the knuckles bristling with red hair—in their own way, Hawke knew, the hands of a skilled surgeon.

"I'm open to suggestion," Hawke said.

"Ever hear of Plastomite?"

"Can't say that I have. A plastic material, I presume."

"Yeah. It's brand-new. Best goddamned stuff around, developed for offshore jobs. I never seen it used on anything as big as a ship's hull, but I'll give you odds I could cut a hole in the *Titanic* and you'll think I'd a done it with a can opener."

Hawke glanced at Lefferts. "Martin, it's looking better and better."

"Just a minute," Caitin growled. "Nobody's told me how we get to where she went down. You keep talkin' about midget subs and big steel platforms and sonar to find the wreck, but nothin' about basic transportation. Sounds like you'll need a battleship to haul all the equipment."

Lefferts said, "Matter of fact, Craig, I did advise John I have a ship in mind, one that I already own, and I'll tell you what I told him. It's a converted minelayer, about eighteen hundred tons."

"Converted into what?" Caitin asked suspiciously. "Hell, that trawler we used down in the Caribbean woulda been fine."

"Right now, the *Pima* is more or less my personal treasure-hunting yacht. Bought her for a song seven years ago, partly to please my wife; she thinks holding cocktail parties on a salvage ship is the ultimate in entertaining. We put in state-rooms and dolled up her quarters real fancy; you'd never guess she was once a minelayer, not from her interior, anyway."

Hawke asked, "Why the devil didn't you go out and buy yourself a regular yacht? I'll wager it would have cost less than what you spent converting her."

"Yep, but that wouldn't have been any challenge. I got myself a good ship's architect and believe me, we had a ball turning her into a working pleasure boat. Christ, every time I take her out, I feel like I'm an admiral."

Caitin's laugh was more of a rumble. "Lefferts, you don't know a fuckin' thing about conning a ship. I remember you on that trawler. You couldn't steer a rowboat across a small lake without gettin' lost."

"I said I *felt* like an admiral," Lefferts explained mildly. "I didn't say I sailed like one. Anyway, I've got me my own admiral—an ex-minelayer skipper, incidentally—Jerry Robertson. I may own the *Pima*, but he commands it."

Caitin rasped, "So now you gotta convert her some more. This ain't no pleasure cruise we're goin' on. You'll need winches to lower the subs and the platform Hawke mentioned. A hell of a lot of communications equipment, too."

Lefferts said calmly, "We'll buy all the necessary communications gear, including a good bottom-scanning sonar unit. She already has radar and a SatNav for navigation."

"Where's she docked?" Caitin asked.

"Long Island Sound, near my home. John and I are going out to inspect her tomorrow. You're invited, too."

"I'll pass. Have to take your word for it that she's seaworthy."

Hawke wondered who the *Pima* was named for and asked Lefferts.

"That was her original navy name. Pima's some kind of Indian tribe in Arizona; the navy uses Indian names for some of its auxiliary ships. I was gonna call her the *Priscilla* after my wife, but she didn't go for it."

"I think we might consider changing it," Hawke said.

"To what?"

"The *Henry Morgan*."

"Who in the hell was Henry Morgan?" Caitin inquired.

"A seventeenth-century British pirate who turned respectable and became the governor of Jamaica. A very appropriate name for our little treasure hunter, I'd say."

Lefferts declared, "Goddamn, I love it!"

"I never heard of the son of a bitch," Caitin complained.

Hawke gave him a mischievous grin. "You should have," he said. "I wouldn't be surprised if you're a direct descendant."

"I don't like it," Caitin said, scowling.

"Why?" Hawke asked.

" 'Cause it's bad luck to change a ship's name. Any sailor'll tell you that."

Lefferts scoffed. "That's an old wives' tale, Craig. Superstitious bunk."

"It ain't superstitious bunk to me. I've seen some funny things happen to ships sailing under names they didn't start with."

Hawke said, "The opposite can be true, Caitin. In World War Two, the Germans had a pocket battleship christened the *Deutschland* when she was launched. She spent more time in dry dock than at sea. So they finally renamed her the *Lutzow*.

She didn't exactly distinguish herself, but at least she stayed afloat almost the entire war."

"Lucky exception," Caitin growled. "I still don't like it, Lefferts, but she's your ship. I just hope I don't have to say I told you so."

When Hawke returned to his hotel that evening, he found a message to phone Trevor Van Buren. He placed the call immediately, figuring that the oceanographer might have regressed to his original pessimism. Van Buren sounded—for him, anyway—positively bubbling, however.

"John. How are things going?"

"First-rate. I believe we have our salvage ship, and damned if Lefferts himself doesn't own her." Hawke was about to mention Caitin's recruitment but wisely decided against it. Trevor may have joined the parade, but he was still a bit out of step in the marching. Revealing that a demolitions specialist had already been brought into the picture could well alienate the scientist, and Hawke wanted to avoid friction if at all possible. There'd be the inevitable confrontation later, he reasoned, if they had to cut through the hull, but by then Hawke would have the tantalizing proximity of the gold in his favor.

He continued, teasingly, "I don't think you called merely to ask how things were going. Something on your mind?"

"Definitely," Van Buren said. "John, is there any chance you could fly out to the Scripps Institute of Oceanography while you're in the States?"

"But that's out in California."

"San Diego. Right." When Hawke hesitated, Van Buren knew he was calculating cost, and the oceanographer added hastily, "I know it's an expensive imposition, but there's someone at Scripps I believe you should talk to in person. Someone who'd make an excellent addition to our complement."

"In that case, I'll go. What's his name?"

From an unseen distance of more than three thousand miles, Hawke still would bet that Trevor was blushing, the stammer in his voice giving him away.

"Well, uh, ah . . . well, the person I have in mind is a lady."

Hawke laughed. "Don't be so defensive, you old fart. Give me her name and background, which must be considerable if you're recommending her."

"A very qualified background," Van Buren said enthusiastically. "Her name is Debra Chaney. She worked with me some years ago as a graduate student. Since then, she has earned herself a reputation in our field. I'd venture to say she's among the top five oceanographers in the United States. A truly brilliant woman, John. Truly brilliant, believe me. She's a specialist in both computer regression and hydrography, and is exceptionally knowledgeable about the *Titanic*, as well as having done quite a bit of deep-sea diving. In my judgment, she's the one we need for the location phase."

"I'll take your word for it," Hawke assured him.

"Call me after you talk to her, will you? I'd like to have your reaction. Meanwhile, I shall cable her and tell her to expect you."

"Righto. Anything else?"

The soft voice was back to normal. "Well, I take it Lefferts is going to back us?"

"Looks that way. I'll know for sure tomorrow after I inspect the ship."

Riding back from Long Island to Manhattan in Lefferts's Mercedes the next day, Hawke almost forgot the California trip, so enthused was he about the *Henry Morgan*. The ex-minelayer wasn't much to look at and still needed a lot of work—for one thing, heavier winches than the ones on her stern would be required. He was impressed with her beam, unusually broad for a ship of this type. His practiced navy eye told him she could accommodate not only the heavy deck gear but the two subs, as well. And she was plenty long enough—well over two hundred feet, he guessed.

Although the billionaire had repainted the former *Pima* a dazzling white, the cosmetic job failed to hide her utilitarian military ancestry. It was her interior that impressed Hawke; the staterooms were large and luxurious, and what had been a starkly prosaic ship's mess had been turned into a dining room that would have done justice to a fine restaurant. A section of the mess hall was partitioned off to form a small cocktail lounge. Aside from the excellent accommodations, Hawke also noted with interest the ship's new Bendex radar, one of many indications that even the Royal Navy would have approved of the spotlessly modern bridge equipment. He wanted to ask the captain about her diesel engines, but Robertson was away on a brief vacation. "They're old but in good shape," Lefferts told him.

Lefferts interrupted his reveries. "You going back to England soon?"

Hawke replied, "Now that you mention it, no. I'm heading for California tomorrow to interview some female oceanographer Van Buren has most heartily urged upon us."

"A woman? She'd be the only one on the ship. Your pal's off his rocker, John. Tell him no dice."

Hawke said firmly, "I've already promised him I'd at least talk to her. She's top-notch according to Trevor, and if she's as good as he says, we're going to need her."

Lefferts grunted unhappily but said nothing. He was driving the sleek gray Mercedes himself, even though he could have afforded a twenty-four-hour shift of chauffeurs. He claimed he could think better when he drove, a statement Hawke accepted as an unfortunate fact, because Lefferts did more thinking than driving. The Englishman was an expert motorist himself and considered Lefferts an accident going someplace to happen.

He wasn't doing too badly today, having run only one red light thus far. Now he was wearing his absentminded look, however, obviously pondering the news that a woman might be invited to join the expedition. The deeper his thoughts, the worse he drove—taking his right hand off the wheel to stroke his chin meditatively while the Mercedes wandered all over the road, and it took a poor driver for a Mercedes to wander at all. Hawke felt relieved when the conversation resumed, Lefferts using both hands again to drive.

"Where in California are you supposed to meet this gal?"

"San Diego, at the Scripps Institute. I'll make an appointment as soon as you drop me off at my hotel. What's the time difference between New York and the West Coast—three hours?"

"Yeah." The right hand left the wheel, moved to the chin, then returned. "Look, I'd have our Learjet fly you out there, but it's down in South America for a couple of days. Tell you what, though. I'll pick up the tab for the trip. After you set up the meeting, call my secretary, tell her when you'd like to arrive in San Diego, and she'll arrange everything."

Hawke dutifully, if not very convincingly, protested. "Damned decent of you, but it's not necessary."

"The hell it's not. We're going to be partners, John. You supply the expertise and I'll supply the cash. For Christ's sake, a first-class round-trip transcontinental ticket would eat up your entire pension for a month, maybe two months."

"I was planning to fly coach," Hawke admitted.

"That's what I thought. Came over in the back of the airplane, too, didn't you? Well, I don't let my partners travel in steerage; you're going first class. Wonder what she's like."

"You mean the woman." Hawke smiled. "Well, I always draw a mental picture of someone I'm going to meet for the first time. I'll wager this Debra Chaney's as flat as a board, very tall and rather horse-faced, with stringy black hair that hasn't seen a good cut for a decade. She wears flat-heeled shoes and tailored suits that would look more natural on a man. Extremely intelligent, so much so that she can be patronizing to those she considers her inferiors, which probably includes not only the majority of her colleagues but ninety-nine percent of California's population. She eats nothing but green salads, does not drink or smoke, and looks down her nose at anyone who does. In short, Martin, I expect our Debra will have the brain of Einstein and the aesthetic appeal of a twig."

"Thank God." Lefferts sighed. "She'd be safe on the *Henry Morgan*."

Debra Chaney was two inches over five feet, with exquisitely coiffured hair whose shade hovered between platinum blond and a soft white. Hawke could not decide whether her pretty, porcelain-complexioned face was elfin or patrician; it was a curious blend of both, perfectly symmetrical and definitely not horsey. The nicely shaped nose fell just short of being pert; the lips were full without being broad. She was wearing a short black skirt and a spankingly pressed white blouse of Sea Island cotton.

It was her figure that jolted the Britisher. She was a relatively tiny woman from the waist down, but full-busted, with athletic-looking shoulders and arms. She talked in low, businesslike tones, but when she laughed, it was almost a tinkling sound that reminded Hawke of tiny Christmas bells. Her obvious intelligence was the only thing he had gotten right in his predictions, and even that forecast was flawed. She didn't flaunt it, and when she showed him around the Scripps Institute, she answered his many questions without a trace of condescension. Hawke also noted how popular she obviously was with her coworkers; the tour was nothing but a steady succession of "Hi, Debbi"'s and friendly waves even when they weren't close enough to talk to anyone.

Trevor certainly had been right about her intelligence and her knowledge of the *Titanic*; she was almost as learned as Montague, who was a walking encyclopedia on the subject. While he was flying across the continent in the unaccustomed luxury of American Airlines's first-class service, he had decided not to mention the sunken ship in any way whatsoever. He would merely get an idea of Chaney's competence, judge whether she'd make a compatible addition to the expedition, and let either Trevor or Martin decide whether to invite her.

He hadn't counted on liking her instantly, and this was prompted more by her personality than by her surprising attractiveness. Debra Chaney had a ready smile, and when she met his flight at San Diego's Lindbergh Field, she made him forget immediately that he was six thousand miles from home, confronting a complete stranger.

Somehow, she had instinctively singled him out amid the crowd of deplaning passengers. Her handshake was firm.

"John Hawke?"

He nodded, surprised at both her recognition and appearance.

"Hi, I'm Debbi Chaney. Welcome to San Diego, and let's get a quick drink while the bags are unloaded. Besides, I need a cigarette."

So much for my teetotaler, nonsmoking theory, he had

thought ruefully, and followed her to the cocktail lounge, still laughing to himself on how wrong he had been. His inbred British reserve dictated caution on how to address her, but his more Australian genes took over.

"May I call you Debbi?"

"Debbi's fine. Technically, it's Mrs. Chaney, but I've been divorced for the past seven years."

"How the devil did you recognize me so quickly? I gave you no clue as to what I looked like and—"

"The cut of your clothes," she interrupted. "Very English, and I'll bet nobody else on that plane was wearing cavalry twills."

It had been merely small talk over the drinks, but later, after the Institute tour and accepting his invitation to dinner, Hawke tossed his cautious game plan aside. In the restaurant she had chosen, he brought up the topic he was supposed to have skirted.

"Debbi, when I arranged this meeting, I said I was doing some research on oceanography from the layman's standpoint and that your old mentor Trevor Van Buren had suggested I talk to you. Only the latter is true—about Trevor, that is. I honestly care very little about oceanography. My chief motive in this visit involves a certain ship."

"The *Titanic*."

"How the devil did you know that?"

"Because there are damned few oceanographers here or anywhere else who wouldn't give up the last five years of their lives to find that ship, and I took a guess. So you might as well tell me. Are you going after her?"

"Yes."

"And where do I fit in?"

He hesitated, tempted to flatly issue an invitation he already had decided Van Buren should be making, never expecting to be so impressed on such short notice. He hedged his answer.

"Trevor tells me you are an exceptionally well-qualified oceanographer, and I think this is something you should be discussing with him. I do know, however, no one could find that ship without the help of capable oceanographers, just as one needs a good detective to solve a crime. So an obvious question is, What do you know about her?"

"I think I've read just about every book and every article ever printed on the *Titanic*. I started with Walter Lord's *A Night to Remember* when it was published back in 1955. For starters, I have a theory as to where she supposedly sank. I say *supposedly* because I have a hunch she isn't where everyone assumes she is."

"An assumption based on what?"

"The position the *Titanic*'s radio operators used when they sent their distress calls. They got the position from Fourth Officer Boxhall. I think Boxhall goofed."

Hawke frowned. He had argued heatedly over this point with Montague, unwilling to believe that an experienced British merchant marine officer like Joseph Grove Boxhall would have made such a crucial error. In fact, Hawke had been quite testy, telling Derek that a layman shouldn't be passing judgment on a professional seaman. Now here was another layperson passing the same judgment.

He tried not to sound defensive. "From everything I've read about the man, Boxhall was considered a most competent, even superior navigator. Botching up that position fix simply makes no sense. It was an exceptionally clear night with many visible stars, ideal conditions for celestial navigation."

She looked at him, a half smile on her lips. "By any chance, did you happen to serve in the Royal Navy?"

A *very* smart lady, he was thinking. "Submarines, as a matter of fact. Am I wearing some kind of a sign proclaiming my former naval career?"

"The sign was in your voice. A little tone of resentment. But please don't take offense. I'm not necessarily suggesting that Boxhall was incompetent. You of all people should know that celestial navigation isn't the most reliable method of establishing a ship's position."

"Boxhall," he reminded her, "also used dead reckoning. He estimated the distance the *Titanic* traveled between the last navigational fix at sunset and where the ship came to a stop after the collision, deriving that distance from her speed and direction."

Chaney nodded. "Precisely my point. Dead reckoning in his case wasn't a very accurate cross-check of a celestial fix, because it failed to include the crucial factor of ocean currents. I'll concede you can't blame Boxhall for not taking currents into consideration; in 1912, oceanography as a science wasn't out of its diapers yet. Do you know why there are a lot of knowledgeable people who are convinced the *Titanic*'s last established position may have been several miles off?"

Hawke remembered a point Montague had brought up. "Something concerning the *Carpathia*; she reached the *Titanic*'s lifeboats earlier than expected."

"Well, that's technically correct, but it's not the whole story. The *Carpathia* was coming from the southeast, heading for the position the *Titanic* had given Captain Rostron. But when he arrived at the position, there was no sign of the *Titanic* . . . no debris whatsoever, absolutely no indication that a giant ship had gone down at that spot. But it was there that the *Carpathia* began picking up the lifeboats that had been rowing toward her for almost two hours. The only explanation is that the lifeboats started from a position other than the one Boxhall gave. Given the location of the rescue and the direction from which the *Carpathia* was approaching, it's my opinion that the *Titanic* actually sank about five miles away, to the west and slightly south of where she's supposed to be. And that, my British friend, is where you should be looking."

Hawke looked at her somewhat in awe before replying. "And that, my American friend, is where I rather imagine we *will* be looking."

"Is that all you came out here for? To get my estimate of the wreck site? Or is this a formal invitation to join the search?"

He hesitated again—this had gone faster and farther than he had intended. He studied her face a moment and made his decision—one based on an instinct that he could trust this woman.

"You're invited, as assistant oceanographer. Your first and primary assignment will be to help Trevor locate the wreck."

"And when do you plan to start looking?"

"We hope to be under way about the second week in July."

"Great! I'll ask Scripps for a few months' leave of absence, which I'm sure they'll grant when they hear why I need one. I can just hear what they'll—"

Hawke halted her enthusiasm in midair. "You may ask for your leave of absence, of course, but you will not say one word about the reason. For if you do, I assure you the invitation will be withdrawn instantly."

"For God's sake, why a hush-hush operation? Discovering the *Titanic* would be one of the greatest events in the history of oceanography. Give me one good reason for keeping it a secret."

"I'll give you one." His voice, like his eyes, had suddenly turned cold, and she almost shuddered at the change. "There's more than thirty million dollars worth of gold bullion aboard that ship and we're going after it. If you have any qualms about joining something that's more of a treasure hunt than a scientific expedition, tell me now and no hard feelings. Provided, of course, that you keep all I've said to yourself."

She stared at him, her eyes wide and her mouth half-open. He was trying to judge the expression on her pretty face— either horror or an excitement that was almost sexual, he couldn't decide which. He got his answer when she finally spoke.

"Count me in," said Debra Chaney.

4

Hawke expected Captain Jerry Robertson to be a competent seaman—Martin Lefferts would have made sure of that.

What he hadn't expected was a ship's skipper who seemed to have a negative attitude toward the entire expedition even before they sailed. This was revealed the day the two midget submarines and dismantled recovery platform arrived at JFK via two British Airways 747 freighters and were trucked over to the loading dock in Bayonne, New Jersey, where the *Henry Morgan* was now moored.

Hawke had watched the captain as Robertson first supervised the unloading and then carefully inspected the tiny craft, checking for the slightest evidence of shipping damage. He was a short but burly, bowlegged man with thin salt-and-pepper hair and the determined waddle of a bulldog. Lefferts fondly called him "Popeye" because Robertson was always puffing on a corncob pipe, of which he apparently had an inexhaustible supply. The inspection process had ended with Robertson's noncommittal grunt and a glance at Hawke that ranged somewhere between sour and doubtful.

He waved a thumb in the direction of the two subs. "I take it they're made of steel."

"Yes."

"Including the ribs?"

"A very thick-gauge steel," Hawke said a bit testily, wondering where this conversation was going.

Robertson squinted at the two yellow-painted craft as if he were trying to peer through their outer skins. "I'll admit I don't know a hell of a lot about submarines, so correct me if I'm wrong, but I thought operating two and a half miles deep, you'd need a titanium hull."

"Titanium would have been preferable but exorbitantly expensive in craft of this size."

Robertson grunted again. "Lefferts could have afforded it."

Hawke openly bristled. "He wasn't around when I helped design these subs. Funding was rather limited and we did the best we could. The best, incidentally, is considerable. The outer hull is actually stronger than steel. It's a double skin with a honeycomb structure between the two skins, and the ribs are twice as thick as the ones you'll find on your own fleet submarines. The hull is stressed to withstand pressure of up to nine thousand pounds per square inch, a more than adequate margin of safety, I assure you."

"They've been tested at nine thousand pounds psi?"

"The smaller of the two craft has made three dives to fourteen thousand feet. Absolutely no problems. If anything, the larger sub is even stronger."

The captain grunted for the third time and shook his head. "Well, you *seem* to have covered most of the bases, but at that depth, a lot of stuff can hit the fan."

"I'm glad you brought that up. Let me show you our emergency ascent system. It's something I'm rather proud of. I've even rigged it so the trim automatically adjusts to the abnormally rapid rate of ascent."

He went over the EAS device with Robertson, who listened and looked without comment. However, when Hawke finished, Robertson said, "You got some kind of schematic drawing of the wiring in this?"

Hawke fished out a paper from a pile of engineering blueprints in a briefcase. "I believe this is what you want to see," he said stiffly. He was beginning to dislike this officious, cynical Yank intensely.

The captain studied the drawing for almost five minutes, looked up, and said in a surprisingly friendly tone, "John, you mind some constructive criticism?"

He had never used Hawke's first name before, and the Englishman replied warily, "Not if it's truly constructive."

"Oh, it's constructive, all right. The way this thing is wired would make Rube Goldberg very proud."

"Rube Goldberg?"

"American slang for something that's unnecessarily complicated—so complicated that it makes Murphy's Law inevitable." He grinned at the Britisher's skeptical expression. "Never mind asking me who Murphy is. All I'm saying is that your wiring scheme is a plumber's nightmare. Too many connections and impulse relays, which means too many things can go wrong. The wiring should be simplified. Also, I'd recommend hooking the system to an auxiliary battery, in case the primary batteries fail. Mind if I borrow this drawing?"

"I suppose not," Hawke said, "but I would like to know what you're going to do with it."

"Modify this wiring. Mostly, it would involve bypassing or eliminating some of this circuitry. If you'd help me, I think we could install a far more reliable system in a couple of days . . . three at the most."

"Offer accepted," Hawke said gratefully.

Robertson smiled. "That's good. When advice collides with pride and ego, advice sometimes doesn't stand a chance. You just earned the right to call me Jerry, but not in front of the crew. Okay?"

They shook hands. Hawke felt relieved; he felt he had found a valuable friend and ally. He had no way of knowing that Captain Jerome Robertson considered him a new friend who also was a damned fool.

On the evening of July 7, 1975, the key members of the expedition gathered in the *Henry Morgan*'s dining room, following the routine that had been established when the ship moved from Long Island to her Bayonne berth—a progress report on the day's activities. Loading of supplies and equipment was virtually completed, and Hawke already had announced that the *Henry Morgan* would sail two days hence.

Tonight, he surveyed his colleagues with a sense of satisfaction. An incredible amount had been accomplished in a very short time, including what at first had appeared to be a major bottleneck: obtaining the 50,000 feet of steel cable for the four new heavier winches. Lefferts had pulled strings—and probably called in a few IOUs—to get the cable delivered on time. "I know the top brass at Bethlehem Steel." This was his explanation for the fast action, and Hawke could only guess at what kind of pressure Lefferts had applied.

The friction Hawke expected had not developed. True, cliques already had formed and Hawke himself—without wanting it to happen—was part of one that included Lefferts, Caitin, and Montague. The second clique consisted of Van Buren and Debra Chaney, but *clique* was not even the term Hawke could honestly apply to the coalescing of individuals into the two groups. Mostly, it had been a case of common interests rather than common beliefs—certainly no indication that they had separated into conflicting "gold versus science" or "destruction versus preservation" segments. Van Buren demonstrated hostility toward Craig Caitin from almost the moment they were introduced, but it was the latter's profanity that apparently alienated the oceanographer. It took the preoccupied Hawke some time to realize that what Trevor really resented was the presence of a demolitions specialist aboard. The crude language didn't seem to disturb Debbi Chaney until she overheard him remark to Lefferts, "No fuckin' broad belongs on a ship." Debbi marched up to him, grabbed his collar, and yanked his head down until their noses almost collided.

"*Mister* Caitin," she said icily, "don't you ever refer to me again in that language. Do I make myself clear?"

Unbelievingly, Caitin blushed the color of his beard. "Yes, ma'am . . . I'm sorry."

Later, he remarked to Hawke, "That Chaney's spunky, ain't she?"

"Very. But if you'll try to limit your four-letter words to, say, one every five sentences, I'm sure you two will get along famously."

Not too surprisingly, they did, for Caitin, as he already had demonstrated with Hawke, had a grudging respect for anyone who stood up to him. To witness the giant demolitions expert struggling awkwardly to curb his profanity in Chaney's presence was to see willpower at it highest level. For Hawke, however, the incident had touched off disturbing warning bells in his bachelor's psyche.

He found himself admitting that he was enormously attracted to Debra Chaney, even though from the very start of their association he had steeled himself against any romantic involvement. It was stupid, he kept telling himself, for the nominal leader of an expedition to go chasing after the only woman in the party—bad for discipline, unfair to the other men, and potentially harmful to the venture's success because it would inevitably involve favoritism.

Besides, he hadn't picked up any indication that Chaney might be interested in him. Hawke, a veteran at casual affairs, was expert at sensing such nuances. Debbi was always friendly in a businesslike way with Hawke, but spent virtually all her time with Van Buren on their mutual assignment: to determine the *Titanic*'s location.

This, in fact, was the chief subject under discussion at that night's debriefing session. After Hawke reported that boarding of food supplies would be completed the next day, Trevor Van Buren cleared his throat.

"I have an announcement," he began. "Debra and I believe we have established the *Titanic*'s probable location, not a precise site but a reasonably narrow search area. If our calculations are correct, I'm confident we can locate the ship within two or three days of sonar search."

A burst of applause was interrupted by the deep voice of Captain Robertson.

"That word *probable* worries me. That's one hell of a big ocean out there. When you say your calculations are reasonably close, I'd feel a bit more confident if I knew how you arrived at your site estimate."

"Gladly." Van Buren beamed. "Debra, here, is largely responsible for establishing that estimate, so I'll let her explain."

Chaney spread a fair-sized oceanographic chart on the long rectangular table and the others clustered behind her. She pointed a pencil at the spot of the chart.

"Gentlemen, this red X marks the *Titanic*'s last reported position, the one she radioed to the *Carpathia* and other vessels. That position, as you'll note, is forty-one degrees, forty-six minutes north and fifty degrees, fourteen minutes west. As Trevor and I have mentioned in previous discussions, we are convinced this latitude and longitude were wrong, simply the result of the relatively primitive navigational methods of that era."

The pencil moved a few inches across the chart, poising over a small blue circle and then descending until the tip rested in the middle of the circle.

"This indicates a latitude of fifty degrees, one minute west and forty degrees, forty minutes north. It is our opinion that we'll find the *Titanic* within a five-mile radius of that position."

The dining saloon was tomb-silent, every mind in the room weighing what she had said: a chance for quick success or, if the oceanographers were wrong, weeks of frustration and probable failure.

Chaney continued. "Basically, we added Trevor's and my knowledge of ocean currents to all the evidence supporting the one salient theory; namely, that Fourth Officer Boxhall's final position fix had to be erroneous. As you've heard me say on more than one occasion, the *Carpathia* came upon the *Titanic*'s lifeboats at the position Boxhall had given his radio operators, yet those lifeboats had been rowing for two hours. There was no sign of wreckage, so the *Titanic* could not possibly have sunk at the spot.

"But this was not the only evidence we worked from. I call your attention to the Leyland liner *Californian*, the infamous ship stuck in an ice pack only a few miles from the sinking *Titanic*, the ship that ignored the *Titanic*'s clearly visible distress rockets, the ship whose captain went back to sleep even after he was told about those rockets. Derek Montague furnished us with a copy of the *Californian*'s official log for the night of April 14, 1912. It shows that she came to a stop at ten-thirty at night and did not start her engines again until six o'clock the following morning, having received word that the *Titanic* had gone down three and a half hours earlier. At that point in time, the *Californian* had drifted approximately five nautical miles, a distance indicating that she had been carried by a south-southeast current running at seven-tenths of a knot.

"Now as I've already explained, we know the *Titanic*'s lifeboats drifted or rowed south; that's obvious from the position at which the *Carpathia* found them and the direction from which they were coming. So Trevor and I fed all this data, plus what we have learned about ocean currents in more recent years, into the computer Martin Lefferts so generously provided us"—Lefferts grinned and bowed his head slightly—"and regression analysis confirmed the position I've just shown you on the chart. Any more questions?"

They resumed their seats and Hawke said, "I've got one. The same question I've asked you and Trevor before, and which you declined to answer until you determined the probable wreck site. What's the sea bottom like in that area? I know the topography of the ocean floor can be as rugged as the Himalayas or your own Rockies, with mountains, valleys, canyons—"

She stopped him. "That's the magic word. *Canyon*."

"Jesus," Lefferts exclaimed. "You mean she's at the bottom of some deep hole where she can't be reached? Maybe even out of sight?"

"It's not as bad as you might think," Van Buren said. "There *is* a submarine canyon in this general area. Oceanographers, in fact, refer to it as the '*Titanic* Canyon,' but actually this is a misnomer. It's more of a large trough or valley running northeast to southwest, with a number of tributaries. The ship may be resting smack in the middle of the trough or perhaps in one of its offshoots. The depth of the canyon, if you want to refer to the valley in more dramatic terminology, does not concern me. But there's something else we haven't discussed with anyone yet, simply because the possibility of its causing us difficulty is reasonably remote."

Hawke already knew—Debbi had mentioned it to him but not in particularly alarming terms—and he decided to let Trevor stay in his unaccustomed spotlight.

Van Buren continued, in the confident tones of a professor, "In 1929, a major submarine earthquake occurred in the Grand Banks area off Newfoundland, about three hundred miles northwest of where the *Titanic* sank. The quake was of such severe proportions that it snapped a number of transatlantic cables and caused large mud slides. The potential exists that some of those mud slides may have reached the *Titanic*'s area and buried her, out of sight and untouchable even if she was found."

Caitin blurted, "Well, now, ain't that just dandy!"

"I said this was a remote possibility," Van Buren assured his audience. "I doubt very much whether the mud slides triggered by the Grand Banks earthquake could have reached the wreck site. Furthermore, Debra and I have thoroughly researched seismographic records of submarine earthquake activity in the North Atlantic in the years subsequent to the 1929 occurrence. There has been none of any significant proportions, so once again I reiterate it's not likely that the ship is buried under mud."

"Thank God," muttered Lefferts.

Hawke said, "This brings us to the subject that I asked Derek Montague to look into—the possible or probable condition of the *Titanic* herself. Derek?"

Montague started to unreel his string-bean frame from his chair, then decided to stay seated—mostly because Van Buren had delivered his remarks while standing and had unwittingly given the impression he was teaching a class. It was one of Trevor's idiosyncracies that could be simultaneously annoying and endearing.

Montague said, "To begin with, all I can offer is conjecture, based on eyewitness accounts of survivors who saw the *Titanic* go down. The trouble is that the accounts themselves are conflicting." He picked up some notes he had made. "Let me read a few examples."

"Here's one from a crew member: 'Stern righted itself without the bow. In my estimation, she must have broken in half about abeam of the after funnel.'

"But according to Second Officer Charles Lightoller, and I quote this highly regarded and very experienced seaman, 'The ship did *not* break in two.' Another eyewitness says, 'Broke in two, after part righted itself, then down.' Yet here's a survivor who insists, 'No breaking up—went straight down.' "

Montague looked up from his notes and continued. "I'm sure we're all aware that eyewitness accounts are notoriously unreliable, simply because people looking at an identical event will see things differently, especially under stress. What I've done to clarify the picture a bit is to tabulate the statements of those who claimed the *Titanic* broke in two as she sank and those who swore she stayed intact throughout the final plunge. The former outnumber the latter by a ratio of approximately three to one."

"Seems conclusive enough for me," Lefferts observed. "If she's in two pieces, does that complicate matters?"

It was Hawke who answered. "It could, but we won't know for sure until we find her. Derek, what's the consensus on where she broke up?"

"I'm afraid there is no consensus," Montague replied. "The eyewitness accounts vary too much. Between the third and the fourth funnels, according to some; aft of the fourth funnel, according to others. A ship in two sections, I venture to say, would make our task more difficult, for it would point to far greater damage than we've been hoping for."

It was Debra Chaney's voice that dissolved the tension. "Well, I've read the same source material Derek told me he's been using—the transcripts of the British Board of Trade inquiry and the U.S. Senate hearings. I agree the evidence is confusing, yet it's not as inconclusive as it might appear. Only a handful of eyewitnesses claimed the *Titanic* sank intact. Derek, I think she broke up at a point about two-thirds of her length, or just behind the fourth funnel. And I'm willing to bet we'll find both sections, maybe several hundred yards apart, with the larger or forward section resting upright on the ocean floor."

"Debbi, why do you think the main section is upright?" Hawke asked.

"Because all that heavy machinery tearing loose toward the bow would have made her descent almost perpendicular. And when her nose hit the bottom, I figure she just settled back on an even keel. I wouldn't vouch for the other third—the stern—to be upright. It's very possible that it'll be on its side. But it's the forward part you're interested in, isn't it?"

Hawke nodded. "Cargo hold three, according to the blueprints Derek obtained, is located ahead of the first funnel on orlop D, or the lowest deck."

Montague said quickly, "Where the first funnel used to be, of course. We have to assume all the funnels separated from the ship when she sank; that's one thing upon which the eyewitnesses generally seemed to have agreed."

Lefferts had a sudden inspiration. "Four missing funnels would result in four very large holes. How far down did those oversized smokestacks go? Seems to me, they'd offer some easy entry points."

Hawke looked at Montague. "I'll let you disillusion him, Derek."

Montague said, "The funnels went down all the way to the boilers, and I assume there are, indeed, four large holes topside. But I don't think they're wide enough to accommodate our smaller submarine, and even if they were, the sub eventually would encounter what remains of the boilers. Your so-called entry points, Martin, would only extend down a few of the upper decks. Now Debbi mentioned the fact that a lot of heavy machinery tore loose as the bow tilted forward at an increasingly sharp angle. This raises a possibility that I discussed earlier with you, John, after we studied the ship's interior drawings. We'd better pray that this machinery didn't smash into cargo hold three. Because if it did, you're going to have one devil of a time breaking into that hold."

Hawke, glimpsing the look of consternation that clouded Lefferts's face, said quickly, "And I informed you, Derek, that I don't think the machinery penetrated as far as hold three. Holds four and five would have served as a kind of buffer zone, and it's my theory that the machinery piled up in those two holds before it reached the others."

Lefferts smiled grimly. "John, I'm spending a million and a half bucks on your theory. Frankly, I don't like the odds."

Hawke rose and began pacing, as he had that day in Van Buren's cluttered study when the venture was first proposed, then he sat down abruptly. "All of you, listen well. I never said this would be easy. Derek and I happen to disagree on the amount of damage that runaway machinery might have caused. If he's right and I'm wrong, it's going to make our job more difficult but not impossible. I don't give a damn if every boiler on that bloody ship wound up in hold three. We still can get in there. Martin, you of all people know we've got a demolitions expert"—he looked at Caitin while Van Buren, following the glance, sniffed disdainfully—"whom I'm convinced could break into America's Fort Knox if he had to. We have those pincer arms mounted on the prows of the subs to clear away anything blocking our path. So let's have an end to pessimism and defeatism. The stakes are too high and too rewarding for anyone to feel negative even before we sail. I have never offered anyone in this room an absolute guarantee of success, including finding the *Titanic*, let alone the gold. But I still consider the odds to be in our favor, in fact, Martin, better than when you first asked me to quote the odds."

Affection and admiration were in Lefferts's voice as he replied, "John, if you're that confident, I'm going to throw in with you. For a million and a half bucks, we're getting a shot at thirty million, maybe even more. Those odds we all can live with. . . ."

There were murmurs of approval, but it did not escape Hawke that none came from Trevor Van Buren. The oceanographer simply lit one of his English Ovals cigarettes and looked pensive—almost glum, Hawke thought, and he knew why. He decided if there was going to be any friction, it might as well surface right now so he could at least control it.

"Martin indirectly has brought up a point that warrants discussion; namely, the disposition of the rewards awaiting us if we're successful. I've broached this subject with him before and got his typical 'Let's talk about it later.' I think we should talk about it tonight."

Hawke paused, trying to judge their thoughts by their expressions. "From the very start, I've always felt this endeavor is both scientific and—how shall I phrase it?—well, monetary. Finding and exploring the *Titanic* will fulfill the mission's scientific goals, but considering the amount of money Mr. Lefferts has put into our venture, recovering the gold deserves equal and perhaps even greater priority. I therefore propose that if we succeed in our treasure-hunting efforts, Martin Lefferts must be paid back in full for what he has invested thus far, plus interest at prime. After that, I suggest that the crew of this vessel receive, in addition to their regular wages, ten percent of the redemption value of the gold. The remainder will be divided equally among the seven people present here tonight, including Captain Robertson. Is this satisfactory to everyone?"

Lefferts said, "Wait a second, John." He was scribbling figures on a piece of paper and finally looked up. "Using a conservative estimate of thirty million for the gold after I'm repaid for expedition expenses, the ten crew members would divide about three million dollars among them. That leaves roughly twenty-seven million to be split seven ways—almost four million dollars apiece. John just asked us if this arrangement is satisfactory. Well, I've got no quarrel with it whatsoever. How about the rest of you?"

A burst of applause was his answer. Out of the corner of his eye, Hawke saw Van Buren clapping, too, and he sighed imperceptibly in relief. Although, he had to admit, Trevor's clapping reminded him of a man who had fallen asleep during a dull opera and had joined belatedly and guiltily in the applause that had awakened him. How could anyone be so blasé about the prospects of getting a four-million-dollar payoff? he wondered.

Captain Robertson, perhaps the only person in the room who didn't have euphoria painted on his face, decided this was an opportune time to bring up something that had been nagging at him.

He asked, "How much of this should the crew know? All they've been told is that we're going after the *Titanic* and hope to bring up some valuable artifacts."

"And that they'll share in some unspecified proceeds, if there are any proceeds," Lefferts added. "I think at this stage that's sufficient information. Actually, I had in mind paying them a small bonus even if we didn't recover any gold. Any pictures we obtain of the wreck should be quite valuable in themselves."

Van Buren nodded energetically as he turned to Hawke.

"John, I trust you'll allow adequate inspection of the wreck before attempting any salvage operations. Taking pictures will be an absolute necessity."

"That's why we acquired the new underwater color camera the Japanese developed. A camera's already mounted on each sub next to the work lights."

"How the hell can you take pictures at that depth?" Caitin wanted to know. "Must be like tryin' to see the bottom of an inkwell."

"Well," Hawke acknowledged, "it's not like walking around Trafalgar Square at noon on a sunny day. Yet in 1963, your own navy obtained photographs of the sunken nuclear submarine *Thresher*, and she was on the ocean bottom at eighty-four hundred feet. We have a superior strobe camera and the added advantage of the working floodlights."

Caitin grumbled. "Eighty-four hundred feet ain't twelve thousand, pal."

Van Buren said, "I doubt whether it's any darker at twelve thousand, Mr. Caitin. I should point out that some years ago, at the request of the Titanic Historical Society, the International Ice Patrol actually obtained pictures of the ocean bottom in the general area of the sinking. It certainly demonstrated the feasibility of photography at that depth. As a matter of fact, if we have problems, they'll be of our own doing—such as stirring up mud or dislodging debris."

The last remark was aimed at Hawke in a tone that somehow managed to sound accusatory. "We'll try to be neat, Trevor," Hawke assured him, hoping he had kept sarcasm out of his voice. "I'd say this has been a most productive session. Jerry, do you think we can get under way the day after tomorrow?"

The taciturn captain nodded. "All supplies should be aboard by fifteen hundred tomorrow. We're still working on that sonar gear, but that's almost finished. I'd say we can weigh anchor within the next thirty-six hours."

Hawke was heading for the cocktail lounge when Robertson stopped him. "Stay behind a minute, John."

"Of course. What's on your mind?"

"The *Thresher*. I knew her skipper—a damned good submariner."

"So what's your point, Jerry? Nobody blamed him for what

happened. That bloody submarine was what you Yanks call troublesome motorcars—you know, a lemon. The *Thresher* was always requiring repairs and if I remember correctly, your navy determined she had been poorly constructed."

Robertson's square jaw tightened and his teeth clamped down on the corncob's stem. "She started breaking up at an estimated depth of less than two thousand feet. At eighty-four hundred feet, she was scattered all over the ocean floor. You're taking those midgets down to twelve thousand—that's my point."

"We've tested them at fourteen thousand, Jerry. Not to worry. Besides, the *Thresher*'s maximum diving depth was only a thousand feet; she would have imploded at two thousand even if she hadn't had structural deficiencies. What is it exactly that concerns you?"

The captain took several puffs on the pipe before replying. "Damned if I really know. Maybe it's because I once saw a hell of a lot of men die. My own men, too. Maybe a surface sailor's inherent distrust of subs. You couldn't have gotten me into the submarine navy if you had promised me the Congressional Medal of Honor for making a fifty-foot dive in peacetime. Or maybe it's the thought of you people working at that god-awful depth. You've all become my friends in a very brief time, even Caitin. I'll bet if I had had him in the navy, he'd have spent more time in the brig than on a deck. And then there's Lefferts. I've never know a finer man, let alone a finer boss. Which reminds me, I know you'll be making the dives, but who else?"

Hawke smiled ruefully. "That has been one of my headaches from the start. Everyone wants to see the *Titanic* firsthand. To answer your question, Caitin, of course. Van Buren and Chaney each have had diving experience and can easily be trained to handle the smaller sub by themselves. We deliberately simplified and automated most of its controls for one-man operation. Montague won't require much training. I'll be taking him with me on the larger sub for at least one exploratory dive, but strictly as an observer and guide."

Robertson grunted unhappily. "Seems to me, you would

have been better off hiring a couple of professionals like Caitin, maybe some guys with actual sub experience. You're putting a lot of faith into a bunch of amateurs."

"Thought about it," Hawke admitted, "but the fewer people involved, the larger our treasure shares. Besides, I wouldn't consider either Van Buren or Chaney rank amateurs; they're no strangers to deep-sea work."

"What about Lefferts?"

Hawke looked surprised. "Martin? Frankly, I hadn't really considered using him. He's done a little diving but he has no special skills."

The captain snorted. "Let me tell you something, John. If you don't let him make at least one dive, he'll tell me to turn this ship around and head back to New York. There's no way you can keep him out of those subs. Hell, he doesn't need the gold. He doesn't really even care if you don't recover a single damned bar. The glory of just finding the *Titanic* is enough for him. But he'll have to see it with his own eyes; he'll consider anything short of that a personal failure. And Martin Lefferts doesn't like personal failures."

Hawke said soberly, "I hadn't counted on that development. Never even discussed it with him, in fact. I've always assumed he'd let others do the dirty work. I'm going to have to think this over."

"Think long and hard," Robertson warned. "Frankly, I hope you can talk him out of it. I'll sleep better."

Hawke said doubtfully, "I imagine it would be rather difficult to talk Martin Lefferts out of anything he's set his heart on. Join me for a drink?"

"No, I'm going to check on that sonar again. I'll see you at dinner."

"Right." The Englishman watched the hydrant-shaped figure of the captain waddle toward the door leading to the deck, then sighed in anticipation of trying to solve this latest problem. It was solved for him in the next ten minutes.

Lefferts, a glass of bourbon and water in his hand, announced, "I've got a great idea. Let's give those two midget subs some names."

"*Captain Kidd* and *Blackbeard* would fit nicely with the *Henry Morgan*," Montague suggested.

Lefferts dismissed this with a wave. "Naw, *Henry Morgan* was Hawke's doing. Look, this is a joint Anglo-American show. Let's call the bigger sub *Winston* and the smaller one *Franklin*. After our two greatest leaders of the free world. They personified cooperation. How about it, Hawke?"

"Not bad. Not bad at all. We were going to name them, anyway, for communications purposes. I rather like *Winston* and *Franklin*. Martin, you have just contributed far more than a mere million and a half dollars."

"Great!" Lefferts enthused. "I think I'll be taking a closer look at *Winston* from now on. She's the one I'll be riding on, right, John?"

Hawke couldn't force either a yes or no out of his mouth and settled for a nod so slight that it fell short of classifying as affirmative. But before they broke for dinner, however, he got Lefferts off to one side, out of everyone's hearing.

"Martin, to tell you the truth, I hadn't planned on your making any dives. I honestly don't think it's a good idea."

"Bullshit! Give me one good reason why I shouldn't."

"For one thing, you're too inexperienced at this sort of thing. If things got a bit sticky, I'd want someone with me who knew what the bloody hell he was doing."

"Come on, John, I've made plenty of deep-sea dives. Just ask Craig."

"You haven't made any in anything like these midgets. They're complex and tricky to handle."

"You're taking Craig, aren't you?"

"Yes, but I've been training him—Trevor and Debbi, too."

Lefferts stared at him, half in anger and half unbelievingly. "You're training them and leaving me on the sidelines? Who the hell do you think's paying for this junket?"

"You are, but—"

"Stuff that *but* up your ass, John. If you're gonna train them, I demand that I get the same chance."

"Debbi's had considerable deep-sea-exploration experience, Martin, and she's a professional oceanographer, as well. I'm sorry, but in my mind, she's more qualified than you are. For the same reason, I consider Van Buren more qualified; like Chaney, he's a trained scientist, and you're not. Neither is Caitin, I'll admit, but you know why we need him down there. As for Montague, he knows more about the *Titanic* structure than the rest of us combined."

Lefferts sat down heavily in the nearest chair. "I wouldn't want to put this matter on a 'take me or else' basis," he said ominously.

Hawke said very quietly, "Martin, I don't like threats, and I'm going to forget the one you just implied. But I do realize how important this is to you. Right after breakfast tomorrow, I'll start checking you out in *Winston*. But no promises; you have to qualify and I'll judge you on performance."

Lefferts appeared mollified. "Fair enough. And now that we've settled that, John, when in the hell have you been training the others? I've never seen anything like that going on."

"You've either been away conducting business as usual in your downtown office, or you've been too busy helping Robertson to even notice. Mostly, they've been familiarizing themselves with the subs' controls and instruments."

"Well, I guess I gotta ask. How are they doing?"

"Better than I expected. Caitin's quick to learn. He has natural mechanical aptitude and an excellent grasp of fundamentals. Chaney's very good, too. Trevor's the one who really surprised me; he's almost as capable as Craig, and with a little more practice, I think he'll actually surpass him. By the time we reach the site, I have half a mind to let Trevor try a solo dive in *Franklin*."

"Jesus, think that's wise? I wouldn't want to go down alone, no matter how well you taught me."

Hawke smiled. "Sending Van Buren down by himself is preferable to sending him down with Craig Caitin. They are not what I'd charitably call compatible."

"Yeah," Lefferts agreed with a grin. "Well, let's go eat . . . and John, thanks."

"Don't mention it," Hawke replied, "but one word of caution."

"Which is?"

"If you pilot a sub like you drive a car, God help us."

* * *

John Hawke stood alone on the deck of the *Henry Morgan*, gazing at the jeweled skyline of New York City in the distance.

It was almost midnight. Although the air was oppressively hot and humid, Hawke preferred it to the more comfortable but confining air-conditioned cabin he shared with Montague. He was enormously fond of Derek, but not as a roommate. Montague snored like a buzz saw and Hawke was too restless to sleep, anyway.

They would sail at 0600 tomorrow morning and Hawke always had insomnia the night before an important mission—not from fear but from the delicious excitement of facing the unexpected. That was the way he had always lived and, he admitted wryly, was probably the way he would die—when the unknown turned out to be more formidable than what he had planned.

Not this time, however. He was confident they would achieve the first goal: finding the *Titanic*. He was equally sure they would recover the gold. The only thing that kept nagging him was the conviction that they would have to ravage the old ship to get at the bullion.

He knew he hadn't been totally honest with Van Buren. He could only hope that cargo hold three was accessible without having to blast a path to it from the outside, yet in his heart he was almost sure the hope was futile. It was too easy to visualize the interior destruction that must have occurred during the final plunge, with heavy machinery smashing its way through weakened bulkheads toward the bow. Those in the lifeboats could hear the sound of steel crashing against steel as the 833-foot liner tilted in its fatal angle—a terrible sound, as if the ship were a giant animal screeching in agony before it died.

Despite the night's heat, he shivered, dimly sensing how Trevor and Derek felt about the *Titanic*—the fascination so many had toward a ship whose brief life and sudden death had kept her name alive for more than six decades. There had been marine disasters involving similar losses of life, yet who remembered the names of those vessels? The *Titanic* was something special—a symbol of nobility, arrogance, bravery, stupidity, of beauty transformed into an ugly, mutilated metal corpse; of proud, indestructible power and strength suddenly drained by a hidden stiletto of frozen water. . . .

"I see you couldn't sleep, either."

Hawke, startled, turned around. Debra Chaney was inspecting him gravely. She had no makeup on and was wearing a light bathrobe over pajamas, looking like a teenager heading for an illegal midnight snack.

"Worried about something?" she asked.

"No, just thinking."

"About what?"

"About the *Titanic*. What it must have been like to be aboard her that night."

She nodded understandingly. "I've often thought about that. How I would have reacted—you know, scared while trying to look brave. I believe in equality, but on that occasion, I think I would have been grateful for the 'women and children first' rule."

"And I wouldn't have blamed you. I suppose that facing certain death poses a unique dilemma for a man, an almost contradictory dilemma. He is more afraid of exposing his fear to others than he is of death itself. It's a situation that makes instant heroes out of devout cowards. I saw that often enough during the war. Of course, I saw the opposite happen, too. The trouble is, no one can predict which reaction he'll have."

She took out a cigarette and he lit it for her. "Thanks. I'll bet I know which way you'd turn. You'd rather be dead than branded a coward. I suspect you've made that choice on more than one occasion."

He laughed. "Silly ass that I am, you're right. I'm an officially certified hero, and I'm the only one who knows how unofficially petrified I was. I would have been that way on the *Titanic* . . . trying to appear desperately noble and unafraid while praying, 'Please, Lord, get me the bloody hell out of this.' "

They stared at the twinkling spires of Manhattan for a few minutes.

"Beautiful sight, isn't it?" he remarked.

"In a way," she said thoughtfully. "The night hides a lot of ugliness. That's why I love flying over a big city at night. You forget what it's really like. You look down and all you see is black velvet studded with diamonds, even the bridges look like strings of pearls."

"Well," he chuckled, "that's a picturesque description."

"John, you've never married, have you?" It was more a statement than a question, and the sudden change of subject surprised him.

He said evasively, "Is that an assumption of yours or did someone tell you?"

"Trevor told me. Said they invented the phrase *perennial bachelor* for you."

"Well, that's exaggerating. I'm afraid I've never met anyone I'd be eager to spend the rest of my life with."

She tossed her cigarette into the water and looked at him with a tiny, enigmatic smile. "I suppose I've gotten cynical about marriage, too, after two divorces. My first husband was an alcoholic and my second turned out to be bisexual. So I keep waiting for the proverbial knight on a white charger."

Hawke said quietly, "I happen to be an excellent rider," and her eyes widened.

"I'll just bet you are," Debra Chaney said. "For the time being, I'll settle for your just being my friend."

He managed to coat his reply with a nonchalance he did not feel. "I think that would be wise, Debbi."

Their eyes met, and both knew they were hiding from the truth. Only the sound of other voices on the deck broke the spell and Hawke looked around for the source.

"On the fantail," he said. "It's Lefferts and Jerry Robertson."

The billionaire and the captain were conversing in tones just loud enough for their voices to carry, but not loud enough to distinguish words. Debra Chaney seemed grateful for the interruption, but Hawke pressed on.

"Debbi, if I'm out of line asking this, forgive me, but is there anything going on between you and Trevor? You've been spending a great deal of time together and, well, sometimes I've caught him looking at you in a way . . ."

He left the sentence unfinished because it didn't need finishing. She said quickly, "John, I adore him as a very gentle, kind person, and I respect him for the brilliant scientist he is. But there's no romance between us—not on my part, for sure. I've noticed the way he looks at me and I just hope he doesn't say something that will force me to let him down as gently as possible." Her eyes glinted mischievously. "Do I detect a glimmer of jealously?"

"Concern, not jealousy," Hawke said with a seriousness that she seemed to find amusing. "Trevor's my friend; he's a lonely man who's just come off a bad marriage, and I wouldn't want anything that might, uh, develop in our own, uh, relationship, to hurt him."

The last was delivered so stiffly that Chaney almost laughed, but she settled for a neutral, "Well, I guess I'd better get some sleep. Good night, John."

"Good night, Debbi."

Once again, their glances collided, but she quickly turned away, a little flustered. He watched her disappear down a gangway leading to the staterooms and resisted a strong impulse to follow her. Sleep might come even harder now, he thought with a stab of annoyance at his own weakness, and to avoid going back to his cabin right away, he found himself straining to hear what Lefferts and Robertson were saying.

They still were conversing earnestly, but their voices had dropped; they almost seemed to be whispering. He finally gave up eavesdropping and headed back to his cabin, anticipating more tossing and turning.

Derek's snoring had subsided to a faint, acceptable rumble and while he did think of Debbi briefly, this immediately detoured his mind in another direction: Trevor Van Buren. Chaney might talk glibly about letting him down gently, but it wouldn't be that easy. He knew how sensitive Trevor was, how badly that failed marriage had scarred him. His wife's infidelity had piled humiliation on top of Van Buren's inherent shyness and inexperience, and the result was inevitable: His self-confidence was demolished.

Yet these scientific chaps possessed the faculty of shutting themselves off from mundane personal tensions. It was a pleasanter thought, and he had another just before falling asleep. . . .

Tomorrow they'd weigh anchor.

However, it was just as well John Hawke hadn't heard that conversation on the fantail. . . .

"Well, you asked my opinion and I'm giving it to you," Robertson was saying.

"Which I appreciate, even though I think you're being too damned pessimistic."

"Realistic, not pessimistic. Look, Martin, this thing has been put together too fast. For starters, the *Pima* or the *Henry Morgan*, whatever you want to call her, isn't really the right ship for anything this complicated. I told you you'd be better off chartering a regular salvage vessel already equipped with the stuff that's cost you a fortune to install on this bucket. Second—"

"Matter of personal pride," Lefferts interrupted. "Besides, chartering another ship would have involved too many people asking too many questions—"

"Second, I don't like the way those subs are built, no matter what Hawke says."

"He dove one of 'em to fourteen thousand feet," Lefferts argued. "What more could you ask?"

"More testing of how well a steel pressure hull will stand up to repeated dives to those depths. I wasn't too impressed with the welding, either. The smaller sub's had three dives; the bigger one hasn't even gotten its feet wet. I don't call that adequate testing."

Lefferts said, a little testily, "Well, John has confidence in them and that's good enough for me. Any more objections?"

"This business of getting at the bullion. Personally, I don't think you stand one chance in hell of getting inside that wreck, even if Caitin blows a hole in her fifty feet wide. I'm no expert on the *Titanic*, Martin, but I'll give you odds the inside of that ship is one mass of twisted metal and debris. There's probably three tons of steel piled on top of those bullion crates."

Lefferts said doggedly, "Remember what John told us . . . that the pincer arms can clear away internal wreckage?"

Robertson smiled a little grimly. "A lot of people are taking his word, aren't they? Very persuasive fella. Martin, are you a football fan?"

"Sure," Lefferts said, surprised at the change of subject. "Why?"

"Because John Hawke makes one hell of a pregame fight talk. The trouble is, he doesn't have much of a game plan."

5

Four days out of Bayonne, the *Henry Morgan* was still several hundred miles short of the planned search area—a turtle pace that exasperated John Hawke.

He was the only unhappy person on the ship. The weather was perfect and the voyage silk-smooth, thanks not only to the gentleness of the Atlantic's swells but to the fact that Lefferts had installed liner-type stabilizers on the old minelayer. The atmosphere was that of a pleasure cruise, not an expedition; the sight of Craig Caitin jogging on the deck every morning, Montague sniffing the sea breezes, and Chaney's daily sunbath on the fantail—they all might as well have been carefree tourists.

Not John Hawke.

"Lefferts told me this bloody scow could do eighteen knots," he complained to Captain Robertson. "We've been averaging ten."

The skipper shifted the ever-present corncob from one side of his mouth to the other. "She'd do eighteen knots easy before she had to carry all the weight you've added—winches, cranes, and damn near eleven miles of steel cable," he said placidly. "Not to mention those two subs; you're lucky she's making ten knots. Anyway, I thought the British were a patient people."

Hawke grinned. "It's impossible to be patient when you're crawling at ten knots toward a thirty-million-dollar pot of gold."

Robertson said seriously, "John, if I ask these engines for any more speed, we're going to break down considerably short of that pot. The head temps already are running higher than I'd like. We're asking a lot of this old gal."

"Yes, I know," Hawke said. "Sorry, Jerry, I'm bitching like an old woman. It's just that I'm damned bloody anxious to get there."

"*There* is nearly fifteen hundred miles from Bayonne. And we don't really know where *there* is located, do we?"

"Ever the skeptic, Jerry. At any rate, everyone except me seems to be having a jolly good time."

"They're sure as hell eating well," Robertson observed.

That they were, thanks to Martin Lefferts's proclivity for seagoing luxury. He had brought along—over his wife's objections—the family cook, which in itself was something of a misnomer. Charles LeBaron could more properly be called a chef, the kind of culinary wizard who could work magic with the simplest ingredients. LeBaron was pencil-thin, in his early fifties, and looked as if he never ate anyone's cooking, including his own. He came aboard the *Henry Morgan* five days before they sailed; up to then, they had sampled virtually every restaurant in Bayonne.

"I hired him right off a French cruise line," Lefferts explained after the first dinner at sea drew raves—a succulent beef Wellington. "He thinks I'm a savage because I'm strictly a meat-and-potatoes man, but he'll fix anything I ask. The guy knows herbs and spices like Dow knows chemicals."

Hawke noted with interest that Lefferts insisted on the crew being served the same meals as everyone else, although they had their own dining quarters. Only Captain Robertson ate with the key expedition members, and sometimes he preferred to join the crew, usually at breakfast.

There was only one other officer aboard, a pudgy, baby-faced recent graduate of the U.S. Merchant Marine Academy named Paul Crippens. Ostensibly, he was second-in-command; on a naval vessel his role would have been that of the executive officer, or the first mate on a civilian freighter. In either case, he would have served as the captain's link to the crew, transmitting his orders and rules, at the same time being the men's conduit to the captain.

On the *Henry Morgan*, he was neither. Crippens was an

excellent ship handler, almost as good as Robertson himself, but he was unusually shy and nervous. This was his first post-graduation job, and he was in awe of Lefferts. He ate in the main dining room, at Martin's invitation, exactly once, but he hardly spoke a word and was so ill at ease that Robertson suggested privately to Lefferts, "I think Paul'd rather eat with the crew from now on." Crippens actually seemed happiest when he was conning the ship alone, usually late at night so Robertson—who gave the impression he practically lived on the bridge—could get a few hours sleep.

Hawke had tried to avoid the frictions of a divided command, not an easy task on a ship carrying its volatile owner, a veteran skipper, and an expedition leader who liked giving orders more than taking them—not to mention a pair of independent-minded scientists who weren't used to taking any orders. Yet he couldn't help the fact that his natural air of authority had enveloped even the crew, to a point where he realized they were giving him equal status to Robertson.

They were a good lot, of that he was sure. Not enough of them, Hawke thought, but this was one area in which Lefferts had exercised his will. "Not one man more than we really need," he had decreed. "I could afford to sign on fifty guys, but we're sailing with three more than I usually use on a cruise, and that's enough." The ten-man complement had been the compromise they worked out, with Robertson doing the selections, and Hawke was satisfied with all of them.

He particularly liked the two topside frogmen who would help in the launch and recovery operations of the two subs. One was a husky black man, Cornelius Jefferson, with an infectious laugh and the bulging muscles of an Olympic weight lifter. Hawke had known few blacks in his life—the Royal Navy's wartime black contingent was rather sparse—but he came to respect this one as much for his intelligence and humor as his awesome strength. At first, Hawke addressed him a bit officiously as "Mr. Jefferson," but quickly changed to "Corny," as did the rest of the crew.

The other frogman was Sean "Tattoo" Ryan, an obvious nickname for a man whose arms and chest were covered with a gallery of needled artwork—if two anchors, a battleship, and three nude women could be classed as artwork. Both Jefferson and Ryan had worked for Lefferts on previous diving trips, yet they, too, had gravitated toward Hawke as the dominant figure on the ship. It was an instinctive response that extended even to Charles LeBaron. Hawke remembered one night in Bayonne, when Lefferts was away, the chef had asked him, not Robertson, to suggest a menu for the evening's dinner.

Robertson's attitude toward Hawke puzzled the Englishman. The captain obviously liked him, and he seldom voiced criticism, yet Hawke was uncomfortably aware that he disapproved of the expedition. Robertson seldom joined in the lively mealtime conversations; he simply sat quietly, puffing on his corncob, and looking for all the world like a grouchy schoolmaster listening to the prattle of children.

Most of those conversations involved Hawke's training sessions on the submarines, although, as he pointed out right from the start, the term *submarine* didn't really apply to *Winston* and *Franklin*.

"Technically speaking," he had lectured, "the submarine actually is a surface vessel that can travel underwater. It dives by filling ballast tanks with water and ascends by expelling the ballast. The angles of descent and ascent are controlled by diving planes. What we're operating are submersibles that dive and rise through a combination of their thrusters and the use of diving planes, like the ailerons and elevators on an aircraft. A submersible actually is a wingless aircraft that swims instead of flies, using the water instead of the air."

The training sessions were thorough, Hawke emphasizing that each one had to be intimately familiar with all controls and instruments—manipulation of the robot arms, camera operation, and use of floodlights; how to read the fathometer and translate its numbers into feet; how to interpret the psi dial; how to monitor the instruments linked to the life-support equipment; how to handle communications and activate EAS, the emergency ascent system, which Lefferts insisted on christening "Popeye" because of Captain Robertson's contributions.

Hawke gave Montague only the most cursory training, knowing he would be accompanying Hawke himself on any dive. The others absorbed instructions quickly, even Lefferts. Caitin was the most adept student, followed by Van Buren, who also was the most curious. Trevor wanted to know how everything worked, why it worked, and what would happen if it didn't work. Typical was a session in which Hawke was explaining the operation of valves that controlled the flow of oxygen into the subs.

"It's not pure oxygen, of course," Hawke mentioned. "Oxygen is too combustible. A chance spark from a short circuit and poof! Remember that American pad accident that killed three astronauts a few years back? The interior of their spacecraft became an inferno when a spark ignited the pure oxygen they were breathing."

"So what will we be breathing?"

"A mixture of oxygen, nitrogen, and helium, the correct proportions measured by a computer that feeds the data to the emissions valves."

"What would happen," Van Buren asked, "if the computer failed to measure the mixture properly? Too much helium or nitrogen, say, or too little oxygen."

"If you fed the wrong data into the computer, you'd certainly end up with various unpleasant symptoms, their severity depending on the extent of the error. Headache, nausea, diminished coordination, grogginess are all possible. We tested the effects on volunteers during the design stages. One chap said he felt rather euphoric. Nothing lethal would result, but you'd want to abandon a dive if any of those symptoms appeared; it should be very obvious something is wrong. Of course, the life-support-system gauges would warn you of any malfunction before those symptoms appeared. That's why I keep emphasizing how very important it is to monitor life-support instruments."

"Very," Van Buren agreed. "Now show me the computer itself. Remarkable machines, computers. They've always intrigued me. And then, if you don't mind, John, I'd like to go through that simulated dive again. I seem to be manipulating the planes too abruptly. . . ."

Since Bayonne, they had settled into a nightly routine of an after-dinner bridge game with a starting foursome of Montague—expert enough to be classed as a tournament player—

Van Buren, Lefferts, and Chaney. Hawke himself detested the game. Robertson always went to the bridge after eating and stayed there until midnight. No one thought of inviting Craig Caitin to play, although Montague was the first to notice that the big man apparently enjoyed silent kibitzing; he'd stand behind each bidder, quietly observing but saying nothing. Then he would move around the table as the hand was played.

The fifth night out, Lefferts had fouled up an easily makeable bid and Montague, his partner, patiently tried to explain where Martin had gone wrong. He apparently was too solicitous, for the billionaire suddenly threw down his cards.

"I quit!" he announced. "I'm through with this goddamned stupid game. I never liked bridge, anyway. I'm ruining it for everyone."

Chaney tried to mollify him. "You're not any worse than I am, Martin. Besides, we can't play with only three people, so don't take the game so seriously."

Lefferts hesitated but looked miserable. In his rumbling voice, Caitin unexpectedly said, "Can't force a guy to play if he doesn't wanna. I'll sit in for a few hands if nobody minds."

Van Buren said, rather nastily, "I would think poker was more your game."

"Like poker, too. Rather play bridge, though . . . too much fu-uh, too much luck in poker. Haven't played bridge in a long time." He chuckled in a self-deprecating way that was touching. "There ain't a helluva lot of bridge players in my social circles."

He stood there, trying to look indifferent and failing miserably. It was Chaney who beat Montague to making the invitation. "Park in Martin's chair, Craig. You're Derek's partner; you've got one leg on the rubber and you're vulnerable."

He looked at her gratefully and sat down, almost engulfing the chair. Then he glanced up at Lefferts. "That last hand, pal . . . you gotta remember to draw the trump out first, or you're gonna be hangin' out to dry with nothin' but your jockstrap. And when you tried that finesse, you shoulda known where the king was. . . ."

They looked at him in amazement. After two more rubbers, they were staring at him in awe. He was almost as good as

Montague, lacking some of Derek's technical skills but possessing incredible card sense.

The final round involved a difficult bid of six diamonds. Caitin had forced the bidding to small slam, played the hand, and made it. Montague shook his head.

"I can't believe you took it to six," he remonstrated mildly. "You and Debbi had only seven diamonds between you, and if you hadn't made that finesse, you would have gone down like the *Titanic* herself."

"Figured on an even trump split. That and the finesse were the only chance I had."

"But Craig, depending on the trump split is like playing Russian roulette."

"Hell, I know it. But the point count was there. I figured if I had a shot at it, I'd better take it."

"Well"—Montague sighed— "I suppose success is an adequate answer to any question. In the previous rubber, when you opened with four spades—a most unusual bid—wouldn't a preemptive bid of three spades have been preferable . . . ?"

They were off on an animated discussion of the night's play, in which Chaney joined briefly before leaving for a nightcap with Lefferts and Van Buren. Hawke, as was his custom during bridge games, was topside with Robertson.

"Aren't you two joining us?" she asked.

"We'll be along in a few minutes," Montague told her. "I'm still fascinated with that opening four bid. . . ."

Caitin, looking at Chaney, said shyly, "Hope my cussin' wasn't too bad tonight, Debbi."

"Well within reasonable bounds," she assured him, then added mischievously, "and I must admit that was, indeed, one beautiful goddamned finesse."

Everyone laughed, except Trevor Van Buren. He said abruptly, "Let's go have that drink," and took Chaney's arm possessively, an untypically macho gesture that went unnoticed by everyone except its target. She felt more pity than annoyance, but she was upset enough to mention it to Hawke later that night.

They were on the deck having a smoke. Nothing had been prearranged, it just happened that way, both gravitating to the spot on deck where they had conversed that last night in Bayonne.

"It was the way he took my arm," Debbi recounted. "There was almost a . . . a kind of anger behind it. I actually believe he was jealous of Craig."

He allowed, "Well, that's understandable. Caitin's a rather dynamic man . . . remarkably intelligent, considering that he's had very little formal schooling. Smooth off those rough edges and you'll find a very decent chap."

She said defensively, "Trevor's a decent guy, too."

"Most assuredly, but I'm trying to look at this situation through a woman's eyes. All Trevor has going for him is a brain, and that mustache of his. I'm afraid he's not very attractive to women and he knows it. That's his problem."

She looked over the deck railing, flicking the remains of her cigarette into the dark water, the sparks glowing briefly like a tiny spent rocket. "I think he's getting to be my problem, John, I can sense it. The last thing I need is for someone on this ship to have a crush on me, especially someone like Trevor, whom I adore but not in the way he'd like."

He observed gravely, "You might have the same trouble with Caitin, you know."

"Craig? Don't be silly; that big gorilla's scared to death of me. Sometimes I think he even resents that fact that I'm here. Maybe he believes in that chauvinistic superstition: A woman on a ship brings bad luck."

"Craig Caitin isn't afraid of anyone or anything on this planet, Debbi. He did resent you initially, but I dare say you're the first woman in his life he ever respected, and for a man like Caitin, respect is a very powerful emotion, so powerful that it's almost a kind of love, because it's the only emotion he really feels. At times, there's an uncanny similarity between the way he looks at you and that cocker-spaniel expression on Trevor's face."

She laughed. Trevor's eyes did have a slight downward slant that made him look mournful even when he smiled. Laughter had become a frequent part of these conversations, just as conversation itself had become a kind of wall they had constructed together, a bulwark against the threat of physical involvement. They were talking again on this clear, calm night and, as always, it was a pleasant stroll down a varied conversational path that ranged from light banter to serious discussion. Pleasant, that is, until Hawke—looking down at the glass-smooth sea and then up toward a sky alight with stars—remarked casually, "Y'know, this is just like the night she sank."

Without warning and for no logical reason, Chaney felt a chill. It had been a perfectly natural and appropriate thing for him to say, yet somehow it had parted a curtain that led to the past. The plodding old minelayer had become a time machine, carrying them relentlessly toward a dead ship, a thing of mystery, sleeping undisturbed and inviolate in the black depths of a grave 12,500 feet down. And suddenly, she was afraid.

She could not control an inadvertent shudder. Hawke said solicitously, "Debbi, are you cold?"

"No." Without looking at him, she asked, "John, how long have you been a sailor?"

The way she asked the question told him her mood had changed, abruptly. He was puzzled, but his reply was casual.

"Since I was twenty. I've already told you my father was Royal Navy, too. So was his father. A great-great uncle of his was a lieutenant on Nelson's *Victory* at Trafalgar, and family legend has it that one of my ancestors served under Sir Francis Drake when the rascal was plundering Spanish galleons. So I guess it is safe to say I have centuries of saltwater genes."

The last was said jocularly, but she was frowning, and for the first time he realized something was wrong. "Debbi, I have a strong hunch you didn't ask that question to learn about my genealogy."

"No, I didn't, but your answer leads me to the next question: Do you believe in that sailor's superstition . . . a woman on a ship means bad luck?"

"It's balderdash," he scoffed. "Sailors are the most superstitious breed on earth."

"San Diego's a sailor's town and I've talked to a lot of navy men. I've asked them the same question. They always laugh and deny it, but sometimes they're lying. I can see it in their

eyes. They're just afraid to admit it. Craig felt that way, too
. . . at least at first. Maybe he still feels it, no matter how much
he wants to accept me."

So does Lefferts, Hawke thought. His instinct was to reassure
her, however. "Debbi, Craig's current attitude is far more
important than any prejudice he might have felt in the past.
For God's sake, you're a scientist; science and superstition are
mortal enemies."

"Not always. Some superstitions rest on scientific fact."

"Name one."

"Well, the superstition that plane crashes always occur in
groups of three. Trevor says there's statistical evidence supporting that belief."

"Trevor?"

"Yes. We were discussing old myths and legends and superstitions, and he brought up the one about crashes. He said
when the airlines go for a long time without an accident, they
get complacent about safety. Then all of a sudden there's a
series of fatal crashes—usually three right in a row—and then
they tighten up and go without one for another long period."

"That's not superstition. It's industrial psychology . . . nothing but pure logic."

"Superstition derived from logic."

"True, but you're talking about a relatively modern superstition. I'm talking about old superstitious beliefs: Friday the
thirteenth, a black cat crossing your path, walking under lad-
ders, break a mirror and you're guaranteed seven years of bad
luck—all bloody nonsense! You might as well tell me you
believe in the legend of the Flying Dutchman. Look, the sea
is vast, lonely, intimidating; you might as well be on a different
planet. But it's treacherous enough without dreaming up jinxes
that have absolutely no foundation."

She tried to smile at him, but the result was so feeble, he
could almost smell her fear.

"Debbi," he asked softly, "what are you afraid of?"

"I don't really know." Her voice was so low, he could hardly
hear her. "It's what you said—about this being like the night
the *Titanic* sank—it . . . it seemed to touch something off. A
vague feeling of uneasiness, like something bad was going to

happen to all of us. I can't even explain it, John, but all of a sudden I felt . . . fear. A kind of dread about going on."

He stared at her, trying to decide whether scolding or simple reassurance would be best. He took the middle road: an attempt at light humor.

"What you just described sounds like female intuition, and I don't believe in that, either."

He wanted badly to put his arms around her, knew that the touch of her body against his would be a dangerous ignition source, and was just about to do it anyway when Robertson's deep voice came out of the night above them.

"Hawke . . . is that you down there?"

He wasn't sure whether to welcome the interruption or curse the captain, but Chaney answered, with obvious eagerness, for him.

"We're both down here, skipper. Come join us." The last was said in a tone that sounded almost desperate. She didn't want to talk about fear anymore.

"On my way." They heard his heavy steps on the steel stairs leading down from the bridge. Debbi said, "John, don't say anything to Jerry about my qualms. He'll think I'm nuts. And probably so do you."

He had no time to reply before Robertson's stocky figure hove into view.

"Hello, you two. My apologies for barging in, but I wanted to tell John something."

"You're not barging in," Hawke assured him. "But don't you ever sleep? It's after one and you've been conning all day."

"Not much else to do. Besides, Paul's still pretty inexperienced. I don't like leaving him alone on the bridge too long with just Pickens to help him." The last was a reference to Tom Pickens, the night helmsman and oldest crew member. He wore a perpetual smile that seemed to have been glued to his mouth. Robertson, like so many veteran seamen, was capable of functioning at full efficiency with only two or three hours sleep a night.

Hawke asked, "What's on your mind?"

"Think I can give you an ETA. By this time tomorrow morning, we should be within fifteen miles of the search area.

We're picking up a little speed as the fuel load lightens. If we're getting this close, I figure we should start dropping that sonar array tomorrow morning and see how it does."

Chaney said, "And I'd better get some sleep. I want to be there when you test the sonar returns, and I assume it's going to be very early in the morning."

The two men said good night to her. Robertson sighed as she receded from sight. "I don't mean to sound like a dirty old man, but that woman is absolutely beautiful."

"A remarkable combination of beauty *and* brains," Hawke said almost wistfully. They talked for another half hour, their pipes glowing in the dark. After the captain left, Hawke remained on deck briefly, thinking about Debbi.

This time not with longing, however, but with a twinge of guilt. Indirectly, he had lied to her, or at least misled her. Until he acknowledged to himself that he was falling in love with Debra Chaney, down very, very deep in his seaman's heart, John Hawke himself always had believed that a lone woman on a ship was nothing but a bloody jinx.

"It's like trolling for safety pins," Hawke grumbled to Van Buren.

They were bent over the sonar-reception unit in the *Henry Morgan*'s darkened radio room just behind the bridge, peering at the televisionlike screen and listening to the "*ping-pong*" acoustical returns coming from the 12,000-foot array trailing under the ship. The converted minelayer had been crisscrossing the search area in a grid pattern for four and a half days without success, commencing the probe at the perimeter of the five-mile radius established by Van Buren and Chaney as the *Titanic*'s probable position.

The sonar-search unit at the end of the array was housed in a tube shaped like a miniature dirigible, and painted the same garish yellow as the two subs. The towing process was laborious, for every foot of the ocean floor in each grid pattern had to be searched. Robertson likened the process to mowing a huge lawn. There had been several visual false alarms, each showing a large mass below them and each setting off temporary excitement that died when the acoustic returns and the magnetic anomaly readings were negative for metallic objects. All they continued to hear were the *pings*. Van Buren was the only one who remained unperturbed by the successive disappointments.

"It's a perfectly natural phenomenon," he explained calmly. "We're over that long submarine canyon with God knows how many tributaries. There are all sorts of subterranean ridges, hills, and valleys and any one of them can give us a false sonar image. Sonar cannot really distinguish between an undersea hill and a ship in terrain like this. You have to be patient."

"Maybe we're moving too fast," Hawke said to Robertson.

The captain shrugged. "She's doing only three knots, John. That's a knot slower than we tried yesterday." He paused, sneaking a cautious glance in the direction of the two oceanographers, as if he was hesitant to challenge their calculations. "Trevor and Debbi, mind if I make a suggestion?"

"Feel free," Van Buren said.

"I think we should swing south a bit, maybe a couple of miles beyond the perimeter where we started this grid pattern, and do another grid search below that point."

Trevor nodded thoughtfully, but Chaney said rather tartly, "Jerry, we didn't use Kentucky windage to establish this search area. Computers don't make mistakes on the order of a couple of miles."

"They can be wrong if the data they're fed is wrong," the captain reminded her. "And it wouldn't take much of an error to throw you way off. One square mile of ocean is the equivalent of almost seven hundred acres, which is a hell of a lot of real estate."

"What wrong data?" she asked indignantly. "All factors were taken into consideration, including currents and—"

Robertson interrupted, "Current may be your problem, from the way the array is streaming. I have a hunch it's running stronger than you figured. That's a mighty small hunk of tin down there in a mighty big ocean. Only the Lord himself knows where that ship really is. I still say let's try farther south."

The only sound in the room was the soft, intermittent pinging of the sonar. For once, Hawke was reluctant to make a command decision, knowing Debbi was on guard, and it was

Van Buren who finally made it for him. "I think the captain may be right," he admitted. "A lot of what we threw at the computer amounted to variables that could have been off a fraction one way or another. John, you're the boss; shall we move south?"

"Let's try it," Hawke said flatly. He saw the hurt look on Chaney's face and added, "Debbi, if it hadn't been for you, we would have spent the last five and a half days groping like blind men miles to the north. You and Trevor always told us to look farther south; we just haven't gone far enough south."

They were manning sonar on a twenty-four-hour basis, dividing the duty among them into three-hour shifts. Robertson, a sonar expert, had given each one a crash course on how to read the display, and he proved to be an excellent teacher, because they all had become reasonably proficient by the second day. Lefferts had purchased a newly developed unit that not only produced acoustical returns but visual blips, like targets on a radar screen.

It was 2:55 A.M., the morning of the second day in the new search area. Montague entered the radio room, where dim red bulbs provided the room's only illumination apart from the green-tinged sonar screen. Caitin was hunched over the screen, half-asleep and kept awake only by its monotonous pinging; without the competition of the ship's noisy daytime activities, the transmissions sounded even louder.

Montague hoped Craig would stay awhile, even though his shift was over. They had become good friends, somewhat to Derek's surprise, because at the start of this voyage, he would have guessed Caitin to be the last man on the ship with whom he'd have much in common. He had been wrong, and more than just the bridge game had revealed the profane, rough-hewn giant for what he really was.

Just before they had sailed, Montague had seen Caitin bring an armful of paperback books aboard and assumed they were literary trash, at best mystery novels. One night, he happened to find Craig alone in the cocktail lounge, reading one of them.

"Murder mystery?" he inquired.

"Naw. Haven't read this for a long time, and felt like readin' it again. " He held up the book for Montague to see.

It was *Moby Dick*.

Montague succeeded in hiding his surprise. "A great novel," he commented. "One of the classic stories of the sea."

Caitin had surprised him again by looking disappointed at this appraisal. "Well, I kinda figured it's more than just another sea yarn. It's . . . it's about somethin' else." He stopped, groping for words. "About a guy's gettin' fixed on one thing, one target, maybe, so it drives him batty and destroys him." He hesitated again, embarrassed. "I can't think of the word that fits."

"Obsession," Montague said.

"Yeah, that's the word. Obsession. This Captain Ahab, he reminds me of someone on this ship."

Montague was startled. "Captain Robertson?"

"Nope. John Hawke."

From that night on, he had spent more and more time conversing with Craig. Found himself telling Caitin about his own life, about Beth and the void she had left. And Craig confided in him, too: that he was illegitimate, never knew his father and hated his alcoholic mother who abandoned him to the unloving care of a series of indifferent foster parents; that he never got beyond the sixth grade but loved to read—when he found the time, because he went to work full-time from the age of sixteen, literally educating himself.

Montague was grateful for their growing friendship. Once the sonar monitoring began, the process of trying to find an 883-foot needle in a 3,200-acre haystack, he had deliberately arrived for his trick ahead of schedule because it gave him more time to chat with Caitin. Tonight, however, he had run late, and if Craig was hungry—which he invariably was after his shift—there'd be no prolonged conversation.

"Craig, here to relieve you," he announced.

The giant yawned and stretched his massive arms. "Thank God. This goddamned sonar's like a sleeping pill that makes noise."

"Anything stirring?"

"Nothin' down there but fish."

"Go get some sleep."

"I will after I stop in the galley. Gonna rustle me up some ham and eggs."

He had just started for the door, Montague waving him good night, when a harsh new sound came from the sonar's speaker.

POING . . . POING . . . POING . . .

Caitin stopped. Montague took one look at the sonar screen and swallowed hard. "Craig—come here, quick!"

They stared at the screen together, and the loud *poings* went up in volume.

Montague muttered, "Look at that return image. It's something huge."

"Yeah. And this other reading here, the one Robertson told us to watch for? Magnet somethin'."

"Magnetic response. That image is a huge metal object."

"Holy shit," Caitin muttered.

"Holy shit, indeed, my friend. Go wake up Hawke and the captain, fast. Get some crew member to rouse everyone else. I think we've found the bloody *Titanic*."

6

Derek Montague spent the rest of that night without sleeping.

Within minutes after news of the sonar contact had spread throughout the ship, John Hawke announced a decision he had made in his own mind not long after the *Henry Morgan* sailed: When the *Titanic* was found, he and Montague would make the first dive.

"It wasn't an easy decision, but it is a logical one," he explained to the six people who formed the core of the expedition. After dancing around the sonar room and shaking everyone's hand when he, too, saw and heard the contact, he had summoned them to the dining room.

"The first dive is of utmost importance," Hawke had told them. "The raising of a curtain that for sixty-three years has hidden the *Titanic*'s secrets. Before we even think about recovering the bullion, it is absolutely vital that we first inspect the wreck, ascertain her condition, look for possible entry points. Derek knows more about that ship than the rest of us combined—her construction, the details of her interior, the possible difficulties we may face getting into cargo hold three. I realize the rest of you who've qualified on the subs are keen to go, but I promise you that before this venture is successfully concluded, anyone who wants to see the *Titanic* will be able to do so."

Montague searched their faces after that announcement and found what he expected. Trevor looked hurt, Chaney seemed resigned, Caitin indifferent, and Lefferts wore a weak smile that somehow escaped from his tightened jaw. Still, Montague thought, their reaction was less emotional than he himself would have expected. It had always been assumed that Hawke would command the first discovery dive, and no one had openly campaigned for the honor of accompanying him. And honor it would be. They all had talked about the sensation that would erupt around the world if the *Titanic* was discovered: acclaim for everyone, but the loudest for the first person or persons to actually lay eyes on the famed liner.

There had been a brief debate over whether to send down the smaller one-man craft at the same time; this was Van Buren's suggestion, but Robertson adamantly opposed it, and Hawke supported him.

"Too much chance of a fender bender with the visibility you'll have at that depth," the captain argued.

Hawke concurred. "It has never been my intention to use both subs simultaneously on the first dive," he said with an admonishing glance at Van Buren. "*Winston*'s primary purpose is to survey the wreck initially and, if it proves necessary, to attach Craig's explosives. *Franklin*'s job is penetration of the ship by whatever means possible and recovery of the gold."

Montague didn't miss the expression on Van Buren's face at that verdict: one of unconcealed disappointment that was almost anger. Neither did Hawke. "First things first, Trevor. Now I suggest you all try to get a few hours sleep. I'd like to dive at dawn."

The suggestion didn't involve Hawke himself. He went straight to *Winston*, accompanied by Robertson, to spend the rest of the night running checks on the submarine's various systems. So Montague lay sleepless alone in the cabin they shared. It wasn't fear that kept him awake, although he admitted he was terribly nervous about the dive. Rather, he was thinking about the conflict that separated Hawke and Van Buren—an emotional chasm of attitude, a canyon of philosophical differences, a breach he had created himself by unearthing the knowledge that the *Titanic* was carrying a fortune in gold.

He had never given much serious thought to the possibility that finding the ship might raise ethical or moral questions.

Why should it? Merely locating her, not to mention exploring her, was the only logical goal anyone had ever had. Virtually every salvage expert in the world had discounted, even scoffed at, the possibility of raising the liner, even though there was no dearth of suggestions for achieving such an impossibility. An appealing fantasy, Montague conceded—raising, then restoring and displaying the magnificent liner in a visible resurrection of her glory! Even if a technical means could be found, however, the cost would be astronomical. "It would be cheaper to lower the Atlantic," one salvage professional had sarcastically declared.

He always had laughed at the various schemes proposed for raising the *Titanic*. The most persistent proponent was an Englishman named Douglas Wooley, a man possessing no scientific background whatsoever but a genius at attracting attention. The British press gave him plenty of publicity everytime he announced new plans to bring the liner up from the bottom by means of huge inflated nylon balloons. At least Wooley was an expert on nylon, being a worker in a hosiery factory, but his brash ambition exceeded his financial resources by an enormous margin.

Wooley had started his salvage campaign in 1966, the publicity apparently infecting numerous other aspirants to such an extent that by early 1970, there had been nine various groups announcing similar projects. One actually was organized under the name Titanic Salvage Company and involved a plan to fill plastic bags with hydrogen to raise the ship. Another outfit came up with the idea of pumping nearly 200,000 tons of molten wax into the wreck; supposedly the wax would harden into weight-lifting buoyancy.

This, Montague thought whimsically, was no less practical than such proposals as pumping the hull full of Ping-Pong balls, or encasing the *Titanic* in a huge cake of ice that would float to the surface. One could chortle at all these examples of misguided ingenuity, but they reflected the endless love affair with the *Titanic* that so many people shared. Of course, motives were seldom altruistic or the product of scientific curiosity; most of the raise-the-*Titanic* proponents envisioned a restored ship as a money-minting tourist attraction.

No, for Montague and the other *Titanic* purists, the only motivation for finding the ship always had been the solution of mysteries, the answer to questions that had gone unanswered since the night of April 14, 1912. Was there really a three-hundred-foot gash in the hull? Was she in one piece or torn apart? Was there anything left of her luxurious interior? What did prolonged immersion at that depth do to a huge ship? What kind of damage might have been inflicted on her structure by almost a two-and-a-half-mile plunge to the bottom? Would there be any evidence of that supposed bunker explosion? Was there any way to get inside the ship? Was she actually salvageable, still so structurally intact that she might not only be raised—if that was possible—but rebuilt? And, ghoulish though it was to consider, were there human remains left?

Good questions, Montague thought morosely. Thanks to him, though, another question had been raised: What would it feel like to loot a wreck that was also a graveyard? Were they legitimate salvagers, or scavengers? The issue had never come up in all the past speculation on what might be recovered if the *Titanic* was ever located, largely because it had been too well established that she wasn't carrying unusually valuable cargo. Maybe the purser's safe—the combined wealth of the American millionaires aboard her had been estimated at two billion dollars. But, Montague reasoned, millionaires didn't haul around their entire wealth on their persons. There might still be jewels in that safe and quite a bit of currency, but this fell far short of classifying the *Titanic* as a treasure-laden wreck.

He found himself straddling that fence he had erected between his two best friends. Until the moment Hawke had announced the selection of his copilot for the first dive, Montague had indulged mostly in fantasizing about becoming a millionaire. Quite natural, he could rationalize, because he hadn't expected to be chosen and actually had assumed he'd be more of a bystander on any dive he did make. That had diluted his excitement at the prospect of seeing the ship; he simply figured others would gaze on her long before he got the chance.

For that matter, with the exception of Trevor, everyone had been talking freely about the gold and the overnight wealth it would bring. The chief topic of conversation at one cocktail hour concerned what each would do with newfound affluence. Hawke and Caitin talked of buying new cars and cabin cruisers; Lefferts confessed he might finally get a real yacht; and Chaney expressed a desire to spend at least a year traveling to places she never dreamed she could afford to visit. "And I'll go first class," she enthused, "including booking the most luxurious suite on the *QE Two*." Montague had confided that he always wanted a home in the country, "not a palatial mansion, mind you, but a small, brand-new cottage with plenty of wooded acreage and every modern convenience money can buy." It was as if they already had accepted Hawke's priorities almost to the same extent, even an oceanographer like Chaney.

However, Van Buren declined to discuss his own dreams. "I haven't given it much thought," he insisted. "Finding and exploring the *Titanic* is all that matters as far as I'm concerned." Montague didn't believe Trevor was as blasé about wealth as he pretended, yet there was a disapproving intensity in his tone. The strange thing was that tonight, only a few hours before the dive, Montague found himself feeling the same way.

He was going to be one of two human beings to see for the first time the immortal liner of the past as she existed in the present. It was an exhilarating yet sobering thought, one of staggering import. He didn't doubt for one second they had located the wreck, in spite of Robertson's caution that "it might turn out to be just a big freighter sunk in the war." Montague knew it was the *Titanic*, just as he knew what lay in cargo hold three. He knew because he *felt* the ship's presence. It was eerie but true; he was as certain as knowing he was aboard the *Henry Morgan*.

His old fascination with the *Titanic* was gripping him again, stirring his imagination—the same emotional surge born the first time he was exposed to the legend of the doomed giantess, acclaimed like a queen in her brief life and vilified like a criminal after her sudden death. All the suspense, mystery, and sadness of the world's greatest ocean liner soared back into his mind—and with it came fear.

Fear of the unknown. Fear of a descent into a very dark, forbidding place. Even fear of the *Titanic* herself, because

even as he gladly welcomed the realization of his own lifelong
dream, he sensed something else.

They were going where they were not meant to go.

He tried to dismiss this gloomy premonition by thinking of
a pleasanter, if more prosaic, picture—that little house in the
country. But this only led his mind back to cargo hold three—
back to the gold and the curious remark Craig Caitin had
made.

"This Captain Ahab, he reminds me of someone on this ship."

"Captain Robertson?"

"Nope. John Hawke."

He felt the old minelayer shuddering as the bridge watch
used occasional applications of engine power to maintain station. She seemed to be stirring restlessly over the tomb of the
even older ship.

So did Derek Montague, tossing and turning until a faintly
pink splash of dawn dissolved the last traces of the long night.

It didn't help either John Hawke's patience or Derek Montague's apprehensions when *Winston*'s launch was delayed
more than two hours by a series of frustrating mishaps involving
the launch equipment. First, one of the winch motors failed
to start, and it took the *Henry Morgan*'s "Mr. Fixit," a seaman
named Dan Ballinger, almost thirty minutes before he could
coax the engines into life. Crewman Ballinger was a dyspeptic-
tempered veteran of the merchant marine, with a tanned face
and a potbelly that made him look pregnant. Robertson swore,
though, that Ballinger must have been born with a wrench
in one hand and a screwdriver in the other. "He can repair
anything," the captain declared.

No sooner had the first motor been revived, the second one
died, too. A cursing, sweating Ballinger labored another half
hour before he got it going. Hawke and Montague finally
climbed into the sub and a crane began hoisting her over the
side. *Winston* was poised twenty feet in the air, just clear of
the ship's side, when the crane cable snagged and refused to
budge another inch forward.

"Jesus, what next?" Ballinger groaned. "Reverse it and lower
the bastard back to the deck," he yelled to the crane operator.

They had to detach the cable from the submarine before Ballinger could find the trouble—a link that somehow had twisted out of place. While Ballinger worked, Van Buren murmured to Chaney, "It would seem this first dive is jinxed."

"Just a little bad luck, Trevor."

"But that's what a jinx is—bad luck for unexplainable reasons. Did you know that the very word *jinx* is derived from a wryneck bird called the jynx, spelled j-y-n-x? The bird was used in black magic, part of voodoo curses, I believe. Hence the origin of—"

Chaney interrupted him sharply. "Trevor, the last thing I need right now is a lecture on voodoo curses."

On the second try, *Winston* was dropped into the water and they watched her disappear under the swells. The sub was only five minutes into the descent when Hawke's voice squawked on the loudspeaker in the sonar room.

"Jerry, are you there?"

"Roger. Anything wrong?"

"Apparently. Exceptionally bad vibration. It feels as if the propeller shaft is out of line, or we have a bent propeller blade. I don't know which, but we'll have to come back up."

"Understand, John. Surface and stand by for recovery."

After the dripping sub was lifted aboard, it took only one brief look to find the cause of the vibration. A propeller blade was indeed bent, and Hawke examined the offender unbelievingly.

He glared at Ballinger. "I checked that bloody prop this morning myself. It was in perfect condition. The blade had to have been damaged when she was hoisted over the side."

"She cleared the side by a good six feet," the seaman retorted. He looked imploringly at Robertson. "You saw the launch, Captain. Did that sub hit anything?"

Robertson said, "He's right, John. The launch was clean. I'd swear to it."

Hawke's gaze swung back to the bent blade. "I apologize, Dan. Can you straighten it out in a jiffy? Doesn't look too serious."

Ballinger's oil-stained hands felt the metal for a few seconds. "Serious enough to take a few hours straightening her out. We have to check the shaft bearings, too. I'll be lucky to finish by midafternoon. Sorry, Mr. Hawke."

Hawke said sourly, "Might as well scrub today's dive. We'll go tomorrow at oh-seven hundred."

Only half in jest, Debra Chaney whispered to Van Buren, "How did you spell the name of that bird?"

For Montague, the delay seemed almost like a reprieve, and he scolded himself for feeling that way. He even managed to catch a few hours of afternoon nap. When he awoke, much refreshed, his gloomy presentiments of the previous night had been pushed aside, replaced by fresh anticipation. Hawke grabbed him late in the day and insisted on going over the ship's drawings again.

"I really don't care one twit about Trevor's sensitivities concerning that wreck," he remarked, "but I suppose I should take them into consideration. Do you honestly think there's any chance of getting inside her without blasting the hull open?"

Montague smiled. "Well, you asked for an honest opinion and I'll give it to you. No, I don't think so, except for one very remote, even farfetched possibility . . . so farfetched that I haven't even mentioned it because I don't believe it myself, and I didn't want to get Trevor's hopes up."

"I'm listening."

Montague's forefinger traced a course down the drawing of the *Titanic*'s hull. "This isn't detailed enough to show the location of the coal bunkers, but there was a fire in the number ten bunker before she sailed. Presumably, it was extinguished before the *Titanic* left Cherbourg and headed out over the North Atlantic, but no one knows for sure. The theory is— and I must caution you it's generally discounted—the theory is that a coal-dust explosion may have occurred in that bunker around the time she struck the iceberg; an explosion severe enough to tear open a fairly large-size hole in the hull, thus adding to the damage inflicted by the ice spur and possibly being a major factor in her sinking. If there is such a hole, it may be an entry point."

"Why don't you believe the hole exists?"

"Because there isn't a single eyewitness account to support

the explosion theory. A blast strong enough to blow a hole in the side of the ship certainly would have been noticed and subsequently reported by survivors."

"However remote, it's still a possibility. Where is the number ten coal bunker located?"

Montague's finger pointed to the hull amidships. "As far as I can determine, approximately there, on the starboard side. And that's one area we could inspect tomorrow."

"That's one hell of a distance from cargo hold three."

Montague nodded. "Much too far. The damage between bunker ten and cargo hold three must be horrendous, very likely impassable. By the same token, I doubt whether it would provide access for exploring other areas of the interior."

Hawke snapped at him. "The cargo area is all that interests me," and Montague once again realized how little the actual discovery of the *Titanic* meant to John Hawke. His own uneasiness returned like the unwelcome recurrence of a bad headache. He said nothing, but Hawke caught his unhappy frown. "Derek, I'm sorry for your sake and Trevor's—maybe Debbi's, too—but you've all known right along why Craig Caitin's on this ship. I can't for the life of me understand how people like you feel so much sentimental rubbish about the *Titanic*."

Montague smiled thinly. "You may find out tomorrow, John," he said quietly, "when you see her yourself."

"*Winston*, what's your depth now?"

"Just passing five thousand feet." The second launch had gone off uneventfully, much to everyone's relief. Hawke's voice sounded metallic on the underwater telephone, almost tinny and not easily heard because of the intermittent crackling static.

Robertson, handling communications from the *Henry Morgan*, was equally hard to understand. His voice was multiplied by an annoying echo in the submarine's tiny cockpit.

"*Winston*, it's been thirty-seven minutes since launch. You're way behind schedule."

"I know, Jerry. I underestimated the bloody descent time. I'm going to increase power a bit."

"Don't hot-rod the damned thing. Save those batteries for the bottom."

"Right." Hawke took his finger off the transmitting button and grinned reassuringly at Montague. "Relax, Derek. It's taking longer than I expected, but it's better than free-falling."

"Not much better." Montague sighed. "My goodness, it's getting cold."

"It's going to get colder. Put on that extra sweater."

Montague laboriously donned the heavy sweater, squirming in the cramped space and bumping Hawke with his elbow in the process. "Sorry . . . this is like dressing in a closet."

The sub's interior had been uncomfortably warm during the first fifteen minutes of the descent, both men sweating under the thermal inner garments Hawke had decreed they must wear. Now they were grateful for that precaution—the thermometer on the sub's instrument panel was registering only fifty-eight degrees. *Winston's* insulation left a lot to be desired.

It was dark, stygian dark. To conserve the precious batteries, only the instrument panel was illuminated, the dials giving off a soft red glow that reflected eerily on their tense faces. The blackness finally got to Montague.

"I say, John, how about turning on the floodlights? Be interesting to see what's out there. I'd even welcome a shark or two for company."

The minute the words left his mouth, he wished they had never been spoken. He was only too well aware that if there was any living thing John Hawke feared as one would fear the devil himself, it was sharks. Just before they had left England, Montague had taken him to a preview of the new American film *Jaws*, despite Hawke's misgivings about the subject matter. John had walked out midway through the picture and Montague found him outside the theater, still pale.

He had told Derek his nightmares were few, but when he had one it almost invariably involved a shark attack. He would dream that his ship had been sunk under him and he found himself trying to keep afloat in a waterlogged kapok life jacket, the oily sea lapping hungrily at his chin. And then he would see that ominous dorsal fin, like the rudder of a submerged airplane, circling . . . circling ever nearer until the great jaw with its jagged teeth would open wide in a hideous smile . . . and he would wake up, bathed in cold sweat.

Montague saw him sweating now, even in the clammy atmosphere of the minisub, and he himself had a sudden vision of turning on the powerful halogen floods and finding themselves staring into the dead, beady black eyes of a shark. . . .

Hawke's terse reply eliminated that potential nightmare.

"No work lights until we hit bottom," he said. "We can't afford premature drain on the batteries. Besides, light attracts predators and I don't want some big bastard of a curious fish bumping us around. A great white shark could really give us a headache."

"A great white? Not at this depth, and certainly not in water this cold. A whale'd be more likely, maybe a killer whale." Montague said the latter almost hopefully; the submarine's claustrophobic environment was unsettling. He wished Hawke could keep him busier.

"Derek, what's our depth?" John must have been reading his mind.

"Almost seventy-five hundred. My word, that's more than halfway."

Hawke pressed the transmitting button. "Jerry, are you there?" There was a pause of some seconds as the underwater sound signals traveled to the transducer on the *Henry Morgan* and back again.

"Roger, *Winston*. Everything okay?"

"We're fine. Estimating eight thousand feet in about five minutes. How do we look on sonar?"

"Tracking you nicely. By the way, Van Buren wants to talk to you."

"Put him on." There was a moment's delay and he could visualize Trevor's earnest face pressing close to the transmitting microphone in the ship's sonar room. The oceanographer's resentment seemed to have dissipated in the excitement of the launch. He had shaken their hands warmly and wished them luck.

"John, this is Trevor. Have you seen any interesting or unusual marine life thus far?"

"Saving the amperage for the big show, Trevor. We're descending slower than I anticipated and any unnecessary drain on the batteries means less time on the bottom."

"I understand." The hell he did, Hawke thought. That "I understand" had a ring of disappointment. He promised himself to remind Van Buren that if he took *Franklin* down alone, under no circumstances was he to turn on the work lights above 11,500 feet.

Robertson's laconic voice resumed.

"*Winston*, for your information, we're tracking you beautifully on sonar. Your decent angle seems a little shallow. Suggest increasing about two degrees. We don't want you coming down right on top of the *Titanic*."

"Two degrees it is. Thank you, Jerry."

Montague suddenly gasped. "My God, I think this damned thing is leaking!" He pointed at the cockpit ceiling directly above the instrument panel. There were droplets of water there, and in the red glow they looked like tiny spots of blood.

Hawke laughed. "That's water condensation from our breath," he explained. "It's probably all over the sub by now. Taste one."

Montague gingerly touched a drop and put the finger in his mouth. "It's not salty."

"Damned right it's not. If it was seawater, we could start humming 'Nearer My God to Thee.' "

Relieved, Montague mused, "You know, that's the hymn they were supposed to be singing on the *Titanic* just before she went down. Except it's one of those many myths told about that night. What they actually sang was an old Episcopal hymn called 'Autumn.' I sometimes get the impression Captain Robertson thinks the gold is another myth, too."

"We both know it's there," Hawke said grimly. "Getting to it is what concerns me. At this very moment, watching us on sonar, sits a well-meaning oceanographer praying for the improbable: a report that the *Titanic* is fairly intact, with easy access to her interior."

Derek started to say something, but Hawke motioned him into silence. At this depth, the mere act of normal conversation consumed oxygen. The cold was now affecting him, too; the interior thermometer read only forty-one degrees. The only comforting thought was that it shouldn't get much colder. He was giving the *Henry Morgan* a descent progress report every five hundred feet and notified Robertson that he planned to test the external lights when they reached 11,500.

They forgot the cold as *Winston* passed through the 11,000-foot level. The blackness was oppressive; to Montague, they seemed to be moving through opaque dye.

"Derek, keep your eyes on the depth gauge. Call out at eleven-five."

"Right. We're almost . . . there! Eleven-five, and I'm getting a corresponding depth on the fathometer."

"Jerry, we're passing eleven-five and I'm cycling the floods. Start vectoring us toward the target."

"Roger, *Winston*. You've got a ways to go."

"I know it. Just keep tracking us, floods are on."

Van Buren's eager voice: "John, any sign of marine life?"

Hawke didn't answer him at first, but gave Montague a resigned "here goes the boffin again" look. They both strained to see what the work lights were picking up—which was precisely nothing except dark water that might as well have been ink. Hawke shut off the lights.

"I think we're too deep for marine life," Montague guessed. "There are probably thousands, perhaps millions of living organisms around us, but to see them, we'd need a microscope."

Van Buren repeated, "I say, anything interesting in sight?"

"Answer's negative, Trevor. It's as lifeless down here as the moon."

Robertson's voice squawked and echoed in their eardrums. "*Winston*, turn right, very slow . . . a little more . . . easy, now . . . that's it! Steady as she goes and maintain your angle of descent."

"Roger."

"*Winston*, have you activated your own sonar yet?"

"Negative. I'm still trying to conserve the batteries for inspection and ascent. Jerry, I'd prefer to wait a few more minutes."

"Understand, and we'll continue vectoring. But don't wait too long; you should be coming up on target within the next fifteen minutes."

Montague could actually hear his heart pounding. Excitement had consumed him, obliterating all thoughts except the closeness of a dream about to be realized. He cautioned himself that what lay ahead might still be a torpedoed freighter, but somehow he knew. . . .

He was watching the depth gauge so intensely that his eyes watered. He blinked away the moisture.

"Twelve thousand, and the fathometer's showing two thousand," he told Hawke, his voice a little unsteady. He recalled Trevor's estimate that at this depth, the pressure reached six thousand pounds per square inch. Montague felt shaky. They were in a fragile eggshell, gripped by an invisible vise.

"Lights again," Hawke ordered. As they had the first time, the twin beams rammed into a wall of absolute darkness. He reduced power and activated the sub's tiny sonar unit, its green screen a miniaturized version of the larger unit on the *Henry Morgan.*

"Jerry, sonar's on but no return as yet," he informed Robertson after a few pings. "What's showing up there?"

"We have your blip about five hundred feet from the big target, slightly to your left. Maneuver that way."

"Acknowledging. Are we lined up with her now?"

"Target's dead ahead, slightly below you. What's your depth?"

"Approaching twelve-five."

"Are your floods on?"

"Affirmative, but they're not picking up a bloody thing. Maybe we're too . . . hold it, Jerry! There's the sea bottom!"

It was as though they had just emerged from a pitch-black tunnel into a night illuminated only by moonlight. *Winston* was crawling slowly over an underwater landscape that was mostly flat—nothing but a bleak, apparently endless terrain of mud. Hawke leveled the sub into a horizontal path, and once again the hundred-foot beams of the work lights were stabbing into the darkness. Tiny particles turned white by the powerful beams swirled around them in a merry dance.

"Christ," Montague blurted, "it looks like it's snowing."

"Sea bottom debris tossed around by the current," Hawke explained. "Trevor told me to expect something like this. Keep a sharp lookout, Derek. Anything on our sonar?"

"Absolutely nothing."

"I wish this sonar unit were stronger. The signal doesn't seem to project much farther than the lights do. Jerry, how's that vector?"

"Target's still dead ahead, about the length of a football field from you."

Hawke turned to Montague. "I assume he means one of his American football fields. How long would that be?"

"About a hundred yards, I believe. What's wrong with this damned sonar?"

The word *sonar* had just left his lips when the screen in front of them suddenly came alive, changing from the flat lines of an empty return signal into a large hump.

Hawke shouted into the mike, "We have a target!"

Robertson's voice was laconic as ever. "Yeah, we show you practically right on top of it. Ease off."

Hawke retarded the throttle. They were scarcely moving and the *Winston* swayed noticeably, the current playing with her as if she were a toy. Both men peered down the bright path of the floods, eyes almost bulging with the effort. Then they saw it, simultaneously.

An enormous mass, like a huge black cliff, its shape indistinguishable at first until the sub inched closer.

"Portholes," Montague gasped.

"It's the side of a large ship, that's for sure," Hawke said cautiously. He turned *Winston* to the right so they were moving down the length of the vessel, becoming slowly aware of its size.

"She's no bloody freighter," Montague muttered. "It *has* to be the *Titanic*."

"*Winston*, what's happening?"

Hawke smiled; Robertson's blasé tone had turned eager. "Stand by, Jerry. Investigating."

He applied reverse power briefly, then moved the sub's nose up and turned *Winston* left so the flood beams were striking the side of the massive wreck. As they climbed slowly, the twin circles of light moved with them, giving them their first glimpse of the superstructure.

Montague, speechless, gulped.

"It's the *Titanic*," Hawke said with forced calmness.

"Absolutely. Look at the number of decks. You'd better tell Robertson and the others."

The finger that pressed the transmitting button was trembling so, Hawke had to calm himself and press it a second time.

"Jerry—and all of you—listen well. It's the *Titanic*. We've found her!"

Dimly, they could hear the cheering through almost two and a half miles of murky water. Montague thought he heard a squeal, and that would have to be Chaney, but he wasn't sure. Over the faint hubbub came the captain's voice, still controlled but tinged with an excitement Robertson was unable to suppress.

"Congratulations, both of you! Van Buren's asking what kind of shape she's in."

A natural question, Hawke admitted, but somehow Van Buren's impatience irked him. "For Christ's sake, we've only had time to identify her. Tell Trevor to keep his bloody shirt on until we've had a chance to look her over."

"Understood, *Winston*. Keep us advised."

"All boffins have one-track minds," Hawke growled. "Let's look this old lady over, Derek. We'll go back toward the bow, get above the ship, and deflect the lights down."

It took ten minutes for Hawke to maneuver *Winston* back toward the bow section and position the sub above the wreck so they could move down its length. "I think we'd better settle for one pass over the ship," he decided. "Look for any entry points large enough for a sub like *Franklin*; I don't think we'll find anything that will accommodate this one. Deflect the floods—that lever there. You take over the voice transmissions; you can describe this better than I."

The sight that passed below them was strangely magnificent, yet at the same time horrifying. The *Titanic* was only a poignant caricature of a once-mighty liner, a half-devoured metal carcass. It was impossible to tell how much of the damage had been done by the collision and sinking, and how much by six relentless decades of immersion in saltwater. They could see the sub's shadow below them as it passed over the wreck like a ghostly caress. Montague's voice, as he transmitted a description to the *Henry Morgan*, was muted with an instinctive awe.

"We're just past the bow. We can see the foremast, although it's more like a long stump, and it's fallen back against the forward part of the superstructure. We can still see what looks like a crow's nest, twisted around the mast. There are two large cargo hatches in the bow section; they might be access points, but I doubt it. Absolutely no sign of the bridge. It's simply disappeared. We're moving aft now . . . the funnels are gone completely, but we can see two large holes where the number one and two funnels once were . . . a lot of jagged metal all the way down the superstructure, like someone went to work on her with a giant tin opener. There's a complete absence of any wood planking; all we can see is bare metal. . . . I'm trying to locate where the—"

"*Winston,*" Robertson interrupted, "are you taking pictures? Van Buren's asking."

Hawke looked abashedly at Montague. Using the special underwater camera mounted on the sub's bow between the floodlights had been the latter's assignment. Hawke should have reminded him, but in the excitement of the ship's discovery, both had forgotten. It was, they both realized, a stupid and inexcusable mistake.

Montague said unhappily, "Van Buren and Chaney will kill me."

"My fault as much as yours. Well, I'd better repair the damage with a little white lie."

"Uh, tell Trevor we had some trouble with the camera initially—couldn't seem to activate it—but I think we've solved the problem now and we've commenced photography."

"I'm sorry," Montague apologized. "Thanks for covering up for me."

"You'd better light off the damned thing right now and keep taking pictures until we leave," Hawke ordered. "I'll have to . . . my God, look at that!"

They had progressed about two-thirds of the ship's length and there was nothing more in sight—the remaining third was gone. Montague gaped at the only too apparent violence of the rupture. The point at which the break had occurred resembled a multitiered cliff, the tiers increasing in length the lower they went. He could only guess at the force required to crack the *Titanic* in two, from her superstructure all the way down through the keel, as if cleaved by a gigantic knife wielded at an angle. Such force, he knew, must have been generated by dislodged heavy machinery tearing loose—boilers, turbines, and God knows what else pulled from their foundations as the liner tilted into her final death throes. The mass of shifting weight had snapped the ship's spine like a matchstick.

He stole a glance at his companion, whose own face was taut. Stolid and unafflicted by the *Titanic*'s mystique he may have been, Montague thought, but John Hawke also seemed shaken. There was a strange air of death around the wreck, a foreboding silence, as if they had stumbled on the remains of a gigantic cadaver that was staring malevolently back at them.

"No stern," Hawke murmured. "She really did break in two, aft of the second funnel." Montague reported this discovery to the *Henry Morgan* and was rewarded by a plea from Van Buren: "He thinks you should look for the stern section," Robertson advised. Montague looked at Hawke, who muttered, "I'll answer that one."

"Negative. We can't spare the time on this dive. I want to get a closer look at the forward hull area first. We're going back toward the bow now and we'll be taking more pictures."

He put *Winston* into a 180-degree turn, poised briefly over the forward superstructure so Montague could photograph what they had missed on the first pass, then descended away from the wreck until the sub was level with the bow. They could see the giant anchors still in place, the bottom tips just above the mud in which the nose of the ship was buried. The *Titanic* was resting on the bottom at a slight angle, her prow digging deep into the muck. But the rest of the bow section—especially the area where cargo hold three was located—seemed fairly clear and, they judged, potentially accessible without having to battle the mud.

"Well, that's one thing in our favor," Hawke grunted. "Have you spotted anything remotely resembling an entry point wide enough and high enough for *Franklin*?"

"The two funnel openings are out of the question and they're too far away from the forward cargo area, anyway. I did notice a fair-sized hole on the boat deck, just about where the Grand Staircase was located. This was the uppermost of a series of staircases leading down to the lower decks. Divers could get through that hole, but definitely not *Franklin*. The same goes for the two cargo hatches we saw on the forecastle."

Hawke licked his lips, digesting Montague's appraisal. "Derek, we're already close to the starboard side of the bow. What say we look for that coal-explosion hole you mentioned?"

Montague said firmly, "John, I'll wager a year's pension there is no such hole. But I'll be delighted to look for it."

Winston, undulating more now in the grip of the surprisingly strong current, crept abeam of the black steel wall, and Montague once again was struck by the contrast between the *Titanic* he had seen in so many photographs—sleek, majestic, and seemingly invincible—and the battered wreck passing before his somber eyes. He had never expected, of course, to see her still in pristine condition, but he never dreamed the giant liner could have been ravaged to this extent. He wondered whether Van Buren would be as shocked when he was able to glimpse what really had happened to this noble ship.

He stared into a line of portholes moving slowly by, speculating what the interior behind them must look like. There probably were third-class or steerage accommodations in this section, an area where hundreds had been trapped—many of them Irish and other immigrants sailing to new lives in the United States. Only 25 percent of the steerage passengers had survived, compared to 53 percent in first and second class, a shocking disparity reflecting the social inequities of that era. Warnings that lifeboats were being launched had reached steerage last, and there were plenty of women and children traveling in steerage. At least some of them might have been—

Montague's heart jumped as if jolted by an electric shock.

He thought he saw a face in one of the portholes. The face of a woman, framed by a shawl. He blinked and the image was gone. He started to say something to Hawke but realized his companion couldn't have seen anything; he was concentrating on piloting the sub, peering straight ahead. Montague decided his own eyes were playing tricks on him, and then got another surprise.

"John, look at that bloody hole!"

Hawke whistled. It was a gash about thirty feet wide and six feet in height. Twisted, jagged metal framed the edges.

"Look at the way the metal curls," Hawke muttered. "It could have been caused by an explosion."

Montague shook his head. "I don't think so. It's too far from number ten bunker. Keep going—I want to look for something else. It's always been assumed the spur tore a continuous three-hundred-foot rip below the starboard waterline, starting just beyond where we determined cargo hold three was located. Thus far, I haven't seen one sign of such a gash."

Winston crawled her way down the hull, Montague peering intently at the side of this black mountain. He saw no continuous gash but he did spot a number of holes, none as large as the first one but faintly visible. He said triumphantly, "John, we're not only making history, we're rewriting it! Unless that supposed three-hundred-foot gash is lower than anyone believed, it simply didn't exist."

"Then what sank her?"

"From what I've observed, the spur didn't stay in the hull as everyone thought for all these years. Rather, the ship kept bumping against it, each impact opening a new hole large enough to admit tons of water. I think the first hole we saw must have been the point of initial contact. We've made an amazing discovery!"

"The hell with your discovery," Hawke said tersely. "That hole is wide enough for *Franklin*, but the conning tower would never clear the top. And look at these jagged edges. Even if we had enough height, I wouldn't try it."

Montague stared at him, hurt by his reaction. They had just solved one of the *Titanic*'s greatest mysteries, and all Hawke could think about was breaking into the ship like some bloody burglar. Well, at least Trevor and Chaney would be excited, but he decided to wait until they surfaced to break the news. Hawke already had maneuvered the sub back around the wreck's prow and to the port side.

They looked in vain for the name of the ship, although

Montague swore he could see the dim outline of a C on this side of the bow. What intrigued him the most, and also moved him the most, were the huge rivulets of rust that encrusted the hull. In the light of the halogen floods, they resembled coral growths.

"Time to go, Derek," Hawke decreed. "It's a long way back to the ship and we're stretching those batteries to the limit."

Montague, still staring at the rust that covered the _Titanic_'s hide like ugly scars, sighed.

"John, I swear those look like dried tears. As if she was crying all the way down and through all these years."

Hawke said quietly, "That ship is going to be shedding a few more tears. I've seen enough of her to know we're going to have to blast our way in."

Montague nodded, only half-listening. He was still thinking about what they had seen—and hadn't seen. He was wondering about the missing stern, to where scores of desperate, frightened passengers had retreated as the _Titanic_ sank by the bow in her steadily increasing angle of death. The stern had remained afloat for a few minutes after the rest of the ship disappeared. Afloat just long enough to give those clinging to this last haven some false hope. Let Van Buren, Chaney, and the others look for the stern, Montague decided. Let _them_ complete the exploration of this desolate morgue at the bottom of the North Atlantic.

All he knew was that he never wanted to return.

Even if he wasn't quite sure why.

7

Trevor Van Buren took the news better than expected—probably, Montague surmised, because the oceanographer was practically drooling at the prospect of inspecting the *Titanic* by himself.

It was a development forced by another annoying mechanical malfunction that had occurred just seconds before *Winston* surfaced from its successful dive. The sub's motor had lost some power for no apparent reason, especially mystifying because when Hawke, Ballinger, and Robertson inspected the motor and its powering batteries later, they found absolutely nothing wrong. It was the cautious captain who finally suggested that they tear it down and start from scratch.

Hawke had protested. "That could put *Winston* out of action for God knows how long. It seems to be running like a jolly top now."

"It wasn't running perfectly two hours ago," Robertson reminded him. "Something's wrong and you'd better know what it is before you wind up losing power two and a half miles down."

Off to one side, Montague and Caitin were listening to this exchange. The Britisher shook his head.

"I don't like it," he said just loudly enough for Caitin to hear. "All these mechanical mishaps. We've just been fortunate they haven't occurred at the bottom of the ocean."

The big man shrugged. "The only reliable tools anyone ever invented are the ones you can hold in your hand, like a hammer or screwdriver."

"Strange there have been so many mishaps, Craig."

Caitin stared at him, not sure whether Montague was serious, and finally decided that he was. "That's bunk, pal. There ain't a machine made that can't blow a gasket for no reason at all. You're gettin' upset over a bunch of coincidences."

"Perhaps," Montague said without conviction. He turned his uneasy attention back to the conferees huddled around the ailing sub.

"How long will it take?" Hawke was asking Ballinger. "I'll help all I can, but I've other things on my mind."

Ballinger shrugged. "I'll get Casey Benton to help me; he's pretty good with power plants. We can start right now, but we'll need time for chow and some sleep. I'd say noon tomorrow, if we're lucky." Benton, a curly-haired young sailor with the chiseled features of a 1925 collar-ad model, was Ballinger's unofficial assistant.

So Hawke had given in. Not willing to waste time, he decided *Winston*'s malaise at least offered an opportunity to make Van Buren happy with a solo assignment that would be purely scientific. Getting Trevor off Hawke's back and out of the way was the real motive, Montague suspected.

He hadn't known of Hawke's decision to send Trevor down alone until that evening, when everyone gathered in the dining room to inspect the photographs taken on the first dive. It was at his own suggestion that the viewers include all ten crew members. "Even if we somehow don't retrieve the bullion," he had told Hawke, "they should know that this expedition has been a success."

"I refuse to consider the former possibility," Hawke had retorted, "but I agree they have a stake in this."

The pictures were spread around the big dining table. Montague was worried that his photographic skills might be on the same level as his manual dexterity, but most of the shots—developed quickly in the ship's excellent processing lab—had turned out surprisingly well. He watched with an understandable sense of pride as he listened to such comments as Van Buren's "Absolutely incredible," Caitin's respectful "Holy cow," Chaney's awed "These will make oceanographic history," and Robertson's "As far as I'm concerned, we could go home right now and be satisfied with what's been accomplished." The last drew a sardonic smile from John Hawke, who finally rapped for attention after the crew had filed out, visibly impressed by the pictures.

He began, "While those photographs were being developed, Captain Robertson and I checked on *Franklin*'s readiness. I've already informed our senior oceanographer, Trevor Van Buren, that he will make a solo dive in that sub at oh-seven hundred tomorrow, for additional exploration and photography."

He had put a gentle emphasis on the word *senior*, and Montague stole a glance at Debbi Chaney, who was smiling without really smiling in Van Buren's direction. He didn't envy Hawke's juggling of diving assignments, especially those involving exploratory work. Everyone wanted a bit of that action, even Caitin, who had confided to Montague during one of their lonely sonar vigils that he, too, was looking forward to seeing the *Titanic*. "Be somethin' to brag about to my kids, if I ever have any."

" . . . and when *Winston* is repaired," Hawke was saying, "all subsequent dives will be devoted to recovery of the gold. Further scientific exploration of the *Titanic* may continue after this is accomplished, weather permitting."

Chaney asked, "Did you find any way to get into the ship without using Craig's charges?"

"No," Hawke said bluntly, "and that's what I told Trevor when he learned he'll be diving tomorrow."

Van Buren said quickly, "But you didn't elaborate on that conclusion, John. You said you'd explain the situation when all of us were present."

Hawke nodded. "I think Derek is best qualified to elaborate."

A neat psychological maneuver, Montague thought admiringly. Hawke had shifted the burden of explanation to the one man who shared Van Buren's and Chaney's reverence for that slaughtered ship. He uncoiled his elongated frame from the chair and faced up to the unpleasant task.

"We examined several potential entry points, hoping we might avoid any blasting operation. There is no access to the interior capable of admitting either of the two subs, and that includes the superstructure as well as the hull. As John announced before you saw the photographs, the *Titanic* lies in two separate sections, and pending further exploration of the site, it is anyone's guess where the stern rests."

He went on to disclose the evidence of the hole in the starboard hull and their important discovery that the *Titanic* was fatally wounded by a series of spur punctures rather than a long, continuous gash. He was pleased to see their looks of amazement at this disclosure. "A monumental revelation," Van Buren said with awe.

A burst of applause greeted him as he sat down, yet for some reason, he had a nagging feeling it was undeserved—as if he hadn't quite told the whole truth. Hawke was speaking now, his words just registering in Montague's brain.

" . . . and on the following morning, Craig and I will take *Winston* and crack open the hull adjacent to cargo hold three. Fortunately, that area of the hull is fairly clear of mud. It's impossible to estimate how many dives we'll need to recover the bullion, but I—"

"Just a minute, John." Montague was on his feet again. "I left something unsaid. It is just as well the ship's crew doesn't have to listen to this, because what I have to say is addressed to those of you who will be seeing with their own eyes what John and I saw today."

Hawke said impatiently, "You've given everyone a most accurate and detailed description, and I can't think of another."

"Please let me finish," Montague said with uncustomary coldness. "Each of you will have intensely personal reactions when you first glimpse the *Titanic*. Initially, a sense of triumph and pride, perhaps, as I did. Then sadness. Awe. Disbelief at the terrible destruction, which is beyond what anyone supposed. I felt all of this. But also something else."

He paused and swallowed hard, as if flushing some obstruction from his throat.

"It is a place of death. It is every haunted house, every abandoned ghostly mansion that gave you nightmares as children. It is a silent tomb down there, so unearthly quiet that the very stillness seems to be the voices of the dead, whispering to the living that they are intruders, trespassers. That the dead wish to be left alone."

Hawke's snort broke the tension in the room. "Derek, you're entitled to your own superstitious fears, but I saw nothing down there but a pile of rusted junk—a pile, I keep having to remind you, containing wealth for all of us. Let's keep that in view, shall we? Derek might as well be telling us the damned wreck is haunted."

Van Buren said slowly, "I think that's just what he means. Isn't it, Derek?"

Montague shook his head, a gesture more of frustration than denial. "I don't know. Sensory impressions can be annoyingly vague and intangible. I am quite sure, however, I do not want to visit that wreck again, even though I may be just a silly old fool, as John suggests."

Hawke said quickly, "I don't think you're any such thing, Derek. Good heavens, man, of course it can get a bit spooky prowling around a ship at that depth. Especially a ship you of all people know so well. Most of us would feel squeamish visiting a morgue, even if we didn't believe in ghosts. We fear the dead because we fear death itself."

Lefferts interjected, "Any sunken wreck will give you the shivers. Hell, Craig, remember that galleon we explored? Jesus, when we broke into the captain's cabin, I expected to be faced by a skeleton swinging a cutlass."

Caitin nodded. "I guess I seen more dead ships on the bottoms of more oceans than the rest of you put together. It ain't no shame if you're scared, and the deeper you go, the worse it can be. That's when the darkness gets to you. Sometimes I've been inside an old wreck and it was like . . . like somebody was watchin' me outta all that black water." He gave Montague a smile of understanding.

Chaney said in her soft voice, "We'll probably all feel the same way, Derek. I know I will. I think all of us picture in our minds the *Titanic* as she was, not as she is. The reality has to come as a shock."

Montague was beginning to feel better—even, perhaps, a little foolish. LeBaron came back into the saloon—his reaction to the photographs had been a murmured and respectful "*Mon Dieu*"—and announced that dinner would be served in thirty minutes. "Filet mignon in honor of today's great event!" he informed them. "The wine will be a cabernet sauvignon I have been saving for the occasion!"

It was not until later that Montague's sense of dread returned. He was alone in his cabin, remembering something Caitin had said.

" . . . *like somebody was watchin' me outta all that black water.*"

That's exactly what it was like, Montague thought. The fleeting impression of a woman's face surrounded by a shawl, staring at him. Out of a porthole.

Hawke didn't see *Franklin*'s launch. He and Trevor had joined the others for dinner after the oceanographer's dress rehearsal, but Hawke never finished eating. He had no appetite, ached all over his body, and felt his sinuses closing up.

He finally had submitted to having his temperature taken and the captain had diagnosed it as a case of flu. "Probably the twenty-four hour variety," Robertson added. "It hit one of the crew the day we left Bayonne, but it didn't last very long."

"It damned well better not," Hawke had said unhappily.

He didn't want to expose Derek to the flu, so he wound up sleeping in Robertson's cabin just below the bridge—small, very Spartan quarters but well isolated—while the captain moved in temporarily with Montague. He slept badly, the fitful, feverish dozing populated by a new version of his recurring nightmare—a shark attacking one of the minisubs, shaking it like a mastiff gripping a toy poodle in its jaws. Eventually, the aspirin broke the fever, the nightmares faded, and he drifted off peacefully. When he awoke, he felt much better, but it was almost two hours past the launch time.

He dressed and hurried to the sonar room. Montague eyed him with disapproval.

"You should be in bed," he admonished.

"Not on your bloody life. Besides, I'm feeling fine . . . no more fever and I got a good night's sleep. How's Trevor doing?"

Robertson said dryly, "He's doing fine, and he'll keep doing fine without you."

The medical discussion ended when they heard a burst of static from *Franklin*'s voice transmitter, followed by an excited voice.

"This is Van Buren. I have the *Titanic* in sight."

Robertson grinned and put his hand over the mike. "He's probably having an orgasm."

The truth was that no one on the *Henry Morgan* could come close to appreciating the intensity of Trevor Van Buren's emotions as he nudged the little sub toward a position above the superstructure.

He already had violated Hawke's orders not to activate the work lights until sea bottom was reached. At fifteen hundred feet, he couldn't resist the temptation to look for marine life. The results were disappointing; he saw a few small fish and what appeared to be a large marlin that bumped against the submarine, apparently attracted by the bright light. The jar had startled Van Buren so, he hurriedly extinguished the floods and promised himself he wouldn't commit the infraction again.

This resolve was forgotten at the two-thousand-foot level when Robertson had advised him *Franklin*'s sonar return had become a shapeless blur on the screen—"like a cloud," the captain had said. Van Buren considered this official permission to investigate and turned on the floodlights again, watching in fascination at strings of tiny lights flashing in sequence. He recognized the phenomenon instantly.

"It's what we call a deep scattering layer," he informed Robertson. "Thousands upon thousands of tiny sea creatures. It's a beautiful sight, really. Some of them are bioluminescent. They light up when frightened. They live at this depth but come up to the surface at night to feed. . . ."

Robertson spoke sharply over the underwater telephone. "Never mind the ichthyology lecture, Trevor. Douse those damned lights."

"Complying," Van Buren had acknowledged, a little reluctantly. The little things had been almost pleasant as well as interesting company. Yet now, as he approached the *Titanic* all thoughts of marine life fled his mind.

Contrary to what Montague had forecast, his initial reaction was neither sadness, dismay, nor disbelief. What he saw instead was an ageless nobility that carelessness and the elements had failed to destroy.

Still in his mind was the image of a *Titanic* that no longer existed, the most beautiful ship man had ever created. Every object, every detail the lights were picking up, became to Van Buren what they once were, and the poignancy intensified with every identification: a bronze steering telemotor that once had been in the wheelhouse . . . rusted winches . . . the collapsed roof over what used to be the ship's gymnasium . . . windlasses and anchor chains and a capstan . . . lifeboat davits, hanging forlorn and empty like long-abandoned gallows. . . .

He spotted what Montague had mentioned: the hole in a deck area directly over where the Grand Staircase had been. He wondered whether that magnificent staircase was still intact. Probably not, because—as Hawke had reported—there was no sign of wood anywhere on the deck itself, and that staircase had been made of polished mahogany. There must be wood-eating organisms at work even at this tremendous depth, he decided, and he added a line to that effect in a notebook he was using to log his observations.

He wished he could squeeze *Franklin* into the distorted cavity that led to the Grand Staircase, but he judged it to be too small. Somehow the ship's ornate, gracefully curved main staircases, each in the shape of a huge Y, had symbolized the *Titanic*'s splendor. He could visualize the gowned ladies sedately descending the staircase that led into the massive first-class dining saloon, on the arms of their escorts dressed with equal elegance. . . .

Trevor Van Buren was looking not upon a scene of devastation but at a faded picture of past glory . . . of an age as dignified and regal as the *Titanic* herself. To him, the ship was no longer a dead thing; it had come alive.

He long since had activated *Franklin*'s camera and was sure he was getting even better photographs than the ones Hawke and Montague had brought back. Van Buren had taken the sub to within a few feet of the deck, and he exalted with each fresh identification of objects and areas, although there were some he didn't recognize. He wished Derek, who knew the *Titanic* so intimately and thoroughly, was with him. Derek could have pointed out things that others might miss, ignore, or misinterpret. Like that hood-shaped structure, he thought. Some kind of vent?

He nursed *Franklin* lower, so the sub was crawling along the side of the black cliff. He was looking for the same evidence of intermittent damage created by the hidden ice spur as the giant liner cleared the berg itself. Van Buren remembered Montague's relating that the *Titanic* was doing just under twenty-two knots when the lookouts first spotted the iceberg—more than 46,000 tons of metal moving at a rate of thirty-eight feet per second. The collision occurred only thirty-seven seconds after lookout Fredrick Fleet notified the bridge "Iceberg right ahead." Even though the bridge rang up an immediate STOP and then REVERSE ENGINES, and the helmsman was told to turn hard astarboard, it hadn't been enough to prevent the disaster. Montague had pointed out that no one, including Captain Edward J. Smith himself, had the slightest notion of what it took to slow down, stop, or turn a ship of that size moving at such speed. During the *Titanic's* sea trials, she had never exceeded eighteen knots, nor had any emergency maneuvers even been attempted; the entire trial procedures had consumed only half a day. Derek had added, "By contrast, today's new liners go through more than a month of trials; it boggles the mind how perfunctory the *Titanic's* were. Absolutely no effort was made to ascertain her turning radius, how quickly she answered the helm, or how long it took to slow her down, let alone stop."

Van Buren finally called out, "Derek, you were absolutely right about that spur damage. Much of the lower hull is plainly visible and there is no sign of a long gash. I can make out the same small rents and punctures you saw. My God, wait until we get back and announce this finding to the world!"

Then the image of a living ship suddenly disintegrated, like the crumbling of burned paper. The nostalgia that had achieved resurrection in his mind was replaced by reality, for *Franklin* had reached the point where the great liner had snapped in two. The floodlights were showing him the end of the severed forward section, and beyond was nothing but the lifeless sea bottom. Now he recognized the *Titanic* for what she was—a water-ravaged giant tombstone. But just as sacred, he thought feelingly. Maybe even more sacred. . . .

He sighed and pressed the transmit button.

"Van Buren, here. I'd like to look for the stern section now. I could use sonar's help. Any other large targets in the area?"

"Give me the mike," Hawke snapped to Robertson. Snatching it out of his hand before the captain could acquiesce. "Trevor, this is John. You don't have the luxury of blundering around trying to find that goddamned stern."

"I don't intend to go blundering around. I expect you to give me some vector guidance to save time. I just want to get a brief look at the stern. It'll tell us a lot about the *Titanic*'s trajectory as she fell to the bottom . . . priceless scientific information, as you must know."

Hawke looked at Robertson, who was bent over the sonar screen. "Getting anything, Jerry?"

"Yeah. A pretty large blip at least two thousand feet to the south of where he is now."

"Two thousand?" Hawke repeated. "That's a hell of a distance to cover in the bottom time he's got left." He hesitated, strongly tempted to deceive the oceanographer, then decided against it. "Trevor, we've got a target to the south, but you're two-fifths of a mile from it, maybe a third. Before we leave here, you can take *Franklin* down again, so please commence ascent." He hoped phrasing the distance in fifths of a mile instead of feet sounded more threatening, but one never really knew how a boffin's mind worked.

There was no immediate response from *Franklin*, and Montague had a strong feeling Van Buren was trying to figure out a logical way to defy Hawke. He was right.

"John, it is absolutely essential that I at least attempt to locate the stern. You people are going to be so busy going after that damned gold, I'll probably never get another chance. I've been down here less than an hour and a half and there's plenty of time. Please begin vectoring me."

Robertson said philosophically, "Well, there's no way you can go down there and grab him by the scruff of the neck."

"I'd like to wring his damned neck when he gets back," Hawke growled. "We'd better keep track of his bottom time, because he jolly well will forget to."

The captain shrugged and spoke into the mike. "Okay, *Franklin,* turn ten degrees to your right."

The blip moved obediently, as if Robertson's voice were a two-and-a-half-mile rope.

"That's it. Now three degrees left and you'll be right on course."

The blip came to a halt.

"*Franklin,* you all right?" Robertson inquired.

Van Buren didn't answer, simply because he had become distracted. Just before moving away from the *Titanic,* he had been taking a last look at the area where the bridge had once stood. He thought he saw a figure up there, a human figure. Some kind of officer? He could see the bridge jacket and a visored cap. He blinked his eyes in disbelief and looked again.

There was nothing there.

A piece of debris, he reasoned, but for some reason, he was sweating and his heart was pounding.

Robertson called out, "Van Buren, are you all right? Why have you stopped?"

"I . . . I thought I saw something, but I was wrong. Will you repeat that vector, please?"

"Repeating, three degrees left. That's it—you're on course."

They waited impatiently for *Franklin*'s next transmission, but it came sooner than expected, and Van Buren sounded as excited as he had been when he first sighted the *Titanic.*

"I say, you people! There's an enormous debris field between the ship and where I'm heading. Absolutely huge. The floods are picking up numerous objects. Derek, you should be with me. You'd be positively ecstatic! You, too, Debbi. I'll try to describe them as I move along. There must be thousands of artifacts in this field. There's a coffee cup or teacup; I can't make out which. I see a closed leather satchel and a vase. I'm slowing down to take some photographs. . . ."

Hawke muttered, "The silly bastard! Twenty-five minutes left to stay on the bottom and he's slowing down to take pictures."

Chaney said sharply, "Those pictures are more valuable to him than the gold itself."

". . . wine bottles still in what remains of their cases. I see enough china to serve the Queen's guards. And here's a . . . my word, I don't believe it! A pair of shoes! And Derek, listen to this. A number of much larger objects. They seem to be bits of machinery of some sort. All kinds of chamber pots and toilets. This field is an absolute gold mine! I can see a silver serving tray. In remarkably good condition, too. As I move—"

They heard him gasp and everyone listening in the sonar room froze.

". . . Oh, my God. It's a child's head!"

Montague gulped. "That's impossible!"

The others exchanged shocked glances, but Van Buren's voice resumed, much calmer and apologetic.

"Sorry, it's only a doll's head. Gave me quite a fright."

"He's not the only one," Lefferts murmured.

Franklin was creeping toward the stern section with her belly less than three feet off the ocean floor. Van Buren's excitement remained unabated.

". . . and I'll tell you one thing . . . from the size of this field, I'll wager that the two intact sections represent only about two-thirds of the *Titanic*. Quite literally, thousands of small items but very few large pieces of wreckage. There's a wineglass. An unopened bottle—champagne, probably. Now there's a large piece. Damnation, Derek! I think it's a boiler but I'm not sure. Oh, my heavens! I see . . . bless me, it's a safe! Derek, I'm taking a photo of it now so you can identify it for certain. I've just spotted more shoes and one appears to be of the high-buttoned type. Strange how leather has been preserved, whereas wood simply disappeared. . . ."

His cataloging of the debris items continued all the way to

the stern section. The litany affected his listeners oddly; if Van Buren had reported only huge pieces of twisted metal, it would have seemed coldly impersonal, but what he was seeing involved intensely personal items that once-living people had used, touched, consumed. Somehow, they spoke silently of tragedy and sudden, terrible death, and for the first time even Hawke grudgingly began to grasp the power of the *Titanic*. It could make one relive that cold night of hell, April 14, 1912.

Lefferts, still thinking of the doll's head, said softly, "I hope he doesn't stumble on a body."

The captain shook his head, more to ward off the thought than to deny the possibility. "Not likely," he growled.

". . . I do believe those are workman's tools. . . and those black things have to be lumps of coal . . . I think that's a windowpane. . . ."

"*Franklin*! Large metallic object dead ahead!"

"Yes, I see it. I see it! I see the stern! My god it's an absolute mess. Far worse than the bow. Just twisted, flattened metal. . . . I'm abeam of it now. . . . The extreme aft section isn't that bad. . . . I can see the graceful overhang curving down toward the rudder . . . but most of the rudder itself appears to be buried, and the propellers, too. . . . I'd love to find—"

"Take your pictures and start your ascent," Robertson barked.

"I'm photographing the rudder area. . . . I think I got an excellent shot. . . . Now I'll try for a shot of the entire stern section from above . . . it's lying somewhat on its side, and off to the left there are much larger pieces of debris . . . huge strips of metal . . . severed tubing . . . a deplorable sight. . . . The structural break-up on the way down was absolutely incredible. . . ."

"*Franklin*, I'll give you five more minutes."

"Understood. I'm moving above the stern now for more pictures. . . ."

Hawke threw up his hands helplessly. "That crazy bastard's liable to stay down there until the batteries go dead."

Lefferts chuckled. "He's having a ball, John. I can't wait to get down there myself."

Montague said worriedly, "Trevor has absolutely no conception of time. Once he gets interested in something, an hour seems like a minute to him. John, he's paying no attention to Jerry, but he may listen to you. I think you should order him up."

Hawke nodded and was about to transmit an immediate ascent command when Van Buren's voice, louder than usual, came crackling out of the loudspeaker on the wall of the sonar room.

"I say, topside—is sonar picking up anything in my vicinity?"

He sounded matter-of-fact to everyone except Hawke and Montague. They were English, and they had picked up a subtle inflection in the oceanographer's voice.

"Trevor," Hawke said calmly, "is anything wrong?"

The answer came back hesitantly. "I don't know. There's something alive down here. It . . . it just passed over the sub like a . . . a huge cloud . . . more of a giant shadow, actually."

"Is it still there?"

"No, but it's around here somewhere. I . . . I can almost feel its presence." His voice went up two octaves and he seemed on the verge of hysteria. "There must be something on sonar. I tell you, it was monstrous!"

Hawke and Robertson swapped worried glances. "Only thing on sonar is the stern and Van Buren's sub," the captain said, puzzled. "I see nothing that's moving, and I'm scanning the whole area."

Hawke said, "Keep scanning a wider radius." Into the mike, he said reassuringly, "We're taking a good look all around you, Trevor, but nothing shows. It may have been a large mass of sea-bottom debris stirred up by the current."

Van Buren's response sounded grateful. "You're probably right. I wish there were time to take one last look at the hull and—"

His transmission ended with frightening abruptness. The next sound was a gasp of sheer terror.

A burst of static came from the loudspeaker, and then Van Buren's voice again, rising to almost a scream.

"It just came back! . . It's something alive, I tell you. It's undulating over me. . . . I can't even see the floods . . . they're blotted out. . . . It's some kind of enormous creature. . . !"

"POPEYE!" Hawke roared into the mike. "HIT POPEYE AND GET OUT OF THERE!"

Two seconds of terrifying silence. Then . . .

CLANG!

The emergency ascent system on the subs was linked electronically to a large firehouse bell in the sonar room; it sounded simultaneously with the pressing of the sub's panic button, accompanied by the flashing of a red light over the bell.

For a moment, they simply stood there paralyzed, the glow from the still-flashing red light reflected on their tense, worried faces. The entire group was stricken into silence, broken only when Caitin muttered, "I hope the little guy's all right."

Just those few words of solicitude, coming from a man whom Van Buren had consistently treated with disdain, seemed to galvanize Hawke out of his numbness. "Track him on sonar," he told Robertson, and the hand with which he clutched the mike was no longer trembling.

"He's on his way up," Robertson said tersely.

"*Franklin*, come in. . . . Trevor, come in, please."

There was no response.

"Got him on sonar," the captain called out. "Ascent looks good. No other target in sight. Whatever he saw doesn't seem to be following him."

Montague cleared his throat, so dry that his voice came out in a rasping croak. "You said it yourself, John, probably a mass of sea debris twisting in a current. The mind can play strange tricks, and Trevor must have let his imagination run wild."

Hawke made no comment. He knew Van Buren, an experienced and brilliant oceanographer, wasn't likely to be fooled by anything as prosaic as bottom debris.

"*Franklin*," he repeated, "can you hear me?"

A burst of static from the loudspeaker startled everyone and they tensed, waiting expectantly for the oddly filtered metallic voice that invariably followed the crackling noise of a transmitter button.

Except there was no voice.

"He's got to be conscious," Hawke muttered more to himself

than to the others. "That static indicates some kind of transmission effort. Trevor, come in. . . . Are you all right?"

The silence continued, for minutes that seemed endless. Twice more, they heard static from *Franklin*'s mike but nothing from Van Buren.

"He may be having communication problems," Robertson said finally. "That equipment's temperamental. One way or another, the sub should be breaking the surface in another twenty minutes. We'd better prepare for recovery. Derek, I'd like you to keep trying to raise Van Buren while the rest of us head outside."

Hawke handed the mike to Montague and started to follow the others out when the static crackled anew. This time, however, it was followed by a voice—a very weak, shaky voice.

"Can you read me? This is *Franklin*."

Hawke grabbed the mike out of Montague's hand. "Trevor, what happened? We've been trying to raise you for over an hour. Are you all right?"

"I passed out, John. That . . . that thing started to follow me and I . . . I just fainted. I'm sorry, but it has been a terrible experience."

"I'm just glad you're safe," Hawke assured him. "We're all glad. We'll see you in a few minutes. Do you remember the prerecovery checklist? If you need help securing for recovery, tell me and we'll go through—"

Van Buren interrupted. "I'm fine, John. I have everything in hand now. And I remember the procedures."

Hawke said to Montague as they hurried out, "I hope he also remembers exactly what the hell happened down there."

Trevor Van Buren remembered perfectly. The only problem was that after recovery, he couldn't even come close to identifying what had frightened him so.

"You say it was alive," Hawke pressed, "and that it seemed to be undulating."

"Not *seemed* to be," Van Buren objected. "It *was* undulating, like some kind of huge snake."

Robertson asked, "Is that what you saw . . . a gigantic snake or serpent?"

Lefferts, the man who loved to chase myths, said triumphantly, "By God, a sea serpent! The oldest mariners' legend of them all!"

Van Buren looked doubtful. "No, the mass was too large, too broad. It definitely was not the shape of a snake."

"Did you see any specific features, like a head, or any kind of body shape?" Chaney put in.

"Something like a gigantic plesiosaur?" Lefferts suggested hopefully, and Van Buren smiled faintly.

"No, and it's futile to ask me for a precise description, because all I got was a rather vague impression. The lights never really illuminated it. Quite the contrary; it was so huge that it felt like a density, a shadow, like an eclipse shutting off moonlight."

Hawke said patiently, "Trevor, that doesn't add up to something that's alive. I still think it could have been a large chunk of sediment moving around in the current."

"It turned around and came back," Van Buren said softly. "You're telling me that current did a hundred-and-eighty-degree turn?"

Chaney spoke up. "There must be an explanation for what Trevor saw. Frankly, from his description, it sounds like some kind of giant manta ray. That would fit his impression of a shapeless mass, and also the abrupt change of direction. Rays are very maneuverable."

"Except," Montague pointed out, "you're talking about a species of manta ray that would have to be the size of a barn. I'm no expert, but I doubt very much if rays that large exist."

"Anything's possible at that depth," Chaney argued. "Oceans comprise seventy-one percent of the earth's surface and we haven't even begun to explore them."

"Well"—Hawke sighed—"no matter what's down there— if anything—Craig and I will take *Winston* down tomorrow and attach our little toys to the hull. If that thing shows up, the hell with it."

Robertson said bluntly, "You're a damned fool making a dive when you've got the flu."

"Dammit, Jerry, I *am* fully recovered. I don't feel feverish anymore and aside from a little weakness I'm—"

"Aha!" the captain proclaimed. "You admit to feeling weak. You can't clear your ears, either, can you? John, let someone else make tomorrow's dive. Wait another twenty-four hours before you go down again."

Hawke started to argue but decided not to. He had to admit he still wasn't quite up to par, and Robertson was right; it would be foolish for him to make the most difficult dive yet attempted until he felt better. "You win," he said simply. "Craig, you'll need to decide who goes with you."

He was sure Caitin would choose Chaney. So was everyone else, including Chaney herself. However, Caitin said to Lefferts, "Martin, I'll take you, and if you screw up, I'll pull out your toenails with my bare hands."

That ended all debate, but Robertson motioned Montague to stay behind when the others headed for the lounge. The captain seemed preoccupied, and Montague looked at him curiously.

"Something bothering you, Jerry?"

"Yeah."

"Care to confide in me?"

"I don't mind, but I'm not sure exactly what there is to confide."

"Worried about what Trevor saw, or thought he saw?"

"More curious than worried. Nobody's ever gone that deep in the Atlantic before, and Christ knows what's swimming around that wreck. But with the sea, you have to take your chances, under it as well as on it. Hawke knows that and so do I."

"So I gather it's not the idea of some monstrous creature that's bothering you."

"Trying to define what's bothering me is about as easy as describing color to a blind man." Robertson paused to relight the corncob, puffing on it as if he were pumping fuel into his brain. He gave Montague a curiously hesitant glance. "Tell me something, Derek, do you believe in premonitions?"

Montague looked at him but left the question unanswered.

"Back in World War Two, I was a mustang officer. Are you familiar with the term?"

Montague shook his head.

"In the U.S. Navy, a mustang is an enlisted man who earns a commission the hard way, by coming up through the ranks without the benefit of a Naval Academy diploma or reserve officers' training. I started out in the thirties as an apprentice seaman and by 1940, I was a warrant officer—the highest noncommissioned rank in the navy. I was serving on a battleship at the time, in charge of an engine-room detail. We were in port and I was at my station below, supervising some maintenance work.

"Anyway, all of a sudden that engine room seemed to close in on me. It wasn't claustrophobia, either. I liked working there and it had never happened to me before. I had this terrible feeling of dread, vague and intangible, but so overpowering, I couldn't fight it. Mind you, I felt like a horse's ass. Yet I was absolutely certain that something bad was going to happen.

"I told the boys to keep working, that I had to go topside for a few minutes. I figured all I needed was a little fresh air, but even when I got outside, the feeling was still there. I didn't know why, but I was convinced I had to get the hell off that battlewagon. So I went up to the OOD—officer of the deck—and mumbled some cock-and-bull yarn about personal business and having to make an emergency phone call to the mainland.

"The OOD was a young lieutenant who just grinned at me . . . figured I was probably going into town for a quick lay. 'Permission granted,' he says with this little wink. So I left my ship and started walking away from her, not going anywhere in particular, just walking aimlessly and still wondering what in God's name had hit me. All I knew was that I had to get away from there."

Robertson banged his pipe into an ashtray. A few grains of tobacco were still burning and he snuffed them out with the corncob heel.

"I finally looked at my watch. It was oh-seven-fifty-five and I had been gone for almost an hour. I decided I had been foolish long enough and started back. I remember wondering what kind of alibi I could concoct for my kids in the engine room. But I never got a chance to make up a story."

The captain closed his eyes for a long, painful moment.

When he opened them, Montague could see they were moist, two tiny twin mirrors of sadness.

"I never saw those kids again, Derek. The date was December 7, 1941, and the name of my ship was the *Arizona*. She blew up when a Jap bomb penetrated a magazine. I was transferred to the *Maryland*, eventually won a promotion to ensign, and wound up after the war commanding a minelayer like this one. But my kids are still buried in the *Arizona*'s hull where, by all rights, I should have died with them."

The two men stared at each other in the silent room. Outside, they heard someone laugh and the sound broke the spell. Robertson sighed heavily, an exhaling of unpleasant memories. He filled and relit the pipe.

"You never did answer my question. Do *you* believe in premonitions?"

The tall Englishman frowned. "Before I answer, I must ask you a question. Do you have a premonition now? That something is going to happen . . . to this expedition?"

"Yes, because too many things already have gone wrong."

"So do I," said Derek Montague.

8

That night's prelaunch meeting started innocently enough with continued speculation over what Van Buren had seen. Chaney still held to her theory of a huge manta ray; Caitin suggested it could be a monster octopus; and Lefferts persisted in believing it had to be a plesiosaur. Montague could see Hawke's annoyance growing in proportion to Martin's enthusiasm for this possibility.

"It has to be a plesiosaur of a size that no one ever dreamed of," Lefferts insisted. "God, can you imagine finding the *Titanic* and a living dinosaur on the same expedition? The press will eat this up when we get back!"

"A plesiosaur would be a devastating discovery," Van Buren agreed, "yet so would the discovery of any hitherto-unknown species." His expression suddenly altered. "Has it occurred to anyone that Caitin's explosives might very well frighten the creature away before we can study it? Or, equally unfortunate, provoke it?"

Caitin shook his massive head. "I'd be happy to scare an oversized octopus away. I seen a movie once, where this big son of a bitch of an octopus goes after a sub; the tentacles were the size of hawser chains on a carrier. I know it was just special-effects stuff but still—"

"For God's sake!" Hawke exploded "You people are giving credence to an illusion. I can understand a pair of oceanographers getting carried away, but you, Martin? And Craig?"

Van Buren looked him right in the eyes. "Suppose," he

asked with deceptive mildness, "this creature doesn't want anyone fooling around with the *Titanic*? That thing was alive, and it's entirely possible it has established some kind of territorial rights to the wreck, a trait that is not unknown in certain sea creatures . . . such as the shark."

Hawke threw up his hands. "Good God in heaven, you're all at it again. This meeting is adjourned. Craig, Martin, I want you to go over Derek's schematic drawing of the *Titanic* once more, also the blueprints. You must be absolutely certain where to place the explosives. Derek will help you convert the scale of the schematic and blueprint drawings to the hull's actual footage, then he'll mark up the photos we made of the hull. That way you'll be able to judge fairly accurately how far you have to progress from the bow to hold three. Remember to—"

Van Buren interrupted. "I say, John, just in case they are, uh, attacked, is there any chance of installing some kind of weapon with which they could defend themselves?"

Hawke burned him with a glare. "They can do what you did—use their imagination."

He was still fuming as he left the saloon with Robertson, grumbling, "Let's go check on Ballinger. I hope the potbellied bastard knows what he's doing with my submarine."

Montague shook his head. He had never seen John Hawke so ill-tempered. He knew Hawke was carrying a mountain of responsibility as the leader of an expedition that had experienced a smashing success but also some baffling bad luck. Yet his attitude toward Van Buren's experience bothered Montague. A trained, observant scientist like Trevor wasn't the type to have imagined anything so bizarre.

He wondered whether Hawke might not be a personification of the British military psyche. Courage had always been a British trait and deserved source of pride in every sailor's heart, but military history was replete with examples of courage taking the form of foolhardiness. Underestimating the enemy had a place in British military tradition, as did the habit of facing danger with a gallant nonchalance that would have courage prevail through anything, including outmoded strategy and poor planning. Come to think of it, arrogant overconfidence

might have described Captain Edward J. Smith of the *Titanic*.
It was said that when the ship was in her death throes and the
end was near, Smith turned to the officers and men still on
the bridge, saying, "Be British, lads. Be British!"

Montague knew this account probably was just another of
the apocryphal stories told about the *Titanic*, yet it would have
been typical for an officer to say something like that. The irony,
Montague thought wryly, was that in this case "being British"
was what had led the ship to her doom.

At 0617 the next morning, a heavy crane hoisted *Winston* over
the side and lowered the submarine into the water.

Caitin was already in the cockpit, but Lefferts was standing
upright in the open hatch, waving good-bye with a huge grin
on his face. "Don't worry, Mother," he yelled at Hawke. "We'll
come home safe and sound."

Hawke had to laugh. He *had* been demonstrating the zeal
of a parent sending two children off to school for the first time.
Long before dawn, he had insisted on more drills, repeating
emergency procedures and—most vital of all—practicing the
manipulation of the robot arms that would attach the explosives
to the wreck's hull.

This would be Caitin's chief task, which meant Lefferts
would be piloting the sub during the attachment process;
Hawke had rehearsed the billionaire relentlessly on the controls. "Craig will be your eyes," he kept emphasizing. "Your
touch on the wheel, throttle, and planes must be absolutely
precise and smooth, and your reaction to his commands instantaneous." Martin had merely nodded. He was delightedly reliving his Loch Ness expedition. More than once he announced
his hope of "meeting Nessie's big brother down there"; he had
even given Van Buren's mysterious creature the nickname
"Plessie."

Van Buren wasn't on deck to see the launch and Hawke
suspected he simply didn't want to witness the start of a dive
that would culminate in the demolition of his beloved ship.

Winston slid gracefully under a sea that had turned a little
choppy; Robertson was monitoring weather reports constantly.
"I think we'll be lucky if this weather holds up for another

week," he had warned Hawke. "You'd better pray recovery operations won't last longer than that."

By mutual agreement, Lefferts was handling communications from the submarine. Relaying *Winston*'s progress gave him a welcome sense of being in command, and his voice came back to the *Henry Morgan*, crisp and authoritative.

"*Winston* reporting. Passing three thousand."

Hawke smiled. "He sounds like he's having fun," he said to Montague. "Reading you loud and clear, Martin. Suggest that when you reach five thousand, run a test on the robots."

"Roger."

Hawke grinned again. He understood Lefferts perfectly. Martin was that rare, fortunate man who could afford to live out his fantasies. Life to him was more of a game than anything else; even in business, the challenge was more important than the monetary reward. It wouldn't have surprised Hawke if Martin was imagining himself at the periscope of a fleet submarine, lining up a torpedo run on an enemy carrier.

"Hawke!" Robertson's interruption was curt. "Their rate of descent is too fast and the angle too sharp. What the hell is Caitin trying—a power dive?"

"That's not like Craig!" Hawke worried. "I'll slow him down." He said into the mike, "*Winston*, sonar has you descending too rapidly. Suggest reduce power and lessen your angle three degrees."

Lefferts turned to Caitin. "You get that?"

"Yeah, I got it. Tell 'em to mind their own business. I'm drivin' the car."

Lefferts looked at him, shocked. "I can't tell them that."

Caitin's response was a cross between a grunt and a chuckle. Then he shook his head as if he were trying to clear it of cobwebs. "Don't know why I said that," he rumbled. "Tell 'em okay."

"Craig, are you feeling all right?"

"Yeah. Go ahead and acknowledge them instructions."

"Roger," Lefferts informed the *Henry Morgan* as Caitin's ham-sized hands closed the throttle slightly and corrected the sub's descent angle. "How do we look now?"

"Descent angle and the rate look good now, and thank you,"

Hawke said after glancing at Robertson on the sonar and getting a nod of approval. He felt relieved; Caitin apparently just hadn't been concentrating, natural enough in the excitement of his first dive. If there was anything to worry about, it would be Lefferts's handling of the sub while Caitin attached his Plastomite charges to the hull. Inside the magnetic disks containing the Plastomite were small, fairly fragile timing devices activated automatically when attached. This gave them fifteen minutes before detonation, sufficient time to move the sub a safe distance away.

Lefferts had to be extremely careful not to nudge the hull too hard or the timing devices could be damaged, resulting either in premature detonation or no detonation at all.

At five thousand feet, Lefferts advised they were testing the robot arms as instructed.

"Test completed and everything worked fine," he announced a few minutes later. "Continuing descent and will report from now on at one-thousand-foot intervals. We're both doing just great."

He sounds positively effervescent, Hawke thought. "Well played, Martin. You seem to be enjoying your trip."

"John, I never felt better in my life. Can't wait to get to the *Titanic*. We'll blow a hole in her a herd of elephants could walk into. Why, I can almost smell that gold, and you can tell Van Buren—"

Hawke cut him off. "Don't get too cocky, friend. And keep your eyes open for that thing Trevor claims he saw. Maybe you can get a better look at it than he did."

"We'll spit in its eye. *Winston* out."

As they passed eight thousand feet, Caitin remarked that he didn't feel the cold he had been warned to expect.

"Come to think of it," Lefferts said, "neither do I. Matter of fact, I'm actually comfortable. Hawke and Montague said they damned near froze at this depth and that it got even colder. Want to try the work lights, just for a few seconds?"

Caitin grinned wickedly. "What Hawke don't know won't hurt him." He turned on the powerful lights and peered ahead. A few small fish swam into view briefly and then hurried away, leaving behind them nothing but inky water.

"Christ, it's blacker'n axle grease out there," the big man muttered, and doused the lights. The descent continued in mutual silence, punctuated only by Lefferts's depth reports and an observation he made at the ten-thousand-foot level.

"Craig and I both noticed it earlier, but we still don't feel that cold even at this depth."

"What's your interior thermometer showing?"

"Forty-two degrees. That can't be right, though."

"I hope you haven't caught my flu bug." Hawke sounded worried.

"I doubt it. We both feel fine; maybe we've hit some kind of thermal layer."

"Not with the cabin temp at forty-two. Trevor's been listening and he says he can't explain it, either."

Montague said in a worried tone, "I've been listening, too. Did anyone except me notice their voices sound different somehow? Pitched a little higher?"

"I did," Chaney agreed. "I thought it must be just the transmission distance."

Hawke, frowning, raised the mike again.

"Martin, check your oxygen-flow gauge, also the computer settings for that flow. Are they both normal?"

There was a brief delay and Hawke guessed Lefferts might be asking Caitin to help him. He was right, for after several minutes, it was Craig's voice heard next.

"Flow's normal and the computer's set just like we left it last night. What's the problem?"

"Apparently nothing. Are you sure you didn't get a warning light on the flow indicator?"

"Nary a blink."

Hawke looked at Montague, but they couldn't argue with dials and gauges that flatly denied trouble. Lefferts came back on.

"The hell with it, then. How are we looking on sonar?"

"Angle of descent excellent. You're right on course and we'll commence vectoring at eleven-five."

"Okay, John. Craig says hello. He's laughing at something, but damned if I know what."

Hawke thought he heard the giant's rumbling chuckle but

he wasn't sure. Few things struck Caitin as funny and he wondered what Craig had found so amusing.

At the 11,500-foot mark, Caitin turned on the floods, took over the mike, and asked for a continuous vector. They sighted sea bottom two minutes later.

"Okay, *Winston*. Reduce descent angle to one degree and turn left . . . nudge her a bit right, now . . . that's it. Steady as she goes and reduce speed . . . you're almost there . . . level off . . . target should be dead ahead. . . ."

"Got her!" Caitin exclaimed. "Holy cow, she's one big motherfucker. . . ."

"Easy now, *Winston*. Be sure you start at the bow and work back slowly . . . remember the footage Derek worked out . . . sixty-eight feet marks the leading edge of hold three and you should—"

"I ain't no goddamned amateur!" Caitin interrupted angrily. "I know where that hold is!"

Well, he's back to normal, Hawke thought. "Sorry, Craig. Start your attachment process when ready."

Winston moved at a snail's pace down the side of the massive, encrusted hull.

"Damn current's strong," Caitin complained to Lefferts. "I'm havin' trouble holding this son of a bitch." Lefferts, who was mentally estimating the distance they were covering, didn't reply. "Fifty-five feet," he called out. "We're almost there."

Caitin, still wrestling the current, cursed.

"Sixty . . . sixty-one . . . sixty-two . . . sixty-three . . . four . . . five . . . six . . . seven . . ."

Caitin clicked the throttle into reverse and the sub came to a wallowing stop. "I'm gonna back her up now," Caitin said, "and I'll tell you when to start the approach."

"Okay. But give me plenty of room so I can adjust if I have to." Lefferts was surprised how calm he was. He had been a lot more nervous simulating the approach with Hawke monitoring his performance, yet faced with the real thing, he had never felt so confident, so sure of himself, so alert and cool. Funny, but Craig seemed more on edge than he was.

"That's far enough," Caitin announced. "She's all yours. Johnny, we're startin' attachment approach. Activatin' arms."

"Roger, *Winston*. Good luck." Hawke looked around a sonar room heavy with tension. There was Robertson, sucking on an unlit corncob; Debbi chain-smoking, discarding one cigarette after another before each was even half-consumed; Montague chewing gum furiously; and Van Buren, rubbing his hands together nervously. Hawke would have bet those hands were oily with sweat.

Hawke turned back to the sonar screen, watching intensely as the tiny blip representing his submarine edged its way toward the battered liner.

Inside *Winston*, Lefferts peered ahead, following the twin paths of their lights. He heard Caitin breathing heavily as his big hands manipulated the robot arms. "The left one's stuck," he grunted in frustration. "Hell of a time for the fuckin' thing to louse up . . . there, she's workin' now! Easy does it, Martin. I got 'em in sync . . . slow, now . . . real slow . . . that's—"

Whatever he was about to say was never spoken, for his voice seemed to freeze in his throat. The white light from the floods had suddenly turned a dull gray and both men saw the reason in the same split second.

A shadow, huge, shimmering, and strangely menacing, like a gigantic ghostly shroud, hung directly over them. It even blotted out part of the wreck's massive bulk.

"Back up and tilt the lights," Caitin said hoarsely.

"Craig, maybe we should get out of here." Lefferts's voice was almost a squeak.

"Not 'til we get a good look at that thing. If it ain't gonna bother us, we can finish what we came here for. Here, lemme do it."

The sub backed away from the *Titanic*.

The shadow moved with it.

"It's following us," Lefferts gulped.

Caitin's hand, normally as steady as an imbedded rock, was trembling as it moved the strobe lever up.

Then they saw it.

On the *Henry Morgan*, Hawke and the captain watched the sub's blip move away from the wreck and they exchanged glances.

"What the hell's wrong?" Hawke wondered aloud.

"Probably repositioning," Robertson guessed. "Approach angle may have been off. Don't bother 'em yet; Caitin knows what he's doing."

They turned back to the screen. The loudspeaker came to life with its warning burst of prevoice static. And the voice was that of Martin Lefferts, a voice of unmitigated terror.

". . . it's a plesiosaur! Oh my God, it's terrible! It must be a hundred feet long and the head—it's bigger than this sub and . . . it's coming right at us. IT'S COMING RIGHT AT US! IT'S OPENING ITS MOUTH. . . . THE FANGS—OH MY GOD THOSE FANGS!"

The voice became a scream.

Then two screams, the second Caitin's but suddenly dissolving into a guttural croak.

"Tent . . ." was all they heard before the final silence.

CLANG went Popeye's panic button bell.

The red light on the wall began pulsating, a steady rhythm like the visible beating of a heart.

Robertson looked at the sonar screen. "They're coming up," he said softly.

Chaney sighed, a sound that also could have been a sob. In a dull, lifeless voice, she said, "Might as well wait for them on deck." She moved toward the door, followed wordlessly by Montague. Van Buren hesitated, then walked over to the screen where Hawke and the captain were still standing.

"I told you so," he said, but his tone was more one of regret than triumph.

Hawke shook his head in frustrated bewilderment. "There were only two targets on this screen—the sub and the *Titanic*," he muttered. "What in the bloody hell did they see?"

"A one-hundred-foot plesiosaur," Van Buren reminded him.

"But it makes no sense. Anything that big should have shown up on sonar."

"Not necessarily, John," the captain said. "Our sonar's designed mostly to pick up metallic objects. I'm not sure whether the signal could reflect something soft-bodied, not on this set, anyway. It's not the most sophisticated rig."

"It's not that unsophisticated, either," Hawke argued. "How the devil could it miss a target that big?"

The captain shrugged. "Damned if I know, but it's the only logical explanation I can think of. One thing's for sure—they got a lot better look at that thing than Trevor, here, did."

They realized something must be seriously wrong when *Winston* popped out of the depths, wallowing like a dead fish about fifty yards from the old minelayer.

The hatch did not open.

Not immediately as expected, nor in the next agonizing ten minutes it took for Robertson to nurse the *Henry Morgan* alongside the submarine so it could be hauled aboard. The frog-suited Jefferson and Ryan dove into the water, climbed onto the sub's deck, and attached a crane hook to a ring on the *Winston's* miniscule conning tower. Jefferson banged on the hatch.

"Hey in there . . . you guys okay?"

There was no reply. The crewmen waved at the crane operator and stayed on the sub as it was lifted into the air. *Winston* twisted toward the ship, rivulets of water glistening as they dripped from its yellow-painted hull, and was deposited gently on the *Henry Morgan's* deck.

"Open up!" Ryan yelled, banging again at the hatch.

It stayed closed.

"Get that goddamned thing open!" Robertson shouted from the bridge, and then raced down the bridge stairs, reaching the deck in only two frantic strides.

Jefferson swung the hatch open. Hawke brushed him aside and peered inside. "Craig! Martin!"

Silence.

He looked forward and saw two limp figures, Caitin slumped against the instrument panel and Lefferts sitting back in his seat, his head dangling to one side like a man who had fallen asleep watching television.

"They're unconscious," Hawke called out. "Someone come down here and help me get them out."

The removal process consumed several minutes. Hawke, still panting from his exertions, was the last one out of the sub and Robertson already had both inert bodies carried to the bridge, where the ship's first-aid equipment was stored. When Hawke got there, the captain was kneeling over the two still figures. He already had examined Lefferts and was now feeling for Caitin's pulse. The very blankness of his expression was more ominous than a frown.

Hawke muttered, "They were as stiff as boards; it was like lifting two big logs out."

The captain looked up, his face gray. "No wonder. Rigor mortis. They're both dead."

Debra Chaney uttered a small cry, half sob and half gasp. Montague closed his eyes. Van Buren turned his head away and whispered, "Oh my God, no." He retched, muttered "I'm going to be sick," and ran outside.

Hawke squatted next to Robertson and looked at the waxen faces of his two friends and comrades. Their unseeing eyes, wide open, stared back at him, and he shuddered in a reflex of pain as much as shock. An old myth—about eyes being a camera that could record the last image a murder victim sees before death—sprang into his mind, and he was almost tempted to look closer at them. As if he was reading Hawke's thoughts, Robertson gently closed Lefferts's lids and then did the same with Caitin's.

Montague, kneeling over Hawke's shoulder, shook his head. "How could they die? There isn't a mark on them. And how could rigor mortis set in that fast?"

The captain rose stiffly to his feet, his expression grim. "All I know is that their hearts stopped beating." He looked at First Officer Crippens, who was staring at the bodies incredulously. "Paul, didn't you tell me once you started out as a medical student?"

"Only for a year, Captain. Even if I could perform an autopsy, I wouldn't know what to look for." He hesitated. "Fast rigor mortis, though; it rings a bell."

"Ring it for us," Hawke said tersely.

"Well, I seem to recall reading that rigor mortis can set in quickly in cases of violent death. Except that it's not true rigor mortis; it's more of a spasm that occurs when the heart suddenly stops beating and the spasm causes stiffening."

Montague said, "You make it sound as if they both were literally frightened to death. That the creature they saw induced simultaneous heart attacks."

Crippens shook his head. "No, I don't think so. Look, one year of med school didn't make me an expert, but I never heard of anyone with a healthy heart being scared into a coronary. And I assume both were healthy."

Hawke said, "Martin had a thorough physical before we sailed. I insisted on it and he showed me the results—a complete bill of health. As for Caitin, I can't believe he had any heart problem. A big man, yes, but without an ounce of fat and he was a physical-fitness freak. You've all seen him jogging around the deck every morning. Crippens, do you have any other ideas? I realize your medical experience is limited, but you're the only one who has any knowledge whatsoever."

The first officer's youthful brow wrinkled. "This is just a guess, mind you, but is it possible they weren't getting enough oxygen? Combine that with a large dose of blind panic and you'd really be raising hell with the old pump. Maybe even cause heart failure."

Hawke's countenance darkened. "Then I'd damned well better have a look at *Winston*'s life-support system, right now. Derek, want to come with me?"

"Gladly." As they left the bridge, Robertson threw canvas over the bodies and one by one, crewmen came over to stare respectfully at the lumps under the coverings. Dan Ballinger was last, his head bowed as he crossed himself.

It was almost unbearably hot inside *Winston*, but Hawke and Montague ignored the discomfort as they bent over the section of the instrument panel housing the oxygen-flow computer. Hawke pressed the key requesting the current flow setting.

They stared at the readout with unbelieving eyes.

"Abnormal," Hawke muttered. "Look at the excessive helium flow. That could explain the way they sounded and the lack of cold. Crippens was right; they weren't getting sufficient oxygen. Yet there was no malfunction warning light. It should have come on as they activated the life-support system, which wouldn't have been more than five minutes into the dive. The light comes on the second the flow deviates from the computer feed."

"Maybe the light's not working," Montague suggested.

"Maybe we'd better find out."

They tested the light. It pulsed a bright red.

Montague said hesitatingly, "John, is there any chance the computer setting was wrong to begin with?" He knew Hawke had personally fed in the flow data, but he had to ask the question.

"Impossible. I checked the flow last night and again this morning just before launch. Martin and Craig watched me do it. And neither one of them would have been crazy enough to change a single digit. Let's look at the valves. Maybe . . ."

The valves were functioning normally.

They reported their findings to the group still clustered around the bodies, Hawke concluding the report by suggesting some kind of funeral service.

Not a sound was uttered until Robertson finally cleared his throat. "We'll have to bury them at sea," he said. "We have no facilities for preserving their bodies. I also suggest we take another look at that sub before anyone else goes down again— if anyone wants to," he added ominously.

"Examine the sub for what?" Montague asked. "We've already done that."

"Check the hull for evidence of teeth marks. You heard Lefferts. He said it was a gigantic plesiosaur with huge fangs. If it actually attacked the sub, it must have left scratches on the hull. And if we find any"—the captain gazed straight into the somber eyes of John Hawke—"you might as well call off this expedition right now."

They went over *Winston* inch by inch.

And found nothing.

At sundown, the canvas-covered and lead-weighted bodies of Martin Lefferts and Craig Caitin were lowered over the side and committed to the deep. Captain Robertson improvised the burial-at-sea ritual, borrowing what he could remember from his naval career. It was a saddened group that assembled in the dining room later for a desultory supper that no one finished.

Le Baron had served it with tear-reddened eyes; he had sobbed openly during the burial. Hawke, sensing defeatism as well as grief, knew he faced a herculean task of restoring morale, not to mention salvaging the mission itself.

At the nightly postdinner debriefing session, Van Buren joined Hawke and Chaney in wanting to continue the operation; Montague sided with Robertson, who was all for returning to New York immediately.

"It's no longer a question of going after the gold," the captain argued. "Even if that loot was worth a hundred million bucks, it wouldn't compensate for the two lives we've already lost. Or the additional lives we could lose if anyone's stupid enough to make another dive."

Hawke said stubbornly, "We have no evidence the creature presents a real danger. Something apparently approached the submarine but—"

"Charged, not approached," Montague interrupted.

"Charged, then. Semantics. The important thing is that nothing ever touched *Winston*. Craig or Martin hit Popeye before they actually determined its intentions. I think they panicked prematurely."

"They panicked," Robertson said dryly, "before the goddamned thing had a chance to strike. If they had waited any longer, they might never have come up." He rubbed his tired eyes as if that could erase a terrible memory. "Jesus Christ, a one-hundred-foot plesiosaur still alive in an age of atomic energy and moon landings—it boggles the mind."

"Correct me if I'm wrong," Montague said, "but wasn't the plesiosaur a carnivorous predator?"

"An ocean-dwelling predator," Chaney said. "One that lived off the smaller, weaker inhabitants of its domain. But that doesn't mean excessive aggression. It's possible the creature Martin and Craig saw was investigating, out of curiosity."

Montague's lips widened in a humorless smile. "It's also entirely possible it mistook the submarine for a new kind of fish, one that would make an excellent meal. Trevor, can you deny this?"

Van Buren stroked his mustache, just as Hawke used the lighting of a pipe to muster his thoughts. When he finally spoke, the words emerged as if they had been carefully measured.

"I suppose any predator of that size must be considered potentially dangerous. However, I must emphasize the word *potentially*. I call your attention to the so-called Loch Ness monster. While its existence has never been proved, there is evidence that something unique inhabits those depths. And if we accept this, we must consider that the Loch Ness monster may be a surviving plesiosaur. The eyewitness descriptions and the few verified photographs taken of the creature all point to this identification. Nessie, as the creature is commonly called, has never shown any aggressive or menacing traits. I'd be willing to accompany John in another dive if Debbi decides not to go."

Chaney said tartly, "Debbi already has decided. I not only want to go but I insist on it." She looked at Hawke as if expecting an argument. "You promised me a dive."

Hawke hesitated. He was willing to risk anything for that gold, yet was he also willing for Debra Chaney to take the same risk? He examined her features, her eyes shining with eagerness and hope. . . .

"I'll keep my promise," he said flatly.

Robertson growled, "Frankly, I think you're all just plain nuts. As the captain of this ship, I have every right to forbid another dive and head for the barn."

"But you won't," Hawke guessed. "Because while you command the *Henry Morgan*, I command this expedition—an expedition commissioned by your boss, Jerry, and one that I'm sure he'd want to continue."

"In a pig's eye he would," Robertson snapped. "If he hadn't died, he wouldn't go near that thing again for all the gold in Fort Knox."

"But he'd let *me* go down," Hawke said. "Chaney's competent enough to pilot the sub while I work the robots. Remember, while I was training Craig, he also taught me a lot about demolition; we must have practiced the procedure twenty times, and believe me, I observed very carefully what he was doing and how he was doing it."

Robertson sighed in resignation. "I still think you're crazy and I still think Martin Lefferts, God rest his soul, would agree with me. But it's your funeral"—he tossed Chaney a grim look—"and yours, too."

Hawke was standing at an amidships deck rail, smoking meditatively on a pipe—one of the Dunhills Martin had given him, he thought gloomily. John Hawke had always accepted death with a kind of graceful resignation, acknowledging its inevitability as a kind of natural law no one could repeal. "Every life," he was told once, "is like a play or book or film, and each has to have an ending."

His father had spoken those words the day he informed his son that he had terminal cancer. Just before he died, he said something else Hawke never forgot: "John, I don't know what's waiting for me but I do know what's behind me. I've lived an interesting, reasonably decent life and I'm not leaving many mud tracks in the path I've traveled. So if there is a heaven, that'll have to be my ticket of admission."

Hawke adopted that philosophy as his own, but it was not foolproof. There were times when he resented death, when it was untimely or cruel or senseless or unexplainably premature. He felt that way now, a grief blended with frustrated anger, a mood of sullen blackness as much as sadness. Martin, a man who had finally found his Holy Grail and didn't live long enough to enjoy it. Craig, a man whose crudeness could never hide his simple dignity—he was going to be a millionaire, Hawke reflected bitterly, and Death had mugged him on the way to the bank.

He looked at his watch. The usually punctual Chaney was late; she had promised to meet him as soon as she changed clothes after spending two hours with him in *Winston*. That was a half hour ago and he was in no mood to put up with any delay. Then, because he had the gift of introspection, he admitted to himself that he was not so much impatient as he was anxious.

She finally showed up ten minutes later, wearing tight-fitting black slacks. A V-neck white blouse topped the ensemble, which he had never seen her wear before, and he could swear it didn't include a bra.

"Hi," she greeted him breathlessly. "Sorry, I'm late, but I took a quick shower."

"All set for tomorrow?"

"I've got mixed feelings, John. I'm excited but I'm also a little nervous. Maybe scared is a more honest word."

He studied her gravely. "Remember what I told the others; we now know what to expect. We won't be surprised and we won't be frightened out of our wits."

"You said something else. That maybe it's moved away. It may sound crazy, but I almost hope it hasn't. God, what a find . . . a live plesiosaur!"

"Unless the damned thing is gold-plated," Hawke said morosely, "I couldn't care less."

Chaney said thoughtfully, "Somehow, the gold doesn't seem as important now. Not when it cost two lives."

"It's even more important," he said testily. "We will have wasted those two lives for nothing if we fail. Everyone seems to be forgetting why we came here in the first place. It wasn't just to take pictures, and it wasn't to gawk at some aberration from fifty million years ago, either!"

She was stung, but she understood his anger. He had been carrying his own burden, walking a command tightrope over the conflicting motivations and interests of his comrades, trying to appease and accommodate a scientist like Van Buren without losing sight of the main mission, soothing easily bruised egos and grappling with the skepticism of a skipper like Robertson. He had spent hours training and fine-tuning a bunch of neophytes in the subs, so quietly firm and patiently persistent. . . .

"I'm sorry," he said. "I'm afraid I must sound rather cold-blooded, emphasizing the gold so much. Matter of fact, when we recover it, I think I'll miss Martin and Craig even more than I do now, knowing they won't be sharing in our triumph."

"John, what happens to Craig's share? He never mentioned having any family, but we should make every effort to locate someone he was close to . . . his parents, for example, if they're still alive."

Hawke shook his head. "Derek told me Craig was illegitimate, that he never knew his father, and his mother died many years ago. Sad case, really. The man personified the phrase *diamond in the rough.* He had the most innate sense of integrity I've ever encountered."

"I liked him," she said in a tone that became a simple epitaph.

"So did I. I think I'll suggest to the others that we donate at least half his share to some charity in his name, perhaps the whole amount, for that matter. There'll be plenty to go around."

"Remember when we were talking about what we all were going to do with all that money? Craig said he was going to buy the biggest cabin cruiser in the state of Florida and spend the rest of his life on that boat, eating, drinking, and fishing."

Her voice suddenly cracked, and Hawke put his arms around her.

Her voice was muffled against his light windbreaker, damp with her tears. "I miss Martin, too, but he already had everything a man could want. Not Craig. There was a whole new life ahead of him, and now . . ."

She couldn't finish the sentence, nor did she have to. Hawke pressed her closer, but she suddenly broke away, looking at him with a puzzled expression. "John, just before they hit Popeye, we heard Craig say something. One word. Something like *tent.*"

"That's what we heard. But damned if I know what he meant. We may have misunderstood, of course. Tent makes absolutely no sense."

"Do you suppose he was trying to tell us something?"

"Probably, but Lord knows what. Debbi, let's go down to the lounge and have a nightcap, you look a bit chilly."

"I should have worn a sweater. Do you really want a drink?"

She had a half smile on her face as she asked the question and he couldn't quite figure out her expression. "Not unless you do," he replied. "What's your preference?"

She said, slowly and distinctly, "I'd like you to walk me to my cabin, come inside, and make love to me."

He had been right. When she unbuttoned the white blouse, there was nothing but bare skin exposed and he swallowed hard at the sight of her large, firm breasts, the nipples already swelling.

She moved easily, swiftly into his arms and kissed him with open mouth, their tongues touching tentatively at first and then writhing in a frenzied dance.

She whispered, "This had to happen before tomorrow. I want you."

"I want you, too, Debbi. I just didn't dare say it until now."

"Help me get these damned slacks off. . . ."

Trevor Van Buren hadn't been able to sleep. All evening he had been worrying about Debra Chaney, and whether she would think him a coward for not insisting that he go in her place. True, he had made the offer, but he wondered whether he should have been more persistent. She seemed to favor assertive men like Hawke and even poor Caitin—especially Caitin. Van Buren never stopped speculating that the two of them had become lovers.

Now Caitin was dead, however, and there didn't seem to be anything between Hawke and Debra. He had seen them talking and smoking together on the deck at night, yet all seemed innocent enough, and they always had gone to their cabins separately. Hawke invariably stayed topside after Debra left, and for a long time, too. If there wasn't anything between them, and with Caitin gone, maybe his own time had come. She might welcome some company right now, he decided. A man to talk to and comfort her; she had been visibly shaken by today's tragedy, and he imagined himself finding her in tears and needing him badly. Needing him for emotional support, of course. A physical relationship could be built later on this first foundation. . . .

He dressed hurriedly and headed for her cabin. He was afraid she'd be asleep, and in his fantasy, he wanted her to be awake, perhaps crying softly so he could hear. Then he would knock on her door and maybe she'd be wearing a flimsy nightgown. She wouldn't bother to put on a robe, she'd be so glad to see him. After all, he was the one man on the ship with whom she had so much in common. Debra Chaney in a nightgown: He discarded this disturbing image with a hurried effort. He couldn't have her opening the door and see him standing there, staring. Or maybe she wouldn't mind. . . .

He stopped in front of her cabin. He heard her voice, so she was still awake, thank God. But what the devil was she doing—talking to herself? His knuckles were less than an inch away from a timid knock when her voice became only too distinct.

". . . that's it, darling . . . yes, use your tongue . . . oh God, that feels good . . . more, John, more . . . faster . . . yes . . . oh . . . yes . . . Oh God, I'm coming. . . !"

The voice of Debra Chaney became a series of guttural gasps. Van Buren, his hand still frozen in its knocking position, turned white.

Her voice, lower and more rasping than he had ever heard, resumed.

"Kiss them again . . . suck them, John, suck them . . . bite the nipples . . . not too hard . . . yes like that . . . now come inside me . . . come deep . . . deeper. . . . God, I love you . . . John, I love you . . . I love y—Jesus, I'm coming again. . . . I'm com—oh darling, darling . . ."

Trevor Van Buren finally unglued the hand that never knocked. *John, I love you*: The words took root in his brain, and he had the bitter taste of bile in his throat.

He turned away and began the long, lonely walk back to a cabin that would no longer harbor fantasy.

Derek Montague couldn't sleep, either.

He deliberately consumed almost a half-fifth of scotch, because when he drank too much, he tended to become pleasantly drowsy instead of pleasantly intoxicated. And he badly wanted the temporary forgetfulness of sleep. It didn't work this time. He would have welcomed Hawke's company, but he assumed John was either having his usual nightly conversational session with Chaney on deck or was sitting in that damned *Winston*, checking out systems for the umpteenth time. So he lay awake, staring at the cabin's pastel ceiling.

Thinking.

At first, about Martin Lefferts and Craig Caitin. Mostly about Craig—the crude, profane, self-educated giant who had read Herman Melville, not the easiest author to understand. His profanity had been a facade disguising a basic shyness that yearned for real and deep friendship. Montague remembered the time Caitin had remarked, "When this thing's all over, I gotta hankerin' to see England one of these days." Then he had added in a gruff, offhanded tone, "Pay you a visit, maybe." The way he said it was a plea hiding behind the casualness of his words.

"Craig, I would like nothing better," Montague had assured him, and he would never forget Caitin's fleeting expression of delight. The knowledge that Caitin treasured their friendship was the greatest compliment Montague had received in a long time. Just as the knowledge that Caitin would never pay him that visit felt like the greatest sorrow he had known since Beth's death.

It seemed impossible that such an apparently indestructible man was dead, and the way he and Lefferts had died made it that much harder to comprehend. Obviously, a malfunctioning life-support system had been a factor. But how? No warning light. Computer input that showed a normal flow during the dive but abnormal when Hawke and Montague had tested it after the dive. No, nothing added up.

He remembered his conversation with Robertson and their mutual foreboding, their sense that something was wrong, without the slightest idea of what it was. He felt like a man trying to recall the details of a nightmare, knowing only that it had terrified him.

Almost subliminally, his mind fought to reject what his intuition was telling him, because it was so illogical and so ridiculous.

It was that decaying corpse of a ship.

9

Derek Montague watched with misgiving as the creaking, straining crane hoisted *Winston* over the side.

Montague hadn't tried to talk Hawke out of making the dive, but Robertson had argued with him right up to the last minute, citing signs of worsening weather.

"Even if you blow her open today," he warned, "you'll need at least two or three more dives to get all the gold out, and there's no way I'll conduct a salvage operation in a storm."

Hawke's eyes were a very pale blue. "Tell me you've got a full-fledged hurricane parked just around the corner and I'll reconsider."

"I don't know what's parked around the corner, but the barometer's dropping, and that means trouble. Besides, weather's not the only reason, and you know damned well what the other one is."

"Yes, some fish or reptile of unknown species, unknown origin, and, above all, unknown intentions, which probably are mere curiosity, not hostility. Well, I'm not afraid of curiosity."

The captain had turned to Montague, hoping for support, then made one final try. "John, the smart thing to do is go home and make another attempt next year. By that time, the creature probably will have moved on to some other playground."

"And who'd finance a second expedition? Martin's widow? We're going to have one jolly time just explaining his death to her. We don't even have a body to take back to his family. No, Jerry, this is our last chance at that gold."

It was a telling point, Montague had to admit, and Robertson emitted an unhappy grunt of surrender. "Join me on the bridge, Derek," the captain said. "Van Buren's already there. You'd think he'd be down here wishing you two good luck."

Montague was thinking the same thing. He hadn't seen Trevor since last night, and the oceanographer had skipped breakfast. Boffin behavior, he decided, and shook hands with Hawke and Chaney. He watched them climb into the sub and was a little surprised when Hawke closed the hatch with a loud bang even before Jefferson and Ryan, the two frogmen, had attached the crane hook to the lifting pads on the submarine's deck. The sound, Montague thought, could have been an exclamation point terminating further argument. As he turned to accompany Robertson to the bridge, he heard Jefferson murmur, "I wouldn't go down there for a mention in Lefferts's will."

"Not for a fifty-percent share of it," Ryan agreed solemnly.

Ship scuttlebutt, Montague realized, had spread the word about a huge creature prowling the wreck. There was an air of tension laced with gloom throughout the ship. It had begun with the two deaths and thickened like a creeping fog as the moment of launch drew near. Montague had noticed the absence of the usual chatter and friendly cursing. The *Henry Morgan*, despite all the mishaps and glitches, had been a happy ship. No longer: The men were going about their duties in almost sullen silence.

He didn't blame them, for he felt the same way. He glanced at Robertson, whose bowed legs were planted firmly against the motion of growing swells. The crane dropped the submarine into the water, Jefferson and Ryan detaching the hitch and winding themselves around the crane cable for their return ride to the ship. Montague turned to find Van Buren next to him, watching the operation wordlessly.

"God be with them," Montague murmured.

Van Buren said nothing. He watched *Winston* slip beneath the waves, turned away, and began walking toward the sonar room, his small fists clenched tightly to his sides.

* * *

Except for routine communications with the *Henry Morgan*, Hawke and Chaney said little during the long descent. It was an uneasy silence, too. An unspoken tension existed between them that both sensed but were unwilling to admit. She was wishing now she had not insisted on making this dive, for Debra Chaney was beginning to feel the constricting chill of fear invading her mind.

Mentally, she scolded herself for this weakness. I should be excited, she thought. The greatest opportunity of my chosen career—everything I've dreamed of, from fame to fortune. Yet I want to go back. God, how I wish John would abort the dive. I'm getting so cold, so scared. . . .

She knew why this overpowering dread had taken over. She had assumed she would feel safe with Hawke beside her, especially after last night when they had become lovers. She had felt his driving energy, a dominance she had welcomed for more than the ecstasy it brought. Her love for him, her confidence in his invincibility, was the armor plate against fear Debra Chaney had carried into the submarine. Except now, the armor plate felt like thin tissue paper and the stolid Britisher beside her was just another vulnerable human being facing, like her, a peril of unknowable dimensions.

She would have been even more frightened had she known what was running through John Hawke's mind.

Guilt had begun to grip him, intensifying as the water around them darkened with every foot of descent. He knew he was reacting to her fear, for she was wearing it like a perfume. It had become part of the oxygen they were breathing, an invisible presence permeating the tiny, cramped cockpit.

The dive was risky, even without the added element of that creature, and this was Chaney's first trip in a craft that had demonstrated an alarming propensity for malfunctions. In truth, one by-product of their satiated passion had been his half-wishing that she'd change her mind about making a dive this dangerous. What he didn't expect was guilt, combined with a growing resentment at feeling guilty.

Maybe it was his military training, he thought with a touch of irony. He remembered telling Debbi once that some courage

was motivated by a man's fear of cowardice. He knew this
applied to him, but it wasn't the whole story. Hawke was more
afraid of failure than of cowardice. The accomplishment of a
vital task whose successful conclusion required absolute commitment and devotion—this had been the heart and soul of
his military indoctrination. This always had dominated his
personal beliefs, his code of honor, which had become almost
a religious conviction.

What might be lurking around that wreck represented danger, but danger to John Hawke had invariably produced a
perverse exhilaration. Only now, his usual exhilaration was
tempered by the guilt he felt toward Chaney, and this was the
conflict he resented. It was interfering with the mission.

Montague, Van Buren, and Robertson, the three men occupying the *Henry Morgan*'s sonar room, were hunched over the
green screen charting the submarine's descent.

"Angle and rate perfect," the captain noted. "Gotta give the
devil his due . . . that Hawke knows how to handle that little
bitch."

"Which one?" Van Buren asked with impulsive bitterness,
then flushed with the realization of what he had let slip.

Montague and Robertson looked up from the screen.

"What the hell do you have against Chaney?" Robertson
asked.

"An uncalled-for remark," Montague said, "and one that
warrants explanation." He had a good idea of what lay behind
it. Hawke hadn't returned to their cabin last night until an
hour before the dive. But how could Trevor have known that?

Van Buren looked flustered. "She's . . . she's been, uh,
rather difficult lately." Sensing the inadequacy of that explanation, he added, "As an oceanographer, she has no right participating in what John is going to do to that ship."

Montague stared at him. "Trevor, you sided with Debbi and
John in wanting this expedition to continue. Why are you
taking it out on her?"

Van Buren retorted, "I was in favor of continued exploration.
I accepted that damnable demolition as the price we'd have to

pay. Chaney's just after the gold, no less than John is. It's . . . it's unscientific of her."

But Montague didn't believe him. What he was seeing in Trevor Van Buren's eyes was not reverence for a ship but jealousy toward two people in a trouble-plagued submarine that even now was edging close to its rendezvous with a place of death.

Hawke's eyes kept roving over the instrument panel, pausing intermittently to inspect the gauge registering oxygen flow. Normal. Everything looked normal, and his tension eased slightly. He even found himself remembering last night: remembering, with a stirring in his loins, Debbi's uninhibited lovemaking; the violence of her orgasms; the silky warmth of that incredible body. Yet for the first time in his life, he had drawn more than desire from the depths of a passionate woman. He had felt a residue of tenderness, of gratitude, and an intense, different kind of desire—to be with her always, after this was over.

Yet even as he remembered these feelings, the guilt returned. His love for Debra Chaney was getting in the way of the mission, and he did not like having to make a choice. Because John Hawke, tormented by the conflicting emotions of love pitted against winning, already knew what his choice would be.

He glanced at her. She was staring at the blackness outside and he wondered what she was thinking. He patted her hand and was rewarded by a squeeze and a smile. It hurt him to realize that the smile was weak and forced.

"Affection or reassurance?" she asked.

"Little bit of both, I guess. Are you cold?"

"Very cold, from head to toes."

"I know. You'll forget the temperature when we reach the *Titanic* and the adrenaline starts pumping."

She decided impulsively to tell the truth. "John, I'm scared."

"Perfectly natural," he said. "But we're going to be fine."

"Let's turn around and go back. Somehow we'll raise the money for another try, and by that time, the creature will have gone away."

He tried chiding her. "Debbi, you're a scientist with the God-given curiosity that makes you people so special. You cannot let fear prevent you from satisfying your curiosity. Remember what I told Robertson last night?"

"You told him a lot of things."

"The most important thing I said was that if I let this oversized fish, or whatever it is, scare me away from becoming a millionaire, I'd regret it for the rest of my life. And you, love, would have the same regrets if I gave into your jitters. You would have lost possibly your last chance to inspect the *Titanic*, plus your last chance to confirm the miracle of a living plesiosaur."

"Not necessarily a last chance," she argued in a weakening tone. "We could still come back next year."

"Only if Martin Lefferts's widow backed us. Which I doubt very much she'll do and, frankly, I haven't the foggiest idea where else we could raise the money. Do you still want me to go back?"

She said, with an uncertainty that ate at his conscience, "No, I guess not. Just promise me if the damned thing seems the least bit threatening, you'll abort."

"I promise."

"Thanks. By the way, I love you."

"It's mutual, I assure you. Now settle back and enjoy the trip." They fell silent as *Winston* continued its steady, slow descent.

"At eleven-five, Jerry. Floods are on. Give us our vector."

Robertson's response, usually so reassuringly calm, was tinged with obvious nervousness—even the impersonal metallic filtering couldn't hide a slight quaver. "Roger, *Winston*. Your descent angle was perfect. Turn right two degrees; target will be dead ahead."

"Two degrees it is."

"Any sign of that thing?" The quaver was noticeably stronger.

"Nary a glimpse."

"Be careful, John. Be goddamned careful."

"I will. How far to the target?"

"About a hundred or so feet. You should be—"

"Got her! Debbi, take a look; there it is. The *Titanic* in all her rusted glory."

Chaney could see only a small portion of the hull, but even this truncated glimpse startled her. It was larger than she had expected, this towering cliff looming high above them with the streaks of rust running down the sides. "My God," she exclaimed, "it's enormous!"

"Hard to believe that an iceberg could have destroyed her, isn't it?"

"Could we make one pass over her? I'd like to get a good look at the superstructure."

"Cargo hold three comes first. Then, if there's time, we'll wander over her a bit." He knew damned well he wasn't going to give her that look. Every instinct told him to get on with the plan he had so carefully—and optimistically—contrived. On this dive, the Plastomite would be attached and the hull blown open. If the bullion crates were within reach of *Winston*'s robot arms, they would retrieve one crate and carry it back to the salvage ship to prove the gold was there for the taking. If the crates were too far inside the hold, tomorrow they'd use *Franklin* to penetrate the interior and start removing the bullion, transferring it to the big recovery platform that would be lowered simultaneously with the smaller craft. After that, things would depend on where in hold three the crates were located; if within reach of *Winston*'s arms, they could use both subs in a shuttle operation and retrieve all the bullion in not more than three dives.

First things first, he reminded himself. The primary task was to open that hole. He maneuvered the sub toward the bow, backed away slightly and began traversing the estimated sixty-eight feet from the *Titanic*'s bow to cargo hold three. The other crucial distance was the two hundred yards of safe separation after the timers were initiated. Hawke could only hope Caitin's calculations had been correct.

"Time to take over," he said to Chaney with deliberate casualness. "Back off for about forty-five seconds and cut power while I adjust the arms." He saw her hands trembling. "Are you all right?"

"I'm fine, still a little cold and nervous, that's all." She gripped the yoke harder and set her jaw.

"Good girl. The robots are activated. Ahead slow, very slow. Jerry, commencing attachment run. Easy does it, Debbi. Easy . . ."

The sub had moved two feet forward when it happened.

Paul Crippens poked his head inside the sonar room, his normally placid face looking distressed. Montague and Van Buren, standing next to Robertson at the sonar screen, glanced at him curiously.

Crippens said nervously, "Captain, I think you'd better come to the bridge and take a look at this sky."

"What's the matter, Paul, haven't you ever seen storm clouds before?"

"Sir, these ones are *green*."

"Green? Good God Almighty, this I've got to see." The captain looked at Montague and the oceanographer. "You two keep your eyes on that screen. I'll be back."

Van Buren said quickly, "I'd like to go with you. This sounds worth seeing."

"Suit yourself," Robertson said. "Derek, let me know what's going on down there."

Van Buren followed him to the bridge, Crippens in their wake, muttering to himself. Robertson wondered whether he was praying, and the minute the captain looked up at the sky, he guessed a few prayers might be in order.

The sky *was* green.

Thick, boiling, angry clouds of a peculiar green shade rolled toward them. The clouds were some distance away, but already the entire ship was bathed in that strange, unearthly color—a color Robertson had never seen in his years at sea. It was pulsating irregularly like flashes of lightning hidden behind approaching thunderheads.

The captain bit down hard on his corncob. "Van Buren, you're the scientist. Any idea what could cause this?"

Van Buren shook his head in awe. "I've never seen or even read of anything like it. Some kind of atmospheric inversion,

I imagine, but the color mystifies me. It's no ordinary forma-
tion . . . not with that unusual shade of green. I'll tell you one
thing, Captain. I don't like the looks of it."

"Neither do I," Robertson agreed. "I'll bet our barometer is
somewhere in the cellar. Paul, what's the barometer show?"

Crippens didn't answer immediately.

"Well? " Robertson demanded impatiently.

"Sir, I had to take a second look. The damned thing's going
up and down like a yo-yo. I can't even get a reading."

"Impossible!" The captain strode over to see for himself. He
took one look and blanched. "Jesus Christ," he muttered,
"what in God's name is going on here?"

Van Buren said in a tone of awe, "Notice how quiet it has
become?"

Neither the captain nor the first officer had noticed, but they
did now. The air was absolutely dead in the eerie light, a
threatening kind of stillness, as if something had just taken a
deep breath.

Even the normal rumbles and creaks of a ship taking the
swells were missing; the *Henry Morgan* seemed to be holding
her own breath, waiting. . . .

The incongruity extended to Robertson himself. He felt curiously lethargic, even peaceful, when he should have been tense
and alert. He couldn't understand it. Like hypnosis, he thought
dreamily. What is happening to us?

He fought an urge just to close his eyes. "Start engines!" he
barked at Crippens. "When this mother hits, we may need
immediate power. I'm going to the sonar room and abort that
dive. Van Buren, you coming with me?"

The oceanographer nodded. As he followed Robertson out,
he took another look at the seething sky. One cloud had taken
on an unusual cylindrical shape. He had to glance again before
he realized what it was.

The shape of a gigantic ship's funnel.

A black mass came between *Winston* and the wreck with devastating speed, moving so fast that neither could focus on detail.
That's all it was, a living mountain of flesh that blotted out the

ship like a curtain dropped in front of a stage. Somewhere in Hawke's brain the thought registered that it was gray and leathery.

Like a shark.

It disappeared and the *Titanic*'s scarred hull came into sight again. Chaney tried to say something, but her vocal chords were paralyzed, quick-frozen with fright. All she could do was grip Hawke's arm so tightly that her fingernails almost reached the skin through two sweaters and a thermal undergarment.

"We've got company."

Hawke's voice sounded in the sonar room, and Montague watched the screen. There was *Winston*'s miniscule blip, but nothing else. It's going to happen again, he thought miserably. He wanted desperately to order Hawke up, but coming from him it would have been a plea, not an order transmitted with authority, and he was glad to see Robertson rush into the room, Van Buren trailing behind. Montague noticed that Trevor seemed spooked, and he wondered with growing panic what was happening outside.

"They've got company," he told Robertson, "but there's nothing on sonar except the sub." He added ominously, "Just like last time."

The captain grabbed the mike out of Montague's hand.

"Hawke, get the hell out of there!"

"Negative. It's out of sight now, and all it did was run by us. Jerry, I'm going to attach the Plastomite. I think the concussion will scare it away and we can get what we came for."

The captain keyed the microphone again. "You crazy fool. Abort while you can."

Hawke ignored him. He held *Winston* steady for a few seconds and looked at Chaney, her face grotesquely sculpted by the red glare of the instrument lights. Her eyes were fixed in a trancelike stare.

"Come on, love," he said gently. "You have to take over. I'm going to have a go at that hull and I can't do it by myself."

Her only response was to shake her head, like a child refusing to obey. "You heard what I told Jerry. Once the Plastomite goes off, that thing won't dare to come back. It's probably gone, anyway. Look, Debbi, I'll show you."

He turned the sub slowly toward the direction in which the creature had disappeared. The twin floodlight beams panned through the darkness, and for once the very blackness was reassuring.

From the *Henry Morgan*, Captain Robertson's voice came over the underwater telephone. "We've got the meanest-looking storm I ever saw coming in from the west. If it's as bad as I think, we won't be able to recover you. John, you might even founder; that sub's not built to take a surface pounding."

"Then we'll stay submerged until the squall line passes."

"Do you have enough oxygen to last two or three days?" Robertson inquired sarcastically. "Because that's how long you might have to stay under. I just told you, this thing's a whopper." He was about to describe the sky's weird color but Hawke cut him off.

"Jerry, I'll compromise. We're ready to move in with the Plastomite. I'll blow open the hull and then we'll come back up. *Franklin* out."

It reappeared with terrifying suddenness, and Chaney's mouth fell open in a silent scream.

Hawke's eyes widened in shock. He was looking into the blunt-nosed head of an onrushing shark that dwarfed the boat he was in. In a split second of awareness, he could see the cold, lifeless black eyes staring malevolently at them. He could glimpse the huge dorsal fin protruding as high as an airplane's tail. A shark almost two hundred feet long was the sickening thought that flashed briefly through his unbelieving brain.

Then all he saw were the jaws, teeth gleaming under the strobes' white glare. Those teeth. The jagged edges of two great saws hinged together by massive muscle and tissue.

The saws spread into a hideous grin.

In the sonar room, they heard a short, half-scream from Chaney, then an anguished cry from Hawke.

"IT'S ATTACKING! IT'S ATT—"

A burst of static, followed by Hawke's voice, still shaky and struggling to sound calm.

"It's gone again. Apparently, this craft's not its cup of tea."

"Was it the plesiosaur?" Robertson demanded.

"Negative." Hawke had regained his old laconic tone, yet they still could sense a residue of fright. "A monstrous shark just made a pass at us. Same thing I saw before. Well over a hundred and seventy feet in length, I'd judge. It's had two chances to botch us up with nothing happening, so we shall get back to the business at hand."

Montague and Van Buren exchanged startled glances.

"My God, there are *two* enormous creatures down there!" Montague exclaimed. With sudden awareness, he remembered Hawke's deathly fear of sharks.

Van Buren's face was taut. "Not even the great white comes close to a length like that."

Montague turned to the captain. "Jerry, you've got to convince them they must abort."

Robertson nearly bit through his pipe stem. "John, you've got more to worry about now. Sea's really getting rough. We may have to unmoor from the anchors and head into the wind under power. We might not be around if you wait too long to surface. For God's sake, man, abort while you've still got a chance!"

"Do what you have to do top side. I'm jolly well going to finish what we came down here for."

If there was one person more upset than the captain at Hawke's doggedness, it was Debra Chaney. She grabbed his arm. "Damn you! Weren't you listening to him? We have to get out of here!"

His response was meant to be reassuring; to her ears, it was something else. "This is no time to panic. I know what I'm doing. The twenty minutes I need aren't going to make a tinker's worth of difference."

She was staring at a stranger—one whose eyes were an icy blue, whose face was as cold as his eyes. His expression was frozen into a grimness she had never seen before, a kind of mad defiance. He looked like a man who believes his secret cowardice has been exposed and who is trying to make amends with one insanely brave gesture.

But the terror that had stricken Hawke with the sight of that one-hundred-and-seventy-foot killing machine was only momentary, replaced by anger. The conflict he feared even more than any shark was upon him, too. The mission was being imperiled, and Chaney unwittingly confirmed his decision. She said hoarsely, "If you love me, you'll surface right now."

He actually glared at her. "Love doesn't have one bloody thing to do with this, Debbi. We're going in, and keep your damned hands away from that throttle."

His own hand closed on the power handle and moved it forward. *Winston* began moving slowly toward the battered slab of metal awaiting them in the darkness.

It was at this moment, almost two and a half miles above them, that the storm reached the *Henry Morgan*.

Its fury was concealed at first, deceptive in its early mildness. The green aura around them was so pronounced that their faces carried a garish tint, as if they had been dusted with a green powder. Yet the most mystifying—and perversely terrifying—element was the sea itself.

The ship had been rolling and pitching with increasing violence until the first storm clouds overtook her. Then, without warning, the waves died. The *Henry Morgan* was riding on glass-smooth water, the sea itself assuming the strange greenish tinge. And with the ocean's sudden calmness came an uncanny silence. The air was motionless, too, devoid of the slightest breeze, but suddenly cold. It enveloped the ship like a huge, choking blanket of icy vapor, so thick they could hardly breathe.

Montague whispered to Van Buren, "My God, Trevor, what kind of storm is this?"

"Take a look outside."

Montague did and returned quickly, his face ashen. Nor did it help when he noticed that the captain's normally ruddy complexion was as pale as his own. Robertson wheeled abruptly and opened the sonar room's door to yell at Crippens. "Paul, tell all hands to don life jackets!"

Conscious of the panicky effect this might have on his two companions, he said, "Just a precaution . . . might as well play it safe. Derek, there are some jackets in that locker over there. Bring out a pair for you and Van Buren, and toss me one, too."

A sensible suggestion, Montague thought. Then he thought of something else.

". . . *don life jackets . . . just a precaution.*" He found himself wondering how many times those words or their equivalent had been spoken more than six decades ago by stewards and stewardesses shaking passengers out of their sleep. The sea had been lifeless that night, too, and there had been a chill in the air that no one recognized for what it was: a warning of the frozen killer lying in wait.

He was thinking foolishly, Montague scolded himself. There were no real parallels to be drawn. Yes, the sea had been unusually calm that Sunday night in April, and yes, there had been a chill in the air, but both were within the bounds of normal oceanographic and meteorologic patterns—nothing like the freakish environment that had gripped the *Henry Morgan*.

Still, he shivered and knew it was not merely the chilled air.

Robertson, looking at the sonar screen, groaned. "They've stopped. Something must have gone wrong."

Even as he spoke, the sea stirred into angry life.

"We've lost power," Hawke said. He scanned the instruments. "Batteries are showing normal output. What the deuce is the matter here?"

"Amps are fluctuating a little," Chaney observed. She sounded almost bored, as if she didn't give a damn, and Hawke threw her a sharp glance before looking back at the electrical readings.

"Not enough to affect main power." He moved the throttle back and forth a few times. Nothing. "I don't understand this. It's as if the batteries have somehow been disconnected from the motor. I'd better go back and check the cables."

It took him several minutes to squeeze out of his cockpit and half-crawl down the narrow aisle that led to *Winston*'s aft section. He had reached the battery area when he heard Chaney banging away at something.

He called out, "Debbi, what the devil are you doing?"

"Oxygen-supply dial seems stuck. According to this, we have only a thirty-minute supply left."

What next? he thought with a surge of panic. "False reading, I'm quite sure. I'll have a look while I'm back here."

His anxiety worsened as he inspected and tested all battery cables and output without finding the slightest abnormality in the motor itself. Nor could he ascertain anything wrong with the life-support system—pumps, tanks, and electrical conduits were functioning perfectly. The trouble must be in that bloody dial registering the amount of oxygen left, he decided. But it also occurred to him that even if the instrument was wrong, they couldn't stay down here much longer, and he glared at the silent motor as if reproach could stir it into life.

Hawke made his way back to the cockpit and squeezed into the left seat. "Well, love, I dare say you're going to get your wish. I think it is time to go home and try again tomorrow after we sort out what's wrong with our power."

She looked at him listlessly. "And how do you propose to go home without power?"

"Popeye. The EAS has a separate battery arrangement . . . one of Jerry's better notions, I must admit. I doubt very much whether the motor's at fault, which means the trouble must lie in the primary batteries themselves." He paged the *Henry Morgan*.

"Jerry, we seem to have suffered some kind of power loss. Don't know the cause. We're going to activate Popeye and surface."

"How much oxygen do you have left?"

"I'm not sure. Supply indicator seems to be acting up. I'd calculate another hour or so. An adequate margin of safety if we come up fast."

"You should have come up when I told you to. We're starting to get our asses kicked but good. I've cast off the anchor buoys because of the waves. Dammit, John, I'm not sure we can recover you until this sea quiets down."

"Understand. We'll take our chances."

Hawke looked at Chaney. He had heard a slight tearing sound, like the ripping of a piece of paper, just above their heads. As he glanced up, several drops of cold water trickled onto his face.

Even under the red glow of the instrument lights, Chaney could swear his face had turned white. She gulped, "Are we in trouble?"

He gave her a single curt nod. "I don't like the look of that. Thank God for Popeye."

He hit the EAS button.

And nothing happened.

10

The storm's stillness had turned violent just about the time Hawke had gone back to inspect the sub's batteries and engines.

Like a man losing his temper in slow stages, the change was gradual—a renewed increase in the *Henry Morgan*'s pitching and rolling that was tolerable at first but ominous in its steadily rising momentum. Robertson kept shuttling between the bridge and the sonar room, concern for *Winston* grappling with fears for his own ship's safety.

Montague peeked outside once more so he could see the storm. The green haze surrounding the ship remained. He felt as if he were on a planet whose sky was unlike anything seen on earth. This was terrifying in itself, but it was only one of the storm's ugly manifestations. The wind had risen to an angry screech and the sound of the savage waves crashing against the ship's old hull was like hearing the thud of metal in a chain-reaction, multiple-car collision.

The wind's force seemed to coincide with the size of the waves, mounting as the sea heaved and convulsed. It was as though an animal had cornered them in a flimsy sanctuary, trying to claw and bite its way in. The *Henry Morgan* creaked and groaned under the ocean's assault. To Montague, she was a living thing caught in a trap and groaning in pain.

He could gauge the extent of the captain's anxiety when Robertson ordered the anchor cables cast off. "Otherwise, they'll tear loose and we need 'em for sub recovery," he explained. "We'll try to maintain station over the *Titanic* by maneuvering with our engines until this damned freak dies down. I'll be on the bridge for awhile."

"What about Hawke and Chaney?" Montague wanted to know.

"They'll be hitting Popeye. I don't know if I can hear the alarm bell above this wind, so when they start coming up, let me know."

But *Winston*'s blip remained motionless, and there was no sign of an EAS signal. Montague paged the sub.

"John, shouldn't you have activated Popeye by now?"

The response came not from Hawke, but Chaney. A curiously listless voice, Montague noted, wondering why.

"It's been activated but we're not getting any power there, either. John's gone back to check on the auxiliary battery. Is this Derek?"

"Yes, Jerry's on the bridge. Debbi, are you all right?"

"Not exactly. We've got water coming in. John thinks the outer hull has cracked. Wait a minute—he's coming back."

Montague snapped to a bug-eyed Van Buren, "Go fetch the captain, quick!"

Robertson burst into the sonar room just in time to hear Hawke's voice, laconic as ever.

". . . bit of a situation. No propulsion response, including Popeye. I heard an outer seam crack a few minutes ago. The pressure hull is holding but I doubt for very long. If you have any great ideas, there's not much time."

"Ideas?" Robertson groaned. "They need a miracle."

Montague said desperately, "Could one of us take *Franklin* down and tow them to the surface?"

The captain shook his head. "Launch another sub in this sea? Not a chance. Even if we did, you couldn't reach them in time. Look at that clock; they'll be out of oxygen before *Franklin*'s halfway to the bottom. If they can't get underway, all we can do is pray they'll implode before they run out of air. It'll be an easier way to die."

He sighed and took the mike from Montague. "John, there's not much we can do to help. Keep hitting Popeye, then see if you can jump the relays. Maybe it's a short circuit and it'll catch. Good luck to you both."

The click of the transmitting button sounded like a thunderclap in the silent sonar room.

"Will they have any warning of an implosion?" Van Buren asked in a quavering voice.

"Maybe a few seconds, when the water starts coming faster. If that happens, it'll be over in the blink of an eye." He banged his fist against the bulkhead. "God_damn_ those subs! I never did trust them."

"How . . . how will we know if it happens?" Montague asked.

"A loud thud, probably. I heard a submarine break up during the war, and that's what it sounded like." He shook his head again, in total futility. "I wish we could do something, but we've got our own problems."

The _Henry Morgan_ yawed sharply to starboard and Crippens's panicky voice came from the embattled bridge. "Skipper, she's broaching and we can't hold her!"

"We're going to die, aren't we?" Chaney said in an emotionless, defeated tone.

Hawke took her hand and squeezed it gently. The madness was gone, but so was all hope. He had been tracing the EAS circuitry for five minutes, to no avail.

"Unless you believe in miracles," he said calmly, "I'm afraid we've had it."

She mustered a wan smile. "I suppose I should hate you. And right now I do."

He felt as if she had stabbed him with a knife. "Right now, Debbi, I hate myself."

"How long do you think we have?"

He looked at the water dripping from the cockpit. They were tiny streams now, and the ominous creaking sounds were louder. "We still have a few minutes."

Chaney's dam of resignation finally broke. She began to sob. As best as he could in the cramped cockpit, he put his arms around her and whispered, "I am so desperately sorry, my love."

As they embraced each other, a sharp spurt of water struck Hawke in the face with the force of a punch. He never felt the icy moisture because it became part of his own tears a split second before *Winston* blew apart in a thousand pieces.

In the sonar room, they heard the fatal thud—more like a loud popping sound, Montague thought with the terrifying realization of what it meant. He tried calling them, but there was no answer from the sub. So now there were two more deaths, a total of four lives sacrificed on behalf of the quest he himself had instigated. Yet with this self-recrimination came a burst of anger. He would have to take at least part of the blame, yet he was harboring an ugly suspicion that had to be voiced.

He said to Van Buren, "We'd better tell Jerry it's over. But first I'm going to ask you a very unpleasant question, and I insist on an honest answer. Did you do anything with *Winston's* computer before Craig and Martin dove?"

Van Buren's eyes blazed. "Are you mad? Of course I didn't! What made you ask such an insulting question?"

"Look, Trevor, after John and I inspected the life-support system, he came back and told everyone we found the computer set to produce an abnormal output of helium and a corresponding decrease in the oxygen supply. John had fed the correct data in himself before they dove. Deliberate tampering is the only explanation I can think of."

Van Buren stared at him, horrified. "I can't believe you could even imagine me capable of such a heinous act. What possible motive would I have?"

"You knew Caitin and Lefferts were going down to blow open the hull. So I'm wondering if you might have rigged the computer to produce a malfunction serious enough for them to abort the dive."

"That's ridiculous! Right from the start, I've hated the idea of mutilating the ship for the purpose of robbing her. I admit that freely. But only a madman would take reverence for the *Titanic* to the point of endangering lives. And I assure you, Derek, I'm not mad. Why would I believe that a single aborted dive would have made John Hawke abandon the whole mission?"

"Trevor, jealousy can be a powerful motive. I think your

feelings toward Debbi were obvious, but I have a strong hunch she and John were more than just friends. Were you aware of that possibility?"

The anger in Van Buren's eyes was replaced by pain. "It was more than a possibility. I knew they were having an affair. Don't ask me how I knew but I did. However, you now seem to be accusing me of tampering with *Winston* before today's dive, as well. Derek, I can't tell a spark plug from an inverter. I couldn't have altered those sub motors if I had wanted to; I wouldn't even know where to start. So for the last time, damn you, *I did not tamper with that submarine!*"

Derek Montague said very slowly, "I believe you and I apologize."

They looked at each other, distrust gone from one, anger from the other. And with the fading of those two emotions came an awareness of something they shared. Montague was the first to voice what already had been gnawing its way into his mind like a malignancy.

"Trevor, do you suppose that someone—or some *thing*—doesn't want looters inside that ship?"

Van Buren's eyes widened at finally hearing from another person what he had suspected himself. "I'd be interested to know how you reached that conclusion."

"The succession of bad luck we've encountered. Our only success has been the actual discovery of the *Titanic*. Everything else has gone wrong, without logical explanations. Mysterious equipment failures, two of them fatal. And those creatures. A strange coincidence that two different species are prowling around that wreck—or maybe guarding it."

Van Buren said cautiously, "Not so strange, Derek. I've said repeatedly that all kinds of marine life may exist at depths we've never explored. The fact that they're gigantic doesn't surprise me. Size would be a logical way of adapting to that environment. There's nothing . . . supernatural about what we've seen down there."

Montague's deep-set eyes narrowed to slits. "Trevor, think back to that awful moment when Lefferts screamed they were under attack by a plesiosaur. But that's not what Craig saw."

"They saw the same thing," Van Buren protested.

"I wonder. Craig spoke one word before he hit Popeye. The word was *tent*."

"So? No one knows what that could have meant."

"I think I do. He started to say *tentacles*."

"Squid," Van Buren said softly. "Or, no . . . octopus."

"Exactly. So now we have three monster creatures, not merely two. And what intrigues me is another coincidence. Martin *wanted* to see a plesiosaur. The night before they dove, Craig mentioned a movie in which a giant octopus attacked a submarine. John encountered an enormous maneater . . . and as both of us know, he was pathologically afraid of sharks. Any logical explanation for *that* coincidence escapes me."

"It escapes me, too," Van Buren admitted. He hesitated. "Derek, I thought I saw something when I was exploring the *Titanic* . . ."

He recounted his impression of what seemed to be an officer-clothed figure. Montague had just started to relate his own story of a woman's face staring out of a porthole when the *Henry Morgan* seemed to go into convulsions, the floor of the sonar room heaving violently first in one direction, then in the other. The second tilt threw them to the floor, their conversation forgotten as charts and test equipment slid off their racks.

Painfully, almost reluctantly, the ship righted herself and they picked themselves up.

"We'd better head for the bridge," Montague said. "If she capsizes, we'd be trapped in here."

Robertson stared at them as they emerged from the sonar room.

"Any word?" The captain's voice was hoarse from shouting over the weather.

"They're gone," Montague replied dully. "We heard that thud. I tried contacting them but . . ." He left the sentence unfinished, and Robertson nodded.

"God rest their souls," he muttered.

Crippens was wrestling with the wheel, aided by Pickens, the night helmsman, who had been pressed into emergency duty. Both, Montague observed with growing panic, looked scared. He stole a glance at the captain, whose inevitable corncob was clenched in his teeth but unlit. He would have needed a blowtorch to fire it up, for the wind was coming in through every crevice on the bridge and one gust already had smashed out a window. The spray felt like a fusillade of cold needles.

"Keep her in the wind," the captain warned Crippens. "Tom, you look beat. I'll relieve you; come back in about twenty minutes." The old sailor wagged his head gratefully and left.

"She keeps broaching," the first officer rasped; his forehead was moist, but Montague could not tell whether it was sweat or spray.

"I know, but if you let her get away from you, she'll roll over like a beach ball." Robertson sneaked a look at the barometer on a cluster of instruments adjacent to the wheel. "It's still fluctuating, but I'll bet we're right in the middle of this sucker."

The *Henry Morgan* thrashed violently to port and collided immediately with a foam-topped wave that struck the side of the bow. The ship keeled so sharply that Montague lost his balance and fell, his long body sprawling ignominiously on the deck. He looked up in panic as Robertson yelled, "Hard right!"

"I can't move her," Crippens gasped, terror now in his voice. Robertson sprang to his side and both men strained against the wheel. Slowly, protestingly, it moved and the tilted bridge came back to level.

"Jesus, that was close," the captain grunted. He noticed Montague getting to his feet. "You okay, Derek?"

Montague merely nodded. He was too scared to speak and could only glance weakly at Van Buren, who seemed more resigned than frightened.

"Maybe you two would be better off in your cabins."

Montague found his voice. "I feel safer up here. Not a hell of a lot safer, but at least I know what's going on."

Robertson released the wheel. "You're doing fine, son," he told Crippens. "Just hang on tight; those wind shifts are tricky."

Pickens popped his head in the door. "Skipper, that last wave took one of the lifeboats clean off. And the other one's hangin' by one davit."

"Shit," Robertson growled. "Well, rig a lifeline and get someone to help you secure it. And close that goddamned door!" The last order was delivered in a bellow, and the crew-man hurriedly complied.

"Fat lot of good a lifeboat would do us in this sea," the captain grumbled. "Here, Paul, let me relieve you for a spell." The first officer loosened his viselike grip as Robertson reached for the wheel, but Crippens had relinquished his hold a second too soon. The perverse wind shifted abruptly, and with devastating strength. Before either Robertson or Crippens could react, the *Henry Morgan* lurched into a spin, like an uncontrollable car on glare ice. The ship turned helplessly ninety degrees, into the path of a huge green wall of water.

Only it was more than just a wall, and Robertson gaped in terror.

The onrushing mass had become a twisting cyclonic tower, a gigantic waterspout bearing down on the helpless ship with the roar of a thousand locomotives. It smashed into the *Henry Morgan* broadside, tearing her in two and lifting the severed stern section twenty feet in the air before dropping it into the boiling sea like the carcass of a slaughtered animal. The bow section coasted forward for a few seconds, then rolled over.

Montague was flung against the bridge door, the impact tearing it off its hinges and hurling him out on the madly tilting deck and against the railing. He knew he was going to die, but he'd be damned if he'd die riding this bloody tub down to the bottom of the Atlantic. Just before she completed the fatal roll, he let go of the railing and fell over the side. He didn't even try to swim; he surrendered himself to the savage sea and was about to make his peace with God when a wave lifted him ten feet in the air and then released him almost on top of an overturned lifeboat—the one Pickens hadn't had time to secure, he realized.

It was not only awkward but nearly impossible to climb onto the boat's belly with his unwieldy, confining life jacket, but he finally made it. Gasping for breath, his eyes still stinging from the salt spray, he clung to the boat's bottom planks and looked around. There was no sign of the *Henry Morgan*, nor any living soul—just a few pitiful pieces of debris from the foundered ship. Van Buren, Robertson, and Crippens must have been trapped on the bridge, he thought: God knows what happened to the rest of the crew.

He murmured a silent prayer for them and himself. He knew he had cheated death only temporarily, but he was determined to stay alive as long as possible. Perversely, as if satiated with the destruction of the *Henry Morgan*, the storm suddenly abated, wind and waves died down, and the strange green aura gradually faded. In what felt to Montague like an hour's time, it had given way to a gray overcast dotted with patches of blue sky.

To bolster his morale, he tried to recall everything he had read or heard about shipwrecked people miraculously surviving ordeals like this one. There was that famous American airman, Captain Eddie Rickenbacker, plucked out of the Pacific after twenty-two days in a life raft. Of course, Montague mused ruefully, Rickenbacker had two other men in the raft with him, and four more in an adjoining raft. At least they didn't have to face death alone—and God, he felt so alone.

He fought against depression, and it helped a little to remember how brave Beth had been. He owed it to her not to crack wide open, letting hysteria and fear drive him mad. He probably would go mad, though. No food. No water. Madness was inevitable and it would be accompanied by excruciating torture. Thirst would drive him to swallow from the sea—a sure and painful way to die. Maybe the others had been lucky, dying with relative quickness. The only ones he didn't envy were Hawke and Chaney; they had had too much time to anticipate death before death came.

Thinking about Hawke led him to think about Caitin. He was almost too tired to think at all. Mostly, he remembered that remark Craig had made about Hawke and Captain Ahab. Very perceptive, Montague decided. *Moby Dick* might even apply to himself. What was the opening line of the novel? Ah, yes, that first sentence might very well be the epitaph of Derek Montague.

"Call me Ishmael."

He sighed, tried not to fall asleep, and lost the battle.

11

The light cruiser U.S.S. *Tucson*, part of a small task force on antisubmarine maneuvers, was heading back to her home port in Norfolk, Virginia—much to the displeasure of her feisty captain.

He was unhappy because the squadron commander had cut the maneuvers short when the four-ship group got caught on the fringe of an Atlantic storm. After the abort signal, *Tucson's* skipper complained to his executive officer, "I'll bet the Russian navy doesn't go chicken in a little rough weather."

The exec didn't want to disagree with his captain, but he remarked, "Might be for the best, sir. Sea's pretty rough. It really looked threatening toward the northeast. I could swear the sky had a green tinge to it. Never saw a sky like that before."

The skipper grunted. "Sea's not *that* bad, and the barometer's rising. Methinks the commodore must have a terminal case of cold feet."

Yet orders were orders, and the trim cruiser plowed her way peacefully on a westerly heading. Flanking *Tucson* were two destroyers, and a mile astern, the flagship heavy cruiser *Sacramento* followed sedately.

The captain was still grumbling over the decision to cancel the exercise when the bridge intercom buzzed and was immediately answered by the exec.

"Sir," he addressed the captain, "bow lookouts report an overturned lifeboat about two hundred yards ahead, just off the starboard bow. Want one of the cans on our flank to investigate?"

"Hell, no. First interesting thing that's happened all day. Advise *Sacramento* we're investigating. All engines stop."

Tucson's momentum faded quickly, the captain peering at the bobbing object in their path. "Jesus," he muttered, "there's a man on that lifeboat. Ahead slow—let's pick him up. I hope the poor devil's alive."

Ten minutes later, the soaked, limp figure of Derek Montague was hauled aboard the cruiser and taken immediately to sick bay. *Tucson* resumed course while the captain paced the bridge impatiently, waiting for word from the ship's doctor. "Can't stand the suspense," he finally told the exec, who knew his captain only too well. "I'm going down to sick bay; you have the con."

He didn't particularly like sick bay, largely because it was the one area of the ship where his authority was somewhat diluted. He also considered the chief medical officer a fussy, oversolicitous mother hen, although he liked him personally.

"How's he doing?" he asked the doctor, a roly-poly man who had all the naval bearing of a shoe salesman.

"Badly dehydrated and suffering from exposure, but I think he'll recover."

"Did he say what ship he was on?"

The chief medical officer frowned in reprimand. "I haven't questioned him, Captain, because I've been too busy making sure he'll live."

"Is he well enough for me to ask a few questions?"

The doctor enjoyed these rare moments of superiority. "Just a few," he warned importantly. "I've already given him a sedative, so I don't know how coherent he'll be. All I got out of him was his name—Derek Montague. Except . . ."

"Except what?"

"Well, he was delirious at first. He kept saying, 'something's alive down there.' Over and over again. 'Something's alive down there.' I asked him what he meant, but he just stared at me and began to sob. That's when I gave him the sedative, although he's still awake."

The captain stroked his chin. "I suppose he was telling you

there were still survivors around, which he must have been imagining. The *John Hughes* and *Emerson* haven't seen a trace."

"Or he may have seen a few men in the water right after his ship sank, survivors who didn't last very long."

"I'll buy that."

The captain knelt beside the cot, studying the weary face of its occupant. "Feel like talking a bit, Mr. Montague?" he asked with unaccustomed gentleness.

The man nodded, and the captain noticed his eyes were filled with tears. "Let's start out with the name of your ship."

"The *Henry Morgan*."

"Freighter?"

There was a noticeable hesitation before the answer came. "No, she, uh, was an oceanography-research vessel."

The captain caught the accent. "British registry?"

"American, privately owned."

"Did she founder?"

The tears spurted, although the voice remained miraculously steady. "She broke in two and rolled over in the storm. I was flung overboard. The doctor told me this is an American cruiser. Are you the captain?"

"I am, commanding cruiser *Tucson*. We're heading for Norfolk, Virginia, and we'll take good care of you until you're well enough to go home. Where is home, by the way?"

The man ignored the question. "Captain, have you . . . I mean, were there any other survivors?"

"We've got two destroyers searching the area." He studied the man's face and decided he could handle the truth. "I wouldn't hold out too much hope. Were any other lifeboats launched?"

The survivor shook his head. "One was washed away before we capsized. The one I was on was torn loose. I guess I was just lucky. I . . . I didn't see anyone else in the water."

The captain frowned. "You told the doctor there was something alive down there. Down where?"

The man's eyes clouded and he shook his head. "I don't remember telling anyone that."

"You did, though. But you were delirious at the time, so don't worry about it."

"I'm awfully tired, Captain. I think I'd like to sleep."

The captain patted his shoulder awkwardly. "Sure thing. You get some rest now, and we'll talk later."

Derek Montague did not fall asleep, however. His tired mind was trying to fasten on the reason he had instinctively avoided telling his rescuers the truth.

Not wanting to relive the nightmare was a partial explanation, but his reluctance went deeper. He could not shake the feeling that they had trespassed on the dead, that they had sought the forbidden. Yet while part of him wanted to bury the real story forever, he also knew he could never stop thinking of the riches that lay within that wreck. The secret of the treasure only he possessed.

He grappled with these conflicting emotions for a long time before surrendering to physical exhaustion and the effects of the sedative. Logic, and Derek Montague above all else was a logical man, told him the Lefferts expedition had been doomed to failure right from its inception. John Hawke had attempted the impossible with the inadequate. Their dream had been a fool's dream.

And what about those strange creatures? The apparitions he and Van Buren thought they had seen? Illusions or ghosts? Harmless phenomena, or some kind of supernatural menace?

He wondered whether anyone would believe his story—the whole story. Perhaps, but it was more likely they'd dismiss most of it as the product of traumatic stress. They might believe the *Henry Morgan* had been looking for the *Titanic*, but no one was going to accept the rest of the story from a shipwrecked survivor presumably on the verge of madness.

No, he decided, he'd not expose himself to ridicule. He would bide his time and keep everything locked within him—for how long, he could not really judge right now. He was convinced there was no feasible way to recover that gold with the technology at hand. Maybe someday there would be, but meanwhile . . .

That night, the captain entered into the daily ship's log the following notation:

> At 1307 Greenwich time, picked up lone survivor of foundered oceanographic research ship *Henry Morgan*, American registry. Survivor, a Derek Montague, is of UK citizenry. Resumed course at 1346, proceeding west at 31 knots.
>
> —Roger Cornell, Cmdr., USN

Part Two

1995

12

Director William Gillespie of the Woods Hole Oceanographic Institution closed the blue-covered folder stamped CLASSIFIED in large red letters. He was sitting in the spartan Pentagon office of Rear Admiral Roger Cornell, a small, wiry man with a face textured like a piece of corduroy.

Cornell took the folder from Gillespie and looked at him quizzically. "Well, what do you think?"

"It's the damnedest story I ever heard. I'm intrigued, but I reserve the right to be skeptical."

"Why? Because you can't believe Bob Ballard wasn't the first discoverer of the *Titanic*?"

Gillespie smiled, softening his somewhat haughty features. Tall and austere, the fifty-one-year-old oceanographer bore a striking resemblance to the actor Basil Rathbone, even to the thin, patrician nose and the air of someone who looked as if he was smelling spoiled fish. The appearance was misleading, as the admiral well knew. It took someone possessing courage, intelligence, loyalty, wit, and objectivity to earn Roger Cornell's respect and friendship—something he seldom extended to civilians.

"I'll admit I'm prejudiced on that subject," Gillespie said. "Ballard's always been something of a hero to me. I owe my job at Woods Hole to his recommendation. That aside, though, I still find it hard to believe that the story this Derek Montague gave your intelligence agents could have been covered up for eighteen years. There were prominent people aboard Montague's ship, Roger. Britain's leading oceanographer, a highly respected American oceanographer, and Martin Lefferts himself. Their deaths made front-page news. I remember reading about them. They were supposed to be on a research vessel owned by Lefferts that sank in a storm, with Montague the only survivor. It was your cruiser that picked him up. What kind of a story did he give you?"

"Basically, the same one he gave at that time to the Lefferts family and the press. And I bought it. I had no reason to believe he was holding anything back."

"So what made you send two agents to England to interrogate him?"

Cornell scratched the bristle on his chin. He was one of those unfortunate men whose five-o'clock shadow sprouted by noon.

"You did, Bill."

"I did?"

"Sure. You told me a publisher in New York had called to ask if you had heard of a secret expedition in the summer of 1975 that tried to find the *Titanic*. He was looking at a manuscript written by Lefferts's son, a biography of his father. The kid had found confidential papers Lefferts had squirreled away, papers containing a reference to a hush-hush expedition his father was planning. It was enough to suggest there had been some kind of search for the *Titanic*, but it didn't say anything about the ship carrying gold. Up to that point, nobody, including his own family, knew Lefferts and the others were after a secret bullion hoard, let alone that they were looking for the *Titanic*. So you came to me, asking if the navy knew anything about a 1975 expedition. And boy, did that ring a bell.

"A secret search, and my plucking Mr. Montague out of the Atlantic, both events occurring at the same time. Damn funny coincidence, I figured, so after I checked and found out that Montague was still alive, I got Navy Intelligence to send a couple of agents over to London, where they interviewed him. Mostly I was curious to know why he had lied about the Lefferts expedition's trying to find the *Titanic* . . . not just to me but to everyone else. And *that*, Bill, is when the old guy spilled the beans, the whole can, starting with the code he broke. The gold, the creatures they saw, four people dying *before* their ship sank in a weird storm, mysterious malfunctions that would have made a gremlin envious . . . I agree with you, it's the damnedest story I ever heard. All written down in that file you just read."

"Written down," Gillespie said, "but not documented. You believe his story?"

"I hope you don't think I'm nuts. But I believe most of it."

"Which parts don't you believe?"

"Well, Montague's thinking there was something supernatural involved. Too much of what he and the others saw can be explained . . . poor visibility distorting natural objects into imaginary ones, hallucinations under severe emotional stress, or the most likely possibility, that imagination can run wild when you're part of this tiny group of amateurs at the bottom of the ocean, staring at a ship holding fifteen hundred dead people."

"It would be difficult," Gillespie observed, "to *imagine* a one-hundred-foot plesiosaur or a hundred-and-seventy-foot shark. I think we have to concede there could be some spectacular marine life at those depths."

Cornell chuckled. "Oh, I don't doubt they might have seen some strange fish down there. But it would have been pretty easy to exaggerate their size or misidentify their species. Put a goldfish in front of someone who's panicking at depth, he'd swear he was looking at a barracuda. Anyway, whatever they saw must have departed the premises years ago. There have been four expeditions to the *Titanic* since the Lefferts fiasco, and nobody saw anything bigger than a sardine."

Gillespie pursed his lips. "Which brings us to the main motive for going. Do you believe Montague's story of the illegal gold shipment?"

"I do now, and I'll tell you why. First, the agents gave him—at his request—a lie-detector test. He aced that. Second, they did some horse trading with Scotland Yard. Everything Montague told about Sovereign came up as gospel. He showed our agents his codebooks and went through the deciphering process with them. It all checked out. The agents even ran down the records on the guy from Sovereign making inquiries on whether the ship could be raised. It was true: Montague even had a legit copy of a letter written to several salvage firms, signed by the man the Yard identified as a Sovereign bigwig. Now maybe Montague hallucinated his monsters, but he sure as hell didn't dream up that bullion."

Gillespie was silent, and the admiral smiled tightly.

"Bill, there are millions of dollars worth of bullion in cargo hold three of that wreck. I'm convinced of it, and so is the Navy."

"You're going after the gold."

"Yep."

"Would you mind telling me why? According to Montague's account, they were expecting to net around thirty million dollars. I know gold's worth a lot more today than in 1975, but even so, I—"

"The bullion in the *Titanic* would probably bring in at least two hundred million bucks."

"Where did you come up with that figure?"

"The current price of gold is just under six hundred dollars an ounce. Up until 1988, the British always shipped bullion in four-hundred-ounce-bars. The *Titanic* shipment weighed some ten thousand pounds, so the bars down there must have a nominal market value of about ninety-six million. But you can double that figure when you take into consideration what a collector would pay for each bar . . . probably triple it, even."

Gillespie shook his head. "Roger, the Pentagon must spend that much every fifteen minutes. Two hundred million is just a comma in the defense budget. Even if you come back with double *that* amount, you couldn't justify plundering a ship that's been declared off-limits by most of the oceanographic community. There's a plaque on that ship, Roger, put there by Bob Ballard seven years ago. In effect, it says grave robbers aren't welcome. Or don't you think going after that gold would be seen as grave robbing?"

"Technically, yes."

"So?"

The admiral leaned forward. "Off the record?"

"Of course. I've never violated your confidence."

"Bill, it's already been rationalized by three people who

outrank me. They're the only ones who've seen the Montague file except for you, me, and the two agents who interviewed him and wrote it up. The first is the Chief of Naval Operations, my boss. The second is the Secretary of the Navy, my other boss. And the third is everybody's boss, including yours—the President of the United States. What I've got is a green light to lead another expedition to the *Titanic*."

Gillespie blurted, "With all the problems he has, he decides to sanction a looting expedition?"

Cornell held up his hand. "Settle down and listen to me. About a year ago, my research people developed the means of sending free divers down safely to depths exceeding fifteen thousand feet. *Divers*, mind you, not just a submarine with robot cameras. Now do I have your attention?"

Gillespie could only nod.

"Good, because the rest of this is top secret. After prototype tests showed the equipment was feasible, I went to my superiors with a proposal that the Navy send divers down to the *Titanic* to photograph her interior. I pointed out that no one had ever seen what she's like inside. The robot cameras used on the previous expeditions penetrated only one area—a few feet into where the Grand Staircase was located. I put it to them as the kind of spectacular stunt that would demonstrate how good this very expensive equipment is."

"They turned you down," Gillespie said.

"I was told that a few pictures of the interior wouldn't justify the expedition's direct cost—which, incidentally, I estimated conservatively would run three to four million bucks. I also was informed that nobody was all that interested in the *Titanic* anymore, and that I should devote further diving research to straight practical applications, such as submarine rescue work.

"I almost came to you for help, but I knew Woods Hole was having its own budget problems. Private funding looked out of the question. I made a few inquiries and got the same reaction as the Navy's. Why spend four million dollars on something that's been done four times? One very rich prospect reminded me that there probably wasn't much left of the interior to photograph."

"He's probably right."

"We can't say that for certain, which is a damned good reason for trying. Anyway, I had to pigeonhole my plan for lack of anyone's interest except my own. And then along came the Montague business. I would have been just as skeptical as you are, except that I was the one who fished him out of the water. That, plus what Lefferts's son unearthed, convinced me there probably had been a 1975 expedition. After our agents finished their investigation, I had all the proof I needed.

"So I showed the Montague file to the CNO. When he didn't laugh in my face, I knew I might have something. He told me he wanted someone else to read it; the someone else was the Secretary of the Navy, who had an idea of his own. He sent that folder you just read over to the White House, with a 'President's eyes only' tag."

Gillespie started to say something but Cornell held up his hand again.

"That's when a minor miracle occurred. Next thing I know, I get a call summoning me to the White House. I'm ushered into the Oval Office, and for twenty minutes there's just me and the President discussing Derek Montague, the *Henry Morgan*, and ten thousand pounds of bullion.

"He asked me if I believed the story, and I said I did. Then he tells me the Secretary of the Navy briefed him on our new diving equipment, and he asks me if I thought the gold was recoverable. I said it would be difficult, but feasible. He says— as you just did—that a potential haul of two hundred million dollars is a drop in the bucket these days, and that it also raised certain ethical questions. Sound familiar?

"But then, he drops the bomb. He says the federal government is having enough budget problems without turning down a chance to bring in a two-hundred-million-dollar bonanza by gambling four million. Then he drops another bomb. He says any moral or ethical objections could be overcome if the proceeds from the expedition were applied to worthy causes. Bill, I was flabbergasted. We talked a little more, and it might interest you to know he shares your moral reservations. He even mentioned Ballard's plaque"—Gillespie's eyebrows went up at that revelation—"and he said normally, he would never sanction such a project. Then he added, and I quote him verbatim, 'But in this case, Admiral Cornell, I sincerely believe the end justifies the means.' He didn't go on to say it in so many words, but I got the feeling he wasn't forgetting the public-relations aspect."

"Roger, what kind of 'worthy causes' are you talking about?"

"The White House is compiling the list. Thus far, a number of high-visibility medical-research projects. The new UN fund for Third World agricultural development. And, at my suggestion, oceanographic research, including your own Woods Hole organization. Feel any better?"

"A little, but not entirely," Gillespie admitted. He was stunned at the prospect of Woods Hole getting a share of something that only a few minutes ago he would have rejected almost with revulsion.

"Well, let's have it," Cornell said brusquely.

"For the time being, my objections are technical, not ethical."

"Shoot."

"Roger, do you have any idea of what condition that wreck must be in by now? If someone did ship ten thousand pounds of bullion on the *Titanic*, I don't think even the Navy stands one chance in hell of getting it out."

"Why?"

"Because you're underestimating by a huge margin the difficulty of getting inside the ship. You're a career naval officer. You should know what happens to forty-six thousand tons of deadweight falling almost two and a half miles vertically. Ballard himself, after he saw the destruction, estimated that the *Titanic* was traveling at almost forty miles an hour when she hit bottom at a thirty-degree angle. And behind her, as she fell, was an immense funnel—a literal cyclone created by the ship's momentum, pushing thousands of tons of water against her structure. In other words, the interior of that ship has to be one unholy mess, and just about impenetrable."

"Fifty percent of what you just told me is correct," Cornell said.

"Which half is that?"

"That the interior is a mess. If Hawke, the Brit who ran Lefferts's operation, had been able to blow the hull open, I don't think he could have reached far enough into cargo hold three to recover even one crate. The wreckage would have blocked the way, and he didn't have the equipment to clear it."

"And you do?"

"You're damned right we do. Lasers."

Gillespie's eyes widened. "You think *laser* beams can cut into that wreckage?"

"Like a Benihana chef. Swish-swish." The admiral's gnarled hands made two quick cutting motions. "We've also developed these carbon-fiber diving suits capable of protecting the human body from pressures as high as eight thousand pounds per square inch—a couple of thousand pounds more pressure than what the *Titanic*'s depth produces. Our carbon-fiber composite is five times stronger than steel, but much lighter."

Gillespie, still doubtful, shook his head. "I would think even a carbon-fiber rig would have to be unworkably thick to withstand such pressures. And the bulkier the suit, the less mobility you'd have—if there's any mobility at all. Why—"

"Only the outer layer is carbon—a metallic mesh about three inches thick, so closely woven that to the eye it appears solid. Under this is a second layer, a newly developed insulating material. That's mostly to protect the diver from the cold. Furthermore, the whole outfit's jointed at the knees and elbows, with oil-filled rotary sockets underneath the two protective layers. The joints utilize movable pistons to equalize internal and external pressures. I won't say a diver could run pass patterns, but for the purposes of maneuvering inside a sunken ship, he can do just fine. He breathes inert fluorocarbon mixed with oxygen, supplied from a titanium tank strapped to his back—a two-and-a-half-hour supply. The fluorocarbon combined with oxygen prevents any buildup of gases in the blood."

"The joints you spoke of. It seems to me you're sacrificing protection for the sake of mobility. Jointing a suit always creates vulnerable areas, like the knees and elbows on a suit of armor."

"You're right; these are the most vulnerable areas if, say, a diver was hit directly on the kneecap by an extremely heavy object. The carbon layer in these areas is two centimeters thinner, to give us the necessary flexibility. Now the shock might over-rotate the internal joints and even fracture a bone, but I assure you the outer layer itself would remain intact and the pressure protection unaffected. The divers move around with tiny impeller thrusters attached to the suit's buttocks . . . like the little rockets astronauts use on space walks."

"What about visibility?"

"Helmets with large, exceptionally strong Plexiglas windows. The helmets are detachable but only from the outside; a diver can't put on or take off a helmet by himself. The helmets are attached to the suit's neck ring by four titanium bolts that are screwed or unscrewed with a special air-driven wrench developed just for these helmets. Any more questions?"

"Yes. What about manual ability? How do they manipulate the thrusters? And how do you protect their hands? Don't tell me they'd be wearing titanium-mesh gloves."

"They won't be wearing any gloves. The suit's equipped with artificial hands—more like claws, really—roughly the same dexterity as the aids a paraplegic uses. The artificial hands are linked to the diver's real hands buried inside the sleeves of the suit. Once a diver's trained to use the robot hands, he can pick up anything from a pencil to a laser gun. A joystick integrated with the hand controls activates the thrusters."

Gillespie couldn't keep growing interest out of his voice. "How do you get the divers down to the bottom?"

"Brand-new research sub. She'll carry up to six divers, plus a four-man crew. The divers depart and reenter via a floodable escape hatch that's the size of a small room. They can work inside a wreck for nearly three hours, then come back to the sub to recharge their breathing tanks. Hell, I'll bet we can get that gold out in two dives, three at the most. If we have to cut into the hull from the outside, the sub carries two larger lasers, more powerful than the hand ones."

Mention of the gold brought the oceanographer back to the prospect of inflicting new indignities on an unhappy vessel. Cornell must have been reading his mind.

"We'd like you to join us on this venture," he said quietly. "I know how you feel about the *Titanic*, Bill, and part of me agrees with you. She ought to be left in peace. She's a forty-six-thousand-ton tombstone. I've asked myself a hundred times why the *Titanic* should be any different than the *Arizona*. The Navy let *her* rest in peace, not just as a memorial to the sailors inside her but as a reminder of what unpreparedness can cost us."

"If you feel that way," Gillespie said, "then why are you going after her again? Have you asked yourself *that* question a hundred times? If you have, then you got the same old answer: greed."

Admiral Cornell said, with more intensity than Gillespie had ever seen him display, "My friend, never question another man's motives unless you really know his motives. I have two, and the first is very simple. I've been ordered to conduct this mission, and I'm going to comply with my orders. The second is more personal. The gold, hell, that's all going to the government—recovering it is just part of my orders, and exploring the *Titanic* is your bailiwick, not mine. What I *do* care about is this chance to prove the capabilities of some revolutionary hardware—the suits and the new sub. That wreck is the greatest challenge to deep-sea exploration and salvage technology since Bushnell invented the submarine."

He stood up, as if a sitting posture was inadequate for his words. "And maybe I have a third motive. If we pull this off, the Navy will get the credit for accomplishing the impossible. I'm only one year away from retirement. This is my chance to pay the Navy back for what it's meant to me since the day I took the oath as a scared, undersized midshipman."

He sat down again, his eyes bright with emotion. The old gruffness returned to his voice. "Sorry, but I figured you'd better know how I feel about this job before you decide whether to join me."

Gillespie was silent.

"I can't believe you'd hesitate," Cornell said. "You scientists are always griping about lack of research funding. Here's a chance to get some real money, and you're going sentimental on me!" He stopped, appreciating Gillespie's dilemma. "I'll level with you, Bill. Woods Hole will get its share whether you go or not. I'm just offering you an opportunity to be there to see what no one else has for eighty-one years."

"You'd let *me* explore the interior?"

"Why not? It wouldn't take long to qualify you on those suits. And you wouldn't be going along just for the ride. We can use you, Bill. You'd be our resident expert on the *Titanic*. Nobody, including Ballard himself, knows more about that ship than you do. I've seen that model you keep in your office; all those books on the *Titanic* in your library. She's been your hobby since you were a kid."

"I know." Gillespie sighed. His mind was in a turmoil. He was thinking about the angry reaction of many oceanographers, including himself, when that 1987 French expedition had brought up artifacts from the *Titanic*'s resting place. A subsequent American television show on the expedition hadn't soothed the resentment, either.

Yet Gillespie knew some oceanographers didn't agree that the French venture had been a grave-robbing job. Their dives had been superbly conducted—the French were unmatched at this sort of thing—and it could be argued that they didn't loot the ship itself, bringing up objects only from the debris field that probably would be buried in a few years and lost forever.

Cornell was right. Sentiment had collided with pragmatism. Gillespie remembered how proud he had been when Ballard placed that bronze Explorers Club plaque near the *Titanic*'s bow capstan, using the submarine *Alvin*'s robot arm. Gillespie could recite every word embossed on the plaque.

In recognition of the scientific effort of the American and French explorers who found the R.M.S. Titanic: *Be it resolved that any who may come hereafter leave undisturbed this ship and her contents as a memorial to deep water exploration.*

". . . *leave undisturbed this ship and her contents*": a warning to those who would for the sake of financial gain sully the memory of a great ship and the souls who went down with her. A plea against commercialization undoing a great discovery and scientific triumph. A prayer for preserving the sanctity of death and the everlasting peace that is its only reward.

He was about to tell Cornell to count him and the Woods Hole Institution out when the thought of his underfinanced facility flashed into his mind. Woods Hole couldn't turn this down, whether he went or not. God, how they could use a share of that gold, and not for anybody's personal gain. No, for oceanographic research projects that were gathering dust because there wasn't enough funding to support them. A *minimum of $96 million* but as Cornell said, there was no telling how much more that bullion was really worth. He recalled reading years ago about a Texas oil baron who offered six thousand dollars for a single piece of thread from one of the *Titanic's* carpets. What would the wealthy give for a bullion bar from the same ship? What would William Gillespie give for a chance to explore her interior?

While the admiral waited patiently for an answer, Gillespie thought of another factor—the strange story Montague had told. The enigma of those four deaths, the creatures—it all defied explanation.

He reached a decision that would have been reluctant no matter which direction it took. "I'd have to consult with our directors, of course, but I'll accept your invitation. When do you—"

Gillespie stopped, for Cornell's grim expression was not of a "welcome aboard" hue. "Sorry, Bill, but you won't discuss this with your board, your wife, or anyone else. This conversation is off the record. For the time being, Derek Montague doesn't even exist, and the expedition itself is absolutely top secret. If any word gets out, the *Titanic's* site is going to look like Times Square on New Year's Eve. Not just with would-be treasure hunters who'd charter every salvage vessel on the face of the globe, but the news media—Jesus Christ!"

Gillespie had to smile. "I suppose I could take a short leave of absence, and if untoward questions are asked, cultivate a deep silence."

"Yeah," the admiral agreed, almost absentmindedly. He was fuming at the thought of reporters getting wind of the venture. "That goddamned press—bunch of fucking wolves!"

"If you want the Navy to get credit for a spectacular mission,"

Gillespie needled gently, "it seems to me you'd want to work *with* the press."

Cornell's leathery features darkened. "That's great if the mission's successful. If we failed on an attempt publicized in advance, which is another good reason for secrecy, they'd be on us like sharks."

"What would you regard as failure—not coming back with the bullion?"

"Bill, I can't separate our two goals. All I can tell you is that if we achieve one, I think we'll achieve the other." Cornell paused thoughtfully. "You know, I think Montague's talk about a haunted ship is bullshit. But I have to admit some mighty funny things happened on that Lefferts mission."

Gillespie almost laughed, but changed his mind—Cornell appeared to be serious. "Roger, you're the last one I thought would believe in ghosts."

"I don't. But I didn't just *read* that interview transcript. I *heard* part of the story from Montague himself—and he tells a pretty convincing story."

"You've met him? When?"

"Two days ago, right here in Washington. Matter of fact, he's still here; we've got him stashed in the Washington Westin, guest of the United States Navy. You'll meet him yourself in about"—Cornell consulted a massive stainless-steel wristwatch—"in about an hour. He'll be expecting us."

Gillespie said, "I'll enjoy talking with him, of course, but don't expect me to come away sold on a haunted *Titanic*." He laughed. "My God, Roger, some of the stuff in that transcript is B-movie material—faces in portholes, for Christ's sake."

"I felt the same way, until two days ago." He hesitated. "I *still* think it's crap but . . . well, you haven't met Montague yet. Listen to him talk and he'll convince you Satan himself is down there waiting for us, licking his chops. It's the man's eyes, Bill. They . . . they look haunted."

"By something he saw?"

"Yes, and by something the others saw, the ones who died while they were at the wreck. It's as if he were looking back at what happened through the eyes of four corpses."

"Roger, he's gone through a lot. That kind of experience leaves marks."

"Yes, it does. That's just what I'm saying. The *Henry Morgan* sank twenty years ago, but listen to the man and you'd swear it happened last week. Look at him, and you start to think it happened yesterday."

Gillespie thought he had just seen the admiral shudder, and he felt chilled himself.

For some reason, Gillespie's eyes wandered to a collection of framed photographs on the wall behind Cornell's desk, all pictures of warships. The ones Cornell had commanded or served on, Gillespie guessed—a small destroyer escort, a pair of destroyers, two cruisers, and a huge carrier, her decks bristling with deadly looking jets. One of the cruisers caught his eyes as he read the tiny brass plate under the photograph that identified the ship.

U.S.S. *TUCSON*

The admiral swiveled his chair around and stared at the same picture.

"That's her," he murmured. "The lady who found Derek Montague."

"I think," Gillespie said, "it's time for me to meet him."

Gillespie's first impression of Derek Montague was that of a man remarkably fit for his age—he was seventy-six, Gillespie learned later. He moved with surprising briskness, his tall frame only slightly bent; his broad face had weathered the years without adding too many lines. He reminded one of a stately elm that had aged gracefully.

Cornell had been right about the man's eyes, though. They were sad, tired, pained. They stared out through a courteous, even cheerful demeanor, and were more poignant for that. Here was a man, Gillespie decided, who had seen too much and suffered even more, yet remained a thoroughly likable person with a quiet courage that had to be admired.

"May I offer you something from this mini bar?" Montague

was saying. He smiled at Cornell. "Bit of an embarrassment; I'm offering you refreshments your Navy's paying for."

"I could use a drink, but not from one of those mini bars," the admiral said. "They charge three bucks for a fifty-cent can of Coke. Let's get down to business and we'll all have a drink in the hotel bar later. Derek, Dr. Gillespie has agreed to join our little foray. I've already given you his background. As oceanographers go, he's the best."

Gillespie looked at Montague curiously. "And how do *you* feel about this affair, which seems to be a combination of legitimate salvage and barefaced sacrilege?"

"The same way I felt eighteen years ago," Montague replied soberly. "I suppose it amounts to justified looting. The stakes outweigh the moral aspects; except . . ."

He left an unspoken thought hanging in the air, and the other two men exchanged glances.

"Except what?" Cornell asked.

"Admiral, we've discussed this before. I still feel strongly that some force does not want anyone plundering that ship." He looked at the oceanographer. "Does Dr. Gillespie know the full story of the Lefferts expedition?"

"I do," Gillespie answered quickly. "But you just said some *force* was present around the *Titanic*. Are you implying something supernatural?"

"I suppose I am."

"A *malignant* force, responsible for the deaths of four people?"

"The evidence," Montague said quietly, "is admittedly circumstantial, but strong enough to have left too many unanswered questions."

Gillespie smiled. "There are a number of those questions that intrigue me. Particularly, the reports of creatures around the wreck. But they were inconsistent reports, weren't they?"

Montague looked weary. He obviously had argued this point with the admiral. "Our sonar never picked up any of them. Captain Robertson insisted this was because our sonar equipment was set up to record metallic objects. But I've always wondered how any sonar could miss anything a hundred feet or more in length. And then we have the puzzle of why my friends saw three different creatures, each corresponding to individual fears or preoccupations."

"Perhaps because there *were* three different creatures," Gillespie said. "Or, it's possible they all saw the same thing but misinterpreted what they saw, influenced by past association with a particular form of marine life. This Hawke's apparent obsession with sharks would be a case in point."

Montague nodded, but without conviction. "I'd be more impressed with that argument if I hadn't heard their screams. If I hadn't listened to their descriptions of what they saw. If I hadn't seen the *Titanic* with my own eyes, sensing the presence of death all around her."

The oceanographer said quietly, "I take it you believe in the supernatural. In ghosts."

Montague managed a wry smile. "I'd venture to say eighty percent of the British population believes in ghosts. Our landscape is dotted with haunted castles and haunted inns and homes. It's a national tradition, and after all, the *Titanic* was a British ship."

Cornell said, "But who ever heard of ghost sharks, or ghost any other kind of creature? The face you thought you saw in the porthole, Van Buren's figure on the bridge—I'd have to call that insufficient evidence."

Gillespie nodded. "The *Henry Morgan*'s divers may have suffered from HPNS. Are you familiar with that term, Mr. Montague?"

The Englishman shook his head.

"HPNS stands for High Pressure Nervous Syndrome. It occurs when highly pressurized breathing mixtures create toxic amounts of inert gases in a deep-sea diver's bloodstream. The usual effects are nausea or convulsions, but HPNS has been known to cause hallucinations. I'll grant you, Hawke and the others were in pressurized submarines, not diving suits, but from your own account, they had trouble with their life-support systems. They may have been exposed to HPNS."

Montague rubbed his jaw reflectively. "All I know is that from the very start I had the feeling something was wrong, that something beyond our comprehension was trying to discourage us. Too many things went wrong. The succession of disasters, the destruction of our ship by a storm so terrible and unique. Captain Robertson was a brave man and a competent seaman, and I remember how terrified he was; he had never encountered anything like it."

Cornell eyed him sympathetically. The admiral, too, was remembering something. Something his exec on the *Tucson* had said: ". . . *I could swear the sky had a green tinge to it. Never saw anything like that before.*"

Cornell had seen the sky, too, casually dismissing it at the time as some kind of freak atmospheric condition. But now . . .

"Sounds as if you were jinxed," Gillespie suggested, and the admiral leaped on that remark.

He growled, "Talk all you want to about busted winches, equipment failing on the subs, brand-new batteries going dead—I'll tell you something. There's really no such thing as a jinx. Jinxes are the result of sloppy planning, human errors, and over-optimistic assumptions, which describes the Lefferts expedition perfectly. I've seen so-called jinxed ships in the Navy. Jinxed, my Aunt Tillie. They invariably had a lousy skipper, lazy officers, and a crew with its collective head screwed on upside down."

Gillespie grinned and said, "Mr. Montague—"

"Derek, please."

"Derek, it is. And I'm Bill. Derek, do you mind telling me why, after all these years, you decided to come forth with the *Titanic*'s secret? You believe there is some supernatural force protecting the inside of the wreck, but you've divulged the facts of the gold shipment and its hold location to the Navy. There was no need to mention the gold at all. You didn't when Lefferts's son contacted you; you merely told him his father died trying to find the *Titanic*. You could have done likewise when Admiral Cornell's intelligence people interviewed you. Instead, you're deliberately inviting another expedition."

"My motives are twofold," Montague answered. "Greed and curiosity. Greed because I'm a rather impecunious man who has made some perfectly awful financial investments, and the thought of that fortune lying untouched at the bottom of the Atlantic has never left my mind. And curiosity? Well, perhaps that is a poor choice of words. It is curiosity, but blended with an element of fear. For eighteen years, I have wondered why so many good people had to die. I am the lone survivor of a group who were doomed, it seems, from the day I broke the Sovereign code. When you, Admiral, assured me that jinxes are created by our own weaknesses, the product of careless planning, I saw that you had logic on your side. I like to think I am a pragmatic man myself. But no amount of logic has been proof against twenty years of terrible memories."

His voice dropped a half octave. "You see, the cross I bear is one constructed of guilt. I instigated that whole ill-fated mess. Yes, I still want a share of the gold as compensation for my knowledge that it exists. But even more than gold, I want help in solving a mystery of my own making. I actually welcomed your Navy's tracking me down. I had been carrying this secret for too long."

The hotel room fell quiet, the men oblivious to the sounds of the late-afternoon Georgetown traffic outside the window.

Cornell broke the silence. "Derek, you could have taken your story to the private sector and made a hell of a lot more money than what we've promised. Or you could have confided in the Royal Navy."

Montague, his voice back to a normal pitch, sounded grateful for the slight change of subject. "I suppose I'm being unpatriotic, but I did have the sense that you might have some specialized technological capabilities. I was right enough about that. And you were the ones who found me . . . first come, first served, as it were. You convinced yourselves—something I was frankly never sure I'd be able to bring off if I'd simply rung up the RN with my story."

Gillespie, who was staring out the window without seeing anything, turned back to the admiral. "Roger, does our technological superiority include the services of a parapsychologist, by any chance? A person trained to study and interpret psychic phenomena?"

"The Bureau of Naval Personnel would have one hell of a time finding someone like that on its roster," Cornell observed.

"Well, I think we should find one and take him along."

"Are you serious?"

"Very."

Cornell started to protest, but stopped when he saw Montague nodding. "Fine, Bill. If you can find one, I'll put him aboard. Now, let's go get that drink before you talk me into hiring a fortune-teller."

As they left the room, Gillespie was asking himself how his attitude could have been changed so drastically. He had walked in convinced that Derek Montague was a well-meaning, harmless old coot with an overly vivid imagination. He was leaving the room admitting that he had in common with Montague more than a mutual love of *Titanic* lore; he shared his instinct that something beyond ordinary comprehension awaited them.

It was then that Gillespie remembered seeing something else besides ship pictures on the admiral's office wall. It was a framed quotation

> *I wish to have no connection with any ship that does not sail fast, for I intend to go in harm's way.*
> —John Paul Jones

13

A fortnight after the Westin meeting, Gillespie found his parapsychologist, a highly recommended psychiatrist named J. Benjamin Henning of Los Angeles.

Gillespie made the contact by phone and visualized Henning as a stuffy, painfully suspicious little man wearing the musty aroma of ancient books on Satanism, witchcraft, and poltergeists. Henning's voice was guarded almost to the point of belligerence, as if he expected Gillespie to burst out laughing momentarily at anyone who would consider parapsychology a legitimate science.

The oceanographer was guarded, too, torn between wanting to arouse Henning's interest and remembering Admiral Cornell's warning—"Don't tell anyone too much." So they dueled warily for some minutes until Gillespie tired of the game.

"Look, this has to do with a certain ship . . . uh, some strange happenings . . . and, uh, let's say unique occurrences of an unexplainable nature."

Henning sounded the type to have hung up by then, except he had seemed intrigued by Gillespie's having identified himself as the director of the Woods Hole Oceanographic Institution. He perked up at the mention of "a certain ship."

"Not the *Queen Mary*, the one docked at Long Beach?" he asked. "She's supposed to be haunted by the ghost of a woman passenger who apparently died violently aboard her on a voyage back in the thirties. Never investigated that one myself, but I know colleagues who—"

"It's not the *Queen Mary*," Gillespie interrupted. "It's—"
He mentally consigned Roger Cornell to purgatory and took
the plunge. "It's the *Titanic*."

Silence. Gillespie thought Henning *had* hung up.

"Now that's interesting," the doctor finally allowed. "Tell
me more."

"I can't discuss it on the phone. I think we should meet. Is
it possible for you to come to Woods Hole?"

This time, Henning sounded more annoyed than interested.
"Look, by profession, I'm a practicing psychiatrist. Parapsychology is more an avocation than anything else. I've got patients to consider; I can't come traipsing across the country just
because you mentioned the *Titanic*. Not unless I get some idea
of what this is about."

"The only thing I can tell you is that this matter involves
the U.S. Navy and is completely hush-hush. It goes without
saying, Dr. Henning, that the Navy will pay all travel expenses,
plus a mutually acceptable fee. I'd go to Los Angeles myself,
but I'm already involved in this . . . ah . . . project and can't
get away."

"It's hard for me to get away, too. What kind of a project is
this, anyway? Is the Navy going to raise the damned thing?
Why would you need a parapsychologist for that?"

"I'm not at liberty to say." Gillespie hoped evasion would
intrigue Henning more than an outright disclosure. He was
rewarded by another moment of silence.

Then: "Has the Navy seen something unusual down there?"

"Not the Navy. Someone else." If that doesn't do it, Gillespie thought, nothing will.

There was the sound of paper being torn from a pad.

"Exactly where is Woods Hole?" Dr. J. Benjamin Henning
inquired.

Five days later, in Gillespie's office, Henning heard from Derek
Montague himself the tale of the Martin Lefferts expedition.

"That's the damnedest story I ever heard," he announced.

Gillespie smiled. He remembered saying the same thing to
Admiral Cornell. "Well," he said, "at least you didn't laugh."

Henning regarded them with surprise. "Why should I laugh?

It's fascinating. But I don't think you're dealing with any psychic phenomena here. In fact, Mr. Montague, everything you've told me could be explained away. The succession of bad luck in the form of so-called mysterious malfunctions, for example. Anything that's man-made has the potential of breaking down for no apparent reason, whether it's a complex piece of machinery or a toaster. Your giant creatures . . . who's to say a shark can't grow to freakish size?"

Henning leaned back in one of the uncomfortable chairs occupying Gillespie's office, an expression on his face that fell just shy of being self-satisfied. He was a big, rumpled bear of a man in his mid-fifties, his burly frame and age offset by a pink-cheeked face and an ingratiating, easy smile.

"I think," Henning said, "that you're both underestimating the power of imagination under stress. If a person is nervous or frightened to begin with, ordinary objects can be magnified into terrifying objects."

"I suppose" said Montague, "you'd discount what I saw, and what Van Buren saw, for the same reason."

"A face in a porthole, and a shadowy figure on the *Titanic*'s deck," Henning said. "Those two incidents intrigue me more than the creatures and all the mechanical problems. But not to the extent of accepting them as legitimate evidence. Look, gentlemen, if you put the average person into a deserted mansion, a place he knows is reputed to be haunted, his mind is capable of conjuring up almost anything. A large piece of cobweb may look like a human face. A curtain fluttering in a draft takes on the shape of a shroud. Now, you park that same person next to the remains of a ship with the reputation of the *Titanic*, and you've got the equivalent of your haunted house. Believe me, I've investigated a lot of houses, and most of them were about as haunted as this office."

Montague said simply, "I was there."

"I'm not doubting your word, Mr. Montague. I'm merely pointing out to you that at least ninety percent of these reported incidents, after they've been objectively investigated, do not involve the supernatural."

Gillespie said quickly, "What about the other ten percent?

Considering the controversial nature of the subject, that seems to be a relatively high proportion."

"Very high," Henning conceded, "but it doesn't mean we wind up with a verified ghost in one out of every ten investigations. Some incidents are simply unexplainable. Or the investigation itself was flawed. It may help if you both understand that competent parapsychologists, and I like to think I'm in that category, are cynical by nature. We see too many alleged psychic phenomena turn out to be the work of charlatans and con artists staging seances, or authors who disguise fiction as fact so they can make a fast buck. On the other hand, if one accepts parapsychology as a legitimate science—as I do—the existence of the supernatural is nothing to laugh at.

"Studies have shown that the human body transmits electrical energy that persists after all organic life has ceased. In rare cases, the energy is so strong that it apparently can form the image of the person who died. Most psychic phenomena are attributed to this residue of electrical energy. There is a fascinating variation of this basic theory, accepted by some parapsychologists. They believe there is an unknown substance present in all space and matter that's capable of preserving the image formed by the body's electrical energy, a kind of intangible photographic medium."

Henning paused, and looked at Montague. "The substance is called psychic ether. The theory is that under exceptionally traumatic circumstances, such as murder, suicide, or other instances of violent, sudden death, the energy is recorded on this psychic ether like a photographic image . . . an image that can move as a living person can move."

He paused again, as if trying to reconcile something. "I suppose," he mused, "the *Titanic* does harbor some interesting possibilities, now that we're talking about it."

Gillespie leaped on that comment. "Doctor, Admiral Cornell has authorized me to invite you to join our expedition. The Navy will compensate you for your services, of course, taking into consideration the time you'll be spending away from your regular practice."

Henning's eyebrows shot up. "I'm a little surprised there's

an admiral in the United States Navy who even admits the possibility of the supernatural."

"He didn't object to my suggestion that a parapsychologist accompany us," Gillespie said.

"Well, he shouldn't. I do serious research, just like you, Dr. Gillespie. But I'd just as soon debunk a ghost story as verify one. Is that understood?"

Montague smiled his sad smile. "I ask for nothing except objectivity . . . and the same open mind both Admiral Cornell and Bill, here, have demonstrated."

"How long do you figure I'll be away? Have to clear this with my wife, of course."

"Admiral Cornell hopes to sail for the *Titanic*'s site early in July," Gillespie said. "You'd better plan on being away a couple of months to be on the safe side." Conscious that he was mimicking Cornell, he added, "The secrecy of this mission is of such importance, I suggest you tell your wife the same thing I'm telling mine—that you're on a special assignment for the Navy and skip any details."

"Psychiatrists know how to respect confidentiality, Doctor. Keeping our mouths shut is an amendment to the Hippocratic oath."

"Then welcome to the party," Gillespie said, shaking Henning's hand. "Frankly, you're not at all like I pictured you when we first talked on the phone. Even your name sounded intimidating—'J. Benjamin.' Mind telling me what the *J* stands for?"

Henning grimaced. "Jeremiah, after a grandfather on my father's side. Personally, I don't think kids should be given names until they're old enough to choose one for themselves. My friends call me Ben."

"Your sense of humor is refreshing," Montague observed. "I've always imagined psychiatrists to be rather dour chaps. Perfectly natural, after spending hour after hour listening to people's phobias, emotional problems, marital difficulties. How do you manage it?"

"Who listens?" J. Benjamin Henning said innocently.

The group gathered in Roger Cornell's office on a warm June day was larger than Gillespie expected. In addition to Montague and the admiral himself, there were three men and a young woman, all in tropical white navy uniforms.

Derek Montague, who had just returned from England and came into the office with Gillespie, did a double take when he saw the woman. She reminded him, with agonizing sharpness, of Debra Chaney at first—tiny and shapely with the same fine, symmetrical features—until he realized the resemblance was mostly superficial.

Admiral Cornell began the introductions. "Well, we're all here except Doctor Henning. He phoned me yesterday that he couldn't make it, seems he got saddled at the last minute with a difficult patient. So, all of you, I'd like you to meet Bill Gillespie, director of the Woods Hole Oceanographic Institution and, I'm proud to say, an old friend of mine."

He turned to Montague. "I'd also like you to meet Derek Montague, and I've already briefed you navy people on his background and importance to this mission."

He next nodded in the direction of the young woman officer. "This is Lieutenant Fay Carlson. She's a navy oceanographer stationed in Pearl Harbor, and I've just had her transferred to my staff. Next, Bill and Derek, this is Captain Charles Bixenman, who'll be commanding our salvage ship."

Gillespie and Montague shook hands with a tall, reed-thin officer with a shock of silver hair that could have been the crest of a wave. Bixenman's narrow, stern face was softened by a pleasant smile, but his pale blue eyes gave the impression they could hurl thunderbolts at an erring seaman.

"Doctor Gillespie, I know of your work, but I've never had the pleasure of meeting you," the captain said. "It'll be an honor to have you aboard my ship. You, too, Mr. Montague."

"May I ask what ship?" Gillespie inquired. "I'm fairly well acquainted with the Navy's salvage vessels."

"The U.S.S. *Chase*," Bixenman said with a touch of pride.

"The *Chase*? An appropriate name, but she's a new one on me."

"She's brand-new, designed for both salvage *and* deep-sea research. Four thousand tons and equipped with—"

Cornell rasped, "Brag about your new baby in a minute, Bix. I want to get past these introductions. He nodded in the direction of another officer, a full commander. This is Steve Jackman, who'll be in charge of all diving operations. He's one of the best men who ever wore a uniform or a wet suit."

Jackman was short—not more than five-eight, Gillespie guessed, but he must have weighed close to two hundred pounds, giving him the appearance of a beer barrel with arms and legs. A crew cut roofed a pockmarked face that could have been a lunar landscape, and a thin scar ran from his left cheekbone down to the corner of his mouth. His nose was smashed almost flat, as if someone had held him down and tried to hammer it into his skull. A bull neck mounted between massive shoulders completed the unattractive picture.

Jackman's handshake was surprisingly moderate, although Gillespie got the impression he easily could have broken the oceanographer's hand. "I enjoyed your history of diving-physics research," the commander said. "It was required reading in UDT/SEAL school."

The third man in the room didn't wait for the admiral's introduction. A towering, handsome black officer wearing the stripes of a lieutenant commander, he shook hands with both civilians. "I'm Ozzie Mitchell. I'll be Steve's assistant in the diving operations. But only because he was one class ahead of me at Annapolis."

"Steve and Ozzie were football teammates at the Academy," Cornell said. "Linebacker and defensive end, respectively. We beat Army in Steve's senior year."

"Army clobbered us the next year, Admiral," Jackman said. "That's because I wasn't around to tell Ozzie what he was doing wrong."

Cornell glanced at Captain Bixenman. "Okay, Bix. Go ahead with your dog and pony show."

Bixenman cleared his throat. "U.S.S. *Chase*: She's absolutely the last word in vessels of this type; twin screws with a pair of General Electric turbines, top speed twenty-five knots, so we won't be wasting any time getting to the *Titanic*'s site. The major piece of support equipment is a deep-sea submersible that'll carry our divers down to the wreck. We've developed a new method of launching the sub that eliminates winches and cranes. The *Chase* has two nylon-covered rails located on the aft deck, hinged so they can be tilted down or up by means of hydraulic jacks. The sub itself is mounted on these rails, the ends of which extend over the ship's stern. All we have to do is tilt the rails and the sub slides into the water. The procedure takes less than a minute."

"How do you recover the sub?" Montague asked.

"She has two steel rings attached to either side of her prow. We manually hook these to a set of twin cables, and a motor-driven winch cranks her aboard over the same rails, which, incidentally, are coated with a special grease to reduce friction. The recovery operation takes about five minutes at the most. The sub takes up almost the entire stern area; she's almost eighty-three feet in length, with a beam of twelve feet. *Chase* is the only salvage ship we've got capable of carrying a sub that size, largely because she's built on what amounts to a light cruiser's hull. We've already given the sub a name, by the way. *Nemo.*"

"The captain of Jules Verne's fictional submarine." Montague smiled. "One of literature's most interesting and enduring characters. Another appropriate choice."

"And an excellent piece of equipment," Jackman put in. "*Nemo* has four storage batteries, any one of which can sustain life-support systems for two full days—fifty hours before recharging is necessary. All-titanium construction capable of withstanding twenty-thousand-foot pressures. *Nemo* is fully operational utilizing only two of her batteries. The other two simply offer tremendous reserve power, an unheard-of margin of safety. Underwater illumination is provided by another new piece of equipment—continuous strobe gas-plasma lights of exceptional high intensity. *Nemo* has two of them, prow-mounted, and each diving suit has a smaller version."

Bixenman added, "Sub-to-surface communications have only a five-second time lag, thanks to a new type of variable-depth repeater transponder especially designed for deep-sea operations."

"When the Navy does something, it does it right," the admiral said, looking at Gillespie, who had enjoyed some heated debates with him over the Navy's poor showing in the early years of World War II. Gillespie was fond of reminding Cornell

of such items as submarine torpedoes that failed to explode
even with direct hits, the flimsy construction of heavy cruisers
built before the war, the failure to equip older carriers with
armored flight decks, and the obsolete or overly cautious tactics
of certain admirals.

Cornell said meaningfully, "I think, Bill, the Navy has
learned from past mistakes, like the ones the Lefferts expedition
made. Such as assuming they could force their way into that
cargo hold with a pair of robot pincers. They might as well
have tried soup-can openers, for all the good it would have
done. Just wait and see how our lasers work on that interior
debris."

Lieutenant Carlson spoke up, her pretty face set in a frown.
"Admiral, I take it those lasers could also be used as weapons?
In case there's some kind of large marine creature that's estab-
lished territorial rights to the wreck."

Montague cringed. He remembered Van Buren making the
same suggestion about territorial rights. He glanced at the admiral to see if his thinking had changed any.

Cornell said sternly, "Let me remind you and everyone else
for the last time, Lieutenant, that the last four expeditions to
the *Titanic* didn't see a damned thing except the ship itself. To
answer your question, yes, if those lasers will cut through six
inches of steel, believe me they'll cut through flesh. Bill, you
have anything to bring up?"

Gillespie was grateful for the question. He had noticed that
Carlson's query hadn't been well-received by Bixenman, Jackman, or Mitchell, all three staring at her with some amusement. He badly wanted to change the subject and get her off
the hook.

"I'm especially interested in the chance to inspect and photograph the *Titanic*'s interior," Gillespie said. "This is something
Ballard and the others merely touched, being limited to the
use of a robot camera that gained access only to a small area.
I hope, Roger, you'll give us that opportunity along with proper
camera equipment."

"Lieutenant Carlson'll be handling the bulk of the photographic work. Kodak has developed a new lightweight underwa-

ter job that's an absolute marvel. They've provided us with three of them." Cornell tossed Gillespie a good-humored, affectionate grin. "Even you could work this camera . . . if I decide to let you poke around the interior."

"Are they still or movie?" Gillespie asked.

"Still. All the portable underwater cameras available are too bulky and too heavy for a diver to lug around in addition to essential equipment, including a laser gun. Lieutenant Carlson will be carrying such a gun along with her still camera, and I can't ask her or any other diver to take on the extra load. I'm afraid you'll have to be satisfied with stills."

Carlson said quickly, "Admiral, we could mount a movie camera on *Nemo's* hull. The attachments and activating electrical connections are already installed for that. We'd get some good exterior shots."

Cornell pondered this a moment. "Seems to me there's plenty of exterior film footage available from the previous expeditions." He took one look at Gillespie's disappointed expression and added, "However, I see no reason why we shouldn't make a compromise. Fay, go ahead with a requisition and I'll sign it."

"Thanks, Roger," Gillespie said.

Montague was thinking, I wonder what a movie camera might have picked up twenty years ago, like Martin's plesiosaur or Hawke's shark. No matter, he decided—those films would have been lost in the sinking, just as the still pictures had been.

". . . must remember the dual nature of this mission," the admiral was saying. "But always bear in mind that our personal priorities may clash with those of our superiors. They regard the *Titanic's* treasure as the primary goal and exploration as secondary, simply because only the former is making the latter possible. I don't necessarily agree with this reasoning, but I'm here to carry out orders and I expect everyone to do the same"—he grinned at Gillespie and Montague—"including the civilians."

Gillespie smiled but Montague thought, again with the uncomfortable feeling of déjà vu, that Cornell sounded like John Hawke.

Commander Jackman cleared his throat, the sound of a man about to bring up an unpleasant subject. "Admiral, isn't this more in the nature of a triple rather than a dual mission?"

"You're absolutely right, Steve." Cornell beamed. "I happen to think the most important aspect of this expedition is that it's a proving ground for our new equipment."

"Sir, that's not what I had in mind. I'm referring to the presence of this Doctor Henning aboard *Chase*."

"What about him?"

"We've all been briefed on what happened during the Lefferts expedition, and I'm not trying to pass judgment. But it seems to me another objective has crept in—to investigate possible psychic phenomena. Which, frankly, I find rather farfetched."

"And on what do you base that opinion?" the admiral inquired.

"With all due respect, sir, what I've heard and read about the Lefferts attempt does not add up to supernatural visitations. I don't think it warrants taking Doctor Henning on this voyage, in either of his professional roles. Unless you believe we're going to develop cases of combat fatigue, we won't need the services of a psychiatrist."

"I agree with that appraisal," Cornell said. "I issued the invitation on the advice of Bill Gillespie, who is a very pragmatic scientist in his own right. We probably *won't* need him, but even as dead weight, he certainly isn't going to interfere with the operation."

Jackman said stubbornly, "No, sir, but he might be a distraction. If Henning is going to conduct any psychic investigations, he'll insist on diving with us. That means some basic training for another neophyte—no offense, Doctor Gillespie—and one inexperienced civilian down there is enough. As I see it, sir, we're in for some difficult and potentially dangerous work."

"Objection noted, Steve. But there's no way I'm going to withdraw my invitation. Let's just hope Doctor Henning's expertise won't be required, in which case there's no harm done. If anyone else has something on his mind, get it over with now."

"Admiral," Montague asked, "how many divers do you plan on using?"

Gillespie observed, with some amusement, that Derek's propensity for first-name informality was never extended to Cornell; whether from respect or because Roger Cornell could intimidate Satan himself, he could not tell.

Cornell replied, "Three divers in addition to Steve, Ozzie, and Fay here. Six in all. The *Nemo* has a four-man crew—two pilots, a communications officer, and a fourth man assigned to the divers' compartment. That's the area I told you about, where the divers leave or reenter the *Nemo*."

Gillespie said, "I've got a question. When do we sail?"

"July ninth. Make your plans accordingly, and Bill, I'd appreciate it if you'd notify Doctor Henning of that date."

"I'll call him tonight."

"Then this meeting's adjourned. Thanks for coming, and navy personnel are dismissed, except for Captain Bixenman. Bix, I'd like to go over the cover story we'll use when we file our movement reports . . ."

That night, William Gillespie and Derek Montague were having a quiet drink in a secluded corner of the Westin's cocktail lounge, the subject under discussion being the session in Cornell's office.

"What did you think of the Navy people?" Gillespie asked.

"Good chaps . . . very efficient, obviously, and like Admiral Cornell himself, delightfully informal. I . . . I was rather stunned when I saw Lieutenant Carlson. For a moment, I thought I was looking at Debra Chaney."

Gillespie studied him. "Stop dwelling in the past, Derek. The present is too interesting, and the future too promising."

Montague took a sip of his iceless scotch and water. "Unfortunately, at my age, the future looks only too brief."

"Nonsense. I hope I can reach your age and look as healthy. I'll bet we could talk you into making one of the dives."

Montague laughed without mirth. "Not likely." He added grimly, "Bill, I never want to see that damn ship again. Nothing in my entire life has ever affected me so. The sight of her, coming at you without warning out of utter darkness, as though you had accidently stumbled on something that was never meant to be seen. The unbelievable destruction of her beauty and grace, like seeing for the first time the rotting corpse of someone you once loved. Worst of all, you see her with the terrible awareness of what happened on a night in April, so many years ago. Awareness of the people who died because she and the men who built her and the men who sailed her betrayed them."

He stared into his half-empty glass. "You know something, Bill? She's haunted even if she's not haunted. Do you know what I mean?"

"I think so. Or maybe the *Titanic* is haunted for some and not for others. Not everyone who's seen her came away feeling as you do."

"True. Only the looters and grave robbers, like myself, have sensed a kind of evil inhabiting that wreck. Perhaps a reflection of our own greed, of which I am as guilty as the others, past and present."

Gillespie signaled to a waitress for refills, welcoming the simple task as relief from his companion's black mood. He wished he could dismiss it as maudlin gloom fueled by alcohol, but scotch had no more effect on Montague than wine has on a Frenchman. No, Gillespie was getting a glimpse of the man's tortured soul.

"Derek, I honestly believe this expedition is different. No personal gain is involved, not even for you. The Navy literally hired you as a consultant, the same status given Ben Henning and myself. Your share is more in the nature of a fee, compensation for your knowledge of the *Titanic* and what she carried. You're not receiving any ill-gotten gains. I understand how you feel, but we have to balance sentiment against reality. That gold is going to accomplish a lot of good."

"If I accept that argument," Montague said, "it would stand to reason that no evil will befall this endeavor. We won't be regarded as invaders because our motives are technically pure." He chuckled, again without humor. "Jolly good try, Bill."

Gillespie said thoughtfully, "You could be wrong, of course—I mean about the supernatural business. Even Hen-

ning seems more curious than a true believer, and he's the
expert on the subject. I'd have to put myself and Cornell in
the agnostic category, too—which is more than you can say
for people like Commander Jackman."

"A veritable doubting Thomas," Montague agreed. "Ah,
here comes the lass with our drinks. I think I shall toast Commander Jackman."

"Because doubting Thomases make the most dedicated con-
verts?"

Montague said very seriously, "No. Because I hope he's right
and that I'm just a silly old fool."

The recipient of that toast was having a late drink of his own
with Lieutenant Commander Mitchell in the Army–Navy
Club. They had dined there earlier with two officers not con-
nected with the *Titanic* mission, so only after their dinner
companions had left could Jackman bring up the subject that
he really wanted to discuss with Mitchell. He was gazing into
his brandy snifter like a fortune-teller. "Level with me, Oz.
Was I out of line arguing with the old man about that shrink?"

Mitchell grinned. "No, because Cornell's a rarity among
admirals. I've never known a flag officer quite like him. He's
willing to listen to subordinates. He'll weigh their opinions,
even take their advice. He sure as hell speaks his own mind,
so he wants us to speak ours. That's all you did today."

"He listens," Jackman commented dryly. "But it's a cold day
in July when he agrees with you."

"That's not always true. Remember the goof-up sailor on
the *Binghamton*—that Kieling kid? Cornell wanted to court-
martial him and the exec talked him out of it. All Kieling drew
was loss of three liberties."

"Cornell's tough but fair," Jackman conceded. "His idol was
Bull Halsey. But I've had people tell me he's actually more
like Chester Nimitz. Which may be true. Can you imagine
Halsey allowing a ghost hunter on a Navy mission? No, not
just allowing him, Cornell actually invited this guy!"

"He's just stroking the researcher contingent," Mitchell said,
"so they won't think too much about what the deep-dive suits
are really designed for, like cable cutting and underwater sabo-

tage. Besides, you know as well as I do, the Navy listens to Bill Gillespie. Cornell trusts him. Roger Cornell doesn't trust many civilians."

"Apparently he trusts our on-board spiritualist, Mr. Montague, too. Don't get me wrong, Ozzie, I like the old guy. But he gives me the willies. I can't help wondering why the Navy's spending four million bucks on the word of an old man who believes the *Titanic* is haunted. Operation after this one, we'll be going after the *Flying Dutchman*."

"To paraphrase Tennyson," Mitchell said cheerfully, "ours not to reason why, so into the valley of death go we gallant six divers."

He expected the commander to laugh, but Jackman only smiled faintly.

"Ozzie," he said softly, "in spite of all the cracks I've made about Montague and Henning, I've got a funny feeling about what we *are* going into. I just hope I'm wrong."

14

The most surprising development aboard U.S.S. *Chase*, as she churned her way toward the *Titanic's* grave, was the popularity of Dr. J. Benjamin Henning.

Few of the ship's personnel were aware of his role as a parapsychologist. Everyone knew the mission's purpose—to recover gold bullion and explore the *Titanic's* interior—but only officers and the three enlisted men directly associated with the diving operations were told of Derek Montague's full background and the events that had led to Henning's presence. On the *Chase*, Montague was known generally as "the guy who found her first," and Henning was thought to be aboard as part of a shipboard habitability research project.

"The Navy's a collection of men, ships, and scuttlebutt," Captain Bixenman told the admiral. "The men will have Henning tagged before we even reach the wreck site."

"They won't hear it from any officer," Cornell said. "And I've already talked to the enlisteds assigned to *Nemo's* dives. I figured they had a right to know about Henning, and I told them to keep their mouths shut. They got the message."

Bixenman looked at him curiously. "Admiral, it sounds as if you're expecting trouble."

"Bix, I never know what to expect, but I'm taking no chances. If word gets out that we've got a ghost hunter aboard, and then something, well, does happen out of the ordinary, we'll have a ship's company ready to panic."

"That kind of panic on a seasoned ship?" Bixenman scoffed. "Not likely."

"Don't kid yourself. Most people are afraid of the supernatural, and that includes sailors. They're superstitious to begin with. It's best we wait, without preconditioning the men to expect something. In which case, they'd start seeing ghosts on their mess trays."

At first, the crew regarded Henning with suspicion, based on a common belief that most psychiatrists were nuttier than their patients. Many held the opinion that medical students who couldn't hack it as real doctors chose psychiatry as the only way to a medical degree. But Henning's friendly personality gradually undid these prejudices. Jovial, informal, and blessed with dry humor, he became known as "Doc" and even won the respect of the ship's chief medical officer, a wiry, tart-tongued surgeon named Cyrus McDonald. A captain by rank, an unbeliever by conviction, and a cynic by experience, McDonald had the snippish features of an unhappy Pomeranian, although—fortunately for the crew—he was mostly bark and very little bite. He actually was too senior to be on a ship the size of *Chase* and had served almost entirely on carriers, but Admiral Cornell had requested him for this assignment.

"Roger, I know why you picked me," McDonald had groused. "It's because I'm the only officer in the whole god-damned Navy who's shorter than you are."

"Not true," Cornell protested in what was a partial lie. "I happen to think you're the best ship's doctor in the Navy, and frankly, Mac, I don't really know what we're going to run into. These dives may involve considerable risk; they'll be inside a ship that's been disintegrating since she hit bottom. Besides, this Henning I told you about isn't a real doctor. I know he's officially an M.D., but I wouldn't want a shrink dispensing anything stronger than two aspirin and a glass of water."

With that kind of billing, McDonald could have been prejudiced against Henning for the duration had it not been for inquiries he had made into the psychiatrist's background. He learned that Henning had a brilliant record in UCLA's medical school and could have specialized in any field he desired, from neurosurgery to opthalmology, but chose psychiatry simply because he was fascinated by its very inadequacies. Henning, virtually every source had told McDonald, was insatiably curious, and this quality attracted him to the most mysterious, unpredictable, and least understood component of human life: the mind.

Two days out of Norfolk, a yeoman reported to sick bay complaining of severe abdominal pains. More as a courtesy than anything else, McDonald asked Henning to join him in examining the young seaman. When they finished, McDonald said offhandedly, "I'd be interested in your diagnosis, Doctor."

"Very tender around the affected area, with a fever as well. A white-cell count would nail our culprit—an extremely sick appendix."

McDonald knew any competent medical student could have arrived at the same diagnosis, yet he still couldn't help but be impressed by the professional manner in which Henning had examined the patient. He asked the psychiatrist, half on impulse and half out of sheer curiosity, to assist him in the surgery, and was even more impressed.

"The guy could have been a surgeon," McDonald told Cornell later. "Don't underestimate him, Roger. Just because he's in the Twilight Zone of the medical profession doesn't mean he isn't a fine doctor. I've had a few talks with him. He doesn't wear blinders when it comes to his field. He thinks there are too many quacks and phonies practicing psychiatry."

The admiral grumbled, "Yeah, but I'm still a little suspicious of anyone who's supposed to be a man of science and then spends half his time chasing spirits."

Yet even the admiral found himself admitting that Henning was one of the most likable, engaging men he had met. At officers' mess, he regaled them with stories of the psychic-phenomena cases he had exposed as frauds, or flights of fancy. One night, when Bixenman was on the bridge because they were nearing the *Titanic*'s position, Henning told his fascinated listeners how an airline hired him to investigate reports that one of its planes was haunted by the ghost of a pilot killed in a previous crash.

"The so-called haunted aircraft supposedly was carrying parts salvaged from the crashed airplane," he related. "That in itself turned out to be totally false. And when I interviewed flight attendants who claimed to have seen the pilot's ghost, I discovered that no one had actually seen anything; they all said they had heard about the sighting from some other flight attendant or pilot. Every bit of it consisted of second-and third-hand stories that had spread throughout the airline."

Gillespie asked, "Did you ever find out how the rumors got started?"

"I did. The dead pilot's name was Frank Clark. A couple of weeks after he was killed, another crew had two of their plane's three engines quit and they had to make an emergency landing on only one engine. The captain happened to be at a cocktail party that night, and someone asked him about the landing— how the plane handled and was he scared. The captain just laughed. 'For a couple of minutes,' he said, 'I thought I had old Frank Clark in the cockpit telling me how to land the son of a bitch.' And from that remark came all the ghost stories. I flew on the suspect airplane five or six times; the only thing haunted on it must have been the coffee maker. I never tasted such lousy Java in my life."

Henning was enjoying himself. It was the kind of audience he liked—pragmatic, hard-to-convince naval officers who had been eating up his debunking tales with the relish of men who were hearing exactly what they wanted to hear.

He shifted gears.

"On the other hand, there are instances that are not so readily dismissed. Houses that appear to be actually haunted, and they aren't the stereotyped deserted mansions of our boyhood fears. The broken shutters, cobweb-covered walls, creaking old floors, and the wind whistling through broken windows like the moans of a lost soul—no, forget that image. Haunted houses in America, and there are a surprising number of them, are usually old but very much inhabited. I give you, for example, a certain house right in the heart of New York City's Greenwich Village.

"It's a small building once owned by the famous, or infamous, Aaron Burr. Originally, it was a stable, but eventually it became the locale of a neighborhood bar. Longtime residents in the area had claimed for years the place was haunted. One night, the bartender and a customer heard strange noises coming from an adjoining corridor. They looked and saw nothing, but felt a blast of icy air. A few nights later, the bartender was going up the stairs to the owner's second-floor office. At the top of the stairs was a figure dressed in eighteenth-century clothes, presumably Mr. Burr himself. The bartender insisted later that the ghost picked up a broom and hit him over the head—a twist that considerably diluted the validity of his story."

Several officers laughed, but Henning wagged his finger at them.

"The fact that the bartender added the unlikely embellishment of a ghost using physical force doesn't negate the possibility that it was haunted. I use the past tense, because when the ownership of the tavern changed hands, the ghostly occurrences stopped. I cited this incident to emphasize that even perfectly sane and sober persons who may have actually seen ghosts tend to exaggerate the event somewhat. Oh, they saw something, but in their fright, they added details of actions and movements that they only imagined.

"Haunted houses—I could take the rest of the night listing them. The Westover Mansion in Virginia, said to be haunted by the ghost of a young woman who died of a broken heart in the seventeen hundreds. She has been seen wandering around the gardens of that estate. The Allen House in Monticello, Arkansas, haunted by the ghost of a girl who committed suicide there. The Octagon House in Washington, only two blocks from the White House, has acquired quite a reputation for being haunted. Before it became an architectural museum, there were all sorts of strange happenings reported by the home's occupants. For that matter, the White House itself is supposed to be haunted by the ghost of Abraham Lincoln . . . and don't laugh"—somebody had snickered—"a reputable parapsychologist I know in the nation's capital told me his grandfather, a prominent businessman, once slept in a second-floor bedroom of the Executive Mansion. He awoke in the middle of the night and saw a tall, bearded figure standing in the doorway. Startled, he spoke to him, but the man shook his head and vanished."

"Holy cow," someone murmured.

Henning shrugged. "Of course, the businessman may have been dreaming the whole thing. That's only too common. Nightmares can be so real that a dream crosses over the threshold of reality. It often is difficult to separate one from the other. Parapsychology is incapable of telling the difference, and no wonder. The cases we investigate always end up with one of two verdicts: no or maybe. Never a flat, definite, unequivocal yes. How, for example, would you judge this one?

"A snapshot was taken of a car in a funeral procession. The driver was alone. But when the picture was developed, there was a woman riding in the backseat. The same woman who was being buried that day."

"A faked photograph," Gillespie suggested.

"Apparently not. A member of the deceased's family took the picture and went into a state of shock when they saw the results. Considerable effort was made to prove it was a hoax, but every expert consulted swore the negative hadn't been tampered with."

Lieutenant Carlson, her expressive green eyes alight with interest, said, "I've heard or read somewhere that it's impossible to photograph a so-called ghost, that they don't register on film."

"That's not entirely true," Henning replied. "Some investigators have taken pictures of plainly visible apparitions and wound up with nothing. Legitimate ghost photographs are virtually nonexistent. Yet other people have photographed apparently normal, prosaic scenes and objects, but when the films were developed, they were looking at the faces of perfect strangers or even of long-dead relatives. I strongly suspect that in many such cases, someone was guilty of a mischievous trick photograph, as Bill Gillespie just suggested. But not in every instance, not when photography experts testified to the contrary."

It began to dawn on all officers, including Cornell, that Henning was a serious, tough-to-fool investigator. The admiral couldn't resist asking a question that was on the minds of all in the wardroom.

"Ben, did you personally ever run into a real haunting—a one hundred percent actual ghost? One you saw yourself?"

Henning nodded, his face suddenly pensive. "Mind you, I've gotten fairly cynical about ghost stories, especially the ones that wind up as best-sellers. Some clown wrote a book about that airline case I just mentioned; wrote it with an absolutely straight face, as if the whole story was absolutely factual. He sold the movie rights and made a fortune out of something that was nothing but a major-league latrine rumor. In parapsychology, though, it pays to be suspicious . . . even cynical. It helps you be more objective when you encounter something that defies explanation."

He smiled in the direction of Gillespie and Montague. "I've already shared some of my less explainable cases with my two fellow civilians. For example, there was an old mansion in the Beverly Hills area. Back in the mid-twenties, it was owned by a wealthy dilettante who had inherited all his money and didn't do much of anything else except commit murder, the victims all young women he had lured to the mansion on some pretense. When the police finally caught up to him, they found the dismembered bodies of at least thirty girls buried in the backyard and cellar.

"Because of all the publicity, the greatest real estate salesman in the world couldn't have given that mansion away. It stayed unoccupied for years until people forgot what had happened there. A bank took it over, renovated the place, and eventually it was sold to a movie producer. He came home one night and found his wife in hysterics; she claimed she had seen the ghosts of two young women. Everyone, including the producer, thought she was either using drugs or had gone bonkers, until the husband saw the same apparitions. I knew the guy casually, and he asked me to investigate.

"I was prepared to stay a week under the roof, but I was there only four nights. The first night, nothing happened. The second night, the producer and his wife had gone to bed and I was in the kitchen getting a glass of water. The door to the cellar was in the kitchen. My back was to the door and I felt a cold draft, as if someone had opened a window. I turned around. There was a young woman standing in front of the closed door, looking as solid as the kitchen table itself. I remember what she wore—a high-necked white blouse and a very short skirt, strictly out of the twenties. Her face was, well, sad.

"For a minute, I thought she must be a maid I hadn't met, or maybe the couple's daughter, except that I remembered they didn't have either. I said something like 'Who are you?' and all she did was shake her head, as if she was sorry I didn't recognize her. I started to say something else and she just . . . just disappeared.

"I said nothing to the producer, but on the third night, after they went to bed, I stayed in that kitchen for six hours. Zilch. I might as well have been waiting for the Headless Horseman. Nothing appeared there the fourth night, either, until around two in the morning. I was sitting in the breakfast alcove having my fifth cup of coffee, trying to stay awake. The alcove had a bay window, and for some reason I happened to glance up. There was a face staring at me through the window. The face of another young woman, different features but the same sad expression. It startled me so, I spilled the coffee and with my pants dripping, I opened the door leading to the back patio and looked outside. She was gone.

"The next day, I told the producer I had seen some funny things and maybe he'd better get a priest. He asked why and I told him that while I didn't quite believe in exorcism, it sure as hell wouldn't do any harm . . . either that or get rid of the damned house. Which he did, with alacrity. The next owners, I'm told, had similar experiences and moved out. The bank decided to raze the place and now there's a new English Tudor home that's been built on the lot. But that's not the end of the story. I knew a few cops in the Beverly Hills police department and one of them got me the file on the murders, including photographs of the victims before they were killed. I found what I was looking for: two familiar faces—that of the girl standing by the cellar door and the one whose face I saw outside the window."

His entranced, almost hypnotized audience was silent until Cornell spoke. "I take it you believe in the supernatural."

"Depends on your definition of the supernatural," Henning

said calmly. "If you're asking me if I believe in life after death, I couldn't give you an answer either way. The only definitive answer any of us can hope for will come when we die, and we find out for ourselves. But if you're asking me if I believe there is some kind of life form that exists after death, yes, I think that's possible under rare circumstances, such as the one I just described."

There was another moment of uneasy silence before Les Scofield, *Chase's* executive officer, asked, "Doc, is there a scientific explanation for what you saw?"

Henning described the theories of electrical energy and psychic ether. "I happen to have my own pet theory," he added, "although it's really too vague and undefined to be categorized as even a theory."

Cornell said, "I'd like to hear it."

"Well, this comes as much from my psychiatric training as it does from parapsychology studies. I think the primary source of psychic phenomena is the human mind, not the human body. I believe the will to live, the urge to survive, the stimulus to resist death—all this is strongest when the mind suddenly comprehends the inevitability of a death that is unwarranted, unjustified, or totally unexpected. Murder, for example. The certain knowledge that a plane is going to crash."

Henning paused, looked at Jackman, and smiled to himself. The commander's expression was a map of skepticism.

He continued. "There is a pattern to so-called ghostly manifestations, and that is the element of violent death. It's not an entirely consistent pattern, but it's frequent enough to be a common denominator. The vast majority of unexplained cases involve the apparitions of people who have suffered violent deaths."

Commander Jackman frowned uncomfortably. "Are you saying that the deceased mind is capable of producing these . . . these apparitions?"

"At the risk of oversimplifying a complex subject, yes, that's what I'm saying."

Jackman's forehead wrinkled. "How about the mind of someone who's committed suicide?"

"Such instances are not unknown. They may stem from a

person who has committed to taking his or her life, and then regrets it when it's too late. The stimulus here may be a tremendous sense of guilt at the last minute."

Lieutenant Commander Mitchell said, "But the mind supposedly dies with the body, Doctor. The Bible teaches us that the only surviving element in death is the human soul."

Henning nodded. "And the Bible may be right," he said quietly. "We may be dealing with a semantic matter here. All I'm saying is that *something* apparently is capable of surviving—maybe we should say transcending—what we assume is the finality of death. If the resistance to death—almost a resentment of death—is strong enough, this will, resistance, or whatever you want to call it can become a visual, physical manifestation. Actually *willed* by the mind with such intensity that it persists even after the mind has ceased to function as a living organism. You might say the triggering mechanism is a last-second, almost desperate refusal to accept death, particularly a traumatic death, one without reason or meaning."

Derek Montague murmured, "Such as the kind of death inflicted upon fifteen hundred souls on the *Titanic*."

Henning squinted at Montague uncertainly, surveyed the solemn countenances of the others, and wondered if he had gone too far. "You all remind me of kids who've been huddled around a camp fire listening to ghost stories. Look, I don't want anyone to assume that what I've said tonight is applicable to the *Titanic*. Legitimate encounters with the supernatural are extremely rare, and even the word *supernatural* is open to varying definitions. In the broadest sense, the supernatural is simply something we can't explain scientifically—*yet*. Personally, I'm convinced you're going to find the *Titanic* exactly what she is: a wreck in a very spooky environment that lends itself to distorted imagination."

A young seaman picked this moment to enter the mess and throw the admiral a crisp salute.

"Begging your pardon, sir, but Captain Bixenman sends his respects and would you please come to the bridge. We've reached the *Titanic*'s site and he says to tell you sonar's already picking up a large object below us."

Officers' mess emptied quickly amid a hubbub of excited

voices. Gillespie lagged behind, out of consideration for the aging Britisher whose steps were firm but slow. Montague hadn't risen from his chair yet, though; he was sitting at the mess table, hands folded in front of him on the table, his head bowed.

From the very start of this voyage, Montague never could stop comparing the *Chase* to the foundered *Henry Morgan*.

The only thing the two ships had in common was their naval origins, but even in this respect the ancient minelayer as he had known her never really reflected her military heritage. She was too fancy, too much—as Martin Lefferts had so often admitted—a personal and extremely expensive toy. Her white hull, the luxurious pastel-painted staterooms, and the plush dining room and cocktail lounge had always given Montague the impression of a dowager whose wrinkles were hidden skillfully under heavy makeup and at least three face-lifts.

The contrast with *Chase*, however, went far beyond the ship's cruiserlike hull and her unaesthetic battleship-gray coloring. *Chase* may have been a noncombat vessel, designed for research and salvage, but Captain Bixenman never let any officer or seaman forget he was aboard a ship of the United States Navy. *Chase* had a three-inch gun mounted forward of the bridge, and a wicked-looking Bofors twin-barreled antiaircraft unit located on a small platform between the bridge and the ship's single funnel. Montague suspected she could be converted into an electronic surveillance ship quickly.

Within five hours after departing Norfolk, Bixenman had ordered gun-crew drills, and this ritual had been followed daily all the way to the *Titanic*'s site. The first time he sounded general quarters, startling the three civilians aboard, Henning made the mistake of jokingly asking the captain, "Are you expecting the *Titanic* to attack us?"

Bixenman impaled him with a glare the captain normally would have reserved for a recruit who spilled bilge water on a freshly mopped deck. "Doctor," he said icily, "if this ship was a navy tug, I'd still insist on a state of combat readiness, and I'll thank you to keep such remarks to yourself."

Cornell was in listening range of the exchange, saw Henning

flush with embarrassment, and later made a point of talking to the psychiatrist alone.

"Ben," he began in a friendly tone, "I overheard Bixenman chewing you out. There's something you should know about him. He had an older brother on the *Pueblo*, the spy ship that surrendered to the North Koreans without firing a shot. That brother spent eleven months as a prisoner and Bix is a bit sensitive on the subject of readiness."

"I'll apologize to him," Henning offered.

"Not necessary. I already told him I'd talk to you."

However, Henning apologized anyway. "I was way out of line, Captain," he told Bixenman. "Admiral Cornell explained about your brother, and I'm sorry I made that remark."

The captain eyed him with a glint of new respect. "The incident is forgotten and your apology accepted. Am I correct in assuming you've never been on *any* ship before, let alone a Navy ship?"

"Nothing bigger than a rowboat," Henning confessed. "Despite my remarkable seafaring ancestry."

Bixenman showed his surprise. "You come from a family of sailors?"

"Bad sailors," Henning said with a straight face. "My great-great-grandfather was a lookout on the *Titanic*, my grandfather was in charge of torpedo warnings on the *Lusitania*, and my father handled radar on the *Andrea Doria*."

It took Bixenman a few seconds to realize his leg was being pulled, and then he burst out laughing.

Montague was one of the first to notice that the captain and the psychiatrist were becoming unlikely friends, but given Henning's personality, it didn't surprise him. In fact, he welcomed the relationship as one of the few light spots in the *Chase*'s businesslike atmosphere. That was another difference between this vessel and the informal, frequently sloppy *Henry Morgan*. The *Chase* breathed efficiency, from her captain down to the greenest seaman. John Hawke had told him once that few navies kept their ships as spotless as the Americans, and he could believe it after seeing the way Bixenman ran the *Chase*.

True, the daily loudspeaker blare of "Sweepers, man your

brooms!" was grating to the civilians, but Montague, for one, found this environment curiously reassuring. He began to feel that Cornell, Bixenman, and all the others knew what they were doing. Yet he also wondered if all this brisk competency had given him a false sense of security. There was no wasted motion in the oil-smooth lifeboat drills, the fast manning of gun stations, the crisp commands and instantaneous responses by bridge personnel. He listened to the effortless humming of the ship's modern turbines and wistfully remembered the *Henry Morgan*'s tired, wheezing engines. And yet . . .

He could laugh wryly to himself when he admitted there was one thing about the *Henry Morgan* he missed: Charles LeBaron's culinary skills. The nostalgia of such remembrances also carried a bittersweet taste, though. Thinking about people like LeBaron and the others on that old ship hurt, for Derek Montague never felt he could become really close to his companions on the *Chase*.

It was not that he was the only Englishman; if anything, the American tendency toward informality eradicated that barrier. Bill Gillespie was especially warm, Henning was more than cordial, and in his own barnacled way, Admiral Cornell treated him with a respect that bordered on affection. Still, Montague couldn't help feeling like an outsider, a man trapped in an unhappy past that refused to go away.

His age was a handicap, he suspected. Everyone on the *Chase* seemed so young, especially the sailors, and he even envied Cornell himself, who was only a year away from retirement. The admiral, perhaps sensing the loneliness behind his natural if courteous reserve, had made every effort to make him feel like a full-fledged partner in this endeavor. So, as a matter of fact, had Jackman and Mitchell. The two chief divers were constantly consulting him on the *Titanic*'s construction, the details of her interior, even the historical lore of that maiden voyage, which fascinated these younger men.

Montague relished the occasion when he got into an argument over Gillespie's insistence that the British inquiry into the sinking had been a whitewash and less objective than the U.S. Senate hearings conducted by Michigan Senator William Alden Smith—the same maritime neophyte who both had amused and outraged the British press by asking surviving *Titanic* officer Harold Lowe, "Do you know what an iceberg is composed of?"

"Ice, I suppose, sir," Lowe had replied—an answer to a question that Montague declared clearly demonstrated Smith's "utter incompetence." Gillespie had argued that the question was logical, inasmuch as another *Titanic* officer—Boxhall—had answered the same question by pointing out that icebergs also contained sand, gravel, and rocks.

"It was still an asinine question," Montague had persisted. "Your Senator Smith's ignorance was abysmal. I recall he even asked one witness if the *Titanic* went down by the bow or the head. Really, Bill . . ."

"Ignorant of matters concerning ships and the sea," Gillespie had said. "But far more thorough than the British inquiry's Lord Mersey, who always seemed ready to vindicate Captain Smith, White Star, and the British Board of Trade. . . ."

The others loved to hear the two experts argue, as well as hear them agree on many points—including the irresponsible actions, or lack of actions, taken by Captain Lord of the *Californian* and his ignoring of the distress rockets. No one enjoyed the exchanges more than Montague, however; such moments made him feel not only welcome but important and needed. They didn't erase his painful memories, but at least they let him forget them momentarily. His chief problem involved an occasional reminder instigated, however innocently, by someone else.

Mitchell once remarked in jest, "You know so much about that ship, Derek, I think you should make one of the dives with us and pay her another visit."

Montague smiled. "I'm too damned old, Ozzie," he said quietly. The very suggestion made him shiver inwardly; he had absolutely no desire to see the *Titanic* again, not even if he were twenty or thirty years younger. Not even though he was vastly impressed with the Navy's technology and an atmosphere of confidence that surrounded him.

He marveled at *Nemo.* She looked more like a wingless airliner fuselage than a submarine, especially the nose section. The upper third consisted of cockpit-type windows providing not only forward vision but side views as well, almost as if the nose of a DC-10 had been grafted onto a submarine hull. There was no conning tower; the hull's cylindrical shape was broken only by an oblong bulge in the top of the midsection—that, Montague learned, marked the location of the diving compartment.

Nemo was painted a bright orange, and this brought back memories, too. Montague remembered Captain Robertson's disdainful description of the yellow-colored *Winston* and *Franklin*: "They look like a couple of bananas," he had snorted. He wondered what Jerry would have thought of *Nemo* with her powerful all-titanium construction. Poor Robertson had never trusted Hawke's two subs, despite all of John's proud assurances. He would have trusted *Nemo* though, with her look of absolute indestructibility. Montague was sure of that. This in itself, he supposed, was a foolish assumption. That's what they had called the *Titanic:* indestructible; unsinkable. He asked himself whether the differences between *Chase* and *Henry Morgan* were more than cosmetic; whether there were any real, deep-seated differences between the two expeditions. And—the most disturbing thought of all—did the Navy's technology and professionalism represent foolproof protection against the unknown?

His mind wandered back twenty years. Caitin's voice . . .

"*Holy shit!*"

His own voice.

"*Holy shit, indeed, my friend. Go wake up Hawke and the captain, fast . . . I think we've found the bloody* Titanic."

A memory of the past that suddenly became the present . . .

". . . *we've reached the* Titanic's *site and he says to tell you sonar's already picking up a large object below us.*"

And once again, a chill of prescience enveloped his body, as if he were being caressed by something cold.

Ben Henning retired to his stateroom after the initial excitement died down, feeling out of things because he couldn't share the general elation. He wanted badly to make at least one dive, but his request for training had been turned down, mostly because of Jackman.

Henning remembered Bill Gillespie's first training experience in one of the new diving suits, which were called AMOS—for auxiliary mobile oceanography suit. Gillespie had been introduced to AMOS on their first day out, Jackman conducting the session with Cornell and Henning looking on.

"They weren't designed for the human body." The oceanographer panted as he struggled his way into the cumbersome outfit. "My God, I feel like the kid in the Michelin tire trademark." Even with the movement of the suit's limbs assisted by servomotors, it was ponderous out of the water.

"Getting into a suit of medieval armor would be easier," Jackman agreed. "Now, extend your arms about three-quarters of the way, until your fingers touch two knobs inside the sleeves. Find them?"

"Not yet."

"Your arms are only half-flexed. Stretch a little more."

"Got 'em!" Gillespie announced triumphantly. "But what the hell do I do with them?"

"If you turn each knob to the right, the claws open. Turn it left and they'll close, like clenched fists. Try it."

Gillespie complied and watched the claws respond obediently. "What happens if I push or pull on this gizmo?"

"Pull toward you and the claws rise. Push forward and they'll go down. Compare it to the up-and-down flexibility of your wrist; that's all there is to it."

"Sounds easy," Henning volunteered, drawing a get-lost glare from Jackman. The commander took a pen from the vest pocket of his shirt and held it in the palm of his hand. "Okay," he told Gillespie, "pick up the pen, but for Christ's sake, don't take my hand with it."

Gillespie managed to lift the pen but promptly dropped it. Instinctively, he tried to bend down to retrieve it from the deck and then realized AMOS wasn't flexible in the midsection.

"Comes with practice," Jackman said encouragingly, retrieving the pen himself. "You'll soon get the hang of it."

Henning protested, "So could I, Commander, if you'll give me a chance."

Jackman glanced at Cornell, who had been watching Gillespie's contortions with amusement. It was a look that hovered between defiance and imploring. The admiral decided vacillation was the best course.

"Ben, why don't we wait and see what develops down there? As Steve's already pointed out, one rookie diver's enough for the time being."

Henning hadn't raised the issue again. So on this night of rediscovery, he resigned himself to the possibility that he might not get to make any dive and settled down to his favorite form of relaxation—reading a murder mystery. An unexpected knock on the door came just as he decided that the killer had to be the airline captain's wife.

"It's not locked, come in."

He did a double take. The squat figure of Commander Jackman filled the doorway, his very size imparting belligerency. But the somewhat gravelly voice was friendly enough.

"Hope I'm not disturbing you, Doctor."

Henning eyed him suspiciously. "Not at all. Just reading." He motioned Jackman toward the only chair in the tiny cabin, and the burly officer just managed to squeeze into it. "What's on your mind, Commander?"

Jackman's eyes narrowed. "I want you to level with me. No parapsychology bullshit, no psychiatric mumbo jumbo!"

Henning smiled sardonically. "You're starting off on a 'have you stopped beating your wife' level. I agree fifty percent of psychiatry is mumbo jumbo, and there's also a lot of crap in parapsychology, but I submit I'm more qualified to separate the truth from the bullshit than you are. What's this about?"

"That story you told tonight . . . about seeing the ghosts of those two murder victims. I want to know if you embellished it to scare a few gullibles."

"Why would you think I'd have to embellish it? What would be my motive?"

"Maybe to condition us. Prepare us for what we might find two and a half miles below this ship."

"I don't have the slightest idea of what you'll find down there. But by the same token, I'm not going to be surprised at anything you *do* find. To answer your question, no, I didn't embellish that story. It happened the way I told it. Are you worried about something?"

Jackman looked at him, momentarily off balance. "That's a damned foolish question, Doctor."

"Is it? Commander, I'm not a mind reader, but I can read faces, and I hear a lot in voice inflections. You have something to tell me, something that made you come to my cabin. Do you want to say what it is? Or do I have to lie awake the rest of the night wondering?"

Jackman lowered his head. Whether it was embarrassment or a natural gesture of recollection, Henning could not tell. When he finally looked up, his eyes were a kaleidoscope of emotions.

"It's something that happened years ago. I was an ensign, not too long out of the Academy. My first ship was a destroyer, the *Donald Smith*, and one of my best buddies was a classmate assigned to the same can. Sensitive guy, not your usual naval officer. Read poetry and philosophy, stuff like that. Well, he committed suicide one night; left no note, and nobody ever figured out why. Two nights after he was buried at sea, I had come off the morning four-to-eight watch and was walking toward my stateroom when I saw someone standing in front of the door, facing it as if he had just knocked. I didn't recognize him, so I called, 'You looking for me?'

"He turned toward me and I stopped dead in my tracks. Stopped, hell, I froze. So help me God, it was my dead shipmate. He—or it—didn't say anything; just stared at me. You remember telling us how sad those two girls looked?"

Jackman paused, and now his eyes showed pain. "I started walking toward him and he . . . just disappeared. I thought I was dreaming. I told myself I *had* to be dreaming. I must have lain awake the rest of the night, wondering what I had seen. The next morning I decided it *was* all a dream. Sunlight has a way of letting you forget nightmares."

Henning stroked his chin. "So that's why you asked me that question about suicide. Did you ever mention the incident to anyone?"

Jackman smiled a little grimly. "Hell, no. I figured a boot ensign who sees ghosts in the Navy is looking at a section-eight discharge. But I'll tell you something, Doctor. To this day, I've always wondered if I was the only one to see what I did.

Over the years, I've run across several guys who had served on that can, but I never had the guts to ask them. She was decommissioned shortly after I transferred to SEAL school. I never did hear whether she was scrapped, but to tell you the truth, I hope so."

"Why?" Henning asked bluntly.

"So maybe my friend's soul will have found some peace. That's one theory you didn't discuss tonight, isn't it? That ghosts are lost souls, looking for everlasting rest that for some reason didn't come with death?"

Henning shook his head. "When it comes to psychic phenomena, Commander, one theory's as good as the next. We can report occurrences but only God himself can explain them. Tell me, why did you decide to unload on me tonight?"

Jackman rubbed his forehead. "Impulse, I guess. That story you told . . . it brought back a memory I've tried to forget. Pragmatists need explanations; I figured you might give me one. I guess I've always been afraid nobody'd ever believe me."

"I believe you."

Jackman stared at him for a long moment. "Yeah, so you do. Doc, you sleepy?"

Henning said, puzzled, "No. Why?"

"Let's go topside and I'll give you a workout on AMOS."

15

From the log of the U.S.S. *Chase*, dated 15 July 1995 . . .

. . . by agreement between Admiral Cornell and Dr. Gillespie of WHOI, it has been decided that the first dive to the site of R.M.S. *Titanic* will be exploratory, for the purpose of (1) determining the best entry point or points for AMOS personnel and (2) if entry points prove feasible and safe, to penetrate accessible areas of the ship's interior and photograph same.

For the record, crew complement of the exploratory submersible *Nemo* will consist of the following personnel:

Pilot: Lt. Jeff Lawrence

Copilot: Lt. (jg) Todd Ellison

Communications officer: Ensign Jennifer Anders

AMOS coordinator: Chief Petty Officer Joseph Kresky

Also herewith logged are personnel assigned to AMOS operations:

Cmdr. Stephen Jackman

Lt. Cmdr. Oscar Mitchell

Lt. Fay Carlson

Lt. (jg) Felix Williams

CPO Bertram Tuttle

PO Robert Nader

With concurrence of Adm. Cornell and Cmdr.

Jackman, Dr. Gillespie will accompany divers Carlson, Mitchell, and Tuttle on the initial exploratory probe, which is under the overall command of Cmdr. Jackman. *Nemo* launch has been scheduled for 0715 tomorrow.

> —Capt. Charles Bixenman, commanding
> U.S.S. *Chase*

Derek Montague was grateful for Admiral Cornell's suggestion that he sit in on the predive briefing.

"Between you and Bill Gillespie," Cornell had pointed out, "you can give the diving team some guidelines on possible entry points. I know the Grand Staircase is the most obvious area, and it's probably the best place for starting the interior exploration. But there may be others, hopefully closer to the forward cargo holds, that we can use when we start the gold-recovery phase."

The briefing was held in the officers' wardroom with all six divers present, plus *Nemo*'s crew, Bixenman, Gillespie, and Henning. Except for Jackman and Mitchell, Montague hadn't seen much of the divers or the personnel assigned to the submarine; they had formed something of a clique aboard *Chase*, necessitated by the nature of their specialized duties. It made no difference that this group's work was ahead of them; Jackman had kept them busy with AMOS drills, equipment inspections, and a daily check on *Nemo*'s complex systems.

They were an impressive lot, Montague had concluded—intelligent, enthusiastic, and superbly trained. Number four diver was Lieutenant (jg) Felix Williams, a stocky, pleasant-faced mustang officer who had won a commission largely as a reward for helping to develop AMOS. He was old for his rank, but Montague knew Cornell's respect for him was unlimited. The fifth diver was chief petty officer Bert Tuttle; in his mid-forties, he had the downcast jowls of a basset hound, but his appearance belied his good-natured personality. The youngest diver was Bob Nader, a dark-complexioned and slender petty officer with slanted eyebrows that gave him a satanic look.

He was—Montague had learned from Ozzie Mitchell—Steve Jackman's personal rehabilitation project.

"A chronic troublemaker heading for a dishonorable discharge until Steve took an interest in him and shaped him up," Mitchell had confided. "Jackman's the one who got him into SEAL school."

Nemo's commissioned personnel was surprisingly youthful. The ranking officer was Lieutenant Jeff Lawrence, laconic and tall, with a shock of blond hair tossed over one side of his forehead. Copilot and second in command Todd Ellison was a six-foot-five telephone pole who looked as if he were two years away from his first shave. The sub's communications officer, Ensign Jennifer Anders, called him "Beans" (abbreviated from Beanpole). Anders herself was a short, attractive woman from Nebraska, with tawny hair and a corn-fed appearance that included the rosiest complexion Montague had ever seen. All three, he had learned, were Annapolis graduates.

Nemo's only enlisted man was Joe Kresky, the chief petty officer who served as the diving coordinator. Burly and totally bald except for a pair of incongruous sideburns, Kresky was aboard *Chase* at Jackman's request. They had worked together on diving assignments for years. He even called Jackman by his first name, which surprised Montague.

"There seems to be an unusual lack of rank distinction among the diving people," he had mentioned to Mitchell.

"There is," Mitchell agreed. "And you'd find the same thing in our submarine service. There's a sort of informality where rank doesn't count as much as ability. I think it's true of your British submariners, too. Any kind of underwater work, where one man's mistake can endanger everyone, it's like that."

True enough, Montague mused as he watched their faces and took in the excited, almost infectious chatter. He admired the way Cornell ran the meeting, more with an air of patriarchal pride than that of a lordly flag officer.

The session lasted more than two hours, most of the time spent studying photographs taken on previous *Titanic* expeditions. There were schematic drawings of the ship's interior, too, created on a CAD computer and blown up to an enormous, easy-to-read size that made Montague wish he'd had such a simple visual aid before the *Henry Morgan* sailed. He remembered Chaney bending over the antique steel-pen drawings with her magnifying glass, passing it around so the others could get a better look.

The mess was darkened while Gillespie showed film footage from the two Ballard expeditions, and the later French and Soviet–Canadian expeditions. The movies were Cornell's suggestion: "to give you people an idea of what it's going to be like down there." Montague had to resist the temptation to close his eyes. It was like reliving his own dive—seeing the ghostly, scarred shape in the dark depths.

They were looking at the French footage when Jackman called out, "Stop the projector a second, Bill."

On the screen was the mysterious hole in the starboard side of the hull that Montague and Hawke had discovered on their first dive, years before the French photographed it.

"It's about thirty feet wide," Jackman said, peering hard at the image. "We might be able to get divers in that way."

Cornell said dubiously, "I dunno, Steve. Look how the hole's framed by jagged metal. Might damage an AMOS. Too risky."

"It still looks wide enough to avoid those edges, Admiral. Derek, you saw that hole up fairly close. Think we could enter there?"

Montague shook his head. "Wide enough, Steve, but futile. It's adjacent to an area we've always taken to be filled with the heavy machinery projected forward when she sank bow first and almost at a perpendicular angle."

Mitchell said, "The hand lasers could cut through almost any obstruction. That's what they're for."

"Not *any* obstruction," Jackman corrected. "We'd need *Nemo's* lasers to break through heavy stuff like piled-up engines and boilers. I guess Derek's right. Even if we tried entering there, it would take too much time to clear a path. Okay, Bill, start up again . . ."

Later, when the projector had been turned off, the mess lights turned on, and the decision made for the divers to use the Grand Staircase entry point, Montague posed something he was almost reluctant to voice.

"Before we break up," he said diffidently, "I was wondering if I could ask a favor of you *Nemo* people. I . . . was hoping you might keep your eyes open for. . . for the *Henry Morgan*. She must have gone down close to the *Titanic*."

Jackman said "Sure thing. I'll be in the diving compartment, but Lawrence and Ellison will be watching for her."

The two sub pilots nodded, Lawrence adding, "I'll let you know if we find anything, Mr. Montague."

"Thank you. I should like to be able to say a prayer for my old friends."

Montague didn't hear what Jackman whispered to Mitchell as they were filing out, but Gillespie did.

"Ozzie, I almost hope we don't spot the old tub. If there's one thing Montague doesn't need, it's another reminder of the past."

William Gillespie was no stranger to deep-sea exploration, but he had never gone exploring in anything as sophisticated as *Nemo*.

For the early part of the descent, he sat behind Lieutenants Lawrence and Ellison, listening to the banter that bespoke their crisp professionalism. Years ago, thanks to an airline captain he knew, he had been privileged to sit in the cockpit of a Boeing 747 on a flight to London; he was experiencing the same atmosphere now, a reassuring blend of camaraderie and proficiency.

For that matter, *Nemo*'s cockpit would have done justice to a 747's flight deck. A bewildering array of dials, lights, buttons, and levers confronted him; he recognized only the most obvious ones, such as the depth meter, whose needle was moving at a faster rate than he expected. He remembered it took Ballard's sub, *Alvin*, two and a half hours to reach the *Titanic*. According to Montague, Hawke's two subs—whose main motors were more powerful than *Alvin*'s—had covered the same distance in about ninety minutes.

"How long will the descent take?" he asked Lawrence.

"Descent angle's thirty degrees, Doctor Gillespie. So, from launch to sea bottom should take about forty minutes tops. You comfortable?"

"Surprisingly so. When Ballard found the *Titanic*, he needed two extra sweaters and a toque around his head to keep warm."

"What's a toque?" Lieutenant Ellison inquired.

"A close-fitting cap. Ballard used a toque that his son wore playing hockey. I guess his sub wasn't very well insulated."

Lawrence said proudly, "*Nemo* is. Look at that cabin temp—seventy-two degrees. It'll stay at seventy-two even when we reach bottom."

Ensign Jennifer Anders looked up from her communications panel. "Seventy-two's too warm, Jeff. Personally, I'd like it in the mid-sixties."

Ellison laughed. "Jenny's an outdoor girl who never should have joined the Navy. She'd rather be riding a horse than a submarine."

"Horses," Anders said, "are more reliable than submarines."

Gillespie said, "I do a little riding myself, Jennifer. Strictly amateur, though; when I get on a horse, John Wayne turns over in his grave."

"Jenny's no amateur," Ellison said. "Got enough horse-show ribbons to cover this instrument panel. Which reminds me . . . advise *Chase* we're at eight thousand, angle of descent thirty degrees, and all systems normal."

"Roger," Anders acknowledged smartly, and turned back to her panel.

"Start making depth reports every five hundred feet when we hit nine thousand, Jenny," Lawrence ordered. "And Doc, I think you'd better go back to the diving compartment and start getting into your AMOS."

Gillespie thanked the cockpit crew and went aft to the diving compartment. He found his heart was pounding, not so much in anticipation of the dive itself but at the prospect of seeing what so few human beings had ever been privileged to view: the remains of what was once the world's greatest ship, that symbol of Edwardian grandeur and complacency. This expedition, he knew, probably would be the last.

The mood in the divers' compartment was the same as that in the forward control room—a lot of joshing mixed with businesslike preexploratory preparations. Joe Kresky was fussing over the divers like a mother dressing her children for school. The analogy was appropriate, for AMOS required manipulation of an ingenious but complex series of locking rings that no diver could open or close by himself, once his arms were inside the suit. Kresky looked up as Gillespie squeezed his tall frame through the diving room's narrow door. "That number five suit's for you, Doc. Nader, help Doctor Gillespie."

Jackman, Mitchell, and Carlson were already in their suits, lacking only the Plexiglas and fiber-composite helmets that would be put on at the last minute. Spread out on a metal table in the center of the divers' compartment were most of the photographs studied thoroughly the night before; Jackman had brought them aboard Nemo for last-minute perusal and they were reexamining them now, Lieutenant Williams sifting through the various shots so the AMOS-clad others could see.

Jackman called out, "Bill, if you're finished come over here; we're still trying to figure out if there's another way to get inside, other than that staircase well."

Gillespie, with considerable effort, waddled over to the table. He was wearing weighted boots, and despite the relative lightness of AMOS, moved like Boris Karloff playing the Frankenstein monster. Williams held up a mosaic of photographs taken from a height of 25 feet directly above the ship, depicting the entire 470 feet of the forward section; the mosaic itself represented some one hundred individual photographs. Gillespie was proud of the fact that a Woods Hole technician had put the jigsaw puzzle together, a task that had taken months.

He scanned the mosaic for what must have been at least the fiftieth time and shook his head. "The staircase is still the only logical entry point."

"Look again," Mitchell said in his soft voice. "Just to the right of the number two funnel hole."

"I see it. The gymnasium roof, partially collapsed. Just twisted metal, Ozzie."

"The roof's not what interests me. Felix, find me that shot of the gymnasium itself." Williams fumbled through the stack of photographs on the table and finally produced the one Mitchell wanted.

"That's it," Mitchell said. "Notice the hole in the deck a

few feet away from the gym? It's directly above the first-class promenade on A deck, a hole plenty large enough for us to enter. Once we get onto the promenade, there's no telling what other entry points we might find."

Gillespie nodded slowly. "Possibly, although I still think the stairwell's our best bet. Ballard's little robot camera penetrated all the way down to B deck and actually got its lights on C deck. But I'd be satisfied just with exploring A deck, even though it's fairly limited. If the damned ship hadn't broken in two, B deck would be a photographic bonanza. The Café Parisian and first-class smoking lounge were all on B deck, but they were aft of where the break occurred. Still, Ozzie, you might have something. There were some swanky staterooms off that promenade. If we can get into one or two—"

His sentence was cut off by the hollow, metallic noise of *Nemo's* intercom.

"Attention divers and *Chase*! We're at sea bottom and we've got some wreckage dead ahead . . . but it's not the *Titanic.*"

"The *Henry Morgan*, or what's left of her," Gillespie guessed, and Jackman nodded.

"How could sonar have missed it?" Gillespie asked. "Or the previous expeditions?"

"Easy. Our descent trajectory was aimed at sighting sea bottom about five hundred yards ahead of the *Titanic*, a sizable distance from the main wreck, the debris field, and the stern where they explored. They had no reason to suspect there was any other wreck in the vicinity. As for our sonar missing it, I'd guess the array just missed something that small and broken-up. Whatever that wreckage is, we've stumbled on it by chance."

There was a fair-sized porthole on each side of the diving compartment and as Gillespie tried to decide which one to use, Anders supplied the answer.

"Divers, that wreck's coming up on our starboard. Appears to be the bow section of a small vessel. Take a look as we come abeam."

Gillespie was the first to reach the porthole, the others clustering in back of him. *Nemo* had come to a dead stop, her lights bathing a sight of horror.

"That's her," Gillespie muttered. "My God."

They had heard from Montague how a strange storm had destroyed the *Henry Morgan*, and as they viewed her remains, they could almost hear his voice describing the waterspout that had finished the old minelayer off.

The forward section was more a lump of tangled wreckage than a recognizable part of a ship. The bridge had fallen through the crushed deck into what was left of the hull, its wheelhouse protruding from a mass of twisted steel and tilted at a crazy angle. There was no sign of the stern.

Gillespie said in a stricken voice, "I suppose we should let Montague know we found her."

"Yeah." Jackman had seen a lot of wrecked ships, but this one he seemed to be looking at through Montague's eyes instead of his own. "Jeff, pass the word to Mr. Montague, but don't bother with the details."

"I already have, Steve. He didn't ask how she looked. He just thanked me. We've got the bow movie camera taking pictures of that mess, not that he'll want to see them."

Gillespie murmured, "I guess Derek must have said his prayer by now. Would one of our own be out of order?"

"A silent prayer would be very much in order," Jackman said. In unison, they bowed their heads in a silence that ended when Gillespie wondered aloud, "Do you suppose there's anything left of the sub that imploded?"

Jackman shook his head. "Not much, at this depth. I saw pictures of *Thresher* once and—"

Mitchell, who was still examining the wreck, broke in. "Hey, take a look at that wheelhouse, up forward. Is that a body in there?"

Jackman peered. "I don't see anything. Bill?"

Gillespie looked, too, straining his eyes in the direction of the wheelhouse. There seemed to be some kind of a shadow inside, hazy and shapeless at first glance. For a heart-stopping second, it seemed to be adding arms and legs, but at that point, his eyes began watering. He blinked to clear them and then found he was staring at a very familiar object.

He blurted, "It's the ship's wheel. Take a look, Steve."

The commander did. "Damned if it isn't," he announced. "Ozzie, you'd better get your eyes checked."

Mitchell snorted, "How come *you* didn't see it the first time?"

"Because all the windows in that wheelhouse are gone. The bottom current's probably swirling debris around, so you never see the same object twice—or you miss things completely."

Gillespie accepted the explanation, yet couldn't prevent a queasiness from settling in the pit of his stomach. He could have sworn that shadow was trying to . . .

But *Nemo* began moving away from what was left of the *Henry Morgan,* and his qualms dissolved a few minutes later with another squawk from the sub's intercom.

"Now hear this." It was Lieutenant Lawrence's voice. "We have the *Titanic* in sight. Divers on the ready."

"Let's get the helmets on," Jackman ordered. "Joe, do Doctor Gillespie first. Nader, you take Lieutenant Mitchell and then Lieutenant Carlson. Kresky will put mine on last and then we'll do a voice-com check. Joe, shift Gillespie's mike a little closer to his mouth. Remember, Bill, we'll be in voice contact only with *Nemo*. The sub will be our communications link to *Chase*."

Kresky adjusted the tiny microphone attached to the upper chest of the suit and linked to a battery buried somewhere in the lower torso. On the back of each AMOS was the battery pack that pumped the breathing medium into the helmet; it began flowing automatically when the helmet was secured.

Lawrence came on the intercom again. "Take a look out the starboard porthole. There she is!"

Those in the diving compartment halted their procedures to stare outside. *Nemo* was gliding past the *Titanic*'s vast bulk, the starboard lights picking out a line of portholes. No one spoke.

Gillespie was thinking, *Now I know how Ballard felt when he first saw this ship . . . the reverence he bestowed on her . . . the pride of finding her, combined with a surge of unexpected compassion for the ship and her victims . . . the mixed blessing of achieving his lifelong dream and reliving the nightmare of that terrible night . . .*

Lieutenant Ellison, his deep voice unfettered even by the intercom, advised them that Lawrence was maneuvering *Nemo* to a position directly above the Grand Staircase entry, as planned. "Let us know when you're ready to release divers."

"Roger." Kresky made a mark on his clipboard checklist and looked up. "Okay, Bob, let's secure those helmets."

During training, Gillespie had found the helmet even more confining than the suit, almost claustrophobic. Once locked in place, it could not swivel. Although it was roomy enough inside for a diver to turn his head, peripheral vision was limited. When Nader secured the helmet with an air wrench, Gillespie resigned himself to staring almost straight ahead for the next two hours.

His heart really was pounding now. He was startled by Jackman's voice, sounding tinny, echoing inside his helmet—almost like the voice of that movie cartoon character, Alvin the Chipmunk. "All set, Bill?"

"Everything's fine . . . I hope."

"Okay. When Lawrence finishes positioning, you follow me to the hatch. Carlson, are you receiving me?"

"Yes, sir."

"You go after Gillespie, then Ozzie and Tuttle. Got the camera?"

"Secured to my belt, Commander."

"Let's hope we find things to photograph. Jeff, are you receiving me?"

"Loud and clear," Lawrence responded.

"Then ready when you are."

"Stand by . . . mark! We're right over your entry point. Divers away!"

"Roger. Keep your strobes on us until after we descend down that stairwell."

"Will do, Steve. And good luck."

"All right, let's go." Jackman moved toward the small ladder that led to the upper compartment, its hatch already open. He skillfully mounted the ladder using one of AMOS's arm claws, while the other held the laser cutter, a wicked-looking affair made of a lightweight alloy, painted black, and resembling a cross between a submachine gun and a futuristic jackhammer.

Gillespie tried to imitate Jackman's effortless climb up the ladder and failed miserably, even though he wasn't burdened with a laser. Kresky shoved at his backside and he finally heaved his way into the compartment.

"Jesus, you have to be an octopus to climb that ladder!" He panted, conscious that his own voice inside the helmet sounded like one of the Chipmunks.

"Comes with practice," Jackman said. When Carlson, Mitchell, and Tuttle climbed up—far more dexterously than he, Gillespie noted sadly—the exit/entry chamber was wall-to-wall with divers standing shoulder to shoulder; five divers were all the compartment would hold at any one time. He had been carefully briefed on the ejection operation, Jackman explaining that the entire compartment actually was an escape hatch. When sea valves were opened, it would be flooded and the divers would leave via another hatch mounted on *Nemo's* upper hull. The latter was not really a hatch but a large horizontal sliding door, wide enough for two divers to exit or enter at the same time, side by side.

"A simple, safe, and virtually foolproof operation," Jackman had told him. "The seawater admitted to the compartment gives you enough buoyancy to float toward the sliding hatch. The reentering procedure works in reverse; we come back into the flooded area, wait for the water to be emptied through counter valves, and then return to the diving room via the first hatch."

The advertised simplicity of the process wasn't allaying Gillespie's nervousness now. He held his breath as Jackman issued a two-word order to Kresky:

"Flood up!"

The sea-admission valves opened noiselessly, but the sound of the incoming water was only too audible, like the dull roar of surf. Gillespie could not feel the water himself, but he could see it rising around Jackman, starting as a small puddle at the commander's boots and climbing with surprising rapidity until it reached Jackman's shoulders. Then it swept over his own helmet and Jackman's figure became momentarily blurred in his Plexiglas.

"Open sliding hatch," Jackman ordered.

"Sliding hatch open," Kresky responded nine seconds later. "Divers are cleared—and have fun, you guys."

"Let's go," Jackman announced. "Bill, come with me."

Despite AMOS's weighted boots, Gillespie found that the thrusters made it relatively easy to move toward Jackman's side and then pull himself up toward the sliding hatch with the handholds on the chamber's bulkhead. The suit's "shoes" were weighted and web-shaped, like those used by skindivers, though not as long. In seconds, the oceanographer found himself outside *Nemo*, looking down on the submarine.

"Divers are clear," Jackman advised, and *Nemo* promptly moved a few feet beyond the entry hole, turning its entire length against the strong current that had plagued the previous, smaller submersibles. The carefully timed maneuver had been planned to prevent the divers from being swept away as they descended toward the crumpled boat deck. They were shoved several feet away from their landing target in the brief time it took Lawrence to position the sub, but with its big hull forming a barrier against the current, they quickly worked their way back to the deck.

All five stood on the rim of the jagged hole above the stairwell, illuminated now not only by *Nemo*'s unblinking plasma lamps but by their own small, powerful lights attached to each AMOS helmet—like a coal miner's. The unit had been activated automatically with the first touch of water on a sensor, and the divers—the first human beings to actually stand on the *Titanic*'s deck in eighty-three years—stared around in awe.

The utter devastation of the scene, the havoc wrought by that two-and-a-half mile plunge to the bottom, was Gillespie's most vivid impression: steel flattened as if a giant fist had smashed down on the superstructure; twisted deck railings, covered with shroudlike rust. Ahead of them, looking toward the bow and outlined by the sub's big lamps, was a single lifeboat davit—a forlorn silhouette symbolizing the futility of that night—only sixteen lifeboats on a doomed ship carrying more than two thousand souls.

"I think that's the davit that launched Collapsible D," Gillespie said in a hushed tone. "It was the last boat to leave the *Titanic*."

"God, what a mess," Mitchell noted sadly. "Some of the rust looks three inches thick."

Jackman said into his mike, "Remember what Bill warned us. Try not to touch anything, if there's anything left to touch. Visibility will be tough enough without stirring up debris. We'll go down to A deck first, in the order in which we left *Nemo*. Then we'll try to reach B deck, and if our luck holds, maybe C deck. Let's go."

"Phasers on stun," Mitchell joked and Carlson giggled nervously.

"Knock it off," Jackman snapped. He stepped into the dark abyss and the others followed.

Gillespie continued to be surprised that he could move about so easily, albeit with frustrating slowness. At first, they saw only what previous tethered cameras had already photographed: the rusticles suspended from the ceiling of the Grand Staircase foyer, looking for all the world like stalactites hanging from the roof of an underground cave; a still-intact chandelier, the bulbless socket of the light fixture plainly visible.

"It looks like it's made of gold," Carlson marveled.

Gillespie said, "Not gold—brass. Brass doesn't oxidize like iron. Everything on this ship that's made of brass looks almost as new as the day she was launched."

The ornate Grand Staircase had rested against a wall that separated the first-class entrance lobby from first-class forward staterooms on A deck, but only the wall had survived. The staircase itself had disappeared, its magnificent woodwork long ago devoured by sea microorganisms, but Gillespie spotted the small pedestal that had been at the foot of the staircase. It had once held a cherub with a lamp. There was no sign of the happy little figure now.

Like others before him, the oceanographer had nursed the hope that some of the *Titanic*'s luxurious furnishings might have been miraculously preserved. Just this initial glimpse told him the great liner was a crumbling, empty shell in its upper areas and, he feared, a dense junk pile in the lower decks. He knew he should not have expected anything else. He had the melancholy feeling that he had entered a long-deserted mansion stripped of everything except memories.

Jackman's voice was muffled, though clear. "Bill, move over

to the right of where the staircase was. There's a passageway. Everyone stay together. I want to see what's down there."

They moved cautiously down what the commander had charitably designated a passageway, occasionally employing the small thrusters for momentum. It was more like a tortuous path through a cavern among jagged rocks, for the corridor walls bulged with distorted metal. The damage was not too extensive in the first few yards as they progressed, and Jackman stopped in front of an open stateroom whose door apparently had been ripped from its hinges, or perhaps had merely dissolved.

He peeked inside, then motioned the others to follow. Gillespie, right behind him, almost gasped at the very emptiness of what had been the last word in ocean-travel luxury: no sign of beds, blankets, nightstands, dressing tables, or anything else except the light fixtures on the ceiling and on the wall over where the beds must have rested. Jackman poked his strobe into a closet, half-expecting to see clothes still hanging there.

"Nothing left," he said laconically. "Not even the hangers."

"They must have been wood hangers," Gillespie said. "What's that in the back of the closet? Those little bright objects that seem to be in some kind of a web?"

Jackman's arm claws, with amazing dexterity, plucked at the material until it came loose from the back of the closet wall, and held it under the light of Gillespie's strobe.

"It appears to be some kind of fabric," Gillespie said.

"What are the shiny things?"

Lieutenant Carlson had joined them. "Beads," she said. "Or, to be more exact, sequins. You're holding what remains of a woman's evening gown." She paused with a sudden thought. "The lady who owned it might have gone to dinner in that dress the night the *Titanic* sank."

Tuttle called out, "Hey, look what I found!"

His claws were holding up a small rectangular object, which Mitchell was examining.

"It's a brass plate," Mitchell said.

"Turn it over," Gillespie suggested.

"A Twenty-seven," Mitchell read. "This was stateroom A Twenty-seven. Wonder who was in it?"

"Someone very rich," Jackman said. "Bill, any idea who was assigned to A Twenty-seven?"

"Not a clue. Most of the wealthy passengers were on C deck, people like the Astors and Mr. and Mrs. Straus. Benjamin Guggenheim and his valet were assigned to B deck. If we can get down there, we'll look for B Eighty-two–Eighty-four and B Eighty-six."

Mitchell said admiringly, "What kind of homework did you do—memorize the entire passenger manifest?"

"No, just the numbers of certain cabins, in case we got any access to them. Ghoulish curiosity, I guess."

Carlson had been taking pictures of the light fixtures and a close-up of the cabin number. "For a first-class stateroom," she said, "this place seems awfully small."

Gillespie explained, "Small by today's standards, but large by 1912 standards. Actually, the fanciest accommodations were on B deck, a three-room suite with its own private promenade. Numbers B Fifty-one, Fifty-three, and Fifty-five, if I remember correctly. Which reminds me, I wonder if we could get into A Thirty-six."

"Why A Thirty-six?" Jackman asked.

"That was the stateroom occupied by Thomas Andrews, the *Titanic's* chief designer. His cabin was a last-minute modification and wasn't even shown on any deck plans, including the ones we have. White Star told passenger agents not to book anyone in that stateroom on the maiden voyage because it was reserved for Andrews."

"A Thirty-six should be around here somewhere," Mitchell said.

Gillespie was trying to remember what he had read about that particular cabin. "No," he said, "we're on the starboard side. A Thirty-six was portside, closer to the Grand Staircase than we are right now. Andrews chose A Thirty-six because it was centrally located and gave him easy access to the stairs and corridors of the lower decks. There were a series of staircases directly under the Grand Staircase where we entered, but I assume there's nothing left of them either."

"We might try moving up this corridor a little farther," Mitchell proposed, "then go portside."

They did try, but could proceed only a few feet beyond A27; from that point on, the corridor ceiling and walls had collapsed completely and all that faced them was tangled metal.

"We might as well go back," Jackman said, "unless, Bill, you want me to use the lasers and clear some kind of path."

"No, we'll just try the other side."

It was heavy going. Every step seemed to dislodge particles of debris and rust, giving them the impression they were trudging through a snowstorm. But to Gillespie's joy, they found A36 approximately where he surmised it was. There was little left to inspect, however—just light fixtures similar to the ones they had seen in A27, plus a few pieces of crusted plumbing. There was no sign of the desk on which Andrews had studied the *Titanic*'s plans and blueprints—the ones he had placed in front of Edward J. Smith after the collision to explain to the captain that the ship was going to sink in approximately two hours because the bulkheads of the watertight compartments went no higher than E deck; as each successive compartment filled with water, the ship's prow dipped lower, and the water overflowed into the next compartment.

The emptiness of the ravaged stateroom could not stop Gillespie from visualizing what it must have been like. This was where Andrews came after his incessant prowling through every area of the great liner. This was where he had dressed for dinner promptly at 6:45 P.M., usually eating with the ship's aged surgeon, Doctor O'Laughlin. This was where he perused the voluminous entries in the notebook he carried with him on his inspection tours. As the managing director of Harland & Wolff, the *Titanic*'s builders, Andrews knew the vessel more intimately than anyone else aboard, including the redoubtable old "E.J." He had jotted down every complaint, suggestion, or observation he heard, from passengers and crew members alike, both trivial and major: Too many screws in stateroom hat racks. Malfunctioning galley equipment. Wrong coloring of the dashing on the private promenade decks—too dark. And the swanky writing room on A deck was too large and should be reduced in size to make room for two additional staterooms. . . .

Gillespie sighed. That Thomas Andrews must have been quite a man. At the last minute, he had given up his life jacket to a stewardess, who made it to one of the lifeboats; Andrews himself had made no effort to save himself, perhaps out of a sense of guilt rather than chivalry.

Suddenly, Gillespie hated this rotted cadaver of a cabin. It seemed oppressively gloomy, the ever-present debris floating around them like remnants of a disintegrated shroud. He felt stifled in the bulky helmet and wondered whether he was getting enough oxygen.

"Steve, let's get out of here," he said abruptly, hoping his voice didn't betray a touch of panic.

"Might as well. We'll head in the other direction. Carlson might get some good shots, if there's anything left to photograph."

Diver Tuttle was the last one out of A36. He turned for a final look at the stateroom and swallowed hard. He thought he saw movement under his light—more of a shadow, actually. A shimmering shadow, like smoke, trying to form a more distinct shape. Just debris, he decided, and followed the others out.

They were back in the Grand Staircase area, debating briefly whether to descend to B deck—as Gillespie was suggesting— or proceed aft toward the writing room that Andrews had wanted to convert to staterooms, between the staircase and the lounge.

Gillespie wanted to see the next level down. "We should at least try B deck."

"Nothing left there but more staterooms," Jackman insisted. "Probably in worse shape than the two we've seen. Besides, if we go any lower, we're asking for trouble. A deck seems reasonably safe, and Ozzie thinks we might be able to reach B deck from the outside, off that promenade deck. It's a safer route, Bill."

Gillespie knew their time was limited. "You're the boss. We'll head aft."

They headed nowhere, for at that moment, Lawrence's voice crackled in their helmets.

"Divers, *Chase*, we've got company!"

"Jesus, now what?" Jackman muttered. "Jeff, what's up?"

"The biggest goddamned fish I ever saw, or maybe a reptile of some kind. Looks like a gigantic eel with a head the size of a Mack truck. Holy cow, Todd, look at those teeth!" The divers heard him gasp. Then . . .

"Todd, arm lasers."

"Back to the boat deck," Jackman ordered. "Fast!"

They reached the boat deck, in time to see the enormous creature flash by *Nemo*, then reverse course swiftly and head back toward the submarine, which had turned to face it. *Nemo*'s own lights were illuminating it perfectly, and the divers stared in utter disbelief at its size. It was eel-like, as Lawrence had described, but the huge body had the girth of a subway tube and Gillespie spotted slimy scales along the writhing length. It was bearing down on the submersible, its ugly mouth wide open. Carlson was so startled, she forgot the camera hanging on her belt.

"Fire, Jeff!" Jackman cried. "Shoot now!"

Two soundless beams of blood-red light flashed toward the oncoming creature, impacting squarely on its head.

It didn't disintegrate.

It simply disappeared.

Nemo's lights were staring at . . . precisely nothing.

"Like a hologram," Gillespie muttered. "Like it wasn't real at all."

"Say again?" Tuttle asked in a shaken voice.

"It looked like a hologram, a three-dimensional image projected by laser light."

His companions hardly had time to digest that statement when Lawrence, sounding rather shaken himself, informed them *Chase* was ordering immediate diver recovery and *Nemo*'s return to the surface.

"If that was a hologram," Commander Jackman muttered, "there's someone else down here trying to scare us away."

Gillespie said enigmatically, "Someone—or something."

16

Admiral Cornell paced the bridge, impatience growing with every tap of his shoes on the linoleum flooring.

It was more than an hour after *Nemo*'s recovery. He had listened without comment to a distraught Lieutenant Lawrence describe the encounter with the strange creature and its equally strange disappearance.

"Was the movie camera on?" he had asked Lawrence.

"Yes, sir. Wide-angle, pointing right at that thing when it came at us."

"Then let's get the film developed so we can see what we're up against."

Bixenman watched him pace, a familiar sight to anyone who knew the admiral. The captain's respect and affection for Roger Cornell was unbounded, but if the man had a weakness, it was impatience—the same characteristic that had marked Cornell's idol, William "Bull" Halsey. The bridge phone finally jingled, answered by a quartermaster who turned to Cornell. "Admiral, it's Johnson in the photo lab. He says the film's ready and where do you want to show it?"

"Tell him to set it up in the wardroom. Then advise *Nemo*'s crew, all divers, Gillespie, and Montague to meet me there on the double." Cornell started to leave the bridge, then halted and snapped, "Add Doctor Henning to that list. Bix, give Scofield the con and come with me."

* * *

The whirring of the projector and an occasional cough were the only sounds heard in the tense, darkened officers' mess as the film neared the point at which *Nemo* had turned to face the onrushing creature. The previous footage was markedly similar to what they had seen from the other expeditions; Gillespie and Montague were quietly supplying a running commentary on the external views of the *Titanic*.

The screen went dark. "This is when it happened," Lawrence said in a hushed voice. "We had turned off the lights and the camera just as the thing went by us for the first time. When I maneuvered to face the direction in which it had gone, it came back toward us and I told Todd to reactivate the camera. I'm not sure I want to see what comes next."

The screen image returned.

They were looking at black water. Occasional swirls of bottom debris danced merrily around in the current, like leaves in a wind.

And that was all.

"Where the hell is it?" Cornell muttered.

The projector whirred on.

"We should have fired our lasers by now," Lawrence insisted. "I don't . . ."

The twin red beams of the lasers flashed on the screen, but they were lancing into nothing but a void. There was no target. There was nothing except darkness. The image remained for another two minutes, then went blank. Carlson, who was running the projector, announced, "That's the end of the film, Admiral."

Ellison exhaled. "That's when I turned off the camera—about two minutes after we fired. I don't get it. How could we see the lasers and not the target? We sure didn't imagine that thing."

Cornell rubbed his forehead, as if to coax out an explanation. "Son, nobody said you did. Somebody turn on the lights."

The overhead mess lights came on, their cheerfulness giving Gillespie the feeling that they had just emerged again from the bottom of the ocean. He glanced at Montague, wishing he could read the Englishman's mind. Except for asking what the *Henry Morgan* looked like, Derek had said little since *Nemo's* return.

He also wondered what Ben Henning was thinking. The psychiatrist had merely listened to the accounts of *Nemo's* crew and the divers, his face impassive except when Jackman mentioned holograms. Henning's eyebrows had lifted a notch at that. But he made no comment.

Gillespie was beginning to have second thoughts about the hologram explanation. For one thing, Montague seemed to know something, or fear something, that he wasn't talking about. His eyes always seemed to be staring not at the present but at something else. And what about the creatures seen twenty years ago? Gillespie didn't know very much about hologram technology, but he suspected it wasn't far enough advanced in 1975 to conjure up moving gigantic sharks and one-hundred-foot plesiosaurs at over two miles down.

"The problem I have with this hologram hoax business," the admiral was saying, "is that we'd also have to assume there's another expedition somewhere in the vicinity trying to scare us away. I find that hard to believe. Captain Bixenman assures me there's no surface target within distance of our radar sweeps. Sonar shows no trace of any submersible in the area. SOSUS has had no sub traffic in or out of this area for the past three weeks. Furthermore, this mission has been top secret from the word go. Only key officers were told in advance what we were going after; enlisted personnel weren't informed until after we sailed. I'm sure none of our three civilians have violated the promises they gave me not to discuss the mission with anyone, including wives."

He threw a quizzical, almost challenging smile in their direction.

Jackman spoke up. "Sir, if anything had been alive, the camera would have picked it up. And there should have been pieces of flesh remaining; not even the most powerful laser strike could cause total disintegration of something that huge. The beams impacted only the head, yet the whole thing disappeared."

"Like shutting off a light," Lawrence put in.

"Scofield told me it didn't show up on sonar, either," Bixenman noted.

"May I say something?"

All eyes turned to Ben Henning. Cornell said, "Psychic phenomena, Ben?"

"Quite to the contrary, Admiral. I was going to say, psychic phenomena don't come in one-hundred-foot sizes. But neither does holography."

Cornell said brusquely, "Steve, you'll take *two* teams down tomorrow. One into the forward cargo holds, and the other for further exploration and photographs of the interior. I'll let you make the assignments. I want some backup down there this time."

Jackman nodded. "I'll take Doc Henning, Felix, and Nader with me into the holds. Dr. Gillespie will go with Ozzie, Carlson, and Tuttle."

The wardroom emptied, except for the admiral and Bixenman; the captain would have left with the others, but he stayed behind when Cornell gave him an almost imperceptible head shake. He motioned Bixenman to sit down and drummed his stubby fingers on the table, his leathery face somber.

He said quietly, "I wish I knew what was happening. A giant eel that doesn't register on sonar capable of picking up a foot-long piece of tin twelve thousand feet below. We take its picture and the camera might as well have been out of film. Bix, I'm supposed to be advising CNO by op-immediate message of all developments, progress or otherwise. The decodes are going straight to the White House. What the hell kind of development would you call today's event?"

"Are you asking my advice, Admiral?"

"I'd *welcome* your advice."

"I wouldn't send CNO anything except routine progress reports. We don't know enough to tell Washington anything else that's meaningful."

Cornell nodded glumly. "I could do that. The trouble is . . ."

He stopped, fingers beating their tattoo again. Bixenman watched him curiously, waiting for him to finish.

"The trouble is," Cornell repeated, "what do we tell 'em if nonroutine things *keep* happening?"

Ozzie Mitchell led his team onto the battered boat deck, landing almost on the rim of the hole in the promenade roof next to the gymnasium. They could see *Nemo*, lights ablaze, repositioning herself above the bow for releasing Jackman's group over the forward hatches—a reassuring yet also discomforting sight, for it gave them the sense of being left alone on the unsafe front porch of an abandoned house.

They were facing the large, arched windows of the gymnasium, most of the glass gone and the frames coated with rusticles. The windows themselves were almost as tall as a man, but too narrow for anyone wearing AMOS to squeeze through.

Mitchell was peeking inside. "Hey, Carlson," he called out. "Get a shot here, you can still see the supporting pillars."

She sighted her camera through one of the windows. "That's all there is to shoot—just the pillars. No sign of any gym stuff."

She was right. Gillespie looked inside and remembered seeing pictures of how the gymnasium had once appeared, with its mechanical horse, newfangled weight-lifting set, stationary bicycles, and a rowing machine. No other ship afloat, except *Titanic*'s sister *Olympic*, had boasted such complete exercise facilities; the mechanical horse, in fact, had been featured in White Star advertisements as the last word in physical-fitness equipment. Most of the passengers had visited the gym merely to gape at its contents; few had actually used them, anymore than they had frequented the thirty-two foot long swimming pool on F deck—open to gentlemen only between 6 and 9 A.M., and to both sexes during the rest of the day, Gillespie recalled reading. It was too dangerous to descend as far down as F deck, he knew, but he speculated on what the swimming pool with its adjoining Turkish baths must be like now.

"Want to try the promenade next?" Mitchell asked.

"Let's go aft first. We're pretty close to where she broke in two. I'd like to see the damage."

They headed aft, moving very carefully and slowly. The strong current had suddenly abated. They reached the point of the structural breakup and peered over the edge. The wreckage sloped down like the side of a large hill, and their helmet lamps gave enough light for them to see torn tubing and wiring at the base. It gave them the gruesome impression that they were looking into a disemboweled beast.

"My God," Fay Carlson whispered.

"Take a picture and let's go back," Mitchell ordered. "It's too risky hanging over this edge. That current's unpredictable."

Gillespie commented, "Very unpredictable, and I don't understand it. Ballard found that it ran in regular three-day cycles—almost nonexistent for about seventy-two hours and then extremely strong for a day. But reliable."

Carlson got a shot and they began moving back toward the hole above the promenade. "Wonder how the other guys are doing with the cargo hatches," Tuttle commented. "Can't see anything except *Nemo*'s lights from this far away. Jesus, this was a big ship."

"And we're standing on less than two-thirds of it," Gillespie reminded him. "Ozzie, let's try that promenade now."

They dropped through the twisted aperture safely and peeked into the windows of several staterooms, disappointed at the results.

"Same mess as the cabins below," Mitchell observed. "Nothing left but light fixtures and a few traces of plumbing. Doesn't seem to be any entrance to B deck from here, either."

Gillespie felt depressed. They were still exploring nothing but a shell, and these close-up views weren't producing much more than what previous robot cameras had recorded. He knew now that any attempt to penetrate the *Titanic*'s lower decks involved big risk, with little chance of reward. He supposed they had no right to expect anything else in a ship exposed to more than eighty years of underwater decay, on top of the damage resulting from the sinking.

"Ozzie," he said, "let's go back to the boat deck and look around the bridge area. We might find the officers' quarters, maybe Captain Smith's cabin."

"Okay," Mitchell said, "but I thought we were planning to hit the Grand Staircase again and head down to B deck."

"We can do that last."

Lieutenant Carlson said, "There might be a way to enter as far down as D deck. I remember seeing an open gangway door on one of those photographs we studied."

"I remember it, too," Mitchell said, "but the consensus was that it's too narrow for AMOS. Besides, D deck was nothing but cabins, and I think we've seen enough of those."

They plodded back to the promenade roof hole and made their way back to the boat deck. The current seemed to be running strong again, and Mitchell had to ask *Nemo* for assistance.

"Can you position yourself just ahead of us, as close to the boat deck as possible; and run some interference for us? We need a screen against this current; it keeps fluctuating, and right now it's murder."

"Don't I know it, Ozzie. We just dropped Jackman's party with no current at all. It's like a Santa Ana wind that can't make up its mind. Hang on and we'll cover you."

They crouched as low as the bulky suits would permit until *Nemo* nosed her way just above them, hovering only a few feet above the deck. Then they resumed their laborious journey along the superstructure, aided by intermittent application of the thrusters, Mitchell finally pausing at a point about sixty feet from where the bridge had been.

"Far enough," he announced. "*Nemo* we're fine now and thanks."

"Roger. We'll move back and cover the other party. They're near the cargo hatches."

They watched the sub edge away and looked around. To their left was a small section of still-intact deck railing and the remnants of a boat davit, another mute, forlorn reminder of the *Titanic*'s fatal inadequacies.

"Davit for number eight lifeboat," Gillespie informed them. "The one Mrs. Ida Straus refused to board because her husband Isidor wasn't allowed to go with her. Second Officer Lightoller was in charge of the loading, and the women were pleading with him to let some men aboard so they'd have a few rowers. Lightoller at that point wasn't putting any male passengers in any boat, and Captain Smith backed him up. So it was finally lowered with less than forty people, and it could have held up to sixty. Still, that wasn't as bad as lifeboat one; it left with only twelve people."

Somehow, his words, delivered in the almost dispassionate recitation of a tour guide, had the opposite effect on the other divers. They stared at the davit transfixed, recreating mentally an eight-decades-old scene of general terror and individual bravery.

In their minds, they could hear voices. . . .

". . . *Please, Ida, get in the boat like the officer said.*"

"*No, I want to stay with you. . . .*"

Mitchell shook off the reverie and surveyed what lay on his right—an apparent cabin with two small windows and a rectangular doorway. "Bill, I'll bet this is the officers' quarters."

"Looks like it. The door's gone, but none of us can get through that doorway."

"Carlson might," Mitchell suggested. "Her AMOS is smaller. Want to try it, Fay?"

"If I get in, just make sure I can get out again." She attempted to squeeze in sideways, but her breathing tank was several inches too wide to get past the doorjamb and she had to give up.

Mitchell said, "I can open a wider hole with my laser."

"No," Gillespie objected. "The agreement was lasers only when necessary to clear away wreckage. Fay, do you see anything inside?"

The lieutenant was still standing next to the doorway, her helmet up against the rusted frame. "Some kind of metal object that might be what's left of a bunk. Two light fixtures, and damned if those don't look like eating utensils. I think I see a fork, there's a spoon, and—"

Carlson screamed.

She backed away from the doorway so fast that she almost knocked Gillespie down.

"A man," she gasped. "There's a man in there!"

The oceanographer shoved her to one side, moved to the doorway, and looked in.

There *was* a man standing in the center of the room—only

a silhouette at first, but becoming more distinct as Gillespie's eyes adjusted to what his helmet light was illuminating.

A man, very definitely. Wearing the bridge coat of the Royal Merchant Marine. A black officer's cap, with the White Star insignia. Under the peaked cap was a face—square-jawed, stern, very British.

Now it was Gillespie who gasped.

On the right temple was a tiny black hole, jagged around the edges as if a bullet had penetrated there.

It had.

Into the oceanographer's numbed mind came the realization that he was looking at William Murdoch, *Titanic*'s first officer.

Murdoch, who had been in charge of the bridge at 11:40 P.M., April 14, 1912.

Murdoch, who had given the fatal command—"Hard astarboard"—the command that turned the ship into the hidden ice spur that ripped out her guts in thirty seconds.

Murdoch, who, according to several eyewitnesses, had shot himself in the temple just before the giant liner sank. . . .

The figure was shaking its head.

It had been an emotional ride to the bottom for Ben Henning. He had never been in water deeper than a swimming pool, and he was almost unbearably nervous. To its crew, *Nemo* may have been the most spacious, comfortable research submersible ever built, but to Henning she was an invitation to claustrophobia—cramped, confining, and vaguely dangerous.

His nervousness began to retreat after the first twenty minutes of the uneventful descent. It was difficult to stay apprehensive in this atmosphere of cool professionalism. The navy people had a way of impressing ride-along civilians like himself. By the time they reached bottom, he was almost enjoying the trip—until he found himself waiting for the diving chamber to flood.

Trying manfully to keep shakiness out of his voice as the water closed over him, he asked Jackman, "Are we going to be able to communicate with Mitchell's bunch after we go out?"

"Negative. Each group will communicate with *Nemo*, but

not with each other; there'd be too much voice clutter. For a two-contingent dive, we use different frequencies, which Anders monitors separately. Ready to go?"

"As ready as I'll ever be."

"No sweat, Ben. Just stay close to me, and for Christ's sake, don't go wandering off. Any questions?"

"Just one. What's the procedure if I have to go to the bathroom?"

"Pray for a strong set of kidneys." Jackman laughed. "Okay, Felix, Nader . . . let's go."

They landed at the foot of the toppled foremast, which rested against the forward part of the superstructure, its partially severed tip lying where the bridge had been. It looked like a fallen tree. The crow's nest from where the lookouts had first sighted the iceberg was still attached to the mast, tilted at a crazy angle.

Jackman led them directly to the smaller of the two forward cargo hatches; Montague had determined this probably led directly down to hold three. They peered into the aperture, until the commander decided they were wasting their time.

"No good, " he announced. "It looks totally blocked by a mass of steel about ten feet down. Thick steel, too; looks like part of a bulkhead. We'd better go down the wider hatch as planned."

"Let's look around a little first," Williams said.

They surveyed the desolate scene. Jackman said, "This seems to be the least damaged area of the entire ship. Look at all this deck equipment—it's hardly touched."

Henning could see capstans, windlasses, winches, and cargo cranes, rusted but amazingly intact and preserved. Large sections of deck railing were plainly visible, somewhat bent yet still attached and recognizable. Looking ahead of them, toward the bow, they saw *Nemo's* lights focus on a triangular object mounted just behind the ship's prow.

"Anchor crane," Jackman said. "From here, it looks brand-new."

"It wasn't used very much," Felix Williams remarked. There was no sarcasm in his voice.

Henning was staring up at the devastated bridge area towering above them, weakly illuminated by his helmet lamp. He could not explain why, but it seemed to be drawing his attention forcibly. He could not take his eyes away, and Jackman noticed his concentration.

"See anything up there, Ben?"

"No, but the funny thing . . . the funny thing is that for some reason I *expect* to see something."

"Huh," Jackman grunted. "The only thing left up there is the telemotor that held the ship's wheel. *Nemo*, do you read me?"

The sub had just returned from screening Mitchell's divers.

"Loud and clear, Steve. Anything wrong?"

"Negative. Turn your strobes on the bridge."

"Roger."

Nemo obediently lifted her nose, bathing the shattered bridge in a white glare. They could see the telemotor, a small, thin brass instrument standing pitifully alone, like the only surviving stump in a fire-ravaged forest.

"That's all there is to see, Ben," Jackman said.

"Okay," Henning replied, breaking his fixation at the spot. He started to move toward his companions and then, impulsively, turned back for a last look.

His heart almost stopped.

"Steve, everyone . . . *there's something on the bridge!*"

Jackman said, before he really looked, "Probably Carlson, taking pictures. . . ."

He blinked his eyes and swallowed hard.

"What the hell?" Williams muttered.

"Jesus Christ," Nader said.

They were looking at the figure of a man, wearing a bridge coat—a stocky man with a white beard and an officer's cap.

"Captain Edward J. Smith, I presume," Henning said in an undertone.

As if the apparition had heard him, it nodded once.

Then it shook its head deploringly, raised one long arm, and pointed at them.

Jackman was the first to recover from the shock. "*Nemo*, are you seeing anything on that bridge?"

Todd Ellison's usually calm voice sounded strange. "Affirmative. Looks like a human figure . . . probably someone from Ozzie's party." The last was spoken in an almost hopeful tone.

"It's a figure, but it's not human," Jackman said. "Henning thinks it's Captain Smith. Or rather, his ghost. It's apparently warning us away."

Lawrence broke in. "Commander, what are your intentions?" He was being deliberately formal, returning them all to the U.S. Navy of 1995.

"We're going into a forward cargo hatch, the one closest to the bridge. It's larger than the other one."

"Roger. Should we advise Mitchell's people or *Chase* what happened?"

Jackman paused, wondering what the others might be encountering. They could be having their own troubles, he decided. "Negative, Jeff. We'll keep this one to ourselves for the time being. We may have been imagining things."

Nader croaked, "Commander, I didn't imagine it. This ship's haunted!"

Jackman ignored him. "Let's get on with it. Ben, are you gonna stare at the damned thing all day?"

"No, sir," Henning replied, unconsciously submitting even his language to naval authority. He took one more look at the apparition, still standing on the bridge and still shaking its head.

Then it vanished.

The four men moved to the selected hatch, three of them with laser guns poised. The hatch was open, its wooden doors long since dissolved. Jackman dropped into the black water, followed by Williams and a reluctant Nader. The psychiatrist glanced back at the bridge, still illuminated by *Nemo's* powerful lights.

With an inner shudder and a stab of fear all his training and experience could not prevent, Henning stepped into the dark void.

17

William Gillespie stepped back from the doorway in horror.

"What the hell's in there?" Mitchell asked.

"Go see for yourself."

The big diver looked—and looked again before turning around, puzzled. "I don't see anyone, or anything. Maybe your imagination . . ."

"Ozzie, Carlson saw the same thing I did. A man in an officer's uniform, one of the *Titanic*'s officers, I might add. You wouldn't believe which officer."

Tuttle said, "Lemme take a look, Doc." They moved aside for the older diver. "I don't see anything, either. Maybe it comes and goes. Like that friggin' current."

Mitchell said, "We're not doubting your word, Bill. Or yours, Fay. Not after what we all saw yesterday. I feel like I'm walking over graves."

"So do I," Gillespie said, his voice a little unsteady. "I've had enough of the boat deck. I suggest we make one last effort to reach B deck via the Grand Staircase. The current's abated again."

Lieutenant Carlson spoke up. "Ozzie, I'm sorry, but I don't think I want to go inside this ship again."

Mitchell temporarily averted a decision by addressing Gillespie. "Bill, did you actually recognize someone?"

"I've seen his face fifty times. His picture's in every book I've read on the *Titanic*. It was Murdoch, the first officer. He reportedly committed suicide as the ship went down . . . and I saw a bullet hole in his temple. Fay, did you spot that detail?"

"No, sir. I was too busy retreating."

Mitchell managed a weak chuckle and then tried to focus on his duty. "Seeing is believing, but we didn't come down here to retreat from something that evidently can't hurt us. Bert, you game for trying B deck?"

"Yes, sir."

Mitchell could sense Carlson pondering the alternative— being left to a lonely vigil on this gloom-shrouded deck, where even the most familiar objects such as the davit, capstans, and windlasses, seemed to be alive.

"I'm game," she finally said.

"Good. Current's still soft, so let's get it over with."

The fractious current stayed mild until they reached the Staircase hole, then struck with such force that it almost blew them into the entrance. They descended into the area they already had explored, and glanced around nervously. They saw nothing. Each of them sensed something, though.

Like we were being watched, Gillespie was thinking.

They dropped to what remained of B deck, once the most luxurious and liveliest level of the *Titanic*, and began exploring.

On *Nemo*, the two strange sightings had been heard only too clearly, leaving Jeff Lawrence with a difficult decision.

"I suppose we should let *Chase* know," he debated aloud, "but the admiral's liable to scrub the whole dive, and if that happens, Jackman will have my ass."

Ellison disagreed. "Cornell's the last one who'd abort a mission, Jeff. A guy who thinks Halsey deserved sainthood? Not in a million years."

"Bull Halsey never faced anything like this," Lawrence muttered. "Anyway, if I don't report it, I'll have him and Bixenman chewing my butt. Jennifer, raise *Chase* on the UQC. We'll let the topside brass fight it out."

Cornell listened to Anders's report with forced equanimity. "Well, is everyone all right?" he demanded.

Anders glanced at Lawrence, who motioned to go ahead. She keyed her transmit button.

"Affirmative at last reports, Admiral. Commander Jackman's group has gone down a forward cargo hatch, and Mitchell's people are on B deck."

Captain Bixenman said worriedly, "Admiral, I don't like what I'm hearing. Maybe we should get 'em back up."

"No," Cornell said. "Not yet. I don't hear anyone reporting there's any danger. Jesus, these are the best divers we've got. What the hell is going on with them down there?" He seemed to be arguing with himself, debating whether to order an abort, or to ignore information that couldn't be explained. Neither tactic sat well with an officer of Cornell's background, and the captain didn't envy him.

Loneliness of command, Bixenman thought. Worse for an admiral than a ship's captain, even. The agony of isolating the mind from emotion, sentiment, compassion—the very qualities that make us human. Not many men could do it well and take their humanity back when the crisis was over.

Cornell turned to the ship's radio operator.

"Tell *Nemo* to continue mission, but keep us posted."

"Aye, aye, sir."

The admiral walked over to the sonar screen and stared at it without really seeing anything.

"There's a cargo crane right below me," Jackman called out. "When that foremast went down, it must have knocked the crane right into the hatch."

"Is it blocking the way?" Williams wanted to know.

"Afraid so. I think it's time to use lasers." He aimed the futuristic-looking device, and a robot claw pressed the trigger. A noiseless blue beam stabbed through the inky water. Jackman held the trigger down for almost a minute. "Not making much of a dent. Felix, get alongside me and we'll fire simultaneously. Aim so your beam converges with mine, right at the center of that crane. Use full strength."

"Right."

"Ready? Fire!"

Now there were two powerful blue-colored beams slashing into the rusted metal, which held for a few seconds, then seemed to melt away. The crane broke in two at the spot where the beams had met and the two chunks fell out of sight.

"I'd hate to get hit by one of those things," the awed Henning remarked.

"That's why Gillespie and you aren't carrying one," Jackman told him. He tapped his mechanical hand against the breastplate of his AMOS. "These suits are vulnerable to a stray beam. Okay, everyone, let's descend, and be careful. It's about six stories down to the holds."

All they saw as they dropped down what amounted to a huge, deep-well were pieces of wreckage and a few glimpses of bent or broken bulkhead walls. The descent was so effortless that Jackman was uneasy.

"I figured a lot of the engine-room machinery might have been shoved this far forward when it broke loose," he remarked. "It apparently didn't get this far."

"We haven't reached the hold area yet," Williams reminded him. "The damage is probably worse the lower we go."

It was, but not to the extent anticipated. Debris chunks were larger and bulkhead distortions more pronounced, yet their descent was virtually unimpeded. Because there were few visual references to guide them, they had no exact idea of their vertical progress, and it came as a surprise when their heavy boots suddenly touched a firm surface. Their strobes picked out the vague outlines of a large room whose walls showed various degrees of damage. The aft bulkhead was the worst; it bulged out as if a locomotive had been trying to push its way in. Numerous smaller blisters were all around the larger one, and Jackman commented, "I'll bet there's a pile of machinery right behind there."

Williams warned, "We'd better stay alert, Steve. That bulkhead looks like it could collapse any second."

"Not if we don't disturb it. If it's held this long, it'll probably hold forever. What else do we have here?"

Henning said something that startled the others. "Is that gold?"

Their strobes followed where he was pointing, and for a moment, they thought they had stumbled on the *Titanic*'s hoard—until Jackman recognized what they were seeing.

"Bronze auto lamps," he said. "Look closer . . . it's an automobile, or what's left of it."

Henning said incredulously, "If I remember Montague's and Gillespie's briefing on what we might find down here, that has to be William Carter's Renault Town Car. Let's see what shape it's in."

Sorry shape, they discovered on closer inspection. The tires and wood-spoked wheels were gone, and the car was resting on its rusted axles. There was no sign of the original leather seats, either. The interior, including the steering wheel, had rotted or been eaten away, except for a few strands of what may have been rubber that were stirring around the vehicle.

Jackman whistled. "Too bad Carlson isn't with us. This, she'd love. Bob, take a few pictures of this car. Give your laser to the lieutenant first."

Nader handed the gun to Williams and began snapping pictures while the others inspected the hold.

"What else was supposed to be here?" Williams asked.

"Bales of rubber, mostly." Jackman said, recalling Montague's inventory of the holds. "They all seem to have disappeared, like the Renault's tires." His strobe picked out a small door on the forward bulkhead; unlike the aft bulkhead, this one looked almost undamaged except for minor dents. "That hatch leads to hold three and the bullion," he said. "It would be easier and a lot quicker to break in right here than go topside again and come down through the other cargo hatch."

"Steve, there's no way an AMOS will get through that door." Williams said, "even if we can force it open."

"Then we'll cut it out. Nader, you finished playing cameraman?"

"Yes, sir."

"Come over here. We'll use all three lasers. Aim a trace around the frame. We'll need a hole wide enough for us to squeeze through. Start at the lower right corner, about six inches away from the frame. Full power!"

Three blue bolts converged with the brilliance of an arc welder, slowly carving an arch-shaped incision around the rusted watertight door.

"The damned plates must be a foot thick," Williams said.

"Just seems that way," Jackman assured him. "It's starting to weaken; look at the crack toward the top."

The hatch gave away and twisted off to the right for a few seconds before settling on the hold floor.

But the large hole that confronted them was not empty. It was filled with a wild-eyed human figure, nude from the waist up, the terrified face blackened hideously.

Instinctively, they back-pedaled through the water, Nader so abruptly that he tripped over Henning's feet and went down on his back, looking up at the apparition in terror.

Without warning, a section of the violated bulkhead broke away and landed on top of the prone diver with explosive force. A jagged piece of metal smashed into the Plexiglas window of his helmet and six thousand pounds per square inch of water pressure instantly compressed Nader's face into an unrecognizable pulp.

There was no scream, only the shock wave from the brutal implosion of Nader's helmet, which they heard through their own helmets like a bottle shattering.

Williams gagged and his two stunned companions, hearing his retching, had to fight off their own nausea. They looked up from Nader's body, into the adjacent hold.

The apparition was still standing where the hatch had been, but it no longer looked terrified.

It was laughing at them. Soundlessly, but unmistakably.

Jackman could hardly get the words out into his mike. "*Nemo*, Mayday. Mayday. We have a casualty and we're coming up."

The apparition laughed again.

And retreated into the dark.

"Where the hell are we going?" Tuttle inquired.

He meant the question for Mitchell, but it was Gillespie who answered. "I'd like to head aft and see if we can't get into the first-class dining saloon. It was the largest room on the

Titanic." He could just barely see the lieutenant commander shaking his head inside the confining helmet.

"Wait a minute, Bill. She broke apart at a point just aft of the saloon. We've already seen firsthand what that area's like; every deck on the ship collapsed downward, creating a slanted roof. Remember when we looked over the edge? Nothing but a huge iron slope."

"Exactly," Gillespie said. "We were standing almost directly over the first-class saloon. And the slope you mentioned forms an artificial barrier against the sea, a kind of protective wall. That's why I think at least part of the dining room may be relatively intact, provided we can get there without too much difficulty. We can always turn back."

The optimism of the scientific mind, Mitchell was thinking—a kind of single-track bravery that left out the military's more cautious factor of calculated risk. He said nothing though, and they resumed their groping exploration. With Mitchell's concurrence, Gillespie decided to follow the starboard corridor that led from the Grand Staircase toward the severed rear of the ship.

It turned out to be a difficult passage; three times Mitchell and Tuttle had to use their lasers to clear away blocking wreckage. The guns were fired a fourth time when they encountered a corridor wall bulging out so far that they could not get by. In single file, on they plodded, occasionally halting in front of an inevitably ravaged stateroom and half-expecting to find something staring back at them.

In one cabin, they caught a glimpse of something other than the usual surviving light fixture—a brass headboard from a bed, gleaming like burnished gold under their strobes.

"Amazing how brass and bronze resist corrosion," Gillespie marveled. "Fay, we should get a shot of that." As she took the picture, he wondered about something. "Ozzie, how long will these helmet lights last?"

"Got about two hours of power left. To play it safe, I wouldn't spend too much time in the saloon."

Tuttle sighed. "I wish it was a real saloon instead of a dining hall. I'd give a month's pay for a boilermaker right now."

Gillespie said, more pedantically than he intended, "We're all getting a bit dehydrated."

"Kinda ironic, Doc," Tuttle ventured. "Dehydration when we're thousands of fathoms deep."

Gillespie started to reply, but the words never left his mouth. The passageway in front of them seemed to widen. Then they were no longer in a passageway. They were looking into a large black void, and Mitchell whispered, "I think this is it . . . the first-class dining saloon. Look overhead, at those chandeliers. Brass again."

"They're all that's left," Gillespie said.

Carlson was peering off to one side. "Not quite, Doctor. Over in the corner; it's a serving table. And right under it, a metal dish cover. Look, there's tableware all over the place . . . knives, forks, pieces of dishes, too. There's one that isn't even broken. There's a cup . . ."

She was cataloging the various objects in view as she snapped pictures, when all four helmet lights went out simultaneously. They were left in pitch-blackness, the equivalent of being in an unlighted cave two miles inside the earth.

Roger Cornell paled at Nemo's terse message: "Commander Jackman is reporting an emergency, and there's been a casualty."

Bixenman, equally stunned, motioned the underwater-communications operator out of his chair and picked up the mike himself. "What's the nature of the emergency, and who's hurt?"

"We don't know, sir. They were in one of the cargo holds when something happened. They're on their way up. Jackman says he'll contact us when they're clear."

"Where's Mitchell's party?"

"Last we heard, they were exploring B deck."

Impulsively, Cornell and Bixenman turned toward Derek Montague, who had the admiral's standing invitation to be on the bridge during all dives.

Cornell ventured, "Well, Derek, when it comes to some bad luck, it seems history's repeating itself."

Montague gave him an almost chiding look. "Let's hope it is merely bad luck, Admiral," he said gravely.

Anders's midwestern twang came out of the bridge loudspeaker. "*Chase*, what about Mitchell's team?"

Bixenman glanced at Cornell.

"Get everybody up!" the admiral ordered.

The captain squeezed the transmit key. "Contact them and tell 'em to return to *Nemo* immediately," he told Anders. "And let us know the minute you get some details from Jackman."

"Aye, aye, sir."

Bixenman and Cornell exchanged looks. "Nothing we can do but wait," the captain said.

"That casualty has to be Henning. An untrained civilian had no business making that dive."

"Jackman vouched for him, Admiral. We don't know for sure it's Henning."

"It had to be him. I'll bet he went snooping off on his—"

"*Chase*, this is *Nemo*."

The men on the bridge stiffened at the panic in Anders's voice

"Commander Mitchell says their AMOS lights have failed . . . all of them, at the same time. They're in the first-class dining saloon on B deck and they can't move an inch. They're asking for help, but we've had to tell them the other diving group's in trouble, too. Lieutenant Lawrence is requesting instructions."

"Stand by!" Bixenman looked over to the admiral. "Instructions? At this point, I can't even think of an adequate prayer."

Cornell mopped his sweating brow. "Only thing we can do is wait for Steve's team to get out of that hold and then send two divers to look for Mitchell's people. How the hell could all four AMOS strobes fail at the same time? Joe Kresky's a perfectionist . . . a maniac. I saw him recharging them last night myself, with Jackman looking over his shoulder. It's impossible."

Bixenman began transmitting the rescue instructions. Montague walked slowly to the open wing of the bridge and stood in silence, staring at the ocean below, its endless waves lapping gently against the side of the world's most modern deep-sea research and salvage vessel.

"Don't anybody panic. Jackman will get help to us eventually."

Mitchell couldn't blame anyone for sweating. They were trapped without warning in total darkness—a suffocating darkness pressing in at them.

Tuttle said, "I wish I knew what kind of trouble the other group's having. It sure as hell couldn't be any worse than this."

"All Anders said was that somebody was hurt," Mitchell reminded him. "Right now, I don't need any details."

Gillespie spoke up for the first time since the strobes went out. "I'd pay a thousand dollars for a good flashlight right now."

Mitchell caught his breath and heard the others gulp in surprise. The cloak of darkness was whisked away, replaced by a phosphorescent glow as if a million fireflies had suddenly invaded the saloon. It was not a very bright light, but sufficient for them to see . . . that they were not alone.

At least a hundred faces stared at them, faces attached to bodies—bodies wearing formal dinner clothes: ladies in evening gowns, men in the stiff-collared white shirts and black bow ties of a tuxedo ensemble.

"Mother of God," Tuttle croaked.

Hologram was the first thing that flashed into Gillespie's mind, brought on by the recollection that he had seen something like this before.

Years ago, he remembered, when he was fourteen, and he almost laughed at the incongruous memory. *It was at Disneyland, and I was visiting the Haunted House. We were riding in one of those cars around a balcony, looking down at this huge dining room. There were transparent figures in evening clothes sitting around a big table, and these other make-believe ghosts flying all over the place. I was only in my teens and I knew it was all faked, but I still was impressed and I remember my much younger brother gasping in horror, not just at the ghosts but the sound effects, like cackling laughter. I think there was a theremin playing spooky music, and my little brother, Chris, grabbed my arm and buried his head against my sleeve*

*and said he wanted to get out of this terrible place. And I just
laughed at him. . . .*

But this, Gillespie realized, was no illusion. These were the
inhabitants of an accursed graveyard, their forbidding presence
filling a room that once had heard the voices of the laughing
living, the tinkle of champagne glasses lifted in sentimental
toasts, the clatter of expensive cutlery, the murmured, respectful voices of obsequious servers, the soft dinner music of Wallace Hartley's eight-piece orchestra. . . .

And William Gillespie, distinguished oceanographer, found
himself wishing with all his frightened heart that he hadn't
laughed at his brother's fears that day they visited Disneyland's
Haunted House. A day that at this moment seemed to be a
million years away, as unreal as this nightmare was only too
real.

Mitchell somehow kept his voice steady. "Easy now. Easy
does it. I don't think they can do anything."

Gillespie wasn't that sure. In less than an hour, all his old
conceptions of the supernatural had come apart. In the past,
he had acknowledged the possibility of its existence, but in a
detached way that cast him in the safe role of observer. A ghost
was something other people had seen, or thought they had.
The living dead belonged in horror films. Apparitions from the
grave were a subject to discuss and analyze in brightly lit rooms.
Not even Ben Henning's chilling experience in that house of
murder had prepared Gillespie for this. That, too, had happened to someone else.

His mind labored to reject the impossible. He had to be
dreaming; he fell back on the age-old trick of waking up from
a nightmare. Force your eyes open, he told himself. You think
your eyes are open but they aren't. Push those lids up and
you'll wake up. Think where you are. You're back aboard
Chase in your quarters, sweaty and shaken. Montague will be
snoring, as usual—that would be the most welcome, beautiful
sound in the world right now. Push now. Push. . . .

It didn't work. They were still inside this dead ship.

"Look at them," Lieutenant Carlson gasped. "*Look at what
they're doing.*"

Gillespie looked: at a hundred or so specters shaking their heads in unison; a hundred or so disapproving, pale faces. He could make out expressions of undisguised hate.

The phosphorescent glow began to fade, until the apparitions were mere shadows. Once more, the utter darkness returned— but only for a few seconds.

Their helmet lights came back on, half-illuminating the saloon. They were alone again.

Lieutenant Commander Mitchell held the hand of his AMOS up into the beam of his helmet light and looked at it.

"Let's get out of here while we can," he said.

Jackman, Williams, and Henning reentered *Nemo* exhausted and depressed.

They had carried Nader's body from the hold where he died to the *Titanic*'s forecastle, trying not to look at the face. They rested briefly on the deck while the submarine swung into position to retrieve them. They said nothing to each other; they were too busy gasping for breath. Henning started to worry about having a heart attack.

Once aboard *Nemo*, as Kresky removed his helmet, Henning promised himself this was the last time he would wear it. Seeing Nader die—and worse, hearing it—had drained the scientific curiosity from him in one sickening moment.

Lawrence came back to the divers' compartment and turned away in horror when he saw what was left of Bob Nader.

"Cover him up, Joe," Jackman said to Kresky.

The chief petty officer grabbed a towel from a stack kept for divers to mop their faces. Kresky didn't attempt to remove Nader's helmet—he dropped the towel over where the Plexiglas had been and left it at that.

"Steve, what happened?" Lawrence asked.

"We were cutting our way into the hold where the bullion's supposed to be. A chunk of the bulkhead came loose and clipped his helmet. We should have tried clearing a way down the cargo hatch above that hold, instead of the adjacent one."

Lawrence said, "Don't blame yourself for this, Steve. The hatch you used was the wider of the two, and presumably safer."

Jackman looked at him, misery flooding his weary face. "*Presumably* is the most dangerous word in the Navy's dictionary."

Henning noticed that Jackman didn't mention the apparition that had startled Nader and put him in the path of the falling steel. It might be said he had been indirectly killed by a ghost, a matter Cornell wouldn't be able to ignore. Henning decided Jackman would get around to it in due time.

Williams asked, "What about Ozzie's group, Jeff? Are they all right?"

Lawrence hesitated before replying. They all looked shell-shocked, anyway, and he wasn't sure whether they could handle another jolt. He said cautiously, "Well, they had a little trouble, but they're okay and on their way back from B deck."

Jackman said sharply, "What kind of trouble?"

"Steve, I'm not sure you want to hear it."

"Try me."

"They lost all their AMOS lights at the same time. Now don't wet your pants"—Jackman's jaw had dropped—"but I damned near had to tell you and Felix you'd both have to go after them and guide 'em back. Then Ozzie advised the strobes were operating again and no help was necessary, to which I might add a simple thank God, because you're too bushed to rescue anyone standing more than five feet away from this sub."

"Amen," sighed Williams. "Nader felt like he weighed a ton."

Nemo's intercom came to life. "Anders here, Jeff. *Chase* is asking, and I quote Captain Bixenman verbatim, what the hell is going on. He wants to know the status of both diving parties. What should I tell him?"

Lawrence murmured to Jackman, "I'll bet the skipper was quoting the *admiral* verbatim. I'd better go forward and give 'em the poop." He turned to the commander. "Steve, do you want me to tell them about Nader?"

"Might as well, but skip the details. We're gonna have one hell of a postdive debriefing. Joe, if you're finished with Henning and Carlson, help me get out of this suit."

By the time Lawrence returned to the pilot compartment,

Anders had heard from Mitchell again. "They're almost back to the boat deck, and they're asking for retrieval as soon as we spot them."

"Okay, acknowledge. What the hell's wrong now, Jennifer?" The communications officer had a strange expression on her face.

"Nothing, really. Except . . . well, Ozzie sounded funny. Real shaky like. I had trouble hearing him."

Lawrence grunted. "I'd be shaky, too, losing all lights two decks down. Does he have any idea what caused the failure?"

"No, sir. I asked him and he said he couldn't explain it."

Lawrence swapped worried glances with Lieutenant Ellison. "I haven't gotten around to telling either of you yet, but you might as well know it now. Bob Nader's dead. A bulkhead fell on him and crushed his helmet. His body's in the diving room. I still don't know how they brought it up through six decks. Even Jackman's exhausted, and that guy could take on six shore patrolmen without working up a sweat."

The copilot and communications officer absorbed this grim news in silence until Anders asked, "Should I advise *Chase*?"

"Tell them the casualty is Nader, he was injured fatally, and we're bringing the body with us. You can add that we're standing by to recover Mitchell's people and will resurface when they're aboard. Todd, let's get into position for recovery; they should be popping up anytime now."

They maneuvered the submarine over to the prearranged recovery point—the Grand Staircase area—and waited for the divers to reappear; Lawrence made a mental promise not to count heads, like a ground crew counting the bombers returning from a mission. He did it anyway.

"There's one . . . two . . . three—where the hell's the fourth? . . . Jesus, I hope . . . hot dog, there's number four! All present and accounted for! Kresky, stand by to receive divers. And Joe . . ."

"Sir?"

"They've had a rough time, too. Get those suits off fast and pour some of that hot Kresky coffee into 'em."

"Aye, aye, sir."

Ellison voiced a thought that already had occurred to Lawrence. "Jeff, I wonder if Cornell will call it quits."

Captain Bixenman posed the same question to the admiral, after *Nemo* reported Nader's death. The answer surprised him.

"I won't make a decision until we find out what happened."

Bixenman smiled. "Yes, sir. That's what I figured."

Cornell sighed. "Bix, not too long ago, I described that Lefferts expedition as a fouled-up mess. I told Montague and Gillespie the whole thing was doomed from the start. The limey officer who ran it was long on guts and short on common sense. Derek said the problem was a lot deeper than inadequate planning and equipment. He said they were opposed by something we don't understand."

Cornell glanced down at the sonar screen. *Nemo*'s image was clearly outlined above the larger mass that represented the *Titanic*. The sub's blip started to move away, and the sonar operator, flustered at having the admiral standing over his shoulder, called out, "*Nemo*'s starting ascent, sir."

The admiral turned back to Bixenman. "We, on the other hand, have the right equipment, the right men, and the right plan. But we also have a fatality, just like eighteen years ago."

Bixenman said bluntly, "Ask yourself a question, Admiral. Is the gold worth losing any more lives?"

"I don't know. I have to ask Jackman what he thinks."

Then another thought occurred to him. "I think I'd also better ask Ben Henning."

18

It was strangely difficult to sense menace or mystery aboard *Chase* that night, as she wallowed peacefully in the Atlantic swells; not in the disciplined atmosphere of a superbly equipped naval vessel with her gleaming brasswork and well-lit corridors, her scrubbed, spotless decks, and that three-inch gun and the Bofors standing like sentinels.

To Gillespie and Henning, reboarding her after today's dive was like waking up from a nightmare; *Chase* became more than a ship; she was a sanctuary now, an antiseptic haven from evil and death. Cornell remarked to Bixenman later that he had never seen anyone so badly shaken as the five navy divers, not even men after the stress of combat. Hard-bitten Tuttle had fallen on his knees and kissed *Chase*'s deck the instant he stepped off the submarine launch/recovery ramp. The four officers hadn't been that demonstrative, but Cornell saw in their tired eyes things he didn't want to see.

Henning was struck forcibly by the incongruity between their protected existence on this tiny metal island of science and the military and what existed beneath them—a slaughtered ship that somehow had become the gateway to a nether world guarded by phantoms. As he listened to Jackman and Mitchell relate the respective experiences of their diving groups, the psychiatrist thought of another contrast, one branded on his mind during his impressionable boyhood.

He was watching, for the first time, a television showing of the original movie classic *King Kong*. He knew the plot in advance and subsequently saw the film so many times that he could recite the dialogue verbatim, but it was the opening scene that became fixed in his memory even more than the ape's battles with dinosaurs and its rampage through Manhattan. That opening scene: the New York skyline at night, a tugboat moving slowly in the foreground, her whistle hooting mournfully. And young Ben Henning had thought, How incongruous—this great, modern city, teaming with complacent life, and thousands of miles away, on the other side of the world, we know at this very moment there exists a monstrous creature beyond the ken of civilized man, holding a tiny island in terror.

He remembered it again tonight in the officers' mess, with Cornell presiding over the postdive briefing, because he was so starkly aware of the same incongruity. They were only seven years away from the twenty-first century, aboard a masterpiece of modern technology, yet overmatched by something that lay two and a half miles below them. The very contrast was frightening in itself, as if they had found themselves existing in two dimensions, separate yet terrifyingly close—one, their own familiar, comfortably safe world; the other, a menacing, dark hell.

The admiral's strained voice broke into his thoughts. "The first order of business, of course, is to bury Bob Nader. I'll conduct the services myself at oh-six hundred." He paused while his eyes searched their frozen, impassive faces. "The second order of business is to evaluate the risks of continuing this mission. You know, I've always believed in the Navy's most sacred motto—'to go in harm's way.' John Paul Jones said that more than two hundred years ago, and it's been our creed ever since."

Once again, he paused, as if mustering some inner strength to admit something he didn't want to admit. "But then, no admiral or captain has faced a situation like this: an apparent enemy that's not of flesh and blood, or steel and shells." He looked directly at Henning. "Ben, I almost regret to say that the decision to invite you on this expedition has been justified. So I'm going to ask you a direct question. Based on your own experience today and what happened with Ozzie Mitchell's group, *are we going in harm's way*?"

Henning had been expecting that question and he dreaded answering it. He even resented *having* to answer it. Psychic phenomena were something to investigate, analyze, explain if possible. Never before had they involved a possible life-or-death decision, and that seemed to be the burden Cornell had just shifted to his shoulders. The burden was too heavy. Yes, the *Titanic* was haunted; he was sure of that. Yet specters spawned by a haunting weren't supposed to pose actual physical danger. . . .

His answer, when it finally emerged, was deliberately ambiguous, and he was a little ashamed of it. He knew in his heart that hedging could be a risky course. "Nader's death appears to have been an unfortunate accident," Henning said. "I'm convinced we've seen ghosts on that ship, but I never heard of ghosts causing accidents."

Gillespie cut in. "We've been seeing more than ghosts, Ben. How about that giant eel? How about four helmet lights failing simultaneously and then coming back on for no apparent reason?"

Cornell winced. Immediately after *Nemo*'s recovery, he had ordered Williams and Kresky to tear them down and look for the source of the malfunction. Felix had helped design them and Kresky could take one apart blindfolded. Lieutenant Commander Mitchell had stood over their shoulders while they worked and reported back to the admiral with bewilderment in his voice. "Sir, they couldn't find anything wrong. The fuel cells still had plenty of power left, and they tested perfectly."

This was the mystery that worried Cornell more than anything else. It represented potential danger. He didn't even want to imagine what it must have been like, being trapped in that darkness. Thank God it hadn't happened to Jackman's team, four decks farther down. On the other hand, the strobes *had* come back on. . . .

"Ben," he said, "if you have any theories on all this, we'd all appreciate hearing them."

"Admiral, I can't tell you what to do. I can't tell you whether to go down there again or just go home. You want interpretations for phenomena I don't understand myself. Remember, we're also looking for the causes behind what happened eighteen years ago."

He looked at Montague as he said it. The old Englishman was wearing a curious half smile—almost a sly one, Henning thought. Montague said, "It is possible one explanation would cover both expeditions."

"I agree," Henning replied, "but I'm not ready to provide that explanation." He turned back to Cornell. "It's your call, Admiral."

"Yeah," Cornell grunted unhappily. "It's not one I particularly like to make either way. Let me give you my own thoughts before I give you a decision.

"The sea always has been full of mysteries, of unexplainable and sometimes frightening events. Even the legend of the most famous ghost ship of all—the *Flying Dutchman*—may have some basis in fact. Certainly not all the mariners who claimed to have seen her were crazy or perpetrating a hoax. You've probably all heard the story of the *Mary Celeste*, the brigantine found deserted in the middle of the Atlantic. Absolutely seaworthy, fully provisioned and cargo intact, yet no trace of her crew or the two passengers aboard was ever found. The so-called Bermuda Triangle may be a bunch of malarkey. I, for one, have always been skeptical of the yarns of ship and aircraft disappearances told about that area. Yet a few of them can raise the hair on your head. Years ago, the Navy lost a collier in the Triangle, supposedly in good weather and for no apparent reason. No wreckage was ever found."

He had his audience spellbound, not so much for what he was saying but because of *who* was saying it. This was a rear admiral in the United States Navy, a most practical flag officer with a reputation for scoffing at anything faintly resembling superstition. Jackman once had heard him refer to the Bermuda Triangle horror stories as "damned bunk," going on to offer logical explanations for every incident cited as proof that the Triangle was a Devil's playground.

The admiral continued, in a calm voice. "I've seen fear on all your faces, especially those of you divers. Understandable. Natural fear—and as far as I'm concerned, acceptable fear. I don't mind telling you I wouldn't want to go down in that hellhole now myself after hearing what it's like. But that's not my job. My job is to weigh the element of risk and decide whether it's reasonably safe to send *you* down again."

His eyes swept the sea of faces. "I'd be a fool to deny that we have an apparently haunted wreck on our hands, whatever that means. But I would argue vehemently against the possibility that Nader's death was caused by some supernatural force. From the evidence I've heard, it was an accident, the kind of accident that comes with the territory. The very nature of deep diving involves far more risk than any encounter with nebulous apparitions. I know these things seemed to be warning us away. But such warnings constitute a risk as nebulous as the specters themselves."

Gillespie started to say something, but Cornell shook his head. "Please let me finish, Bill, then you can have your say. As a matter of fact, I think I already know what's on your mind. The strobe failures."

Gillespie nodded.

"So let's talk about that. No, I never heard of four of them failing simultaneously and then reactivating themselves for no reason. But those new helmet lights are a mechanical device, and mechanical devices can be weirdly temperamental. Just look at the epidemic of Mark-Fourteen torpedo malfunctions in World War Two. Drove the sub fleet crazy, until the desk sailors in Washington finally got around to admitting their vaunted new magnetic exploders weren't worth a damn, and neither was the Mark-Fourteen itself. I think it's fair to draw an analogy from this. The AMOS lights are a brand-new type, but like virtually all new technical hardware, they can develop some mighty mysterious ailments until the bugs are identified and eliminated. I hope Lieutenant Williams, here, won't take offense, because these strobes are very much his baby. But he knows as well as I do that no amount of bench testing can duplicate the rigors of actually operating equipment in the environment for which they were designed."

Williams looked relieved, and Mitchell patted him on the back. Beautiful, Ben Henning was thinking. Cornell had them eating out of his hand with this adroit approach to an explosive situation: first, an admission that they had a right to be scared, then the theme that strange things always have happened on the sea, and finally, an explanation for the light failures, which actually wasn't even an explanation but was phrased so that it almost made sense. The tension had dissipated noticeably. Still, Henning knew that this didn't apply to himself or his two civilian companions. Gillespie still wore the expression Henning had seen immediately after the dive—that of a shaken man whose structured scientific world, a world enshrining logic, facts, and technological perfection, had just been turned upside down and demolished.

And Derek Montague. A face that always seemed to carry two expressions—one of perpetual sadness, the other synchronized to what Montague was hearing or seeing. Right now, the eyes were sorrowful, but the mouth was set in a faintly sardonic smile that told Henning he hadn't accepted Cornell's appraisals.

Henning's thoughts were interrupted by a question from the admiral. "Ben, has there ever been a case in which a ghost physically harmed the person who saw it? Or tried to harm him?"

"No," Henning admitted. "Lacking any bodily mass as we know it, I suppose a punch from a ghost would feel like a light blast of cold air . . . if that."

It was a lousy simile, Henning realized, and someone chuckled. Too supercilious, too glib. Maybe even dangerously misleading.

Cornell said in a brisker tone. "Bill, you had something to tell us a few minutes ago."

"I just hope you're not underestimating the situation," Gillespie said.

"I don't think I am, but I don't want to overreact to it, either." Cornell's tone was level and reasonable, yet shaded with resolve. Their eyes locked, but if Gillespie saw a trace of defiance in the admiral's Cornell saw fear in the oceanographer's.

His voice turned gentle again. "Bill, if it'll make you feel any better, I'm willing to request volunteers for tomorrow's dive. Because there's going to be another dive, and cargo hold three is the target."

Commander Jackman said, with a quickness that reminded all three civilians they were on a navy ship, "I don't think it's necessary to ask for volunteers, Admiral." He looked questioningly at his fellow divers, and the nods they returned could have been salutes. There was one exception—Bert Tuttle. The older diver's acquiescence was hesitant and halfhearted, and Jackman caught it.

"Doubts, Bert?" he asked.

The hound features were more mournful that ever. "You want an honest answer, Commander?"

"If you don't want to go, say so. I won't hold it against you."

Tuttle looked not at Jackman but at Cornell. "Admiral, I guess I'd rather French-kiss a wall socket than go inside that wreck again. But I'll dive with the others; that's *my* job."

"Well, that's a salty description of courage, Bert, but I must admit it's appropriate." Cornell's eyes fell on Gillespie again. "Bill, exploration won't be part of tomorrow's agenda, so you and Ben aren't invited."

Jackman spoke up to forestall any protests.

"We'll give each of you a full report for your files when we get back. Admiral, I'll want all divers with me tomorrow. We'll proceed down the same forward hatch we entered today. It's adjacent to hold three, and we've already opened an access hole."

"But you didn't actually get into hold three, did you?" Cornell asked.

"No sir. But it looked clear before that . . . the event when Nader got hit. Your recall was sent before we had a chance to inspect it."

Montague spoke up unexpectedly. "The 'event' was an interesting apparition, from your description earlier. A man crazed with fear, face dirty and covered with a black dust. One of the *Titanic's* so-called Black Gang—a coal stoker. Most of them were trapped because they stayed at their posts feeding the boilers until the last possible moment. That's the only way they could provide electrical power for the ship's wireless and lights."

Cornell saw the divers shift uneasily in their chairs at this. He squinted at Montague reproachfully and turned back to Jackman. "It's not certain you people would encounter it again. Remember, that big eel showed up only once."

"That's what I'm thinking, sir. As soon as we find the bullion crates, we'll signal *Nemo* to drop the recovery net down the hatch where we entered. We'll carry the crates from hold three to the adjacent hold and load them onto the net. Montague's already provided us with the probable dimensions of each crate, and we figure the net will hold two at a time. *Nemo*'s estimated weight-carrying capacity is twenty crates, so the full salvage operation will require a maximum of two dives if all goes well. We might have to take time to replenish diver oxygen if moving and raising the crates is tougher than we expect."

Captain Bixenman, a silent observer of the proceeding up to now, wasn't satisfied.

"Admiral, I suggest we keep all divers aboard *Nemo* while the sub's lasers open the hull from the outside. Then Steve and his people can just walk laterally into the hold, get the gold out, secure the crates to *Nemo*'s topside, and resurface. The net wouldn't be needed, so we could complete the job with a minimum of risk to all concerned. The entire operation would be faster, and far better illuminated because we'd be using *Nemo*'s strobes in addition to the divers' units."

"Sorry, Captain, but I can't buy it." Jackman toyed idly with a pencil that looked like a matchstick in his big hand. "The one factor Captain Bixenman hasn't taken into account is the enormous power of *Nemo*'s lasers. I've worked with those lasers more than any of you, and I can testify that at full strength, they can create havoc with any object they strike. Instantaneous disintegration."

Cornell scowled. "You shouldn't need full strength. Hell, a little iceberg spur ripped that hull wide open."

"No, sir, it didn't. We know now the so-called three-hundred-foot gash supposedly made by the spur was an erroneous assumption. It was a series of small but fatal gashes that got her. And I'd estimate that the kenetic energy of forty-six thousand tons colliding with the spur would just about equal a full-strength laser hit. What I'm saying, sir, is that only full-power beams will carve up that hull, and that's where we could run into a major problem. If we cut into the side with *Nemo's* lasers at full strength, we stand a very good chance of inflicting beam damage on the bullion crates."

Cornell's face fell. "Dammit, Steve, you've know all along we might have to use the sub's lasers. Now you're telling me we can't."

"With respect, Admiral, I said *Nemo's* lasers should be a last resort, if we couldn't penetrate the hold with divers, and in that case they'd be used at a maximum of half power. Half power would be the equivalent of full power on the hand lasers, and in my judgment, now that I've seen things up close, that won't open a hole. The outer skin is tougher and thicker than you might think. We had one hell of a time cutting up a lot thinner metal with our hand units."

"If you're right," Cornell said, "we *have* to send the divers down the forward cargo hatch."

"That was our battle plan from the start. I don't think it's necessary to change that. We cleared a way into cargo hold three today. Access tomorrow should be relatively easy. A longer, more difficult process, I'll concede, but a safer one."

Bixenman said, more cuttingly than he intended, "The hell it is. Going down that hatch is the riskiest process, Steve."

"For personnel, yes, but not for what we came after." That remark drew an impulsive nod from Cornell, and Gillespie reluctantly smiled to himself.

But the captain wouldn't let go. "I'd rather take a chance on damaging the gold than losing more lives."

"So would I, Captain," Jackman retorted. "I'm pointing out the serious drawback of using the big lasers. The choice is not mine, sir."

"Nor mine," Bixenman added, shifting his gaze to Cornell.

"We'll proceed with Commander Jackman's plan," the admiral said. He rose and once again Gillespie was struck by how much taller Cornell seemed at certain times. "This meeting is adjourned; and I suggest diving personnel get some shut-eye."

He walked out of the room with the purposeful strides he used to mask his real emotions. They stared after the stubby little figure, and no one spoke until Felix Williams voiced what all the divers were thinking:

"I just hope I *can* shut my eyes."

Ben Henning already knew he wasn't going to get much sleep. He spent more than an hour entering notes into the journal he had begun the day *Chase* sailed. He described everything that had occurred, then added a concluding paragraph.

"*. . . and in the back of my mind, there persists a theory so bizarre, I hesitate to voice it. The evidence is circumstantial, yet in this peculiar avocation everything is. Derek would believe it, and Bill Gillespie's so badly shaken, I thing he's ready to accept any explanation. Cornell and Bixenman? The divers? I don't know if the military mind is equipped to deal with this. Eventually, I suppose, I will have to confide my suspicions, vague and unconfirmed though they may be.*"

He closed the notebook, realized that his mind was racing, and looked around for something to read. He had exhausted the supply of mysteries he had brought aboard and momentarily considered visiting Jackman who also liked mysteries and might have something Henning hadn't read yet. No, he decided, Jackman needed his rest, and it would be unfair to bother him.

Henning was about to undress when he spotted a book on the small table that stood in a corner of his cabin. Maybe Steve had left it there for him; if not Jackman, it must have been someone else, for Henning had never seen it before. He picked up the book, surprised at its obvious antiquity. It was a weather-beaten hardback volume with a thick cover that felt almost like heavy cardboard. The binding was still intact but loose, and Henning knew it had to be very old.

He didn't recognize the title, nor were the author and publisher even remotely familiar. *Futility*, it was called, written by a Morgan Robertson and published by M. F. Mansfield. Printed a hell of a long time ago, Henning guessed as he opened the book to its title page. And there was the publishing date. 1898, London, he read. Which seemed to establish Morgan Robertson as some kind of obscure British author. Without bothering to disrobe, Henning lay down on his bed and began to read—still wondering who might have left the book in his cabin. He wondered even harder as its subject matter unfolded. . . .

Futility was a novel, written rather ponderously in the fashion of that era and not very well. Dialogue was stilted, the characters stereotyped. But the plot . . .

He couldn't believe this had been written in 1898, fourteen years before the *Titanic* disaster. A brand-new giant British ocean liner filled with very rich and complacent passengers strikes an iceberg in the North Atlantic and sinks with a terrible loss of life. The similarities between fiction and future fact were uncanny.

Robertson's ship was eight hundred feet long, a triple-screw vessel with twenty-five-knot speed. She almost could have been the *Titanic*'s twin sister.

Her total capacity was two thousand passengers and nearly a thousand crew members. On the night she sank, the total aboard was two thousand passengers and crew—a lot like the *Titanic*.

She sank on an April night; so did the *Titanic*.

She carried only twenty-four lifeboats, four more than the *Titanic* if you counted the latter's collapsibles; her builders said no more were needed because she was unsinkable.

Her fatal wound was caused by an iceberg spur piercing the starboard hull—same as the *Titanic*.

And what did Robertson call his fictitious ship?

The *Titan*.

Henning continued to read until his eyes became heavy. He dozed off and the book slipped from his chest to the floor.

He didn't see it fade into nothingness.

19

He was dreaming.

At least that was what Henning surmised, except it was unlike any dream.

He was conscious of being in a huge, high-ceilinged room—a restaurant, obviously, for it was filled with tables set for dinner. It was a very swanky restaurant, too: snow-white linen, silver tableware gleaming under ornate chandeliers, crystal glasses, and well-dressed patrons. Well-dressed, indeed; they were in formal attire whose style was definitely in the category of antique; early nineteen hundreds, Henning guessed.

What he couldn't understand about this dream was his own presence in it, or rather, his absence. He didn't actually seem to be a part of the opulent scene. He wasn't standing anywhere. He wasn't one of the diners. The thought occurred to him of the life-after-death accounts of people who had been declared dead, were brought back to life, and later described how they were able to look down on their own bodies.

Henning knew he wasn't dead, however. He was observing the great room and its occupants without being there, a peculiar sensation that became even stranger when the scene shifted.

Now he was seeing one table in particular, a table occupied by six men—five in tuxedos and the sixth wearing some kind of dress uniform. For some reason, Henning's attention went to one person: a tall, portly man with a whitish-gray beard of monumental proportions. He felt his mind gravitating toward him, like water circling around a drain.

The picture he was seeing began to fade. He was starting to think *his* thoughts, to see the others at the table through *his* eyes. It came to Henning that somehow he was being absorbed, that he was becoming someone else. The last thing he saw before losing his identity altogether was the seal on one of the dinner plates.

It was an embossed red flag, with a white star in its center. Underneath were the words:

R.M.S. *TITANIC*

William Thomas Stead, eminent journalist, lecturer, student of the occult, and devout disciple of spiritualism, couldn't have been happier.

On this, the third night of the *Titanic*'s maiden voyage, he had been invited to dine at the captain's table. A great honor, he well knew, for unlike most British liner masters, Captain Edward J. Smith did not hold court over a huge table populated by rich, influential passengers and attractive women.

E.J. never invited more than five guests to *his* coveted table, located near the center of the first-class dining saloon. His very presence was a reassuring sight to any passenger who had sailed with him before. Smith would dine in public only when the weather was clear and all was well with his ship. The six-place table reflected the captain's love of good dinner conversation, far easier and more intimate than would have been possible with a larger number of guests.

Stead, an imposing man whose own thick white beard gave him a fleeting resemblance to E.J. himself, was curious to know what other guests the captain had chosen—and gratified when he arrived at the table and recognized his dinner companions instantly.

First, there was none other than J. Bruce Ismay, the tall, handsome White Star board chairman whose stiff, ramrod carriage always reminded Stead of a Buckingham Palace guard. Next to Ismay sat Benjamin Guggenheim, the enormously wealthy American who had made his fortune in the smelting industry. Stead didn't know him well but already had formed a favorable impression. Guggenheim was a pleasant-faced, square-jawed man with impeccable manners softened by a dry sense of humor.

The other American at the table was John Jacob Astor, probably the wealthiest person aboard the *Titanic*, with a personal fortune estimated at $150 million. In the eyes of many, it was a tainted fortune; it was not only totally inherited, but much of Astor's current income was derived from vast real estate holdings in New York that included some of the city's worst slums. Stead had recently read an article that described him as "the world's greatest monument to unearned increment."

Unlike Guggenheim, who lived well (he had his own manservant with him) but tended to avoid ostentatiousness, Astor seemed to flaunt his wealth. He owned eighteen automobiles and a private railroad car. At state functions, he wore a colonel's uniform that would have made a South American general envious with its splendor—never mind that Astor's military service had been as a noncombatant inspector general during the Spanish-American war, a commission he was said to have literally purchased just so he could wear a fancy uniform.

Yet Stead felt sorry for this tall, imperious scion of wealth. He had recently gone through a scandalous divorce and married an eighteen-year-old girl, Madeleine Force, who was younger than Astor's own son. The Astors, in fact, were returning home on the *Titanic* after a tour abroad that John Jacob took to escape the gibes and insults of New York society—directed mostly and unfairly toward his young bride. From what Stead had been able to observe on this voyage, the couple were very much in love.

The fifth dinner guest was Thomas Andrews, Harland & Wolff's stocky, easygoing managing director and the *Titanic*'s "father." Throughout dinner, he kept glancing around the huge 532-seat saloon and scribbling into the notebook he always carried with him.

"Thomas," the captain said teasingly, "I can't imagine what faults you can possibly find in this magnificent room. Are the tables too close together?"

Andrews hastily closed the notebook, like a child caught reading illicit material in a classroom. "Nothing involving this saloon, E.J.," he explained with his ingratiating little grin. "Merely a few notes I made on an inspection prior to dinner. Not all the kitchen equipment is functioning as well as it should."

"The roast lamb certainly was excellent," Guggenheim observed tactfully.

Astor wiped his fleshy lips with a linen napkin and nodded. "A remarkable cuisine, Captain Smith. White Star must be complimented; my wife and I didn't dine any better in Paris."

Stead, who by nature couldn't stand anyone else dominating a dinner conversation, jumped in like an actor hearing his cue. "A pity your lovely bride couldn't join us, Mr. Astor."

Astor's smile seemed to erase his air of arrogance. "She is, as you may have heard, with child and not feeling too well." He glanced at the book Stead had carried with him to dinner and placed next to his wineglass. "I see that your dinner companion is a book, Mr. Stead. You must have expected this to be a dull gathering."

Stead laughed. "Quite the contrary. I brought it along so I could recommend it to all of you, especially Captain Smith."

E.J.'s frosty eyebrows rose. "Me?"

"Yes. It's a remarkable novel titled *Futility*. About a great British ship, amazingly similar to the *Titanic*. Almost the same length, tonnage, and capacity . . . even her name is a fascinating coincidence. The author—an American, incidentally—calls her the *Titan*."

"I trust she's a great success," the captain said dryly.

"I'm afraid not. She strikes an iceberg in the Atlantic and sinks. Because there are an insufficient number of lifeboats aboard, most of her passengers and crew perish." Stead couldn't forego a glance at John Jacob Astor. "Many of the passengers are extremely wealthy, and sublimely confident that the *Titan* is unsinkable."

Ismay had said little up to now, but he was glowering. "Sounds like literary rubbish to me, Mr. Stead. It is a mystery to me why you'd recommend such a work to anyone at this table, especially Captain Smith. When was it written?"

"Fourteen years ago," Stead said calmly. "The parallels were so striking, I merely wanted to draw the novel to your attention. I'm not saying the author was capable of premonition."

Captain Smith snorted indignantly, "I certainly hope not! I must say, Mr. Stead, you make it sound as though the physical similarities between the two ships must inevitably be followed by similar disaster. I assure you, sir, it's a damn sight easier to sink a ship with a pen than to sink one as safe as the *Titanic!*"

Andrews's own rather bushy eyebrows had narrowed. "Mr. Stead, I seem to recall reading a story you wrote some years ago . . . one with roughly the same plot. As a matter of fact, you used E.J. here as a character; he commanded the ship that rescued the survivors."

"I did," Stead admitted. "Pure fiction, though. I apologize, Captain, if my mentioning *Futility* has offended you or this noble vessel in any way. I myself have been most impressed with her magnificence. Why, I can quote you verbatim from letters I've already written to my wife. I said the *Titanic* was as 'firm as a rock'—those were my exact words—and in a subsequent letter, I called her 'a monstrous floating Babylon.' "

"Babylon," Andrews frowned, "was destroyed."

"I was referring to Babylon's fabulous beauty, not its eventual fate," Stead said in a conciliatory tone. He was conscious of Ismay's glare and suspected that J. Bruce, like so many people these days, considered him something of a blithering old idiot. Stead was only sixty-four but looked much older with that great beard, and in recent years, his increasing involvement with spiritualism had given him the reputation of a man who had gone a bit daft.

Not that Stead cared. He was financially secure, albeit a pauper compared to the Astors and Guggenheims of the world, and he possessed considerable clout in political, diplomatic, and journalistic circles. He knew people laughed behind his back because he professed to be in frequent contact with a spirit named Julia, but let them laugh; his writings still swung elections and moved public opinion. He sensed the antagonism at the table, but to him, this was a challenge to stimulate further conversation and debate.

He asked innocently, "Captain, we *are* taking a northward track that will carry us into iceberg territory, aren't we?"

"We'll stay well south of icebergs," E.J. said a little sharply.

Ismay blurted, "We wouldn't be moving at this speed if there was any danger."

"Are we trying for some kind of crossing record, Captain?" Guggenheim inquired. Smith looked a trifle embarrassed, and Stead caught the captain's side glance at Ismay—a warning glance, the journalist thought uneasily. And when E.J. hesitated, Ismay answered for him.

The White Star chief looked around the table in a manner of a man about to impart a great secret, and lowered his voice. "This is something to be shared only among the four of you," he said importantly, "but I have suggested to Captain Smith that setting a new speed record would be a splendid climax to this maiden voyage. This is quite unofficial, I must emphasize. I would not want you to confide our attempt to other passengers. If we succeed, I shall make the proper announcement myself. It would be distracting and unwise to create false hopes. I'm sure you all understand."

The others nodded, but Smith noticed that Stead's nod was perfunctory, decidedly unenthusiastic. The captain said quickly, "Trying for a crossing record depends on continuance of our excellent visibility. If the weather should change, we shall have to slow down." He glanced at Ismay. "I've said as much to Mr. Ismay, and he agrees that caution will prevail over ambition."

"Of course," Ismay said in a slightly disappointed tone that somehow irked Stead.

"It is said that truth is stranger than fiction," he remarked. "It would be interesting to speculate how each of us would react if this novel I've mentioned should become fact . . . a most unlikely fact, I hasten to add."

"I'm not sure what you're driving at," Guggenheim said.

"Well, it is no secret that the *Titanic*'s lifeboats could not possibly carry all the people who are aboard. So for the sake of a friendly discussion, suppose she were to sink. Many of us would be faced with certain doom. A most premature, unexpected, and unwelcome form of death that by its very nature would bring out the best in some and the worst in others. I myself, I fear, would probably exhibit sheer panic and hysteria."

Guggenheim said thoughtfully, "Damned if I know how I'd react. Indulge in some devout prayer, I imagine. But applying the situation you describe to this vessel, we have a premise so outlandishly hypothetical that it doesn't warrant discussion."

"Not only hypothetical, but downright ridiculous," Smith said reprovingly. "Really, Mr. Stead, I do believe you are letting that writer's imagination of yours run a bit wild."

Thomas Andrews nodded. "The idea of this ship sinking strains my credibility, Mr. Stead. I would feel secure even if we were carrying no lifeboats whatsoever. The final parallel you drew is unthinkable."

"To be sure," Stead agreed. "Yet however farfetched a similar disaster might be, I am of the opinion that each of us, under the circumstances related in *Futility*, would have a rather common reaction."

The captain's eyebrows arched again. "Such as?"

"Guilt."

His five table companions stared at him. "That's a strange conclusion," Andrews remarked. "Why should I, for example, feel guilty?"

Stead took a sip of wine. "Most applicable in your case, Mr. Andrews. Let us assume the impossible happens. You, sir, are the chief designer of a supposedly unsinkable ship. Her destruction, for whatever reason, would imply flaws, erroneous assumptions, perhaps an inexcusable overconfidence. Hypothetically, of course. You could not face your Maker without confessing your sins of commission and omission . . . your personal flaws, along with those of the ship you helped create. And I daresay the same would be true for Captain Smith, for equally obvious reasons."

Smith, trying to hide annoyance behind his beard, said nothing—after all, William Stead was a respected first-class passenger.

Guggenheim looked more amused than annoyed. "In other

words, Mr. Stead, you are saying it would be God, please forgive me my sins, particularly at the last moment before death and our consignment to a common grave."

"Precisely. But more than that, a sense of guilt would afflict virtually all on the *Titanic*, not merely those of us at this table."

Astor sniffed disdainfully. "Well, I can't speak for anyone else, but I am quite sure guilt would not be among my final emotions. Concern for my wife, of course, would be uppermost. Remorse that I would not live to see my unborn child—a son, I hope, who will carry on the Astor name. But guilt? Ridiculous!"

"Come now, Mr. Astor," Stead chided. "Certainly you have done things in your life for which you are sorry."

"My first marriage," Astor snapped impulsively. Guggenheim chuckled, and even Captain Smith hid a smile behind his beard.

Stead pressed on. "An unhappy marriage is something you'd regret, but not necessarily a source of guilt as I imagine it here. Could you really meet your God with an absolutely clear conscience? I doubt that any of us, good Christians though we may be"—he smiled at Guggenheim —"or good Jews, could honestly claim our lives have been without blemish or blame."

Astor's handsome face clouded. "Only a fool would boast of his own perfection. But guilt is a matter of degree. I can think of no major offense I've committed, no heinous acts deserving of either legal or celestial censure. Wealth, Mr. Stead, is not a crime."

"Granted," Stead said, "and I yield to no man in the delightful pursuit of wealth, which, unfortunately, I have not been able to attain as successfully as you. Perhaps what I am referring to is the use of wealth. Or its misuse."

Astor, his face coloring, started to speak, but Ismay broke in. "I don't see *you* traveling second class or steerage, Mr. Stead. And I find your remarks concerning Mr. Astor dangerously close to insulting."

Stead bowed at Astor. "I meant no disrespect, sir. I intend this to be a friendly discussion of a very important topic. I am merely making the point that this imperfect world is populated by imperfect beings, all of whom, including myself, have something to feel guilty about . . . and including you, Mr. Astor, if you'd be willing to admit it."

Again Ismay interrupted before Astor could reply. "I challenge your assertion that this is an imperfect world. We have no reason to feel defensive about society's achievements in these first years of the twentieth century. Just look at this ship! The very essence of scientific progress!"

"Science represents only a small segment of society," Stead said gently. "Society also includes people like those traveling steerage on this same vessel, mostly Irish and other emigrants to the New World, fleeing the poverty and oppression of the Old. The *Titanic* is a cross section of 1912 society, representing both its faults and its virtues."

Guggenheim said, "Well put, Mr. Stead. But not all of us are as blind as you seem to think. I'd like to believe we wealthy have a sense of *noblesse oblige*. I am quite sure that Mr. Astor, like myself, has always made generous contributions to worthy charities."

"With admirable motivation on your part," Stead said quickly. "Your family was not always wealthy and you understand the privations of the poor."

"Meaning I do not?" Astor asked. Yet there was no rancor in his tone, and Guggenheim looked at him curiously.

Stead said, "It is decidedly unsporting to judge a man without knowing him intimately, Mr. Astor. But your reputation—unjustified, perhaps—is that you are somewhat lacking, shall we say, in social conscience."

Captain Smith's beard seemed to bristle, like the fur rising on the back of an aroused animal. "Now see here, Mr. Stead! I will not have you casting aspersions on a fellow passenger. This conversation has stepped over the boundaries of good manners."

"If I have offended, I ask your pardon," Stead murmured. "Nevertheless, I firmly believe that guilt in one form or another would be dominant within the breast of anyone who knows he or she is going to die. They would be seeking divine forgiveness."

"They'd be seeking divine intervention more likely," Andrews commented dryly. "Tell us, Mr. Stead, would this guilt theory of yours apply to the poor on this ship, as well as the rich?"

"Of course. The poor commit transgressions, too. The Irish emigrants aboard are predominantly Catholic, I'd venture. It certainly would hold true for them, and the Italian steerage passengers, as well. You would have an avalanche of last-minute confessions, including a few from Mr. Astor, here. Come, sir, admit it."

"Let it go, Stead." Guggenheim sighed. "You've made your point. It's time to change the subject."

Astor cleared his throat. "I would prefer not to change the subject," he declared, and the others—including Stead himself—stared at him in surprise. Astor picked up his wineglass and twirled the stem thoughtfully. "Mr. Stead, I would appreciate your telling me why you believe I would feel guilt under the stress of impending death."

The journalist gave him an admiring glance, not expecting this from the imperious American millionaire, but admiration didn't soften his reply.

"Because, sir, I believe you are aware that your great fortune is employed mostly to increase that fortune. I believe that in the deepest recesses of your Christian heart, you know you could have helped the unfortunates of this world far more than you have. And finally, I believe that in those same recesses, you have not been truly proud of the fact that your wealth is the product of fortuitous inheritance, rather than solely of intelligence and hard work. I do not indict you for this, Mr. Astor. I only ask that you acknowledge the truth—if only to yourself. Sometimes I think we should all search our hearts, for there we might expose the self-satisfaction that marks this era in which we live."

The table fell silent, and it was Astor who finally spoke. He said quite calmly, and again with no trace of resentment, "The only admission I can make, Mr. Stead, is that I fear I have never looked into the deep recesses of my heart to the extent you have. Perhaps I should. At any rate, I doubt whether any man can really foretell his thoughts or actions when faced with his ultimate fate."

"A noble response," Stead acknowledged, "and one I shall accept as sincere."

Ismay rose from his chair. "More than you deserved. I must say you have raised a most depressing topic, and I refuse to discuss what is impossible to begin with. Gentlemen, E.J., I bid you all good night."

His abrupt departure achieved its purpose. Captain Smith said his own farewells and Andrews, after a few minutes, muttered, "Must get back to work." He left and the others followed suit. Stead decided to enjoy the night air before retiring.

He walked to the promenade deck and stared down at the dark water through which the *Titanic* was plowing her swift way. They did seem to be moving quite fast, Stead thought with a strange glumness. And it was getting rather cold—so cold that he shivered.

Why did he know that the book he carried under his arm *was* a premonition?

Why did he know that they were not "well south" of the iceberg track but heading right toward it, and that Captain Smith would ignore all ice warnings?

Why did he know that the *Titanic* was as doomed as the *Titan*?

And why did William Thomas Stead know he was going to die when the fictitious *Titan* became the real *Titanic*?

He shuddered again and returned to his C deck cabin, where he lay awake for a long time.

Henning was dreaming again, but the setting had changed. He was conscious of the cold night air and then he recognized his surroundings, both from sight and sound.

He was on the boat deck. It was on a marked slant toward the bow of the giant liner, and the raucous blast of the ship's steam whistle assaulted his eardrums. It was a deep, melancholy, frantic, and futile cry for help: the sound of a ship about to die.

He saw a row of lifeboats swinging from their davits, and officers trying to load them, mostly with women and children but a sprinkling of men, too. Then he saw a familiar figure standing off to one side, calmly surveying this scene of growing panic—the same man who had sat at the captain's table in the other dream and had talked about a book he had just read.

Henning's consciousness began to fade as what came to him in the form of a dream became reality once more. . . .

William Stead had been in his stateroom, trying unsuccessfully to concentrate on Gibbon's *Decline and Fall of the Roman Empire,* when he heard the faint grinding noise coming from somewhere in the bowels of the ship.

He knew.

He reached for his gold pocket watch resting on the nightstand and consulted the tiny black hands. 11:40 P.M.

He dressed without haste and made his way toward the boat deck. At the B-deck level, he encountered the American millionairess Margaret Brown of Denver, and noted with some amusement that she seemed dressed more for a fashionable luncheon than someone heading for a lifeboat. Molly, as everyone called her, was wearing a two-piece black velvet suit with black and white silk lapels—very attractive outfit, Stead thought, although it would have looked better on a more aristocratic woman. Stead considered Mrs. Brown a bit vulgar, typically *nouveau riche* by his standards. Yet he liked her breezy informality and good humor. She'd be the last one to panic, he guessed. Her calm greeting confirmed his appraisal.

"Hello there, Mr. Stead. I hear we've struck an iceberg and we're sinking."

Stead nodded, not bothering to tell her how he knew. "I'm afraid it's true, Mrs. Brown. I suggest you not dally, for lifeboat capacity is limited."

"How the hell could we run into anything on such a clear night?" she demanded. "The lookouts must have been asleep."

"Possibly." He was tempted to mention the speed record, but decided not to. True, she might survive this terrible night, and someone should tell the world about Ismay's pressure on Captain Smith. Yet he had too much admiration for old E.J. to let his reputation be sullied in this fashion. Ismay deserved the blame far more than Smith, and if Mrs. Brown talked, the captain probably would get most of the blame.

When they reached the boat deck, Mrs. Brown disappeared amid a cluster of friends, and Stead had a strong hunch she'd forget she had seen him on this night. For what seemed to him an interminable length of time, he watched the lowering of lifeboats, the steadily increasing manifestations of panic as wives and children were separated from husbands and fathers, the women suddenly realizing the numbing truth: There weren't enough lifeboats.

"Well, that book of yours turned out to be the real thing, eh, Stead?"

The journalist turned to find Benjamin Guggenheim standing by his side, and next to the millionaire was his valet—both were in immaculate evening clothes. Stead, who was wearing a heavy wool sweater, suddenly felt shabby, but he had to smile. "I see you are dressed for the occasion, Mr. Guggenheim."

"Dressed up in our best and prepared to go down like gentlemen," Guggenheim said cheerfully. "I gave a woman in one of the boats a note to my wife. I said if anything happened to me, I wanted her to know I've done my best to do my duty."

"Your courage is commendable," Stead said sincerely.

Wallace Hartley and his musicians had come on deck, and the cold air filled with the incongruous sounds of lively music. They should be playing hymns, Stead thought gloomily, but he kept that sentiment to himself.

Guggenheim said, "I assume, of course, there are several vessels rushing to our rescue. I heard the *Capathia* is only a few miles away."

Stead said nothing. He hadn't heard about the Cunard liner, but he was quite sure she would not reach them in time. Then he spotted the tall figure of John Jacob Astor. He was putting his pretty wife into lifeboat 4, being loaded by Second Officer Charles Lightoller. In the clear night air, their voices carried.

"I'd like to join her," they heard Astor say. "She is in a delicate condition."

"No, sir," Lightoller said firmly. "No men are allowed in these boats until the women are loaded first."

Guggenheim murmured, "John will probably file a complaint with White Star when this is over."

However, they saw Astor step back without protest, smiling

at the officer. "I don't think so," Stead ventured. "Mr. Astor seems to be taking this quite calmly. Listen. . . ."

". . . I'll go in one of the other boats, my dear," Astor was saying reassuringly. He gave his wife a fond look, blew her a kiss, turned away, and was lost to their sight.

One by one, with agonizing slowness, the lifeboats on their side of the ship creaked and groaned their way down to the dark water, leaving behind a mass of bewildered humanity who could not believe what was happening.

Stead suggested, "Let's see what is transpiring on the other side. I understand there are four collapsible boats in addition to the regular lifeboats. We might find space in one of them; they have wooden bottoms and canvas sides, but they would be preferable to swimming."

Guggenheim shook his head sadly. "Take a look around us, my friend. There must be hundreds of women still aboard. No, I think I might as well stay here." He gave a wry chuckle. "You know, I have more than four thousand dollars in cash right here in my pocket. I wonder if I could buy my way into heaven."

"If that is the case," Stead sighed, "I had better be prepared for rejection. Good-bye, Mr. Guggenheim. It has been a privilege to know you."

"Likewise, Mr. Stead." Guggenheim hesitated, his eyes somber. "About guilt; there *is* something in my past that has always bothered me. I found myself recalling that certain episode as soon as I heard we were sinking. I'd like to think my last thoughts will be of my wife and children, but who knows? Good-bye, sir."

They shook hands warmly and Stead walked to the other side of the boat deck, where a new and most interesting scene greeted him. Lifeboat 5 was all loaded and just starting down under the direction of Fifth Officer Harold Lowe, a hot-tempered young Welshman. Lowe was issuing orders in a calm voice when J. Bruce Ismay moved in front of him, waving his arms frantically and almost screaming in hysteria.

"Lower away! Lower away!"

Stead saw Lowe's face turn purple. "If you'll get the hell out of my way," the officer snarled, "I'll be able to do something!

You want me to lower away quickly? You'll have me drown the lot of them!"

Ismay flushed but said nothing and walked over to another boat. Stead heard a seaman whisper to another sailor, "Blimey, Mr. Lowe just insulted the president of the bloody company! There'll be hell to pay when we get to New York."

The journalist watched in silence as the last lifeboat disappeared down the side. Only one sanctuary was left: collapsible C, and the crew was having a devil of a time freeing it for transfer to an empty davit. Most of the worried passengers on this side became convinced it would never be launched and they wandered away, leaving only a handful willing to wait for this frail refuge to be readied. Among them was Ismay, and Stead looked on curiously as collapsible C finally was lifted into a davit. Several passengers climbed in.

Ismay glanced around, saw no one except Lowe, and stepped into the boat. Lowe gave him a contemptuous glare and barked, "Lower away!" Collapsible C dropped from sight.

Stead decided he did not want to face the end on the boat deck, not with the mournful honks of the funnel whistle and the pitifully futile bursts of the white distress rockets still being fired into the night sky; not with that band of musicians playing gay tunes, a false cheerfulness that grated on his nerves. With some difficulty, for the ship's forward list was increasing, he wandered down to the smoking lounge, expecting to find a few fellow males there. He was surprised to find that its lone occupant was Thomas Andrews.

The builder was sitting at a card table, his elbows resting on the green felt cover. He looked up as Stead approached.

"Aren't you going to have a go at saving yourself?" Stead asked.

"That's what a steward asked me a few moments ago. I didn't bother to answer him."

"Where is your life jacket?"

"I gave it to a young lady who did not have one."

Stead nodded understandingly. "I left mine in my stateroom. The water must be freezing and a life jacket would be useless. Mind if I join you?"

Andrews motioned him into the chair on his left. "I was just thinking about our discussion of last night. You were right. Guilt is what I feel now, more keenly than I ever expected. And I would say old E.J. must be sharing that feeling. Frankly, I am going to welcome death."

"Not me." Stead smiled. "I do not fear death, because it is merely a threshold to a new kind of life. But I did not expect that the transition would occur so soon . . . on this voyage and on this ship."

"Neither did anyone else," Andrews remarked sadly. "My God, what sublime overconfidence we have displayed! What grossly false assumptions we have made! And yet as despairing as I feel, others must share the blame—especially Ismay."

"For convincing Captain Smith to try for a crossing mark?"

Andrews glanced up at the magnificent oil painting that hung on the wall he was facing. *The Approach of the New World*, it was called, and he studied it for a long moment before replying.

"He bears guilt for more than that speed-record foolishness. This ship's original plans called for forty-eight lifeboats, with a total capacity of more than three thousand souls. She could carry sixty-four if need be. But someone at White Star made the decision to carry only sixteen, and if Ismay didn't make it himself, he should have sacked the blighter who did. Of all the people who dined with us last night, his is the greatest guilt and I hope he remembers this in his final moments."

Stead said dryly, "His final moments will not occur tonight. Ismay left in the last collapsible."

Their eyes met. Andrews murmured, "The cowardly bastard."

"When the end comes," Stead observed, "at least our pain will be over quickly. Ismay will carry his for the rest of his life."

Andrews gave him a quizzical look. "What makes you think our own deaths will bring forgiveness and peace? God may well damn many of us to eternal perdition. I do not know what guilt lies in your heart, Mr. Stead, but I know the everlasting shame that rests in mine."

Stead never had a chance to reply, for at that moment, the giant liner's bow plunged deeper under the black water and the stern rose into the air. There was a screech of tortured metal as boilers and turbines tore loose and smashed forward. Stead and Andrews were thrown to the floor and hurled with violent force against a wall.

All lights went out. Stead never saw the heavy brass spittoon that came flying out of the dark, crushing his skull.

Ben Henning awoke with the worst headache in his life.

He knew he had been dreaming, and he rubbed his throbbing temples, trying to remember the details.

He had fallen asleep with a book on his chest. It was no longer there. He sat up and felt under his pillow. The book must have fallen to the floor, but there was no sign of it. He looked under the bed and throughout the small cabin without finding it.

The book must have been part of the dream, he reasoned, yet he could so clearly remember reading it, turning the yellowed pages. Come to think of it, there had been two dreams, or at least two parts in a single dream, like separate chapters in a book.

He sat on the bed, sweating profusely and heart pounding. He was waiting for the unbidden thoughts to finish—thoughts that now replayed both dreams in all their clarity, thoughts that told him the truth.

Then he went to fetch two people: Bill Gillespie and Derek Montague.

The three civilians were sipping scotch in Henning's cabin, Gillespie and Montague looking at the psychiatrist apprehensively. He was pale, and they saw his hand trembling as it held the glass.

"Ben, are you all right?" Gillespie asked.

"Not quite. I think I've just had the psychic experience of the century."

They stared at him expectantly.

"I feel like I've been run over by an eighteen-wheeler. I have to ask you something. Derek, did you leave a book in my cabin earlier tonight, and then come back to pick it up while I was asleep? Or Bill, maybe?"

"I didn't," Gillespie said.

"Nor I," Montague added. "What kind of book are you talking about?"

"An 1898 novel called *Futility*."

Their eyes widened in recognition. "The most astounding literary coincidence in history," Montague said. "You saw a copy tonight?"

"I thought I did. I remember reading it. I fell asleep, and now it's gone. It must have been part of the first dream I had. Or "—his face turned grim—"part of the psychic experience." He saw their bewilderment and shrugged. "Look, I'll fill you in, but for now let's refill these glasses. I have a hunch you're going to need a few more drinks before I ask you to swallow more than scotch."

He poured out three more hefty slugs of the amber whiskey and began, in a low, intense tone.

"I think I finally know what those divers are going up against. I started with a vague theory, but after what I've experienced tonight, it's no longer a theory. I've had a dream, really two dreams. In the first, I was on the *Titanic*, yet not in a physical sense. There was this dinner in the first-class saloon, hosted by Captain Smith, Let's see . . . I remember who was there. Guggenheim, John Jacob Astor, Andrews, and . . . I can't think of his name. The guy who was head of the White Star line."

"J. Bruce Ismay," Montague said.

"That's the one. Anyway, I could see and hear what was going on at their table, but I wasn't taking part. I guess I was kind of an unseen observer, except . . ." He stopped, coming up against a blocked memory. "There were six people at the table. I can't remember who was the sixth."

"Yourself, perhaps," Gillespie suggested.

"No, it wasn't me. Someone else. An elderly man with a huge white or gray beard."

Gillespie and Montague exchanged glances. "Isidor Straus had a beard," Montague said.

"No, it couldn't have been him. This man had a decided British accent. Very imposing fellow, I seem to recall. Dominated the conversation. Some kind of writer, I think. . . ."

Identification flashed on the faces of his two companions. "William Stead!" Montague exclaimed.

But Henning's strained expression remained one of effortful recollection that hadn't quite succeeded. "Maybe. I just don't *know*. Why the hell can't I remember him? He must have been there, just like the others."

Then his face slackened. "Unless," Henning said slowly, "*I* was William Stead."

Gillespie learned forward. "Ben, what was said at the table?"

"They were talking about that book; there was a copy of it next to a wineglass. Smith didn't take very kindly to the similarities between the *Titanic* and the make-believe *Titan*. Then . . . then Ismay let a cat out of the bag. He said they were trying for a speed record."

"A speed record?"

"That's right. Ismay said not to mention this to any other passenger; if they set a crossing record, he wanted to announce it himself. The captain didn't look very happy. I got the impression this was Ismay's idea, not his—that Smith was following orders."

"My God," Gillespie said, "if there was one thing that's always been conceded about the *Titanic*, it's that no such effort was ever even considered, let alone attempted."

"The subject was brought up at both inquiries," Montague said, "and there was press speculation that a crossing-record attempt may have been a factor. But every surviving *Titanic* officer denied it. All the testimony indicated that the ship's speed entering a known iceberg lane merely reflected common practice by North Atlantic captains of that era: If the visibility was good, there was no need to slow down."

"And for that matter," Gillespie added, "the *Titanic* was never built for speed. White Star emphasized comfort, not speed."

Henning said solemnly. "I'm just telling you what was said at that table. They got to talking about the book, how they'd react if something happened to the *Titanic*, like it did in the novel. How each would face certain death. Then . . . then Stead argued that guilt would be a very powerful emotion in anyone who knew he was about to die. Guilt for different reasons, depending on the individual, but it would be the predominant experience as they died."

He hesitated. "Then there was a second dream. I was on the boat deck. Once again, I seemed to be in Stead's mind, seeing and hearing what he did. When the ship sank, he was in the smoking lounge with Andrews. They were talking about guilt, just as they all had at dinner the night before. Then she went down and Stead died when some heavy object fractured his skull. At that point, I woke up. And that's when the cabin turned cold and I began to feel thoughts . . . *feel* them, mind you. I didn't hear words, but I sensed them. Someone was putting thoughts into my mind . . . his thoughts." Henning drained what was left in his glass. "William Stead, I suppose. I remember your mentioning him in one of our historical bull sessions, Derek. He never made it to a lifeboat, did he?"

"No, he didn't," Montague replied. "Ben, what were the thoughts he put into your head?"

"The spiritual agony of the people who died that night. Guilt was very prevalent, extremely powerful in men like Smith and other officers. Andrews, too. There were other emotions, of course—fear, bewilderment, resentment—but some degree of self-reproach was a very common factor. Remember, I was sensing all this. I wasn't listening to some disembodied voice, and don't ask me what it felt like, because it's impossible to describe. The closest I can come is to liken the experience to the vagueness of a premonition. He—or it—didn't tell me in so many words what's been going on down there. Somehow, I just got the idea that he knew what I had been theorizing and that I was right. I felt his presence and I began to understand everything that has happened—to the Lefferts expedition, to our own, and why."

Henning chose his next words carefully.

"You remember the most common explanation for the psychic phenomenon we call a ghost—a form of energy persisting after death. We don't know, and probably won't know in our lifetimes, whether there is some kind of conscious thought behind this energy.

"But there is one common denominator in all spiritual manifestations: the element of violent, traumatic death. So let us go a step further. Suppose within the same framework of time, there were hundreds of such deaths, hundreds of victims perishing almost simultaneously in a single disaster.

"Such circumstances were present eighty-three years ago, the night the *Titanic* sank. More than fifteen hundred persons meeting a common fate, made inevitable by the sins of omission and commission perpetrated by those in whom they had entrusted their lives. Fifteen hundred souls united in powerful emotions—guilt, fear, anger, futility, helplessness, disbelief, all accumulating into the enormous realization of certain doom. And then the final piece in this mosaic: *Fifteen hundred victims assigned to a common grave.*

"It is my conviction that the psychic energy of the more than fifteen hundred people who died that night has somehow formed a confluence of wills capable of taking on any shape they desire. It's a kind of collective conscience—those were the words put into my head—that forms itself into this convergence of souls, all for the purpose of protecting the ultimate thing they share: their grave, and what lies with them in it. And by protecting that, they are trying to expunge their own collective guilt, shame, and sorrow."

"Such as thirty-four crates of bullion," Montague murmured.

"Exactly. This Entity—it's the only word I can think of—this Entity can be a prehistoric beast or a giant shark. It can be a single apparition or a hundred—whatever shape or shapes will frighten and deter anyone regarded as a despoiler. It seems capable of looking into the minds of the living. I give you Derek's friend John Hawke. He feared sharks, and the Entity gave him one, in a king-sized model."

Gillespie's mind rebelled. "I find it impossible to believe that this all-embracing conscience, or Entity, as you call it, could have the ability to think and reason."

"I can't tell you whether it thinks or reasons the way we do, Bill. In all my investigative experience, I've never encountered a phenomenon of this magnitude. Nevertheless"—Henning's eyes narrowed almost to slits—"there is no other explanation.

Think back to what happened in 1975. Think back to that monstrous eel of two days ago. Think back to what every diver who's gone into the *Titanic* has seen—including you."

Gillespie *was* thinking: of the bullet hole in William Murdoch's temple; of a hundred spectral faces glaring at them out of the dining saloon's dimly reflected darkness; of the terror that gripped them when the helmet lights went out. . . .

The strobes.

"If you're right," he said slowly, "the Entity also has the power to kill. I'm thinking of the lights. If they hadn't come back on, we'd still be down there. And very deceased."

"Jackman's party would have found you before you ran out of oxygen."

"Provided their own lights didn't fail!"

Montague's lips formed a knowing smile. "Which could also explain the mishaps that plagued our venture."

Henning's headshake was more vigorous this time. "Gentlemen, it's difficult enough for me to accept what I've postulated, let alone attributing to the Entity a power beyond all natural laws of physics. There was nothing about helmet lights in the thoughts I was receiving, which is why I don't intend to say anything to Cornell or anyone else until I see solid evidence that the Entity can really harm somebody. And I'd appreciate both of you keeping your mouths zippered."

"You're the paranormal expert," Gillespie said, "but I'm afraid I'm agreeing under some duress."

"Derek, mum's the word?"

"Yes," Montague replied, "but I share Bill's doubts. Tell me, Ben, when you were experiencing these thoughts, was there any sense of a warning or threat?"

Henning rubbed his jaw. "No. They were more of an explanation. That's another reason why I don't feel it's necessary to mention any of this to Cornell. The theory's tough enough to accept without adding the dream and the postdream communication. He's been amazingly open-minded up to now, but I think he'd draw the line at my hearing a voice from the dead."

"Perhaps," Gillespie said. "But I wonder if we're all underestimating Roger Cornell."

Montague didn't seem to be listening. He wore a faraway expression. "Curious thing about William Stead. No one among the survivors saw him after the third night. He told friends he wasn't feeling well and would have all meals in his stateroom for the time being. Perhaps he really was ill, yet this was totally out of character for him. I wonder what was bothering him."

Another conversation was taking place on the portside wing of the bridge, the participants being a sleepless flag officer and an equally sleepless ship's captain.

Admiral Cornell, puffing meditatively on a cigar, knew he was groping, temporizing, and avoiding the truth, but he said it, anyway—out of desperation.

"Bix, maybe I shouldn't be taking Steve's advice. What would you say to using only partial power from *Nemo* first, and see if it cracks the hull? Then we wouldn't have to send the divers down the long way, or at least we'd send 'em down only as a last resort."

Bixenman wished fervently he could encourage this fantasy. "I'm afraid Jackman's right, Admiral. I don't think even three-quarter power could do the job. I should have thought of internal laser damage before I made the suggestion." Bixenman took a deep breath. "Permission to speak frankly, sir?"

"Come on, Bix, you know that kind of protocol isn't necessary with me."

"Yes, sir, I know that. I just . . . well, I think you should have informed CNO of what happened today. The eel incident was one thing—an unexplainable sighting, okay. But those divers stepped into something on the second dive, and God knows what they'll run into tomorrow. All you told CNO was, and I quote, 'Despite some unexpected difficulties, mission progressing according to plan.' Shouldn't you be preparing Washington for possible failure?"

"Failure?" Cornell's voice was sharp, as if the captain had just uttered an obscenity.

"It's possible," Bixenman said doggedly, aware he had touched a nerve. "This mission hasn't gone according to plan. If we don't come back with the bullion, you've got some tall explaining to do . . . and most of it's going to come as a distinct shock, to put it mildly."

"Don't I know it." Cornell sighed. His jaw tightened. "But we're not going to fail. I have absolute faith in Jackman and the others. They're not going to be defeated by a collection of spooks, however real they are."

He stared into the starlit horizon. "I must sound like a heartless fight manager telling some palooka, 'Go back in there and kill the bum; he can't hurt *us*.' But Bix, we can't fold yet. This mission's my swan song, and I've got the top brass *plus* the White House expecting us to get results. This expedition was wholly my idea. If we succeed, I'll gladly spill the whole incredible story, but not while we're still piecing this together ourselves. It . . . it would be as if I was setting up an alibi in advance, an excuse that nobody in his right mind would accept. I don't think I'm immune to failure, Bix. It wouldn't be the first time. But not because of something like this."

Bixenman had an inspiration. "Admiral, aren't the brass and the President already prepared? They read the Montague file."

"Yeah, they read it. But all they believed was that Derek broke the Sovereign code. They dismissed the rest of his story the same way I once did."

The last sentence hung between them like smoke and they fell silent for a long time.

"The proverbial penny for your thoughts, Bix."

"They're probably the same ones you're having."

"You go first."

"I was wondering what surprises are waiting for those divers tomorrow."

Cornell grunted. "I was thinking that, too. But also of something else. Something Joe Kresky suggested before we left Norfolk."

"That ace up your sleeve?"

"A mighty small ace, I'm afraid. A real, honest to goodness last resort."

20

"**K**eep in close contact with *Nemo*," Cornell cautioned Jackman—unnecessarily, the commander thought. Cornell was sweating the load about this dive, and he looked as though he hadn't slept for a week. He hadn't even shaved this morning, heresy for a man whose own morning inspections had been known to make senior captains feel like raw boots.

"And for God's sake, be careful," Cornell added, also unnecessarily.

They were standing next to the launch ramp; *Nemo*'s crew and the other divers had already boarded the sub. Jackman was still thinking of the nightmare he had experienced after Tuttle left his cabin. It was a dream in which he had a visitor: Bob Nader had knocked and then entered his quarters without invitation, looming over his bunk and smelling like putrid, decayed flesh. The sickeningly sweet stench remained in Jackman's nostrils even after he awoke, although he was sure he was imagining it. He remembered how Nader looked—no face at all, just pulp, like a squashed tomato.

". . . Steve, you all right?" Cornell was asking.

"I'm fine, sir. I didn't get much sleep."

Cornell smiled wanly. "I doubt if anyone did. I feel a little guilty sending Carlson on this one."

Jackman said, "Just having her helmet light in the hold will help, and she has the camera with her."

"All right, Steve. I guess we might as well launch."

"Aye, aye, sir." Impulsively, Jackman saluted. Cornell returned it, then shook Jackman's hand. "Good luck, and God be with you."

"Thank you, sir."

Cornell watched the launch from the bridge. Bixenman, by his side, said, "They'll be fine. Jackman's the best there is."

Without looking at him, as if voicing a wayward, inconsequential thought, Cornell said unexpectedly, "I'd kinda like those two to get together some day."

"Who?"

"Steve and Fay Carlson."

Bixenman laughed. "Considering the fact that he's got a puss only a gorilla would want to kiss, that's the most unlikely romance I can imagine. Jackman's the toughest, most cynical bastard I ever met. I've known him for years, since before his divorce."

Cornell smiled wisely. "I've known him even longer than you have, Bix. He's cynical, that's for sure. What you don't know is how hard that divorce hit him. Typical navy-marriage bustup; she didn't cotton to his long absences, and so she started shacking up with some civilian who owned a chain of shoe stores. Finally married the guy. Steve told me once—after seven or eight bourbons—if he ever married again, it would have to be a woman who understands the Navy and loves it as much as he does."

Bixenman laughed again. "Admiral, you're an incurable romanticist."

"Yeah, well, I just hope nothing happens to them . . . any of them."

As Jackman had predicted, the descent into the hold adjacent to the bullion area was uneventful—if any drop through that stygian six-deck inkwell could be classed as routine. Their greatest fear was another helmet light failure, however unlikely, even though they knew Jackman and Cornell had agreed on an emergency plan if it happened again. Carlson would remain stationed at the bulkhead hole blasted open on the previous dive, and her voice-radio signal would be a safety-beacon line to the four divers working in the bullion hold.

As the party reached the lower cargo area, their strobes fell on the bulkhead breach where Nader had died. The jagged rent seemed to be beckoning them.

"Let's get to work." Jackman scanned his little group. "Fay, follow us through that hole but stay close to it."

"I might not get any good camera angles from that position, Steve." Her voice was steady and he had to admire her presence of mind.

"Maybe not, but I want you to stay put. Take your pictures from where you're stationed."

In single file, they stepped warily into cargo hold three for the first time.

The first object they sighted was almost an anticlimax: a bottle of champagne. Jackman picked it up with his arm claws. "It's unopened," he noted. "Wonder what it tastes like after all these years of aging?"

Mitchell was examining the rest of the hold and whistled. "The whole damned floor's littered with bottles!" He picked one up, too. "Scotch," he announced. "Talk about aging. . . an eighty-three-year-old bottle of Dewar's!"

Tuttle said eagerly, "Commander, how about taking a few of those topside along with the gold? Boy, I'll bet that stuff would grow hair on a bowling ball."

"Orders are to touch nothing except the crates." Jackman said it sternly, but he had a suspicion Cornell was one of many topside who'd regard a bottle of vintage Dewar's as a treasure second only to the bullion itself. "I'll have to think about it, Bert. Where the hell are the crates?"

Williams called out, "That mass of stuff against the forward bulkhead, Steve. Aren't they boxes of some kind?"

Jackman turned slowly to see. "Let's take a look . . . and be careful where you step. There's no telling what a breaking bottle might do at this depth."

Mitchell observed, "A lot of the liquor the *Titanic* was carrying must have been stored in this hold. The containers disintegrated but the bottles stayed intact. Remarkable."

The four men left Carlson by the entry hole and picked their way cautiously through the bottle-strewn obstacle course. The metal crates, piled high against the bulkhead, were covered with rust streaks, copper-colored under their lights and so thick they resembled fungus. Jackman was eye level with one of the crates and took a closer look at some lettering on its side, most of it obliterated.

"I can make out a few letters," he told them. "There's an *e* followed by an *r*. That's a capital *M*, I think. Nothing more until the last two letters—*t* and *d*."

"*T d*," Mitchell repeated. "The gold-shipping outfit was Sovereign Metals, Limited. Abbreviated to *L t d*. The capital *M* could be the first letter of Metals. Steve, this ought to be the bullion."

Jackman looked up at the mountain of crates. "Anybody bring a forklift?"

Mitchell was staring at one of the crates just below eye level. "Steve, take a gander at this one. The top's sprung. I can almost see inside."

The commander crouched slightly, as best he could in AMOS. Almost, he decided, was not quite enough, but he could swear he could see the tip of a bullion bar—a faint but tantalizing impression of burnished gold.

He straightened up. "Well, it would seem we've hit the jackpot, but let's not do any premature celebrating until we get this stuff out. Ozzie, how the hell are we gonna work this?"

Admiral Cornell was pacing the bridge like a caged panther when *Nemo* flashed the word.

"*Chase, Nemo.* Jackman's found the bullion crates."

Cornell stopped pacing long enough to stride over to the underwater-communications operator, ignoring the cheers from bridge personnel and the wide grin Captain Bixenman was sporting. "Ask 'em if they're all right, if there's been any trouble."

His voice had carried into the operator's mike, and Anders answered promptly. "We hear you five-by-five, Admiral. Commander Jackman reports everything routine, and they're trying to get the first crate secured for lift-up to *Nemo*. We're positioning over their entry point now and preparing to lower the recovery net."

* * *

"Steve, we're ready to drop the net anytime you give the word."

The announcement from Anders aboard *Nemo* brought an annoyed response from Jackman. "Keep your shirts on! We're having one hell of a time getting a crate loose."

The problem was the way the crates had been loaded aboard eighty-three years ago. To save space in a hold already crowded with liquor cartons, the cargo handlers had piled Sovereign's shipment into a high, relatively narrow stack, with the top crates a good two feet above the reach of even a tall man like Mitchell. Dozens of rope tie-downs, long since dissolved, had probably held the boxes in place during the sinking. There was nothing in the hold to stand on, and Jackman swore under his breath as he pondered the next move.

Williams suggested, "How about prying one of the lower crates loose first?"

"Negative," Jackman said. "The whole damned stack could collapse, and I'd hate to get hit by one crate, let alone a bunch of 'em. Ozzie, you're tallest. How about getting on my shoulders so you can reach a top crate?"

"Either that or you stand on mine," Mitchell said. "The trick is to secure my boots somehow so I have something to push against. What worries me is the bulk of these suits. I'm not even sure I could make it to your shoulders. AMOS wasn't designed for aquabatics."

Jackman grumbled, "We should have brought some kind of hook, like a long marlin spike. But I think I can give you enough leverage. I'll hoist you."

Nemo picked this inopportune moment to relay a message from *Chase*. "Divers, Admiral Cornell wants to know what you're doing."

Mitchell's waist was level with Jackman's helmet and he looked like a man trying to climb a battleship funnel. He paused long enough for the commander to snarl, "Tell the old son of a bitch we're playing pinochle! What the hell does he think we're doing?"

Anders chuckled. "I'll rephrase that answer for you, Steve."

"Keep going, Ozzie." Jackman panted. "Are you almost

there? My suit servos are straining; I can hear them. I feel like I'm lifting a goddamned rhino."

Mitchell's knees had reached Jackman's shoulders and he hoisted himself the rest of the way, now standing upright and actually looking down on the top layer of crates. One arm of AMOS reached out, claws extended to grab the edge of a crate, and then froze as Carlson's half scream rattled their helmets.

"Look behind you! *There's someone else here!*"

Williams and Tuttle were the first to turn around, staring in horror at what faced them.

Jackman tried to turn but realized he might dislodge Mitchell. He managed to swivel his head inside the bulky helmet just enough to see the object of Carlson's warning.

Mitchell got the worst view; he was too high, and from this angle, he couldn't see what the others had seen with terrifying clarity.

It was a man, yet not really a man: a man wearing an officer's coat; a man with a face that was not a face but a mask of rotting flesh. It was the face of a decaying corpse, almost but not quite a skeleton's hideous skull. The nose was gone, and where the eyes had been were two bony sockets, gazing at them malevolently under the glare of their strobes. Weedy tendrils of hair still clung to the top of the skull, and what remained of facial flesh hung like melting wax from the cheekbones and jaw.

It was grinning—a fixed, humorless, toothy cadaver's smile, with teeth that could have been tiny tombstones. It shook its head menacingly, the movement dislodging strips of flesh that drifted close to their helmet visors. Tuttle gagged and closed his eyes. Williams fingered the trigger of his laser gun, an instinctive gesture even as he realized a weapon was futile.

The thing wheeled to look at Carlson, who was still standing transfixed at the entry hole, and its obscene smile became an obscene leer.

Jackman's voice sliced into the tension. "Stand fast, people; it can't hurt us." His words were aimed mostly at Carlson, who proceeded to perform one of the most nerveless acts he had ever witnessed.

She calmly lifted the camera from her belt and snapped a picture. The built-in flash lit up the cavernous hold for a split second, revealing the loathsome envoy of the walking dead in every detail—so vividly they could almost smell it.

As if startled by the exploding light, it vanished.

"Jesus Christ," Tuttle mumbled.

It suddenly occurred to Jackman that the underwater camera Carlson had used previously didn't have a strobe flash, relying instead on a lower-powered continuous lamp for setting up a shot in darkness and using exceptionally sensitive high-speed film.

"Fay, where the hell did you get that camera?"

"It's my own, a backup . . . something I bought in Pearl Harbor. I . . . I felt more comfortable with it, but I didn't say anything because I figured you might insist on the assigned equipment." She dredged up a chuckle. "You didn't notice the switch."

"No, I didn't."

Mitchell said, "I wonder if that shot even registered. Henning told us it's hard to take a picture of a ghost."

"Who'd want to see that thing again?" Jackman said acidly. "Ozzie, let's get one of those crates down."

Working with his clawed arms, Mitchell finally shoved a crate away from the top pile. It fell with surprising speed to the hold floor, and while Carlson's camera flashed again, Williams inspected the padlock attached to the lid.

"Lock's rusted solid," he announced. "We can cut it off when we're back topside. We mess with it here, everything might spill out."

Jackman said, "Right, keep it intact. We don't have time to open anything down here. *Nemo*, you read me?"

"Affirmative. How you doing?"

"We've got one crate ready to load. Drop the net."

"Roger."

Moving the first crate to the adjacent hold was more of a task than anticipated. They had difficulty grasping the edges with their robot claws, and the crate itself proved surprisingly heavy even in the weight-reducing buoyancy of the water. By the time they finally got it out of hold three, the net was waiting for them—a hammocklike affair made of a titanium-alloy mesh, its ends attached to a four-pronged steel cable.

"We're going back for another load," Jackman informed *Nemo* after they heaved the crate into the net.

"Steve, you sound winded. How many do you think you can load on this dive?"

"Four, if we're lucky. The damn crate weighs a ton and it's awkward as hell to pick up. It'll go faster after we get the top layer off the stack, but you'd better tell Cornell we'll probably need more dives than we figured before we're finished."

"Jolly Roger will spit harpoons when he hears that. Hang on a sec. . . . Steve, he's asking if you've had any company yet."

Jackman debated briefly whether to describe their repulsive visitor, and decided to hedge. "Tell him company dropped in but didn't stay long."

"He's going to want details, Steve."

"He'll have to wait. We're going back to hold three."

They repeated their improvised process of getting the crates off the top of the stack, Mitchell bracing himself on the commander's shoulders and working a crate loose until it fell unimpeded to the floor. It went faster this time as he gained dexterity with his claws.

"Want to get another one down while I'm up here?" he asked Jackman.

"Might as well clear the whole top layer while we're at it. That's one less job to do on the next dive. Can't understand how they drop so fast. You'd think they'd be more buoyant; they must weigh a ton."

Mitchell had just dislodged the third crate when it happened.

Not quite like the last time.

Williams's helmet light went out first.

Then Carlson's.

Followed by Tuttle's.

Next Mitchell's.

Jackman's was the last.

And down came the heavy crate, unseen, falling through the

dark water toward the most vulnerable spot on the commander's suit: the AMOS helmet.

Instinct and athletic reflexes saved Jackman's life. Even as his own strobe failed, he knew Mitchell already had loosened the crate. He never saw it fall, but he sensed its oncoming mass, as a veteran quarterback can sense a blind-side hit from an oncoming tackler. A second before the impact, he fell back and took the blow on the left leg of his suit, the crate striking just below the kneecap, where AMOS's armor was thinnest.

Excruciating pain shot up his thigh to his groin and he cried out as the lower leg of the AMOS bent forward, past its electronic and mechanical safety stops. Mitchell shouted frantically, "Steve, was that you? Are you hurt?"

Jackman ground out an answer through gritted teeth, "I think my leg's dislocated or broken, Ozzie. I got hit by that crate. My suit's knee joint is jammed; it's bent out in the wrong direction."

"Oh shit!" Mitchell groaned. "We've gotta get you out of here."

Tuttle said in a defeated tone, "A goddamned bat couldn't find its way out of here."

Anders's anxious voice sounded in their earphones. "Steve, we heard that . . . about the broken leg. Jeff wants you to go back to the other hold, and we'll lift you out on the net."

Jackman took a deep breath. "Didn't you hear what Tuttle said? Our helmet lights are out."

There was no reaction from *Nemo* to that news. He could imagine the consternation it had caused. He added, "Don't say anything to Cornell yet. Maybe we can figure a way out of this before we get him tying up the comm circuits."

Lieutenant Lawrence came on. "Steve, is Fay still stationed at that bulkhead hole?"

Carlson answered herself. "Affirmative . . . I think. In this darkness, I'm not sure where I'm at."

"Keep talking and let the others see if they can navigate from your signal strength."

Mitchell barked, "That won't do Steve any good. I'm on top

of these damned crates and we have to get him up before anyone can get to Carlson."

Jackman could almost visualize Lawrence running a hand through his blond hair in frustration. "Sorry, I didn't realize that. Steve, how about you tapping on something metal so they can find you? Bang on your suit if you have to."

"I'll try it," Williams volunteered. "Steve, hit your free claw on the deck plates."

Jackman complied, cycling his mechanical arm back and forth to clang his suit's manipulator onto the metal floor of the hold.

"Keep pounding."

They heard a thud, followed by an expletive. "I just hit a wall or something," Williams announced. "Steve, am I getting close?"

Jackman, trying to keep the pain out of his voice, said, "You sound farther away than before. It's no use, *Nemo*. We're totally disoriented, and if we start moving around in this black muck, someone else could get hurt. Ozzie, I can't think straight; this leg's killing me. Any ideas?"

"None right now," Mitchell admitted. "Unless"—he paused in full cognizance of what he was about to say—"everyone stay where you are, drop to the floor, and let *Nemo*'s lasers cut us an escape route."

"And where the hell does that leave you?" Jackman demanded.

"Up here on top of the pile."

Jackman said angrily, "That plan's predicated on *everyone* being able to lie prone. You'd better get the hell down before I ask for those lasers."

"No dice, Steve. I'm liable to come down right on top of you . . . and from the way you sound, you can't stand any more pain."

"Ozzie, that's an order."

"Order refused. Use your head. I could put a boot through your helmet visor."

Lawrence broke in. "Steve, you've been in that hold for almost two hours. You're gonna have an oxygen problem in another thirty minutes."

Jackman's heart sank. With rare carelessness, he hadn't kept track of the time, and this was a new and terrible danger. The laborious task of getting at the bullion crates had devoured not merely extra minutes but precious oxygen. Normally on a prolonged dive, they would have returned to the sub, replenished the oxygen supply, and returned to the salvage job. Now they'd be lucky just to get back to *Nemo*. He felt like an animal who had blundered recklessly into a trap. Despite his rank, he had never been faced with many life-or-death command decisions; Jackman was more of a doer than a planner, the recipient rather than the instigator of orders. The pain of this reality was sharper than the agonizing pangs shooting through his leg.

Hate began flooding his mind: hate for whatever was toying with them; hate for this cadaver of a ship, a killer now just as she had been eight decades ago; and, most of all, hate for this whole damned mission and where it had led them.

He made a decision. "Everyone lie flat. *Nemo*, move down to the hull and stand by to fire lasers."

Lawrence came back. "Steve, we should clear this with Cornell first."

"Negative. Get going and advise when you're in position to fire."

"Roger, but we'll have to raise that net first."

"Okay, but don't waste any time. Ozzie, one last time— GET THE HELL DOWN HERE!"

Mitchell didn't reply. But Fay Carlson did.

"Hold up, *Nemo*! I want to try something."

Jackman said instantly, "Belay hoisting the net, Jeff. What have you got, Fay?"

"The strobe flash on my camera. It'll give us enough light for all of you to see where I'm standing . . . and Ozzie can look where to jump without landing on top of you. I'll keep flashing the strobe while you head toward me. Steve, when the first one goes off, Felix and Bert can help you. Do you want to try this?"

From his perch, Mitchell sighed. "It's better than playing laser tag with *Nemo*."

Reprieved, Jackman thought gratefully—until another grim

possibility came to him. Carlson's camera might fail, just like the helmet lights.

"Fay, how many flash discharges do you have left?" he asked through clenched teeth. "We'll need more than one to light up this dungeon."

She was mentally calculating how many pictures she had taken. The strobes flashed only as long as film was in the camera, but she decided this was no real problem. As best as she could remember, she had taken not more than a dozen shots of her thirty-six-exposure roll. "No sweat, Steve. The batteries are fresh." Provided they worked, she thought grimly.

"Jackman to *Nemo*: You reading this?"

Lawrence's acknowledgment came in a moment. "Standing by."

Tuttle murmured, "I wish there was some way to cross these claw fingers."

"Amen," agreed Williams.

Jackman took a deep breath and tried to forget his throbbing leg. "Everyone, get set. Ozzie, jump with the flash. Fay, you ready?"

"I can't find the damned button," she muttered. "I think . . ."

One claw hit the button before anyone was ready—except for Mitchell. He jumped the instant the flash lit up Jackman's prone figure below him, twisting to the right as he fell and landing only inches away from the commander.

"Again!" Jackman ordered, and a second flash lit up the hold. Williams didn't see Jackman, but Tuttle did and he started toward him, calling out, "Come with me, Lieutenant."

The third flash gave them all the orientation they needed. Each succeeding flash guided them closer to Carlson as Mitchell and Tuttle half-carried Jackman with them. When they reached her, the commander warned, "Don't use any more until we're all out. We'll need a couple to locate the net."

One more flash illuminated the net. The first and only bullion crate they had recovered was still nestled in its metallic web.

Mitchell, almost out of breath, grunted, "Might as well go

first class, Steve. We'll hoist you on top of that crate. Okay, Bert, heave!"

Carlson used two more flashes while they were loading Jackman. When she pressed the button again, nothing happened. They were in that black vacuum again, as sightless as if their eyes had been gouged out.

"That was the last frame," she said.

"Stay where you are," Jackman told her. "Now everyone move toward me, as best you can, until the net stops you." They complied. "Drop your claws a little and move the arms back, very slowly. You should feel the claws catch on this mesh."

"Mine are hooked," Williams called out.

"Mine, too," Tuttle announced, and Mitchell came in a few seconds later. But Carlson inadvertently had moved not only her arms but her feet, losing contact with the deck for a long moment. When her boots finally found a foothold again, panic crept into her voice for the first time. "I can't find the net."

"Come forward again, very slowly. Don't worry, you know you're close to us. Take it easy. . . ."

Tuttle called out with relief, "You just bumped into me, Lieutenant. Commander Mitchell's on my right. Move sideways to the left, just a little, then come forward."

"I've got the net!" she said triumphantly.

"Good girl!" Jackman sighed. "*Nemo*, hoist away!"

With agonizing slowness, the net began its upward journey. They had progressed only a third of the way when it came to a jolting stop. Blind though he was, Jackman sensed what had happened. One edge of the net had caught on a piece of metal, probably jutting out from an E deck bulkhead, he imagined. It was impossible to fend things off in the darkness. Hanging precariously as they were, only Jackman had any chance to reach the obstruction and free them. He groped futilely in the pitch-blackness, waves of pain invading his body as he twisted his upper limbs, trying to find where they were caught.

In *Nemo*'s cockpit, Ellison had realized the net was no longer coming up, and he shut off the raising mechanism. "Something's gone wrong," he informed Lawrence. "They're not coming up."

Lawrence swore under his breath and barked into the intercom mike, "Steve, you okay?"

Jackman gasped, "The net's caught on some obstruction. I can't find it in this goddamned darkness."

"Oh boy," Lawrence groaned, looking at Ellison and Anders with a "What next?" expression. "Can one of the others help you?"

"Negative. They've got all they can do just hanging on to the net. I . . . I can almost sense where we're caught, but I can't reach it. Lemme try again."

He groped blindly again with his right claw, opening and closing the metal fingers, heedless of the throbbing pain that the slightest movement ignited. He thought the obstruction was just above him, to his right, but the fingers kept closing on nothing but water. Once he felt them hit something solid, a moment of exultation that was wiped out when he realized all he had touched was the net itself.

He began feeling faint and stopped to rest. Carlson called out weakly, "Steve, any luck?"

"Not yet," he muttered grimly. Maybe, he thought, the hang-up wasn't where he had sensed it was—it was too easy to become disoriented in this well of utter darkness. He shifted to his left claw and resumed groping.

In and out went the steel claws.

In and out . . . in and out . . . touching nothing.

The net swayed once and tilted. Jackman knew one of the other divers—Mitchell, probably—was trying to climb into it and help him. Then the motion stopped, and he knew the attempt had failed.

An electronic tone sounded in his helmet.

They had only ten minutes of oxygen left.

Roger Cornell felt powerless.

Nemo's terse message disclosed more than the latest mishap; Lawrence had discounted Jackman's orders and transmitted all the bad news: another strobe failure, the injury, and the jammed cargo net, leaving the admiral stunned. Bixenman saw this and took over communications with the sub.

Shoving the radio operator aside, he grabbed the mike. "*Nemo,* this is Captain Bixenman. Can you depress your strobes so they get some light down there?"

"We're trying that right now, Captain," Ensign Anders assured him.

"Well, give us your status!" Bixenman barked. He stared at Cornell. "The sub's strobes will pull them out of this, Admiral," he said. "All Jackman needs is some light to work with."

They waited impatiently for another two minutes. Then the intercom speaker came to life with nerve-jarring abruptness. It was Anders's voice again, this time filtered through layers of panic.

"Captain, our strobes are almost dead. They're giving us less than five percent of normal intensity; we might as well be using a flashlight."

Cornell groaned. *"They're goners."*

Jackman was starting to feel faint again. He had consumed more oxygen through physical exertion than the others, and he knew he had little time left—or little strength, either. The tiny red CO_2 warning light had blinked on inside his visor, and he felt his breathing speeding up uncontrollably.

He whispered, "Ozzie, I'm running out of gas. Any way you can boost yourself up here and help?"

"I'll try again." But in the attempt Mitchell nearly dislodged Tuttle from his hold on the net. The effort left him as exhausted as Jackman, and he began to pray silently. A minute later, his own oxygen warning light began blinking. Into his dying brain came something he remembered from the Old Testament's Book of Genesis. . . .

". . . *and darkness was upon the face of the deep. And the Spirit of God moved upon the face of the waters. And God said, let there be light . . .*"

He said the words only to himself, even as Jackman pronounced their epitaph. Aboard *Nemo,* they could barely hear the commander's fading voice. "It's no use; say good-bye to everyone."

Their strobes came back on.

So did *Nemo*'s with full power.

Jackman saw the obstructing spur of metal now, and with a last surge of strength, he reached out with a claw and freed the net. He didn't even know he had simultaneously gasped, "*Nemo*, bring us up."

21

Admiral Cornell watched impassively as the lone bullion crate was hoisted from *Nemo* to *Chase*'s deck, dripping and foul-smelling.

"Hose it down," he ordered two sailors standing nearby. "Then I want a couple of armed guards stationed here until I send for it in the wardroom."

One of the sailors, his nose crinkled disdainfully, said, "Admiral, you'd need a blowtorch to break into that thing."

Cornell said curtly, "There's a goddamned fortune inside that crate and I don't want anyone on this ship getting curious. Understood?"

"Aye, sir."

The admiral wheeled and marched down to sick bay, where an exhausted Steve Jackman lay on the examining table. Cornell hovered over Cyrus McDonald's shoulder while the doctor made his examination.

"Admiral, would you kindly go topside and let me finish my work in peace?" McDonald finally snapped.

"How bad is it?" Cornell asked for the third time.

"Well, he won't be doing any diving for a long, long while. I could give you some fancy medical terms for what happened to his leg, but it all boils down to a crushed kneecap . . . badly crushed, I might add."

The little surgeon glanced at Ben Henning, whom he had asked to be present during the examination. "I can do some patchwork on you, Steve, but you're going to need a good orthopedic surgeon to repair that knee. Ben, you concur?"

Henning nodded. "I saw the X rays, Steve. The kneecap looks like spaghetti. It's a temporary cast and crutches for you until we can get you to a hospital."

Cornell put a hand on Jackman's shoulder. "This is tough luck, Steve. I'm sorry."

"What about the rest of the gold, Admiral?"

Cornell wasn't sure what Jackman wanted to hear. The divers were the ones who had risked their lives, as Cornell was only too painfully aware. Sending men into harm's way was item one in an admiral's job description, but against what kind of enemy?

"Steve, I don't know. I want to hear what Ben has to say before I decide anything." Henning started to speak, but the admiral cut him off with an upheld palm. "Not now. I've already asked Captain Bixenman to have all divers, *Nemo*'s crew, and officers not on watch meet me in the wardroom . . . and it's just about that time."

Through gritted teeth, Jackman said to the ship's surgeon, "Doc, hurry up with that cast and get me some crutches." He had half-risen from the examining table when Cornell shoved him back to a prone position.

"You're not going anywhere, sailor," he said, not unkindly. "It's bed rest for you for at least twenty-four hours. Right, Mac?"

"Right," McDonald agreed, but without much conviction. He suspected it would take a twenty-man shore patrol to keep Jackman away from the debriefing. "I'll give you a shot of Demerol to relieve the discomfort, Steve. What you need is sleep."

"What I need," Jackman said, "is assurance that my divers won't be asked to go inside that hell ship anymore."

"I can't call off the mission yet, Steve," the admiral said. "But I won't endanger lives again. That I promise you." He turned to the others. "Mac, give him that shot. Ben, I want to talk to you privately."

He strode out of sick bay with Henning trailing him. Jackman grabbed McDonald's arm.

"Doc, belay that shot. *Please.*" Uncharacteristically, the ship's surgeon hesitated. When it came to medical decisions, he usually rode roughshod over men who outranked him. "The pain's going to get worse, Steve."

"That kind of pain I can stand. Just put the cast on."

"Patients like you I can do without," McDonald said sourly. He wondered what Cornell wanted to tell Henning as he started applying a cast to Jackman's leg. McDonald worked efficiently but faster—he decided he didn't want to miss the debriefing, either.

"Okay, Ben, if you have the slightest suspicion of what's making those lights fail, tell me now!"

Henning told him. He told him everything: about a collective consciousness; about his contact with the dead, and a dream that had carried him back to April 1912; about the supernatural motivation behind the things that had happened to the two gold-hunting expeditions.

Cornell listened without a flicker of disbelief in his eyes. After a moment, he asked the same question Montague had posed. "Ben, did you sense any real hostility? Any kind of warning that if we tried again, this presence, or whatever it is, would lower the boom?"

"No, but after what happened today, what kind of warning do you need? Those lights didn't fail by themselves."

Cornell said quietly, "I don't suppose they did; I'll admit that. Jesus . . . a force that can appear in any shape, and even screw up equipment. This thing's rewriting the book."

Henning studied him gravely. "This particular book has to have a final chapter, Admiral. And the author, I'm afraid, has to be you. What's the ending going to be?"

The stern, crevassed face sagged a little. "What kind of an ending would *you* write?"

"Finally, you ask me an easy question. You brought me along to advise on psychic phenomena. Well, this particular manifestation has indirectly killed five people and injured one, and I'm not counting the ones who died in that freak storm back in 1975. So I'll give you advice. Leave the *Titanic* alone before anyone else gets killed or hurt."

Cornell shook his head like a groggy fighter trying to clear his brain. "I don't know why I asked you when I already knew the answer. The gist of it seems to be that the United States Navy, the same Navy that has lost battles but never a war, has been defeated by fifteen hundred ghosts. Kind of ironic, wouldn't you say?"

"But unfortunately, true."

"Maybe," Cornell said enigmatically. "Do me a favor, Ben. Lay up to the bridge and tell Captain Bixenman I want to see him and Joe Kresky in my stateroom immediately. And tell him the debriefing will be delayed thirty minutes. I'll see you in the wardroom then."

He strode off, leaving Henning staring after him. The admiral, he thought, might as well have been whistling "Don't Give Up the Ship."

En route to the bridge to deliver Cornell's message, Henning passed by the lone recovered bullion crate, still being cleaned up after a fashion. He paused long enough for a cursory glance, slightly intimidated by the two burly, armed sailors guarding the rust-encrusted rectangular box.

"Hi, Doc," one of the guards greeted him. He noticed Henning eyeing the crate almost distastefully. "Hard to imagine there's enough in there to buy every guy on this ship a Rolls-Royce," he said.

"Yeah," the other sailor said, "provided it ain't haunted like where it came from."

Henning smiled to himself. He had advised Cornell and Bixenman to let the crew know, in outline at least, what was happening 12,500 feet below *Chase*, and they had followed his recommendation. The men seemed to be taking it in stride.

He left the guards and continued on his errand, finding Bixenman pacing the bridge. Henning repeated the admiral's instructions.

"Did he tell you what it's about?" the captain asked.

Henning sensed the bridge personnel watching him. He motioned toward the open starboard-bridge wing, and Bixenman moved outside with him.

"I'm afraid he's going to keep going after that damn gold," Henning said bluntly when they were alone.

"And you think he's crazy."

"Both as a psychiatrist *and* a parapsychologist, yes."

"Did he say he'd order more dives in so many words?"

"He hinted at it."

"Then I think you'd better wait and see what he has in mind specifically before you jump to conclusions."

"Let me tell you something, Captain. In a few minutes, I'm going to be in the officers' mess announcing to you and all personnel concerned what is *really* throwing overalls in their chowder. Cornell already knows what I'm going to say and apparently thinks he should ignore it."

The captain's eyes narrowed. "Ignore what?"

"I have to tell you when I tell the others, not that it'll make any difference. Cornell will probably give you a speech about duty, you'll say 'aye, aye, sir,' and poor Ozzie Mitchell will have to lead four other divers right back into that hellhole again. And for what? Because Admiral Cornell is afraid to admit the Navy is up against something its weapons and tactics can't handle. Do a few crates of bullion mean more to him than his people?"

Bixenman's pale blue eyes turned icy. "Let me tell *you* something, Ben. There's no flag officer in this or any other navy more compassionate, and more dedicated to the men under him than Roger Cornell. He won't squander any more lives for that gold. But if there is any way to get inside cargo hold three with a *minimum* of risk, he'll grab it. What else should we expect from the man? He's in command of a mission that's been ordered to recover that gold. The orders came from the President. If he called it off right now and the real reason for failure ever leaked out, the fleet would become the laughingstock of every son of a bitch in Washington. Try explaining to the politicians and the news media how the world's best-equipped deep-sea salvage vessel came home empty because of a haunted ship. That's what Cornell's afraid of here: They can laugh at him all the way from Capitol Hill to the White House and he wouldn't flinch, but he can't stand them laughing at the Navy. If you'll forgive my psychoanalyzing, he's probably looking for some way to salvage not just the gold but the Navy's reputation."

"Captain, *is* there a way into cargo hold three without risking lives?"

"Maybe," Bixenman said enigmatically. "Joe Kresky's the key to that. Look, I have to get down to the admiral's quarters. I'll see you in the wardroom. We're late."

Steve Jackman, accompanied by an apologetic-looking Cyrus McDonald, hobbled into the wardroom on crutches, his left leg swathed in a cast. His face had regained a little color and, Henning noted with interest, bore the expression of a man itching for an argument.

"I thought I confined you to sick bay," Cornell said sternly.

"You suggested it, sir. You didn't make it an order."

McDonald said quickly, "Commander Jackman has medical approval to be up, Admiral." He smiled slyly. "Reluctant approval, I'll admit, but I have to agree with him—he's strong enough to be here."

Cornell had half-expected Jackman to show up anyway, so he shifted ground. "Well, you're here. You might as well stay."

Fay Carlson motioned the commander to sit next to her. Bixenman smiled to himself—Cornell might have been right about those two.

The admiral rapped for attention.

"Before I discuss with you the future of the mission, Doctor Henning will tell you something he already has imparted to Derek Montague, Bill Gillespie, and myself. It's a theory, and theories are not necessarily facts. However, I think there's something to this, incredible as it seems. Ben, you have the floor."

Henning repeated what he had related to Cornell and the two civilians. As he talked, he watched faces. On many of them, he saw a kind of reluctant surrender to what he was saying, but the divers kept turning toward Cornell, clearly wondering whether they were going down again.

That stirred Henning to recklessness. "In my opinion," he concluded, "it would be useless to attempt any further penetration of the *Titanic*'s interior, *and that includes cargo hold three.* Another equipment failure could be disastrous, as it almost was today. In fact, I would expect things to get worse if we persist."

He sat down, suddenly weary. As weary as Montague, Henning thought, which figured—he felt he had aged ten years since *Chase* weighed anchor at Norfolk. He had just openly challenged Cornell—a heresy even for a civilian—before he even knew what the admiral's plan entailed.

Yet all Cornell did was nod thoughtfully. "Thanks, Ben. I appreciate your counsel, and in a roundabout way, I'm going to follow it." There were two discreetly feeble handclaps from Bert Tuttle, but Cornell ignored them. "I agree with Doctor Henning that it would be foolhardy to continue diving operations as originally planned. I also agree with Commander Jackman that the alternate plan of using *Nemo*'s lasers is impractical. But I believe there is another approach, one presenting a minimum of risk to all concerned. I've discussed this with Captain Bixenman, and he concurs it's worth trying. Certainly preferable to quitting now"—he ached when he saw the doubt in the faces of the divers—"and going home with our tails between our legs."

"We have aboard *Chase* a supply of plastic explosives that can be detonated by short-range radio signal. We also have aboard a man with considerable demolition training and experience. I refer to our diving coordinator, Joe Kresky, who has agreed to perform the planting operation. He assures me he can blow open a hole in the hull at a point where the divers can simply walk laterally into hold three. They will work under *Nemo*'s lights and they won't have to move the crates very far. After we crack the charges, *Nemo* will be positioned not more than ten or twelve feet from the opening."

He gave them a moment for it to sink in. Ozzie Mitchell broke the silence. "Joe, are you going to do the planting alone, or will you need help?"

Kresky glanced at the admiral and got a go-ahead nod. "I'll arm up just before I leave *Nemo*, and I'll do the attaching myself. But I'll need two divers to carry the explosive disks out of the sub. They'll be in a small box that's easy to lift. After the disks are rigged, we'll go back to *Nemo* and move far enough away to avoid any compression damage when they're detonated."

Jackman spoke through his pain and fatigue, "What kind of distance are you talking about?"

"It has to be at least a hundred and fifty yards." Kresky looked at Cornell again for permission to say more.

Cornell understood. "Go ahead, Joe. Tell him the whole drill."

"Well, the only problem is whether the radio signal will carry as far as a hundred and fifty yards. It's never been tested beyond that distance or at that depth. And we can't move in any closer, because when those explosives go off, you might as well be dropping depth charges on *Nemo*. Also, we have to hope the shaped charges do their job of directing most of the force outward, or we'd risk blowing up the hold itself."

Questioning eyes turned toward the admiral. "*Nemo*," he said, "is going to maintain a safe distance, period. If the signal doesn't carry, that's the ball game. And this is the reason Joe and I haven't even mentioned the plastics being on board until now. I never thought we'd have to use them, and that if we did, it would be only as a last resort . . . and a pretty unreliable one to boot."

Mitchell said, "Joe, I don't like the idea of arming those devices inside the sub. Can't they be armed after they're attached?"

"Not necessary. You could drop one of these babies off a thirty-story building and all you'd get is a thud. They can be detonated only by a coded radio signal."

There was silence again as divers, sub crew, and the three civilians digested what they had heard. Gillespie couldn't believe that no one had mentioned the most obvious drawback. He sensed that the navy people were reluctant to challenge a flag officer, so he spoke up himself.

"Great plan, Roger, except for the other very large flaw. What happens if *Nemo*'s strobes dim down to weak flashlights again? Or fail completely? And then the AMOS lights go off? Both of those things have happened already. Then you'll have everyone trapped in a darkness you have to experience to comprehend its terror. That's what the divers fear most, Roger, and I'm saying it for them."

Cornell was prepared for this. "We've got a way for the divers to find their way back to *Nemo* even in pitch-blackness, if it comes to that. They'll work with long tethers attached to their belts, the opposite ends linked to the top of *Nemo*'s diving compartment. There's no way anyone can get lost. We ought to be willing to take *that* much of a chance. If I thought this plan carried an unacceptable exposure to casualties, I'd secure this expedition right now."

Gillespie pressed him. "Roger, even with tethers, we have no way of predicting what those forces might let loose next."

"No, we don't, but our lights appear to be their major and favorite target. It's a *known* hazard against which we can take precautions. We can rig some auxiliary floodlights on the sub to use if her main strobes quit again." He saw Gillespie's dubious look. "Yeah, I know the auxiliaries could fail, too. Look, it's obvious to everyone that if we suffer mass equipment failure again, we're licked. But we've already managed to bring one crate up, haven't we? So let's do it, people. Ozzie, with Steve *hors de combat*, you'll be in charge of the divers tomorrow."

"Aye, aye, sir," Mitchell acknowledged, his face blank.

"Let's look at the bright side of things," Cornell said. "We did achieve exploration of the *Titanic*'s interior, and if we're stymied tomorrow, we're still going back with at least one crate of gold. I think it's time to see what one-thirty-fourth of a fortune looks like. Bert, would you get some help and bring that crate here?"

Tuttle returned in a few minutes, the two guards in tow carrying the crate.

"Put it on the wardroom table," the admiral ordered.

Despite the wash job, the crate still smelled clammy and stale, a stench not unlike decaying seaweed. Only a few spots of metal peeked forlornly through the scales of rust.

Lieutenant Ellison whispered, "It looks like a small coffin."

"Smells like one, too," Jeff Lawrence grunted.

Cornell said, "Okay, Bert, use that laser gun; aim at that padlock. Everyone else stand back and look away."

Tuttle stepped forward and fired. After a five-second burst, the padlock simply disintegrated. Mitchell tugged at the freed lid in vain. "The whole damned lid's rusted solid," he finally announced. "We'll have to cut around the edges."

"Then do it," the admiral said impatiently. "Just make sure the beam doesn't go any lower than the lid edge."

Tuttle hesitated; it was one thing to knock open a padlock, but removing the lid required far more precision and he had a mental image of the admiral's wrath if the contents were damaged.

Mitchell sensed his discomfort. "Give me the gun, Bert." He bent down to get an eye-level aim and fired a steady beam at one edge, repeating the process at the other three edges. They could see the lid begin to loosen, until it seemed to rise a fraction of an inch above the sides.

"That should do it," Mitchell said. He got to his feet, gave the laser back to Tuttle, and lifted the lid in the air, holding it to one side while he peered at the contents. He reached down and picked up a bar, holding it so everyone could see. A bar with a moldy gray color, pitted with rust spots.

Cornell turned white.

"Admiral, it's lead," Mitchell announced.

Every bar in the crate was lead, and when they pulled the last one from the bottom, Cornell glared at Derek Montague.

"Holy Christ!" he growled.

Montague shrugged helplessly. "I can't explain it. I *know* I broke their code. Thirty-four crates of gold bullion shipped on the *Titanic*. I'd stake my life on it. Except"—his voice almost cracked— "I also staked the lives of others on it."

Gillespie took pity on the shattered Englishman. "Derek, do you have any possible clue to what went wrong?"

Montague shook his head dejectedly. "It was a very simple code, one of the easiest ones imaginable."

Cornell looked at the slabs of lead piled on the table. "All those lives, all that money, wasted going after a nonexistent pot of gold at the bottom of the North Atlantic . . ."

His voice trailed off and he looked as if he was about to

crack. Bixenman, studying him anxiously, said, "Admiral, it wasn't your fault."

Cornell seemed not to hear. "Wasted," he repeated, "and I assume the rest of the crates are the same. I'll be damned if I'm gonna go after thirty-three more crates of lead. Bix, I suggest you make preparations for returning to Norfolk."

"Wait a minute."

All eyes swiveled toward Commander Jackman.

"How do we know all the other crates are filled with lead?" he asked. "I got the barest peek into one of the bottom crates—the lid was sprung just a fraction of an inch—and so help me, I thought I saw the tip of a real gold bar. Maybe only one or two of the crates are phony."

"Are you sure you saw gold?" Cornell demanded.

Jackman hesitated. "No, sir, not one hundred percent sure. It could have been the light from my helmet lamp playing tricks."

"Or wishful thinking," Gillespie murmured, and Cornell nodded.

"Pretty inconclusive," he grunted. "Sorry, but I don't buy it. I only wish I could." He turned to Bixenman. "Captain, I'll see you on the bridge. And while we're at it, put those bars back and somebody take that damned crate topside. I want it out of my sight."

He left the mess. McDonald sighed and said to Jackman "You're overdue for that shot, Steve. Back to sick bay for you." The commander didn't argue, hobbling after the ship's surgeon in obvious discomfort.

No one spoke until Bixenman ventured, "Cornell took it better than I would have expected."

"He looked off to me," Ozzie Mitchell said. "When I held up that bar and said it was nothing but lead, I figured he'd have a stroke."

Bixenman shook his head. "Nothing that drastic. But he's been hit hard. The admiral knows the mission's a bust, and Roger Cornell does not suffer either failure or fools gladly."

The captain rose. "Time to go to work. Lawrence, Ellison, Kresky—and you, too, Anders—I suggest you make sure

Nemo's all buttoned up and secured for departure. All divers are off duty until further notice, except for Lieutenant Carlson."

"Me, sir?"

"Yes, you. I want you to go to the photo lab and ride herd on Bob Johnson, especially now that we're standing down from dive ops. The admiral will be very unhappy if he doesn't see the results of what you shot today by oh-seven hundred tomorrow—including whatever you got of that last apparition."

"Aye, sir."

After the naval personnel had filed out, Bixenman sat down again to talk to the three civilians, addressing Montague directly.

"Derek, there's no denying that you made a bad call here, though God knows what went wrong. If you insist on blaming yourself, be my guest. But you've got to let go of those fatalities. You didn't have any more to do with what happened around the *Titanic* than I did. Yes, you led two expeditions down a false trail. But even if there had been gold, the deaths still would have occurred. Do you understand what I'm saying?"

"Yes," Montague said, so softly that they could barely hear him.

"Good, because guilt is nothing but one long migraine headache, and unwarranted guilt is even worse—a malignancy that has to be excised before it destroys you. Now, do I have your word of honor you won't do something foolish?"

"You have it." Montague's words were sincere, even though the sadness remained on his face.

Bixenman paused to light a cigarette, then turned to Henning. "Something's been bothering me since we opened the crate. Something I don't understand. Maybe you have the answer. Or maybe Bill and Derek can explain it."

Henning said, "I wonder if it's the same thing that's been bugging me. You go first."

"Whatever's in the *Titanic* seems to be motivated by a single goal: to keep anyone from plundering that ship. It can differentiate between what it perceives as harmless expeditions like Ballard's and raiders like us. It seems to me that once it learned we couldn't be frightened away, it changed tactics. It began to make things outright dangerous. It struck at our most vulnerable spot—the lights we took down there. Yet at critical moments, today's events being the best example, it let us off the hook. Why? To me, that was a remarkable display of what you can only call compassion. So all of this implies some kind of intelligence, right?"

"Right," Henning agreed.

"A rational capability?"

"Yes."

"So if it's intelligent and rational, why in God's name did it try so hard to protect thirty-four cases of lead?"

Henning looked past them. "Exactly what I've been asking myself. A corporeal intellect with an amazing inconsistency: Its motivation stems from an ability to sense the motivation of others—to test, in our case as well as the Lefferts expedition, for what it considers to be greed. Yet it can't tell gold from lead. In effect, it's been guarding nothing of any value."

Gillespie said thoughtfully, "I think you've both misinterpreted the Entity's motives. It isn't guarding any treasure. It's guarding the *Titanic* herself. The ship is its tomb, something it does not want violated. It doesn't mind visitors, but it does oppose anyone who comes to steal. Apparently, it doesn't make any difference what they're stealing."

"Then why did it let that French expedition remove a number of artifacts?" Bixenman asked.

"Those were recovered from the debris field. I think the *Titanic's* dead may not regard that as sacrosanct, as part of their crypt. It reminds me of the famous curse placed on the archaeologists who discovered and then, you might say, robbed the tomb of some Egyptian pharaoh. They all died mysteriously within a year. I've always considered that story pure hogwash, but after what we've been seeing down there, I wonder if there's an analogy to be drawn."

Bixenman said, "We're never going to know." He rose, regarding Montague with an enigmatic smile. "When it comes to ghosts, Derek, one of your own countryman said it best. Fellow by the name of Shakespeare. Goodnight, gentlemen, I'm going to the bridge—which is my own form of hallowed sanctuary." He gave a mirthless laugh. "Horatio on the bridge."

Gillespie stared after him. "What did he mean by that?"

Montague said softly, "I believe he was referring to the quote from Hamlet. 'There are more things in heaven and earth, Horatio, than are dreamt of in your philosophy.' "

He gave a deep sigh and looked at his two companions. Gillespie noticed that the old man's eyes were no longer sad, but puzzled instead.

"If you're still bothered by that code business," he said, "there could be a dozen explanations, a dozen reasons why the gold was never shipped."

"Bill's right," Henning said. "Maybe there was a double cross within Sovereign itself—thieves within a band of thieves. Maybe they sent the bullion on another ship and used a fake code to throw off the ones they cheated."

Gillespie leaped on this with alacrity. "That's a possibility. You could have broken the code correctly and been fooled like everyone else."

Montague's sad smile returned. "You chaps are just trying to make me feel better, and I'm grateful. But Sovereign was not the kind of organization to have tolerated cheating within its own ranks. Their operations depended on complete internal loyalty. It was a lot like the Mafia. It was a true brotherhood of thieves. Jolly good try, Ben, but it won't wash."

He paused and said very slowly, "Something is still very wrong here."

22

Derek Montague lay restlessly in his cabin later that night, listening to the waves lap at the ship's hull. The temperature had dropped a little, and the lowering cloud deck seemed to be moving more quickly as the wind came up.

He went over the Sovereign code in his mind again, trying to figure out what mistake he might have made. He reviewed the method he had used to break it—the juxtaposition of numbers and letters that came so naturally to him, and especially with this particularly simple code. He was positive there had been no error.

He rehashed the evidence supporting the *Titanic* gold shipment, Sovereign's *modus operandi*, the new code put into effect shortly before the ship sailed, the failure of any bullion-supported conflict to occur; and the most irrefutable confirmation possible—Sovereign's salvage inquiries. Why would anyone who had shipped thirty-four crates of lead be that interested in recovering them?

He pondered Henning's explanation, too. An interesting theory, but Ben didn't know Sovereign as well as he did. There had to be another answer. But not even Montague's sixth sense, as acute as a cat's sight in the dark, could supply it. All he had, as the Americans would put it, was a gut feeling.

The ocean's swells had picked up, and the gentle sway of *Chase* riding to her deep anchors finally lulled him into a welcome sleep.

It was then that Derek Montague, like Ben Henning, began to move across time. . . .

He was standing near Berths 43 and 44 at the Southampton docks. The giant liner towered above his line of sight at such a sharp angle that he had to look up at her in progressive stages; the mammoth black hull, the gleaming white superstructure, and the tall buff-colored funnels were too much for the eye to absorb in a single glance.

It seemed to Montague that he had been there for hours. He knew it must be sailing day, for he had seen the crew streaming toward the piers as early as 6 A.M., marching up the gangways that led to crew quarters. He also had seen Captain Edward John Smith arrive, surprisingly unimpressive in his presailing civilian attire—a bowler hat and a long overcoat that made him look more like a civil servant on the way to work than a lordly ship's master.

The person who most attracted Montague's attention, however, was Second Officer Charles Lightoller. The stocky, broad-shouldered seaman was supervising cargo loading from the dock, bellowing orders at the crane operators as they lifted a half-dozen metal crates in a cargo net and lowered them into a forward hatch.

Montague realized he must be dreaming in much the same way Henning had. He was an invisible presence, watching the unfolding scene without being in it. He waited for his focus on Lightoller to draw his mind into that of the square-jawed officer, the way it had happened with Henning and Stead; now Montague expected to become Lightoller.

It didn't happen. He remained a bystander, and he watched Lightoller turn as another officer approached and slapped him on the back. Montague recognized him: Chief Officer Henry Wilde, a slender man with slightly stooped shoulders and a prominent nose.

"Hallo, Lights. Everything going well?"

"Well as can be expected," Lightoller grunted. "We're boarding everything but Windsor Castle's furniture and I shan't be surprised if even that arrives on the next batch of lorries."

"More income for the company," Wilde said philosophically. "What the devil's in those crates?"

He was pointing at the last load of metal containers awaiting the return of a cargo net. Lightoller consulted his manifest and shook his head doubtfully. "I couldn't believe it the first time I saw the manifest, and I still don't. According to this, thirty-four boxes of nails, screws, and bolts being shipped by Sovereign Metals to someone named J. Smyth in New York. Doesn't make bloody sense, if you ask me."

"Seems in order to me, Lights. What's wrong with it?"

Lightoller frowned. "Well, the Yanks do pretty well manufacturing all this themselves. Why would they be buying carpentry materials from a British firm? And another thing, Henry, look at the heavy padlocks on those crates. The crates are metal, too. Any wooden box would suffice. Makes me wonder what's really in them."

Wilde laughed. "You're a suspicious sort, my lad."

"You'd be suspicious, too, if you had seen the bloke who showed up here at dawn with the two lorries brought the crates. He fussed over the unloading as though they had the Crown's own jewels inside. Tried to slip me a five-pound note, the bugger. Said he wanted to make sure the crates weren't damaged during loading. Furtive little bastard, he was."

"Did you keep the five-pounder?" Wilde asked with a smile.

"I refused it politely." Lightoller grinned back.

"Foolish decision," Wilde said. "I think I would have kept it. Well, if I don't get back on board, E.J. will have my head. We have to man and partially lower two lifeboats to satisfy those pencil-pushers at the Board of Trade. Lowe and Moody are in charge, but I'd better be there to make sure it goes off smoothly. Silly regulation, isn't it?"

"Silly as far as this ship is concerned, I suppose," Lightoller said.

Wilde rubbed his thin hands together. "Bit chilly. This breeze goes right through you."

"Colder than I'd like on the tenth of April, but I expect we'll survive," Lightoller said laconically.

You will, Montague thought, but Wilde won't.

Without warning, everything turned black . . . and much colder.

He knew, even before the blackness turned gray like the birth of a gloomy dawn, where he was.

Back to the present, in cargo hold three.

The grayness became a pale glow.

And he was staring at the face of John Hawke.

"Hello, Derek."

Montague could not hear him, but the words registered in his mind as if they had been spoken. He understood now with startling clarity what Henning had experienced. He did not even question the impossibility of breathing normally more than twelve thousand feet down in the Atlantic, unprotected by a pressurized suit and seeing without artificial light in the unimaginable darkness. He told himself he was dreaming, which blocked out sheer fright; yet he also was aware it was no dream.

"You're one of them, aren't you?" he asked simply.

"One of whom, Derek?"

"The *Titanic*'s dead. The self-appointed guardians of a treasure that apparently does not exist."

"In a sense, yes. I'm the only one here from the *Henry Morgan*. A lately arrived guardian who shares the guilt that spawned what you call an Entity. We who haunt are also the haunted, Derek. Doomed to relive our last moments as the living. I have died a thousand times in that submarine, knowing I also doomed Debbi. Those who died on the *Titanic* must play back their own terror of helplessness, of the bitterness of broken trust, or the shame of their empty boasts. To hear always the sounds of their violent end: the ship tearing herself apart . . . the screams of the last to die, huddled together on the stern . . . the cries of the dying trapped in icy water, pleading for the lifeboats that never came back for them."

"That was eighty-three years ago. You died sixty-three years later. Why should you be part of this?"

"Because I died with the same guilt, didn't I, convicted of blind greed by a higher power than any court? The avarice that killed the innocent woman I loved and all my friends on the *Henry Morgan*—except you, thank God. Guilt is the reason for our existence in this nether world, just as protecting our common grave may be the road to atonement."

"Protecting your grave is one thing, John. But why do all this, even kill, to protect thirty-four crates of nothing? That code I broke was as worthless as the lead in those crates."

The ghost of John Hawke smiled. "Just now you dreamed you were on the docks at Southampton. Did you not?"

"Yes, but—"

"Apparently you learned nothing from it. Lightoller's open suspicions. The unusual behavior of the Sovereign representative. The use of metal crates instead of wooden ones. The oversize padlocks, totally unnecessary unless they were trying to hide something."

"They were probably hiding the fact that they shipped lead, not gold. Which would mean the bullion went on another ship, and the code was a deception."

"Look at the crates against that bulkhead, Derek. Look at them."

Montague looked. The remaining crates were as transparent as glass, and he could see the contents—the muted, burnished glow of solid gold.

He gaped. "The one we brought up was filled with lead bars," he said unbelievingly. "What kind of trick is this?"

"The transparency is the only trick. You're looking at the real contents."

The words marching through Montague's mind became a low chuckle.

"Come now, Derek. If the dead can make monsters and apparitions, they can create other illusions. Tomorrow morning, that admiral of yours is going to throw overboard not lead but pure gold. Alchemy in reverse, you might say. A final, harmless illusion intended to discourage further dives. But for you, as for me, the illusion is only that, Derek. If you open that crate again, you'll see what's really in it."

Montague's head was spinning. "Why are you taunting me this way? Why are you telling me the truth now? Admiral Cornell has given up the quest, and no one will ever threaten this ship again. The dead have won."

The ghost's sardonic smile, the same smile he had seen John

Hawke wear so many times, dissolved. "Let's call it a case of poetic justice, Derek. I am tempting you, just as all of us were tempted twenty years ago. I think my presence here, and yours, has made the dead tired of fighting the living."

"What are you trying to tell me?" Montague whispered.

"That it's all over, Derek. This thing down here doesn't have unlimited power. The gold is yours for the taking. Nothing will interfere any longer, if you can get a grip on your mind. You, Derek, you were the catalyst right from the start, and you still are. When this link with me is broken, you will awake and be free to tell the admiral the truth. Then you'll be vindicated."

"You're inviting us to grave-rob. No two-ways about it now."

"I'm trying to play fair with you. Remember, I wasn't on the *Titanic*. I never did think we were desecrating this wreck, so I shall leave this to your own moral judgment."

Montague said desperately, "If I keep quiet, will this assure the dead the peace they seek—the peace you must be seeking yourself?"

"I don't know. The dilemma you and the others on that ship up there still face is the same one we all have faced since you broke the code. Is the gold worth violating the resting place of the dead? Does worthwhile motivation justify desecration? The final answer is in your hands, Derek. You can keep silent, or you can tell the admiral his mission is not over."

The ghost of John Hawke smiled again, but this time it was a smile tinged with sadness. "I would find it difficult to condemn you, no matter what you decide. Good-bye, old friend."

The glow in cargo hold three began to fade, until Montague was staring into the suffocating blackness and its utter silence.

He found himself outside the *Titanic* again, on the battered forecastle next to the cargo hatch—the gateway to hell, he thought, but no longer. Hawke was saying there would be no more danger, no more failures of the precious lights.

He awoke, bathed in sweat. Blessed sunlight was streaming into the cabin and *Chase* still swayed peacefully on station. He dressed quickly and hurried toward the bridge.

* * *

Admiral Cornell and Captain Bixenman were exchanging post-mortems.

"I feel rotten," Cornell was saying. "We were so damn close."

"Admiral, what are you going to tell Washington?"

"I'm not sure it matters. Will anyone believe me? If that shot Carlson took of the apparition in the hold on that last dive had shown anything but Mitchell's feet, I'd have some visual evidence."

"You've got the lead crate. You've got eyewitnesses to what happened. The Navy's not going to call all of us crazy."

Cornell shook his head. "Maybe not, but I'm strongly tempted to hang it all on Montague and let the rest of the story die with us."

"There are three civilians aboard this ship who might not cooperate. Oh, Montague, perhaps, but not Gillespie or Henning. For that matter, there's the crew. Most of these kids are technicians, not combat people. Hell, five of the sonarmen have electrical-engineering degrees. They think for themselves, and they know we're not at war. There's too much chance of somebody leaking the real story, and if the news media get hold of it, they'll never let go. We can't cover this up."

"Yeah," Cornell said glumly. He looked at the captain. "Maybe I'll take Henning and Gillespie with me to the White House and have *them* tell the whole story. Then I'll let the President decide how much of it should be made public. For now, I'll advise CNO I called off the mission because of excessive risk to the divers." The admiral squinted uncomfortably into the glare of the early-morning sun. "Lousy way to wind up this mess."

"I wouldn't call it that. We proved what AMOS and the sub can do. And it seems to me we've been told there *is* some form of life after death."

"Apparently for those with something on their conscience. Somehow, the idea of spending eternity trying to atone for my sins doesn't appeal to me."

Bixenman said soberly, "That has applied to the *Titanic*'s

dead, but who's to say what lies beyond death for all of us? A different kind of eternity, perhaps. And for those down there, too, now that we're leaving. Nobody's going to visit that wreck again, Admiral. I think they may have found the kind of peace we all want."

Cornell was about to say something when the tall figure of Derek Montague charged onto the bridge. The captain and admiral regarded him with startled glances.

"Where's the crate?" he demanded, without pausing to catch his breath.

Cornell looked at him in disbelief. The ancient Britisher had sprinted up the bridge stairs like someone thirty years younger.

"Calm down, Derek. It's out on deck, portside amidships."

"We have to open it again. That's not lead in there; it's gold!"

"What the hell are you talking about? You saw for yourself last night—"

"I've had the same kind of psychic experience as Henning. I know something. I was right about the code. I saw the gold being loaded at Southampton on April 10, 1912. Then I went back to cargo hold three. That gold was shipped on the *Titanic*, I tell you!"

For the next five minutes, Cornell and Bixenman listened to his account. "You can send the divers down again," he finished. "Hawke said the Entity has lost its powers."

Cornell, for once in his life, seemed befuddled and uncertain. It was the captain who responded.

"This Hawke, or his ghost, told you the lead is illusionary?"

"Yes. All the crates are filled with bullion, including the one we recovered. The illusion must have been so complete, it discouraged all of us, so we wouldn't make any more attempts."

"Then let's take another look and find out for ourselves."

It took them less than a minute to reach the deck area where Ozzie Mitchell and Bert Tuttle were standing by the crate, still discussing Cornell's decision to abort the mission. Tuttle thought the admiral had acted wisely; Mitchell wasn't so sure.

"I keep remembering what Steve saw, or thought he saw," he was saying.

"He saw zilch," Tuttle said. "Montague's code was a bucket of bilge water."

The debate ended when Cornell, Bixenman, and Montague hove into view. Mitchell noticed the Brit's distraught look and Cornell's strained expression even as he tossed a salute, which the admiral didn't bother to return.

"Open that crate up again, Ozzie," Cornell ordered.

Mitchell stared at him incredulously.

"Just get the lid off. I'll explain later."

Mitchell lifted the lid effortlessly and stood to one side, holding it. Bixenman reached in and pulled out one bar, then another and another until the entire top layer had been removed.

"They're still all lead," he said quietly, looking at Montague, whose jaw had gone slack and whose eyes seemed wild. Bixenman had the sailor cut into the bar with his folding pocketknife. The soft metal was uniformly gray—apparently to everyone except Montague.

Cornell said in the tone of someone comforting a child awakened from a nightmare, "It was just a dream, Derek. A real, genuine dream this time. Not a psychic experience, if that's in fact what Henning went through."

Bixenman added, "Don't take it too hard. We're going home with some incredible photographs, and a major victory for deep-sea exploration."

Montague, his broad face flushed, found his voice. "Those are bullion bars, damn you! I'm not blind! Look at the sheen. That dull gold coloring. The—"

He stopped, miserably conscious that they were staring at him as they would at a madman. "You aren't seeing the same thing I'm seeing, are you? I'm looking at gold. You're looking at lead."

Cornell said gently, "You've gone through a lot, Derek. You must be tired, and your eyes are playing tricks on you."

"Maybe a little wishful thinking, too," Mitchell suggested.

"Stop patronizing me!" Montague shouted. "I'm not crazy.

I was talking to John Hawke's ghost, and it was no dream. You people are looking at an illusion, and you're wrong. And even if that is lead in the crate, the bullion is still in cargo hold three. I saw it!"

"How could you see inside locked crates?" Mitchell asked.

"The crates were transparent. I've already explained that to the admiral and Captain Bixenman. You have to believe me. You're leaving a treasure down there untouched."

Cornell's tone stiffened. "We're going home because of the evidence sitting here in this goddamned box. I'm not sending divers down again on the basis of what you've told me. I'm sorry, Derek, I really am, but I think you've distorted a normal dream into something else."

The fight was still in the old man. "You believed Henning at the time. Why don't you believe me?"

"Because I can see what's in front of me," Cornell said bluntly. "And because Ben Henning is trained in this and you're not."

"Then let Henning look at those bars. If he sees lead, I will admit I am wrong."

"Fair enough," the admiral replied. He turned to the sailor who had been listening wide-eyed to all this exchange. "Son, go find Dr. Henning and bring him back here on the double."

They waited in uncomfortable silence. When the seaman returned with Henning, they had Gillespie in tow, as well.

Cornell spoke without preamble. "Ben, Bill, take another look at the bars on the deck. What do you see?"

They swapped puzzled glances at each other, then peered at the bars.

"They're the same lead bars we saw last night," Henning said.

Gillespie nodded. "I agree. What's this all about?"

Cornell had a sudden surge of pity for Montague. "Nothing," he said. "I just wanted to make sure we weren't walking away from anything valuable. Ozzie, put the bars back. We'll need them to prove we did our damnedest."

"You're all blind!" Montague cried, forgetting his promise. "You're seeing what the dead want you to see!"

Henning had figured out what was happening. "Admiral,

he could be right. I'm not saying he is, but it's possible. We've already seen the unlikeliest things become reality out here."

Mitchell, on his knees with Tuttle as they restored the bars to the crate, looked up. "These may be lead, Admiral, but that's no proof the other thirty-three crates aren't legitimate."

Bixenman said, "He has a point. Maybe Jackman *did* see bullion under that sprung lid."

"My God," Gillespie muttered, "I'm ready to believe anything."

This, Cornell thought, from a man opposed to continuing the mission. Henning, too, and even Mitchell—he'd have to lead the divers down again if the abort was canceled. The admiral's resolve wavered. He said, "Jesus, we'd be stupid to run away if we think the divers would be safe."

They stared as one into the open crate.

Cornell's jaw tightened. "Let's go for broke. One more time."

Until the captain looked up and out to sea, no one noticed that the sky had begun to take on a strange green hue.

"What the hell . . . ?" Bixenman wondered aloud.

Tuttle muttered, "Never saw anything like that in my whole life."

The air was absolutely still, not a languid quiet but the same smothering, oppressive silence of the depths that lay almost two and a half miles below them. From a horizon that seemed to be disgorging green-tinted clouds, the disturbance was rolling in almost at sea level. Surging whitecaps had replaced the easy swells, sounding more like punches against the ship's hull than playful slaps.

"I think I'd better get to the bridge," Bixenman said. Cornell, hesitating briefly, with a knowing glance at Montague, followed the captain. The others just stood around the crate, mesmerized by the oncoming fury as if they were staring helplessly into the eyes of a cobra.

It was a bewildered executive officer who greeted the captain.

"I'm glad you're here," Scofield said. "I figure we're about to get clobbered, but damned if I know by what."

Bixenman gave him only a brusque nod. "What's the barometer doing?"

"You tell me, sir. Quartermaster can't even get a steady reading. We might as well be on a roller coaster . . . up or down. In the attic one minute and the cellar the next. Craziest thing I ever saw. And that sky . . ."

Bixenman wasn't listening anymore. He was too busy remembering, in chilling detail, Montague's description of the storm twenty years ago.

Montague shuddered as the unearthly green aura settled over the ship, and the ocean began stirring into angry life. He was reliving the worst nightmare of his life, his fear intensifying with the earsplitting crescendo of the wind and the vessel's sudden bucking. He scarcely heard Mitchell ask of no one, in an awed voice that was almost a gasp, "What in the hell's happening?"

He knew the truth now.

The *Titanic*'s dead were not powerless. John Hawke had lied.

And with that sickening knowledge, *Chase* ceased to be a sleek steel sanctuary protecting them from terror out of the past. They all had become part of that past, as helpless as the men on the *Henry Morgan* twenty painful years ago. From the ship's topside loudspeakers, metallically and defiantly audible over the storm, came Captain Bixenman's voice. It could have been Jerry Robertson's, Montague thought miserably.

"Sea-and-anchor detail on deck for emergency breakaway from anchor cables! All hands . . ."

The rest of that command was swallowed into the maw of the screeching wind. The green hue darkened, as though they were on an airliner that had blundered into a thunderhead, its darkness hiding terrible power. *Chase*'s pitching and rolling worsened.

Mitchell shouted, "We'd better find some life jackets before . . ."

There wasn't time for anyone to respond; *Chase* lurched violently under the impact of a foam-topped wave, and all they could do was hang on to whatever secure object they could reach. The storm seemed to have moved in faster than it had on the *Henry Morgan*, Montague realized. He had the insane notion that the dead were striking hurriedly, before the ship's powerful engines and sturdy structure could thwart them. He couldn't hear the turbines but he could feel them throbbing under his feet, and he said a silent prayer that Bixenman somehow would save them.

The captain was doing some praying himself. He had ridden out a few typhoons in his career, but never anything like this fury that had come from nowhere. The ship was reeling under cliff-sized waves that rose out of the depths like giant disemboweling claws.

Chase lurched into a 360-degree spin that sent unsecured equipment crashing against bulkheads and onto decks.

"Keep her into the wind!" Bixenman bellowed to the taut-faced helmsman.

Panic was in the sailor's voice. "I'm trying, sir, but there's no rudder response."

"Help him with that goddamned wheel!" Another crewman stumbled and almost fell before he reached the helmsman's side and added his strong hands and arms to the wheel. The ship steadied but only for a moment as an immense wave struck broadside. *Chase* heeled to starboard so sharply that the small group still huddled around the *Titanic*'s crate were hurled to the deck. The crate itself narrowly missed crashing into Montague, who was saved from the blow when Mitchell, in a split-second dive, stopped it with his massive shoulders.

"Thanks, Ozzie," Montague gasped.

Gillespie, also sprawled ignominiously on the tilted deck, glared at the Britisher. "Lost its powers, Derek?"

Montague couldn't think of a suitable reply. His mind was filled with an unanswered question. Why had Hawke lied to him? The dead were as strong as ever, still taking their revenge as they had two decades ago when the *Henry Morgan* was ripped apart by the same kind of weird storm. Why, indeed, had Hawke lied?

Or maybe, Montague was thinking, John had also lied to himself again, judgment and reason distorted by his unquenchable passion to complete the mission at which he had failed. Maybe he had used Montague in one final attempt to achieve it, if only indirectly, knowing that Derek wanted vindication even more than he wanted gold. Maybe it was Hawke's obsession that had them trapped in the same green hell of twenty years ago.

Or maybe not.

The huge hydraulic-powered rudder and shuddering turbines were fighting back, bringing *Chase* into the wind and meeting the storm head-on. Another wave swept over the cruiserlike prow and cascaded almost to the bridge, but the ship shook off the blow and began to pick up speed.

"Good work," Bixenman rasped to the sweating helmsmen. "We may ride out this sucker yet. Keep her—"

Whatever order he was about to issue died in his throat.

"My God," he whispered.

Off the port side, bearing down on them with sickening speed, was a cyclonic waterspout many times the size of the ship.

"Right full rudder!"

Not even his instinctive command nor the lightning response of the helm could match the pace of the onrushing mass of destruction. *Chase* turned obediently and quickly, but Bixenman knew it was too late.

Those on the port side, watching horrified as the living, twisting tower of seawater bore down on them, reached the same conclusion.

With one exception.

Ozzie Mitchell, with a strength born of desperation, picked up the crate and hurled it over the side. As it fell, the lid came off and bars began dropping out. Mitchell looked at Montague, awe in his eyes.

The bars disappearing into the foaming sea were gold.

There were several seconds when nothing could be heard above the roar; then the spout suddenly slowed and veered away, its height diminishing with the change in course. *Chase* rocked convulsively from the force of the near-impact but stayed upright. The now-collapsing wall of death moved off and began to come apart.

"God, that was close," Henning muttered. He gave Mitchell a look of understanding and gratitude.

The green aura around the ship began to fade.

It had not quite disappeared, giving way to a gray overcast, when a final wave lashed out from the subsiding ocean like the last swipe of a dying tiger. It was strong enough to engulf the port-side men who had just struggled to their feet. When the wave receded, Mitchell saw it taking with it a single figure, arms and legs thrashing wildly.

"Man overboard!" he shouted.

He already knew it was hopeless. They all watched the last victim of the *Titanic* disappear as soon as he hit the water.

Epilogue

Rear Admiral Roger Cornell sat across from the massive desk in the Oval Office and gave the President of the United States what could have passed as a "do with me what you will" look.

"That's the whole story, Mr. President. I bear responsibility for the mission's failure. The officers and crew, and especially the diving personnel, performed brilliantly and bravely. And I can't speak highly enough of Bill Gillespie and Doctor Henning; they were real troopers."

The President smiled. "I agree with that assessment, Admiral, and I'm writing those two personal letters of commendation and thanks. I'm also suggesting to CNO that he officially commend all divers. As for you, my friend, I appreciate your accepting full responsibility, but I don't think you should be accepting any blame. You were up against some mighty unusual circumstances."

Cornell's return smile was tinged with wryness. "Unusual is a pretty mild adjective, sir. The question remains, how much of this should be made public?"

The President frowned thoughtfully. "We never did announce that such an expedition would be attempted. I'm thinking we could just keep quiet about the whole affair."

"I would agree, Mr. President, except we face the likelihood that someone who was on *Chase* is going to be a blabbermouth. Remember Howard Hughes and the *Glomar Explorer*? The CIA tried secretly to raise that sunken Soviet sub, and ended up with a huge intelligence flap. If the media get wind of what really happened, they'll have a circus. I can just see the headlines: NAVY RUNS FROM HAUNTED SHIP."

"I understand you've already sworn everyone to secrecy until we decide on the best way to handle this."

"Yes, sir, including the civilians. But that's no guarantee, even with my officers. Let just one man confide in his girlfriend or wife, and the next thing we get is the press opening up our can of worms."

He hesitated. "You might as well know, Mr. President, Henning wants to write a book about our expedition eventually, and I'm not sure we could legally stop him. There was a screwup with his in-processing, and nobody had him sign any oath or waiver."

For the first time, the President looked displeased. "That may have been a rather serious omission, Admiral."

Cornell flushed unhappily. "I'm afraid it was, Mr. President. But I never dreamed events would occur as they did. Sir, may I make a suggestion?"

"Feel free."

"We've got some great pictures of the *Titanic*'s interior. Let's release them, along with details on how we accomplished this feat with our new diving hardware. We can say there also was an attempt to recover gold supposedly shipped in 1912, but that there was no sign of any bullion. Which may or may not have been true; we'll never know whether that crate contained lead or gold. I suspect the latter, but we have no proof. Nor do I blame Lieutenant Commander Mitchell. As I indicated to you, sir, impossible though it sounds, I think he saved the ship when he threw that crate overboard."

The President shook his head, but it was more a gesture of wonderment than disbelief. "The supernatural aspects of this just defy the imagination. I agree with you that the press would have a field day. That's what I fear most from any kind of a leak, just as you do."

Cornell took the deep breath of a man about to plunge into icy waters. "Sir, I'd be willing to chance a leak. If it happens, it can be handled. As far as the Navy's concerned, we can just say some unusual things happened for which there are no scientific explanations. I'd even be tempted to refer all media queries to Dr. Henning. He'll write that book anyway, and I'm sure he isn't going to do a hatchet job on the United States Navy."

The President sighed. "It will be quite a book. Well, Admiral, it's probably the best course, but let me talk to the CNO before I make a final decision. By the way, what was the name of that diver who was killed?"

"Robert Nader, sir."

"Have someone in your office get me the names and address or addresses of his next of kin. Today. I'd like to write them personal notes."

"Thank you, Mr. President. I'll do that."

Cornell sensed the meeting was over and rose to leave. The President stopped him.

"Admiral, how about the next of kin for the other fellow who died? A similar letter might be in order."

"Sir," Cornell said softly, "Derek Montague had no living relatives."

Author's Postscript

It is possible that *Titanic* buffs more expert than I will find technical lapses in this narrative. Yet this is a work of fiction based partially on fact, and I can only ask their indulgence toward one who shares their love of the great liner.

The truth about the exploration of the *Titanic*'s interior is that no human being has ever entered the sunken ship. Thus, the interior scenes, like the characters participating in the two expeditions, are totally imaginary. (However, there really was an 1898 novel called *Futility*, which uncannily predicted the *Titanic*'s fate.)

I must pay special thanks to Jared Kieling, an editor of consummate skill, who detoured me away from many false paths as we explored the *Titanic* together.

My sincere appreciation to the following:

Thomas "Speedy" Rice for valuable legal background on the rules of salvage.

John Chase and William Felix for data on gold value and bullion shipments.

Aaron Priest, agent and old friend, for his usual support, encouragement, and advice.

Megan Hughes, Todd Ellerman, Joey Arone, and my incredibly patient wife, Priscilla Serling, for their aid with a word processor.

Mac Plus, which made rewriting easier if not pleasurable.

Of the many books on the *Titanic* disaster I consulted for background material, by far the most valuable was Ballard's own *The Discovery of the Titanic* (Warner/Madison, 1987).

Other excellent research sources were John P. Eaton's and Charles Haas's *Titanic—Triumph and Tragedy* (W. W. Norton, 1986), the most definitive account of them all, and Walter Lord's two brilliant classics, *A Night to Remember* (Holt, 1955) and *The Night Lives On* (William Morrow, 1986).

To all *Titanic* buffs, I recommend a work I found not only valuable but stirring: Charles Pellegrino's *Her Name, Titanic* (McGraw-Hill, 1988).

Additional reference material included: *The Titanic, End of a Dream* by Wyn Craig Wade (Rawson Wade Publishers, 1979); *The Maiden Voyage* by Geoffrey Marcus (Viking, 1969); and *Titanic, The Death and Life of a Legend* by Michael Davie (Henry Holt, 1986).

Robert Serling
Tucson, Arizona

About the Author

ROBERT SERLING is the author of six airline histories and several novels, including *The President's Plane Is Missing* and *Air Force One Is Haunted*. He lives in Tucson, Arizona.

BESTSELLING BOOKS FROM
ST. MARTIN'S PAPERBACKS—
TO READ AND READ AGAIN!

—————————⟨∿⟩—————————

NOT WITHOUT MY DAUGHTER
Betty Mahmoody with William Hoffer
_____ 92588-3 $5.95 U.S./$6.95 Can.

PROBABLE CAUSE
Ridley Pearson
_____ 92385-6 $5.95 U.S./$6.95 Can.

RIVERSIDE DRIVE
Laura Van Wormer
_____ 91572-1 $5.95 U.S.   _____ 91574-8 $6.95 Can.

SHADOW DANCERS
Herbert Lieberman
_____ 92288-4 $5.95 U.S./$6.95 Can.

THE FITZGERALDS AND THE KENNEDYS
Doris Kearns Goodwin
_____ 90933-0 $5.95 U.S.   _____ 90934-9 $6.95 Can.

JAMES HERRIOT'S DOG STORIES
James Herriot
_____ 92558-1 $5.99 U.S.

Publishers Book and Audio Mailing Service
P.O. Box 120159, Staten Island, NY 10312-0004
Please send me the book(s) I have checked above. I am enclosing $ _____ (please add
$1.50 for the first book, and $.50 for each additional book to cover postage and handling.
Send check or money order only—no CODs or charge my VISA, MASTERCARD,
DISCOVER or AMERICAN EXPRESS card.

Card number _____

Expiration date _____ Signature _____

Name _____

Address _____

City _____ State/Zip _____
Please allow six weeks for delivery. Prices subject to change without notice. Payment in
U.S. funds only. New York residents add applicable sales tax.

BBOOKS 7/91

The SILENCE *of* *the* LAMBS

THE ELECTRIFYING BESTSELLER BY
THOMAS HARRIS

" THRILLERS DON'T COME ANY BETTER THAN THIS."
—*CLIVE BARKER*

**"HARRIS IS QUITE SIMPLY THE BEST SUSPENSE NOVELIST
WORKING TODAY."** — *The Washington Post*

THE SILENCE OF THE LAMBS
Thomas Harris
_____ 92458-5 $5.99 U.S./$6.99 Can.

PETER JAMES

INTERNATIONALLY BESTSELLING AUTHOR OF POSSESSION

DREAMER

What's a beautiful, happy, successful woman to think of her dreams? Samantha Curtis lives in fear of her childhood nightmare, the one she had just before awakening to learn of her parents' deaths. And now she dreams again, of a mysterious hooded man, of tragic disasters and heinous crimes—that begin to spill over into reality. And as she watches her perfect life drift over the edge of sanity, Sam scrambles in search of answers, a mere heartbeat ahead of her bizarre vision portraying her own terrible death....

blindsight: residual vision following lesion of the striate cortex. *that is, the ability of a blind person to see.*

Guy Sullivan is slowly going blind. His only hope lies in possibly dangerous experiments in blindsight. But with each jarring headache that heralds his coming darkness, Guy is haunted by bizarre flashes of the future…a future that beckons his son to a horrifying destiny….

MICHAEL STEWART

BLINDSIGHT

"CHILLING!"
—*Washington Post Book World*